Secrets

Satisfy your desire for more.

Out of Control
by Rachelle Chase

Astrid's world revolves around her business and she's hoping to pick up wealthy Erik Santos as a client. Only he's hoping to pick up something entirely different. Will she give in to the seductive pull of his proposition?

Hawkmoor
by Amber Green

Shape-shifters answer to Darien as he acts in the name of the long-missing Lady Hawkmoor, their hereditary ruler. When she unexpectedly surfaces, Darien must deal with a scrappy individual whose wary eyes hold the other half of his soul, but who has the power to destroy his world.

Lessons in Pleasure
by Charlotte Featherstone

A wicked bargain has Lily vowing never to yield to the demands of the rake she once loved and lost. Unfortunately, Damian, the Earl of St. Croix, or Saint as he is infamously known, will not take 'no' for an answer.

In the Heat of the Night
by Calista Fox

Haunted by a century-old curse, Molina fears she won't live to see her thirtieth birthday. Nick, her former bodyguard, is hired back into service to protect her from the fatal accidents that plague her family. But *In the Heat of the Night*, will his passion and love for her be enough to convince Molina they have a future together?

Romantic Times BOOKclub 4½ Stars—Fantastic Keeper

Reviews from Secrets Volume 1

"Four very romantic, very sexy novellas in very different styles and settings. … The settings are quite diverse taking the reader from Regency England to a remote and mysterious fantasy land, to an Arabian nights type setting, and finally to a contemporary urban setting. All stories are explicit, and Hamre and Landon stories sizzle. … If you like erotic romance you will love *Secrets*."

— *Romantic Readers* review

"Overall, for a fan of erotica, these are unlike anything you've encountered before. For those romance fans who turn down the pages of the "good parts" for later repeat consumption (and you know who you are) these books are a wonderful way to explore the better side of the erotica market. … *Secrets* is a worthy exploration for the adventurous reader with the promise for better things yet to come."

— Liz Montgomery

Reviews from Secrets Volume 2

Winner of the Fallot Literary Award for Fiction

"*Secrets, Volume 2*, a new anthology published by Red Sage Publishing, is hot! I mean *red hot!* … The sensuality in each story will make you blush—from head to toe and everywhere else in-between. … The true success behind *Secrets, Volume 2* is the combination of different tastes—both in subgenres of romance and levels of sensuality. *I highly recommend this book*."

— Dawn A. Long, *America Online* review

"I think it is a fine anthology and Red Sage should be applauded for providing an outlet for women who want to write sensual romance."

— Adrienne Benedicks,
Erotic Readers Association review

Reviews from Secrets Volume 3

Winner of the 1997 Under the Cover
Readers Favorite Award

"An unabashed celebration of sex. Highly arousing! Highly recommended!"

— Virginia Henley, *New York Times* Best Selling Author

"*Secrets, Volume 3* leaves the reader breathless. Each of these tributes to exotic and erotic fiction offers a world of sensual pleasure and moral rewards. A delicious confection of sensuous treats awaits the reader on each turn of the page. Sexy, funny, thrilling, and luscious, Secrets entertains, enlightens, and fuels the fires of fantasy."

— Kathee Card, *Romancing the Web*

Reviews from Secrets Volume 4

"*Secrets, Volume 4*, has something to satisfy every erotic fantasy… simply sexsational!"

— Virginia Henley, *New York Times* Best Selling Author

"Provocative…seductive…a must read!" **4 Stars**

— *Romantic Times*

"These are the kind of stories that romance readers that 'want a little more' have been looking for all their lives without crossing over into the adult genre. Keep these stories coming, Red Sage, the world needs them!"

— Lani Roberts, *Affaire de Coeur*

"If you're interested in exploring erotica, or reading farther than the sexual passages of your favorite steamy reads, the *Secret* series is well worth checking out."

— *Writers Club Romance Group* on AOL

Reviews from Secrets Volume 5

"*Secrets, Volume 5*, is a collage of lucious sensuality. Any woman who reads *Secrets* is in for an awakening!"

— **Virginia Henley,** *New York Times* Best Selling Author

"Hot, hot, hot! Not for the faint-hearted!"

— *Romantic Times*

"As you make your way through the stories, you will find yourself becoming hotter and hotter. *Secrets* just keeps getting better and better."

— *Affaire de Coeur*

Reviews from Secrets Volume 6

"*Secrets, Volume 6* satisfies every female fantasy: the Bodyguard, the Tutor, the Werewolf, and the Vampire. I give it Six Stars!"
— Virginia Henley, *New York Times* Best Selling Author

"*Secrets, Volume 6* is the best of *Secrets* yet. ...four of the most erotic stories in one volume than this reader has yet to see anywhere else. ... These stories are full of erotica at its best and you'll definitely want to keep it handy for lots of re-reading!"
— *Affaire de Coeur*

Reviews from Secrets Volume 7

Winner of the Venus Book Club Best Book of the Year

"...sensual, sexy, steamy fun. A perfect read!"
— Virginia Henley, *New York Times* Best Selling Author

"Intensely provocative and disarmingly romantic, Secrets Volume 7 is a romance reader's paradise that will take you beyond your wildest dreams!"
— *Ballston Book House* Review

"Erotic romance is at the sensual core of Red Sage's latest collection of short, red hot novels, *Secrets, Volume 7.*"
— *Writers Club Romance Group* on AOL

Reviews from Secrets Volume 8

Winner of the Venus Book Club Best Book of the Year

"*Secrets Volume 8* is simply sensational!"
— Virginia Henley, *New York Times* Best Selling Author

"*Secrets Volume 8* is an amazing compilation of sexy stories discovering a wide range of subjects, all designed to titillate the senses."
— Lani Roberts, *Affaire de Coeur*

"All four tales are well written and fun to read because even the sexiest scenes are not written for shock value, but interwoven smoothly and realistically into the plots. This quartet contains strong storylines and solid lead characters, but then again what else would one expect from the no longer *Secrets* anthologies."

— Harriet Klausner

"Once again, Red Sage Publishing takes you on a journey of sexual delight, teasing and pleasing the reader with a bit of something to appeal to everyone."

— Michelle Houston, *Courtesy Sensual Romance*

"In this sizzling volume, four authors offer short stories in four different sub-genres: contemporary, paranormal, historical, and futuristic. These ladies' assignments are to dazzle, tantalize, amaze, and entice. Your assignment, as the reader, is to sit back and enjoy. Just have a fan and some ice water at your side."

— Amy Cunningham

Reviews from Secrets Volume 9

"Everyone should expect only the most erotic stories in a *Secrets* book. …if you like your stories full of hot sexual scenes, then this is for you!"

— Donna Doyle, *Romance Reviews*

"*Secrets 9*…is sinfully delicious, highly arousing, and hotter than hot as the pages practically burn up as you turn them."

— Suzanne Coleburn, *Reader To Reader Reviews/*
Belles & Beaux of Romance

"Treat yourself to well-written fictionthat's hot, hotter, and hottest!"

— Virginia Henley, *New York Times* Best Selling Author

Reviews from Secrets Volume 10

"*Secrets Volume 10*, an erotic dance through medieval castles, sultan's palaces, the English countryside and expensive hotel suites, explodes with passion-filled pages."

— *Romantic Times BOOKclub*

"Having read the previous nine volumes, this one fulfills the expectations of what is expected in a *Secrets* book: romance and eroticism at its best!!"

— *Fallen Angel Reviews*

"All are hot steamy romances so if you enjoy erotica romance, you are sure to enjoy *Secrets, Volume 10*. All this reviewer can say is WOW!!"

— *The Best Reviews*

Reviews from Secrets Volume 11

"*Secrets Volume 11* delivers once again with storylines that include erotic masquerades, ancient curses, modern-day betrayal and a prince charming looking for a kiss. Scorching tales filled with humor, passion and love." **4 Stars**

— *Romantic Times BOOKclub*

"The *Secrets* books published by Red Sage Publishing are well known for their excellent writing and highly erotic stories and *Secrets, Volume 11* will not disappoint. "

— *The Road to Romance*

"*Secrets 11* quite honestly is my favorite anthology from Red Sage so far. All four novellas had me glued to their stories until the very end. I was just disappointed that these talented ladies novellas weren't longer."

— *The Best Reviews*

"Indulge yourself with this erotic treat and join the thousands of readers who just can't get enough. Be forewarned that *Secrets 11* will wet your appetite for more, but will offer you the ultimate in pleasurable erotic literature."

— *Ballston Book House Review*

Reviews from Secrets Volume 12

"*Secrets Volume 12*, turns on the heat with a seductive encounter inside a bookstore, a temple of naughty and sensual delight, a galactic inferno that thaws ice, and a lightening storm that lights up the English shoreline. Tales of looking for love in all the right places with a heat rating out the charts." **4½ Stars**

— *Romantic Times BOOKclub*

"I really liked these stories. You want great escapism? Read *Secrets, Volume 12*."

— *Romance Reviews*

Reviews from Secrets Volume 13

"In *Secrets Volume 13*, the temperature gets turned up a few notches with a mistaken personal ad, shape-shifters destined to love, a hot Regency lord and his lady, as well as a bodyguard protecting his woman. Emotions and flames blaze high in Red Sage's latest foray into the sensual and delightful art of love." **4½ Stars**

— *Romantic Times BOOKclub*

"The sex is still so hot the pages nearly ignite! Read *Secrets, Volume 13*!

— *Romance Reviews*

Satisfy Your Desire for More... with Secrets!

Did you miss any of the other volumes of the sexy **Secrets** *series? At the back of this book is an order form for all the available volumes. Order your* **Secrets** *today! See our order form at the back of this book or visit Waldenbooks or Borders.*

Rachelle Chase

Amber Green

Charlotte Featherstone

Calista Fox

Volume 13

Secrets

Satisfy your desire for more.

SECRETS Volume 13
This is an original publication of Red Sage Publishing and each individual story herein has never before appeared in print. These stories are a collection of fiction and any similarity to actual persons or events is purely coincidental.

Red Sage Publishing, Inc.
P.O. Box 4844
Seminole, FL 33775
727-391-3847
www.redsagepub.com

SECRETS Volume 13
A Red Sage Publishing book
All Rights Reserved/July 2005
Copyright © 20054 by Red Sage Publishing, Inc.

ISBN 0-9754516-3-4

Published by arrangement with the authors and copyright holders of the individual works as follows:

Book typesetting by:
Quill & Mouse Studios, Inc.
www.quillandmouse.com

Contents

Out of Control

by Rachelle Chase

To My Reader:

I find the concept of control—giving it up, taking it—intriguing. Which made me wonder… what if a woman who thrived on being in control met a man who challenged her to give it up?

To my family, who has always stood by me, loved me, encouraged me, and supported me, I love you.

Chapter One

"I find it interesting that you sent a resume."

Astrid frowned, not understanding. "Would you prefer to see photos of events I've arranged?" She bent down to retrieve her portfolio.

"No," he said.

Astrid straightened.

"While your qualifications are impressive, they aren't required for the position."

Disappointment settled in her stomach. She stared at the Adonis seated across from her. At the wavy black hair that she'd bet felt like silk. At the thick, perfectly arched eyebrows above intense ebony eyes. Fathomless eyes that scattered her thoughts. And those lips...

She reminded herself that her disappointment was strictly professional, that landing this contract would be a major boon for her company.

"Why are you here, Ms. Thomas?" He set her resume down on the desk and leveled his intimidating stare at her.

"Excuse me?"

"You've talked about events you've planned, and now you want to show me your portfolio." Erik shrugged. "Why?"

What did he mean? Wasn't that the whole point of this interview? She forced a polite chuckle. "Well...that's usually what convinces clients of my competence. Is there something else you'd like to see?"

His gaze drifted over her face, lingering on her lips, before lazily returning to her eyes. His eyes seemed darker, his look...sexual.

Astrid gave herself a mental shake. Her imagination was on overdrive. From what Suze had told her and the articles she'd read, Erik Santos was all business.

She blinked.

The sexy gaze was still there.

"Tell me about your other...skills." Sensuality dripped from the word "skills."

Surely she was mistaken, reading sexual intent where there was none. "I can't think of any other skills more applicable to event planning—"

"But we both know you're not here for the event planning position."

"I don't under—"

With a flick of his wrist, ecru stationery fluttered to rest in front of her. She read the words with mounting horror.

"I didn't write that!"

Paper rustled. Her gaze flew to the name scribbled in blue ink.

"I didn't sign that!"

His lips twisted. "Ms. Thomas, don't waste my time."

She glanced back at the signature—at the big loopy 'A' and the flamboyant 'T'—and fought the panic threatening to overwhelm her.

How totally embarrassing. How utterly humiliating. How was she going to explain this? She straightened her shoulders and lifted her chin. "Mr. Santos, I'm afraid there's been a mistake."

His eyebrow arched. Ebony eyes watched. Waiting.

"Suze sent that letter," she said, keeping her voice matter-of-fact.

His eyes narrowed. "Suze who?"

"Bobby's girlfriend. We—"

"My brother, Bobby?"

She nodded.

"I find that hard to believe."

"Suze is my best friend, and we—"

"Fascinating, Ms. Thomas, but that explains nothing."

Astrid bit back her annoyance. "If you would let me finish, Mr. Santos." She paused and took a deep breath, striving to keep her professionalism in place. She'd pretend that this conversation was like any other, that Erik was…that Erik was…a disgruntled client. Yes, that was it. A disgruntled client who was unable to understand why orchids were more fitting than paper whites, or why baked chicken was more practical than barbeque ribs for his soirée.

With that image firmly implanted in her mind, she gave Erik a polite smile. "As I was saying, Suze and I were at a bar and I was complaining about the lack of contracts for Event Planners. She found an ad in the Personals column of *The Santa Barbara Tribune* and we joked about responding…"

The disgruntled client image unraveled.

"We dictated a letter…" Her face grew warm. "We were joking…" Her palms felt moist. "I don't know why Suze gave you that letter."

His dark eyes stared, seeming to sift through her thoughts. "Don't you, Ms Thomas?"

Actually, she did. This was obviously another one of Suze's convoluted matchmaking schemes, but there was no way she was going to tell him that. But why would Suze put her in such an awkward situation? Why give Erik that letter?

Oh. My. God.

At the dawning revelation of the obvious, her mouth dropped open. "She told you I was responding to the personal ad? *You* placed that personal ad?"

His jaw clenched.

She hadn't meant to blurt that out. But the thought that this wealthy, gorgeous man—a man who could probably have any woman he wanted—would resort to placing a personal ad...why, the idea was preposterous.

About as preposterous as the idea that she—logical and rational, Astrid Thomas—would answer a personal ad. No one would believe it.

No one had to know of it.

The unbidden thought caused rivulets of...*excitement*...dismay to stream through her. She attempted another polite smile. "Well, now that we've cleared that up—"

"Was this really a joke, Ms. Thomas?" he asked, gesturing to the letter.

Her heart fluttered at the silky tone.

No...I mean...Yes...I mean...

Well, they had joked about responding—or so she'd thought—but the things she'd said had an ounce of truth. Like how exciting it'd be to have a strong, incredibly sexy man take control for a change, a man she didn't have to tell what to do or how to do it.

Thank God, Suze hadn't included that!

A shaky sigh escaped her as his gaze returned to the letter. A letter containing her words. A letter she didn't write. Hysterical laughter bubbled in her throat. She was going to kill Suze, just as soon as she got out of here. If she got out of here.

Do you want to get out of here?

"For example..." he began.

She watched him rake his fingers through his jet-black hair. Fingers that tousled more than smoothed. Her hand itched to smooth it back, to comb through his hair, tracing the path his fingers had made. His lashes, so long and dark, quivered as his eyes traveled the page. Almost feminine on such a masculine face. An exciting contrast.

If I had answered a personal ad, he would be the perfect playmate. Strong, compelling, and self-confident. A man she couldn't easily bend to her will. A man she could definitely imagine taking control.

"You start your letter—"

Astrid jumped. "It's not my letter."

"Excuse me. Suze starts the letter with 'All my life, I've been responsible, done the right thing.'" He lifted a brow quizzically. "That doesn't seem like a joke."

Working sixteen hours a day nearly seven days a week for the last five years. Forgoing sex for over a year...

"Of course not. Eventures is very successful. It didn't get that way by my being irresponsible."

Amusement flickered briefly in his eyes before he continued. "'...I've never had a desire to be submissive.'"

Her breath caught as his smoldering gaze captured her startled one.

"'But your ad made me wonder. What would that feel like?'..."

To listen to his deep velvety voice murmuring her name? Telling her what to do? Her gaze dropped to his mouth. Maybe ordering her to kiss him? If he did, she'd tease him. She'd trace his mouth with her fingertip, following the rolling 'm' of his upper lip to the delectably rounded lower lip. Then, she'd nibble their fullness, telling him how good he tasted, asking him if he wanted more. And he would want more. A groan would rumble in his throat—

His lips curved into a knowing smile.

Heat rushed back to her face.

"Is that a joke, Ms. Thomas?" he asked softly.

Astrid forced her breathing to remain even. He shouldn't be speaking words never meant for him to hear. Secret desires never meant for him to know.

She wanted to leave.

She wanted to stay.

"'To let go and do something wild. Something so totally unlike me.'" An invitation beckoned in his smoky eyes. "How would that feel, Ms. Thomas?"

Decadent. Indulgent. Titillating.

"I told you that I did not write that letter," she said. Her voice cracked.

"Then what did Suze write?"

Astrid remained silent.

"I'll tell you. She wrote—"

"'I think it would be exciting,'" Astrid quoted in a strangled voice.

"Is that a joke, Ms. Thomas?"

Her face burned. The trance broken, she grabbed her purse and portfolio. "I'm sorry to have wasted your time, Mr. Santos. I'll—"

"I don't think any of this is a joke, Ms. Thomas."

She paused, sending him what she hoped was a cold glare. "You don't know anything about me, Mr. Santos."

"Only what's in the letter."

The smugness in his tone forced her to respond. "Mr. Santos, I have an active social life." *Liar.* "I have no need to answer personal ads."

"Well, judging from your resume, you've arranged some pretty large events for major corporations. Unless you have a large staff, that doesn't leave much time for…how did you put it?" Lean fingers stroked his chin while he pondered the question. "Oh yes. An 'active social life.'"

Astrid stiffened. Unwanted images of her personal life flashed through her mind—weekend pizza deliveries to her office, the occasional girls-night-out with Suze, daily 6:00 a.m. coffee runs to The Java Cup. "My personal life is not your concern, Mr. Santos."

"But it is, Ms. Thomas. For the Weekend Trophy Wife position."

"Goodbye, Mr. Santos." Astrid stood and walked to the door.

"I'm offering you the opportunity to be someone else. For forty-eight hours, you'll give up control."

The seductive tone. The compelling words. Against her will, Astrid paused. To be someone else…

"It's an erotic game, Ms. Thomas, with one major rule."

Curiosity made her turn back around.

"That you enjoy it. If, at any time, for any reason, you do not, just say the word and it's over." He snapped his finger. "Just like that."

An erotic game, complete with an out.

No one had to know of it.

He leaned back in his chair.

"Sit down, Ms. Thomas."

Sit down, Astrid.

"I prefer to stand, Mr. Santos."

A slight upward lift of his lips. "Before we move on to a trophy wife's... 'duties', there are a couple of other points in your letter that I find intriguing."

She didn't bother to correct him on the ownership of the letter.

"It goes on to say, 'But I believe there's a part of all of us that fantasizes about giving expression to the opposite of who we are. Isn't that why you placed the ad? I mean, if I saw you right now, would I see a mild-mannered man who fantasizes about being dominant? Or would I see a powerful man who fantasizes about taking his dominance to a different level?'"

He raised his head and smiled. A cocky smile. "Do you know which one I am, Ms. Thomas?"

A rhetorical question, as they both knew. If her heart wasn't banging against her ribcage, and her head wasn't spinning, she'd laugh outright at the thought of Erik Santos wishing to be dominant. Why, the man sweated dominance from his pores.

No one had to know of it.

Those words again, her unconscious mind encouraging her to give in to the fantasy. Erotic play just between the two of them.

"And now we come to one of my favorite parts. '...But the possibility of giving up control in such a non-threatening way excites me. It's all a game.'" He paused meaningfully. "'A game in which physical and/or sexual control is relinquished, but emotional control remains intact. The best of both worlds.'"

After a few seconds, she remembered to breathe, forcing her breaths to remain even.

"Why is it that emotions scare you, Ms. Thomas?"

Because they'll overtake me, suffocate me, devastate me, and undo everything that I've accomplished. It was a family lesson she'd learned well.

"Emotions don't scare me. I just prefer to avoid them." She laced bravado into her tone. "Why do they scare you, Mr. Santos?"

Something flickered in the depths of his eyes, fading too quickly for her to read. "What makes you think emotions scare me, Ms. Thomas?"

She lifted an eyebrow. "You're seeking a weekend liaison, Mr. Santos. No chance of emotional involvement within forty-eight hours, is there?"

"A fascinating speculation." His smile goaded. "But are you sure that you're talking about *me*, Ms. Thomas?"

She masked the shocking accuracy of his statement with a careless shrug.

"Which brings us to your "duties." You'll dangle on my arm, looking beautiful. You'll do what I say, when I say it. You won't give your opinion unless I ask for it." He stopped to take a sip of his drink. "I'm not interested in your mind, Ms. Thomas."

I'm not interested in your mind. How politically incorrect. Her heartbeat quickened.

"Why me? Why not just find someone who already has these admirable qualities, Mr. Santos?"

His gaze rested once again on her mouth before returning to her eyes. "You are the epitome of control, Ms. Thomas. Taking away that control is the ultimate turn on."

Astrid shrugged, clearing her throat. "But what's in this for me, Mr. Santos?" Her voice trembled.

His eyes told her they both knew what was in it for her. He rose.

While her mind directed her legs to the door, her hormones led her to the chair she'd previously vacated. Astrid sank into the chair before her legs buckled under her.

As he walked to the bar, she admired the fit of his pants—the way they outlined his ass. His long fingers circled the bottle, pouring the clear liquid. "Why, you get to be taken care of and pampered. In short, you get to live the lifestyle to which you are *not* accustomed." Ice cubes clinked against the glass. He turned, facing her. "And," he continued, swirling the glass, "you get to have sex with me. Often. When I want it."

Her eyes widened.

His glittered.

His words were meant to shock—they did. His words were meant to tantalize—they did. His words appealed to a side of Astrid that she'd never expressed. To be taken care of, to be pampered. Astrid had never let a man do those things. Not because she'd never wanted to, or never fantasized about it, but rather because it meant giving up control.

She wanted it.

No one would have to know.

But the sex. Having sex when he wanted it…

She snorted. The snort sounded like a gasp. "How do I know you're any good?"

He shrugged.

She swallowed. "I think I'd like a drink."

He walked over, stopping in front of her chair. As she took the glass from his outstretched hand, her fingers brushed his, tingling on contact. She swallowed a mouthful of alcohol, fighting the tears that threatened to fill her eyes as the liquid burned her throat. He remained in front of her. Waiting. His thighs mere inches from her mouth. The expensive trousers hinted at the hardness of his thighs, drawing her gaze to them, around them, up to the bottom of his zipper.

Astrid quickly averted her eyes before they traveled any higher, and gulped down the last of his drink.

Erik leaned over, tilting her chin up with his forefinger. The pad of his thumb caressed her bottom lip. She held her breath.

"Would you like me to show you?" he asked quietly.

"Sh-show me?"

His finger dipped between her lips. She fought the urge to suck it. "Show you how good I am."

Yes! Images flitted through her mind. Of Erik gliding his hand down her neck, sliding over her breast, stroking her nipple, pinching it...Instead, she said, "No. I...I need to think about this. Sleep on it."

"No," he said, taking the glass from her nerveless fingers and setting it down.

He leaned toward her.

Astrid willed her body to remain motionless while her fingers gripped the armrests.

Strong hands pressed down over hers, holding her captive.

He leaned closer and the woodsy scent of his cologne wafted under her nose and entered her body, igniting nerve endings. Astrid leaned back.

He chuckled. There was no humor in the sound. "If I let you leave, Ms. Thomas, you'll talk yourself out of it before you reach the lobby."

If he let her leave? Tingles skipped up her arms at the forcefulness of that statement. His warm breath bounced off her lips, enticing her, drawing her closer. A slight tilt of her head and she would be able to taste him, just as she'd fantasized about doing.

One tiny movement.

Unwillingly, her eyelids lowered, her head tilted, and her lips brushed...his cheek.

Her eyes flew open.

His tongue flickered against her earlobe.

"Did you want me to kiss you, Ms. Thomas," he whispered huskily into her ear. "Like this?" he asked, letting his lips nibble and his tongue swirl their way down her neck.

Astrid shivered, a moan escaping her.

"Was that a yes?" he rasped, his mouth moving across her collarbone and up her throat.

What was happening to her? "Oh..."

He suckled her chin. "Say it."

Kiss me.

She wouldn't say it.

His tongue moved up, tracing her lower lip. "Say it," he said hoarsely.

She struggled to free her hands.

His grip tightened.

Kiss me.

If she didn't get away from him, she was going to say it. She was going to arch toward him, strain to meet his lips…

His hold on her hands loosened, lightly caressing, no longer restraining. He pulled back and stared unsmilingly at her. The hunger radiating from his gaze stunned her.

Abruptly, her hands were free. "You've got ten minutes," he said. His voice sounded rusty.

"Ten minutes?" she asked drunkenly.

"To think about it." He left the room.

Astrid's head lolled back against the chair, and she closed her eyes, feeling the heat in her stomach spread through her body. She ran a shaky hand over her hair, absently noting that every strand seemed neatly secured at the back of her head. Which surprised her. Given that her insides felt all jumbled, it seemed only fitting that her external appearance should match. She ran trembling fingers over her ear and down her neck, still feeling lips that were no longer there.

She shuddered. What had happened to that control she prided herself on having? She'd been on the verge of begging him to kiss her. She couldn't remember the last time she'd wanted to be kissed so badly. Had she ever wanted a kiss—or a man—like this?

Shifting her focus from her throbbing body, she concentrated on getting her brain to function. Erik's words echoed in her mind. To be someone else for forty-eight hours. A man's plaything. *His* plaything. How humiliating. How exciting.

No one would have to know.

She sank deeper into the chair, letting snippets of his personal ad flit through her mind.

Tired of the same old thing?

Yes, she was. Well, maybe not of Eventures. She loved her job, even with its long hours and working weekends. But lately, restlessness had crept in, distracting her, confusing her, making her wonder if something was missing.

Want to try something new?

Yes, she did. Something spontaneous and totally out of character. For once in her life, she wanted to live in the moment and ignore the consequences. And fate—or rather, Suze—had offered up the perfect opportunity, the chance to indulge in sexual gratification and get whatever was distracting her out of her system, and then return to Eventures, refreshed and enthused.

With her emotions still intact.

Single, professional male seeks single, submissive female…

But did she want to be submissive? Her professional life—which was her whole life—revolved around instructing others, making things happens, insuring success. What would it feel like to give up control? Sexual control. With him. Sexy, masculine, wealthy Erik Santos. A shiver rippled through her.

…for Weekend Trophy Wife.

An attractive woman. Desired for her body, not her mind. A symbol of a man's success. A thrill of the forbidden tickled her spine.

Your slavish devotion will be rewarded with orgasmic feasts.

Orgasmic feasts with Erik Santos. A man she could imagine knew what to do without being told. She had only to bury her hands in the thickness of his hair and draw his head down to hers, touching her lips to his, teasing, nibbling, before he would take over, going lower, over the swell of her breast...

She heard him enter the room. Felt him standing in front of her. Imagined his hips, lip level once again...

"I want you to wear these," he said.

Her eyes snapped open, darting from the three-inch heels he dangled from one finger to the skimpy bit of material hanging from the other. Spandex knit. Skin tight. Candy apple red. Astrid had never worn anything so indecent in her life.

"I haven't given you my answer, Mr. Santos."

A sly smile. "I already know your answer, Ms. Thomas."

Astrid Thomas was ripe for fantasy.

Erik watched her. Confusion, indecision, and apprehension flitted across her face in a matter of seconds. It was the last one, the apprehension, that concerned him. But he was sure he'd gauged her right. The knack for reading people that served him so well in business was at work here, telling him that the letter was not totally a joke. Astrid's blushes, her defensiveness, and the fact that she was still here all convinced him that she was interested. Even if she didn't want to be interested. Only a take-charge man could get a no-nonsense woman like her to give in to fantasy.

And he was the man to give it to her.

His gaze dropped to her mouth, mesmerized by the snowy white teeth nibbling her lower lip. Lips he had teased, only to have them tease him back, nearly shattering his control. He wanted to crush them under his. Again and again.

The thrill of the challenge shot through him, and a slow smile spread over his face.

"Am I wrong, Ms. Thomas?"

She stared at him, the faint flush to her skin the only crack in her unflappable composure.

"Why would an obviously wealthy man like you place a personal ad for a playmate, Mr. Santos?" she asked, ignoring his question.

His smile froze. She was incredulous, just as she'd been when she'd first discovered that he'd placed the ad. Just like Natalie would be if she were here, disbelieving of his ability to be spontaneous, to have fun. Well, Natalie wasn't here.

But what to say in answer to Astrid's question about the ad?

He wouldn't. I didn't.

Here was another opportunity to tell her the truth, to explain the mix-up with the listing.

He opened his mouth to do so, then masked the effort with a yawn. He couldn't do it. The game would be over before it even started. And this self-contained, self-controlled woman would walk out the door.

Out of his life.

She couldn't. Not yet. What had started out as mere curiosity as to why such an attractive, self-possessed woman—a woman who had come highly recommended by a respected colleague—would answer a personal ad, had now become an…obsession. An obsession to see what she would be like if she let go of that cool, controlled façade. Like she'd almost done when he'd pinned her to the chair.

The words that he had blurted were true: relieving Astrid Thomas of her control suddenly was the ultimate turn on.

Her molasses brown hair, secured neatly with a clip, invited his hands to free it. The sensual full lips begged him to taste them. To have her pliable and yielding, her luminous chocolate brown eyes pleading for him to touch her, her urgent cries begging for him to take her…

Blood rushed to his cock.

Sanity fled from his mind.

Erik sat in the chair opposite her. He stared at her, noticing the rapid rise and fall of her breasts beneath the crisp, white blouse. An innocent, unassuming blouse. Underneath that was…a lacy, frilly confection that barely covered perky nipples? A practical white cotton bra hiding voluptuous breasts?

He shifted in his chair.

His eyes traveled lower, to the slim legs pressed together and crossed primly at the ankle. Unbidden images of crotchless panties and g-strings drifted through his mind—shocking items received in response to the personal ad. Items that now excited him as he pictured them encircling Astrid's hips.

He stifled a groan.

He'd find out soon enough. As soon as he got her hot little body into the sexy red dress. Lucky for him that the shop next door had been able to deliver it within ten minutes. He ran an assessing eye over her body. Yes, she was definitely a size six.

Reluctantly, he returned his gaze to her face, watching in amusement as her chin lifted defiantly.

"Surely you aren't that desperate, Mr. Santos."

He settled back in the chair and gazed at her between half-lidded eyes. "Quite the opposite, Ms. Thomas."

She frowned.

He smiled. "It's my fantasy, Ms. Thomas." *Well, it hadn't been until you walked through the door.* "I've never had a plaything just as you've never been one."

Apprehension returned to her gaze.

He twirled the red shoe around the tip of his finger. "Are you brave enough to exchange control for passion, Ms. Thomas?"

Astrid's gaze escaped Erik's intense stare, attracted to the shoe, to its gravity-defying heel. She watched it go round and round, like a hypnotist's hypno-disk. Did she have the courage to give in to fantasy?

Fantasy in the mind differed from fantasy in action.

She let her gaze travel from his rotating fingertip to his unbuttoned collar. His tie hung askew, loosely knotted at the neck, revealing the round top of a plain t-shirt. Astrid imagined crinkly black hair crushed beneath the cotton, imagined her fingers threading their way through the curls, parting and smoothing, before glossing over a pebbled nipple.

She forced the curling hairs from her mind, her gaze returning to his face. Drawn once again to his brooding eyes with their long lashes, to his perfectly chiseled cheekbones, and his luscious lips. Lips that kept beckoning to her, inviting her to explore, to taste, to finish what he had started.

God, he was gorgeous.

Her heart thudded in her chest. One didn't run into men like Erik Santos every day. Well, at least she didn't. To let fear cause this opportunity to slip through her fingers would be silly, wouldn't it? She'd always wonder 'what if.'

But could she really do it? Be totally submissive?

Astrid drew in a deep breath and let her gaze drift back to his face. Currant-black eyes stared back at her, devoid of expression. Expressionless now, but she'd seen them shine with awareness. As he'd stared at her mouth, her breasts, her legs.

Coldness to desire. Desire to coldness.

She smiled.

"I will be your puppet, your plaything, on one condition."

His brows drew together. "You aren't entitled to conditions, Ms. Thomas."

"Ahhh, but we haven't started 'playing' yet, Mr. Santos."

His frown deepened.

Her smile widened. "Here's my condition: I'll be your plaything for the first twenty-four hours. But you'll be mine for the remaining twenty-four."

He abruptly stilled. His eyes narrowed. Astrid counted the seconds as they passed.

Finally, the corners of his mouth lifted. "No conditions, Ms. Thomas."

Fear grasped the edges of her heart.

"It's time for your first lesson."

Excitement roared through her veins. "My first lesson?"

"In being submissive."

He stood and motioned to the left.

It was starting.

Astrid willed her muscles to relax. She could do this. After all, wasn't the submissive one the one who was really in control?

She shrugged, striving for indifference.

And failed.

She walked in the direction he indicated, feeling his eyes drill into her back. At the closed door, she turned the doorknob and stopped abruptly as the door swung open.

Her astonished gaze circled the room. A bedroom.

Whereas the office, with its leather and chrome, projected an image of sterile professionalism, the bedroom seemed...intimate. The oversized pillows on the king size bed were dented, as if someone had sat against them. A navy blue suit jacket sprawled against the sage comforter, as if absently tossed there, while the heel of a shoe stuck out of the parted closet doors. Mirrored closet doors.

"Is there a problem, Ms. Thomas?"

She quieted her panicked breath. "I wasn't expecting a bedroom, Mr. Santos. How...convenient."

"Yes, it is." As his hand at her waist propelled her forward, her gaze skimmed over the bed, refusing to linger, refusing to wonder what it would feel like to lie on that bed with his body on top of her. His hand tightened, forcing her to stop in front of the closet. She met his gaze in the mirrored surface.

His lips quirked into a half-smile. "I work long hours. I use the bed for sleeping, not entertaining."

Did that mean that she was the first woman to be here? An irrational buzz of pleasure skittered through her.

He moved behind her and dropped the dress and shoes to the floor. "Do you know what I'm going to do to you?"

No, but she knew what she wanted him to do to her: Turn her around and capture her lips, finally giving her the kiss she'd been craving, the—

With both hands on her waist, his fingers freed the blouse from the waistband of her skirt.

He meant to undress her.

Astrid stiffened.

His fingers continued undeterred, unbuttoning the bottom button of her blouse.

"I'm going to take off all your clothes..."

He released the next button.

"I'm going to look at every inch of your body..."

His eyes dared her to stop him.

"And you are going to stand here and let me."

Another button popped loose.

"Aren't you, Ms. Thomas?"

No!

But she had to. This was the game, a game that she had agreed to play, a game that she was suddenly afraid to play. Not trusting herself to speak, she gulped and gave him a terse nod.

His fingers paused over the last button. "A trophy wife doesn't issue ultimatums, Ms. Thomas. But if she does, she has to be punished."

The last button was freed.

"Do you like being punished, Ms. Thomas?" He undid the clasp of her bra. Hooking his fingers under the straps, he slid both bra and blouse off her shoulders. Instinctively, she raised her arms, hugging her chest.

She couldn't go through with this.

His hands moved down, caressing her upper arms.

"What's the word?" she blurted.

"What word?"

"The word that I say to end this."

His hands stilled. "Is that what you want? To end this?" he asked quietly.

Astrid paused, confused by the sudden tension in the air. Excitement and anxiety battled for control. Did she want him to stop? Was that really what she wanted? "I…I just want to know what the word is."

The mirror reflected his dark eyes staring intently into hers.

"You choose the word. A unique word that's unlikely to be used during our game or in a moment of passion."

"The word will be…bubbles."

Will be referred to the future—an unconscious indication that she did not want to stop.

"Drop your arms."

Desire burned in his eyes.

"Please."

Need laced his voice.

Desire and need for her. Because of her. The force of her sexuality surged through her veins, empowering her. She lifted her chin and dropped her arms. Her clothing fell soundlessly to the floor.

His gaze dropped to her breasts, his long, dark lashes sweeping his cheeks. Seconds ticked by as he stared.

She felt her nipples harden involuntarily. The blood rushed to her face, and she looked away, unwilling to catch his gaze. She felt him unzip the back of her skirt. His hands slid her skirt, pantyhose, and panties over her hips and down her legs. They pooled around her ankles.

Astrid stood completely naked.

She closed her eyes and remained still, hands clenched by her side. Waiting for him to do something, anything. Her skin tingled, burning where his gaze had rested, aching for him to touch her, to cover every inch of her body with his fingers, his lips, his tongue.

"Open your eyes."

She forced her eyes open and gazed sightlessly at the brocade edge of the comforter visible in the mirror.

"Look at me."

She didn't want to look at him. She didn't want him to see the need blazing in her eyes, uncontrollable need that threatened to consume her.

"Now." The urgency in his voice drew her focus to him. Kneeling beside her, the top of his raven head level with her thighs, should have made her feel dominant, the controller. Instead, the searing heat burning in his gaze weakened her, leaving her willing and wanting to do whatever he asked.

He held her gaze in the mirror as his tongue lapped lightly along the side of her thigh. Long lashes moved downward, hiding his eyes, while his tongue drew circles of wetness along her parched skin. Nerve endings she'd never been aware of shot darts of pleasure through her and Astrid stumbled, breaking contact.

Strong hands gripped her thighs, steadying her, before sliding downward.

"Your body is delectable, Astrid," he said, his voice as unsteady as her legs had been.

Delectable. As in, delightful, delicious, good to eat. Her starving body demanded to know: Which parts of her body were delectable?

He lifted her foot and ran a finger lightly under her toes. "This part," he said, answering the question she was unaware that she'd asked, before slipping a red sandal over each foot.

He picked up the red dress. After tearing off the price tag, he lifted one stiletto-clad heel, then the other, into it. Once again behind her, he pulled the clingy material up over her hips, standing as he went. She watched in the mirror as he slid his hands up her inner thighs, stopping short of her swollen sex, and squeezed lightly. "And this part," he said hoarsely.

His fingertips continued up, trailing over her stomach, to the underside of her breasts. Skin quivered at his touch.

"And especially this part..." He caressed the tip of each turgid nipple.

Astrid gasped.

"Which parts of your body do I like, Astrid?"

"All of them," she whispered.

Satisfaction gleamed in his eyes as he pulled the dress up, guiding her arms through the openings. Hands once again on her hips, he pulled her back against him. His erection pushed against the thin fabric of the dress.

Astrid moaned.

"Do you feel how much I like your body?"

"...Yes."

He ground his erection harder against her. "I didn't hear you."

"I said...yes."

He stopped.

Astrid's eyes flew open. An objection hovered on her lips.

"Let's go," he said.

"Go where?" she asked, forcing her eyes to focus.

He shook his head with mock sadness. "Ms. Thomas, have you not learned anything from your first lesson?"

Yes, she had. She'd learned that she could be turned on more than she'd ever thought possible. By a stranger. Albeit, an incredibly sexy stranger with probing dark eyes and sensually lethal fingers, mouth, tongue—

She pushed aside the arousing thoughts, along with the unfulfilled ache in her body, and attempted to remember the lesson he'd just taught her.

A lesson on how to endure sexual frustration?

"Your answer, Ms. Thomas?"

"Yes."

"Yes, what?"

"I've learned my lesson."

"Which is?"

Astrid swallowed hard, working up the nerve to utter the words he wanted to hear. *To obey, no questions asked, no requests made.* "To do what you say," she said tightly.

"Good,' he said, moving away from her.

Her gaze went from him to her appearance in the mirror, from her ridiculously arched feet to her scantily clad body. One deep breath and her nipples would pop out of the bodice. Within two steps, the hem of the dress would ride up her thighs, making her lack of underwear clearly visible. "I can't leave the room looking like this," she said, instantly forgetting the recent lesson.

"Yes, you can," he said, scooping her clothes from the floor.

"Wait!" she cried, as he left the room. Astrid hobbled after him as quickly as she dared. She entered the office just as he locked the wet bar.

Erik dangled the key from his finger before slipping it into his pocket. He smiled evilly. "Unless you want to leave the room naked."

He held out his arm to her.

The indistinct murmur of simultaneous conversations greeted her as they entered the bar. Astrid heaved a sigh of relief. Though she'd mastered the stilt-like heels in the ninety-three steps she'd taken to get here, her ankles throbbed. She was convinced that these shoes existed solely as props in porn movies. No real-life woman could wear them and remain alive.

She glanced curiously around the crowded room. Men in suits filled most of the barstools surrounding the U-shaped bar while couples took up the booths. The glow cast by the recessed lighting on the dark cherry wood bar and tables soothed. The classical chords struck by the pianist relaxed. The overall effect calmed.

She met the gaze of seated patrons as she passed. Men stared, lustful eyes lingering on her breasts, her thighs, and her barely concealed crotch. Women glared, envy passing through their eyes before they looked away. Her little red dress accomplished what her tailored suit couldn't. Astrid shook her head in amazement.

Erik stopped at an empty table. She pulled ineffectively at the dress before sliding into the booth.

She listened to the seductive timbre of Erik's voice as he ordered their drinks. With a flash of irritation, she noted he didn't ask her preference. He draped an arm around her shoulders and remained silent.

"You have an admirer at the bar," he observed once their drinks had arrived.

Astrid looked, eyes drawn to a bald, pudgy man. Staring at her. The blatant hunger in his gaze took her by surprise.

Erik handed her the swizzle stick from her drink. "Put this in your mouth. Suck it. Move it slowly in and out," he murmured in her ear.

A bolt of excitement sizzled through her at his words. Moisture formed between her legs. She took the swizzle stick from him, slipping it between her lips. She pursed her lips and twirled the stick, moving it in and out, sucking deeply with each stroke.

"Good. Now, look at him. Make him imagine it's *his* stick in your mouth." Erik's lips traveled down her neck, nipping. Shivers quaked through her body. More wetness pooled between her legs.

She stared at the barfly.

He stared at her lips.

After a couple of deep strokes, she withdrew the swizzle stick and licked the bulbous tip. The barfly gaped at her.

She jumped as Erik's hand fell to her thigh.

"Open your legs," he whispered, his breath fanning her neck.

She parted her legs.

His hand slid to the side, caressing her inner thigh, moving higher, under the hem of the skirt. She spread her legs wider and tipped her hips upward, the swizzle stick motionless at the side of her mouth.

"How does this feel?"

Her body begged for his touch. "G-good."

"Only good?" His tongue traced her jaw line.

Silence.

He bit her ear in warning. She shivered.

"Unbelievable," she breathed.

His lips replaced his teeth, nibbling, soothing. "What do you want?" he asked in her ear, following his words with his tongue. A feather-light lick.

Astrid stifled a moan. "Y-you," she panted.

His fingers rewarded her for the correct answer. She gasped. The bald man's gaze darted under the table, seeking what remained hidden. Erik's fingers parted the lips under her skirt, exploring, stroking...

Ignoring the hard nub.

"Oh...please," she breathed. She reached for his hand. Pulling. Guiding.

He avoided her grasp. His hand left her skin and Astrid whimpered in protest, ripping her gaze from the flushed barfly.

Erik raised his finger to his lips. He sucked the tip. "It's not so hard to play the part, is it, Astrid?"

Reality crashed down on her.

Erik rose from his seat. He withdrew a bill from his pocket and tossed it onto the table. "The forty-eight hours begin tomorrow." He leaned down, his mouth near her ear. "*Now* you can go home and sleep on it."

He straightened and left without looking back.

Chapter Two

The forty-eight hours begin tomorrow.

Dazed, Astrid opened the door of her condo. She flipped on the light and absently walked through the living room. Water. She needed water to moisten her suddenly dry mouth.

As she entered the kitchen, a plaintive meow sounded from the end of the breakfast bar.

"Hi, Grumpy," she said, reaching down to scratch his ears.

Golden eyes stared morosely up at her before he showed her his backside and walked away.

Someone had an attitude tonight. Maybe he was jealous.

"I know what will make you feel better," she said in a singsong voice, popping the lid on a can of his favorite cat food. Grumpy sauntered to his food bowl and sat, refusing to look at her.

Astrid laughed, relieving a little of the tension she felt.

While Grumpy ate, she pressed a button on the answering machine sitting on the counter. Voices pierced the still air. Ordinarily recognizable voices that tonight sounded foreign. She grabbed a bottle of spring water as the voices died. A glance at the digital display indicated that she'd listened to three messages.

No one would have to know.

She had to tell someone.

Astrid picked up the phone and dialed. A swig of water soothed her throat while electronic ringing buzzed in her ear. Seconds later, the recorded voice of her best friend answered.

"Suze, I don't know whether to strangle you or kiss you. Call me," she said, her voice quavering. She hung up.

She finished the water just as Grumpy finished his meal. She scooped him up in her arms and floated down the hall to her bedroom. Setting him on the antique white comforter, she quickly undressed and slid into bed. As she stroked his soft fur, Grumpy purred his forgiveness.

She closed her eyes.

They snapped open.

What had she done? Prim and proper, responsible and levelheaded Astrid

Thomas had never done anything so totally bold. And yet tonight, she'd been stripped and dressed, then nibbled and fondled. In public. By a stranger.

How shameful.

How sinfully delightful.

Buttons popping. The soft brush of fabric against her body...

She turned onto her side.

Strong fingers painting cottony strokes against her starved skin...Soft lips kissing, but not satisfying...

She turned to the other side.

Eyes, glazed with lust, staring from across the bar...Fingertips inching up her thigh, circling inward, igniting sparks of fire...Her burning need for Erik to bury his fingers deep inside...

Astrid groaned and flopped onto her back.

Grumpy jumped off the bed in disgust.

Ringing invaded her obliviousness. Astrid ignored it and snuggled deeper into her pillow. The ringing continued.

Her fingers groped the nightstand in annoyance. "Hello," she croaked, receiver in hand.

"Hi, Astrid. What's up with the cryptic message?"

"Later, Suze. I'm tired."

"It's 6:00 a.m."

"It's Saturday, Suze."

"Yeah, but you never sleep in."

"Well, I am today." Astrid hung up the phone.

The ringing started again. She ignored it. It persisted. Astrid sighed and picked up the receiver.

"Yes, Suze?"

"This sounds serious. Just give me a hint and I'll stop bothering you. At least until 7:00."

Yawning, Astrid stretched and sat up. "Thanks to you, I'm awake now." Grumpy, also awake, hopped up on the bed with a soft meow. Astrid rubbed his belly.

"Great. Then meet me at The Java Cup. I'll make it up to you with caffeine."

Suze's hearty laughter ended with a click.

Forty-five minutes later, the whoosh of the espresso machine, the aroma of fresh coffee beans, and the distinctive crooning of Bob Marley greeted her as she entered The Cup. She spotted Suze's flaming red hair by the shelves of coffee-themed novelties.

"Hey, Suze."

Suze turned and hugged her. "You look like shit."

"Thank you."

"Oh, I'm just jealous," Suze grumbled. "No one should roll out of bed—"

"I didn't just roll out of bed."

Suze held up her hands. "Spare me. I'm fully aware of your thirty-minute beauty routine. Which never fails to disgust me, I might add."

"Well, if I had your sex kitten look, I'd-"

"A look for which I have to labor hours in front of the mirror. Unlike your naturally fresh and innocent, girl-next-door image." Suze sighed dramatically.

Astrid rolled her eyes. "This conversation is like a scene from *Groundhog Day*."

"*Groundhog Day?*"

"You know, the movie where Phil Connors relives the same day over and over?"

"Oh, yeah." Suze squinted at the ceiling for a second. She smiled slyly. "Actually, I think it's the beginning of a scene out of *Envy*, where the jealous friend—"

Astrid groaned. "Can we just go get coffee?" Without waiting for an answer, she turned and zigzagged her way through the round tables, heading for the counter. She heard Suze trailing behind her.

Coffees in hand, they snared their favorite table.

"Well?" Suze asked, once they were seated.

"As you well know, I had a job interview yesterday that was no job interview."

"Huh?" Suze raised her cup to her mouth.

"Oh, don't play innocent."

Suze stared at her blankly.

"You know. The letter and resume you gave Bobby's brother in response to his personal ad. Without my knowledge."

"Oh, that." Suze waved her hand dismissively. "So how'd it go?"

Astrid frowned. "'Oh, that.' That's all you have to say, after transcribing a letter we dictated in jest? After forwarding said letter without my permission?"

"Well, it's obvious you needed my help."

Astrid snorted. "Just like I needed your help the time you set me up with Joshua Jamison?"

"One small mistake," Suze muttered.

Astrid shook her head. "The name itself should have been a clue. And then there was that surprise party-"

"All right, already. This was different. Astrid, will you please tell me what happened?"

Astrid smiled and raised her coffee cup in an imaginary toast. "You are looking at the new, adventurous, fun-loving Astrid Thomas. Weekend Trophy Wife extraordinaire."

Suze choked on her coffee, tears filling her sea blue eyes. Astrid pounded her on the back.

"He asked you to be his sexual playmate?" Suze asked, once her coughing subsided.

Astrid frowned. "What else would he ask me to be?"

"His event planner?"

Astrid laughed. "Well, for a moment there, I thought he might. He was pretty impressed by my professional accomplishments."

"So what happened next?"

"I had a playmate audition."

"No!"

"My sentiments exactly. But I passed."

Suze's mouth dropped open.

Astrid grinned. "So you see," she said, once she'd finished giving Suze a summary of the interview. "I might be Trophy Wife material after all."

Suze rolled her eyes, no longer shocked.

"Well, I did strut my stuff in that slutty red dress. And I followed orders to a 'T' with that swizzle stick."

"Only because it turned you on."

"True. And Erik Santos turns me on." Her cheeks felt warm. She changed the subject. "Suze, why'd you do this?"

Suze smiled. "Because I thought the two of you would make a great couple. So when we were joking about it that night at The Red Rooster, I had an idea. I passed your letter—"

"It was not exactly my letter."

Suze rolled her eyes. "Astrid, you dictated ninety-nine percent of it. Anyway, I gave him the letter and your resume—"

"But why? If you wanted us to meet, why not just invite the two of us to dinner with you and Bobby and…and let whatever happened happen?"

Suze closed her eyes and exhaled noisily through her mouth. "It is obvious why I'm the matchmaker in our relationship."

Astrid waited patiently for the theatrics to end.

Suze opened her eyes. "Astrid, were you not just whining about Joshua Jamison and—"

"I was not whining."

"Astrid!"

"All right. I was whining."

Suze smiled smugly. "Exactly. Which is why you would never have agreed to another blind date and, for reasons of pride, neither would Erik. So I thought that if he saw the letter and the resume together, it might stimulate interest in you."

Astrid shook her head at Suze's reasoning. "Well, you definitely stimulated interest."

Suze pursed her lips thoughtfully, obviously ignoring Astrid's sarcasm. "Only I didn't expect him to ask you to…Oh well, who cares? Look how well things turned out."

Astrid took a sip of coffee. "You would say that."

"Well, I'm right, aren't I?" Suze's eyes sparkled mischievously.

Astrid snorted again. "Well, Bobby may care. He may not approve of your meddling."

Suze scoffed. "He doesn't care. In fact, he encouraged me. Thought of it as a suitable payback for Erik's interference in his life." Her smile had an inquisitive edge. "I bet Erik came across all stoic and tough during the interview, didn't he?"

"That's an understatement."

"Well, it's all an act. Erik's a big softy."

Visions of Erik making her stand still while he undressed her, feeling his hardness pressed against her, ordering her to taunt the guy in the bar with the swizzle stick. There was nothing soft—either literally or figuratively—about Erik Santos.

Astrid chuckled.

"What's so funny?"

"You know that part of the letter that questioned whether the ad owner was a wimp who dreamed of being dominant? Well, according you, I've obviously misjudged Erik."

"There's a big difference between a wimp and a softy."

"Well, you'll never convince me that Erik is either one." Astrid took a sip of her coffee. "What I can't figure out is why he placed the ad in the first place."

"He told you he placed the ad?"

"What? Yeah…Well, he didn't come right out and say it but…" Astrid frowned. "Why would you ask that?"

"I just wondered…Oh, forget it. Just tell me you're going to do it."

Astrid's frown faded.

The forty-eight hours begin tomorrow.

Tomorrow was today.

"Will you watch Grumpy?"

Suze nodded rapidly. "Does that mean you're going to do it?"

Astrid smiled weakly. "I'm going to do it."

Suze let out a whoop and the woman at the table next to them shot her an irritated glare.

Astrid grimaced. "Suze, please."

Suze laughed loudly. "Well, this is worth causing a scene. Finally, my best friend is going to do something…wild."

Black eyes appeared in her mind. Eyes that promised wild and much more. Astrid shivered.

"So what happens next?" Suze asked.

"I don't know. I guess he'll call me." She flipped open her cell phone. No new messages. "Look, let's change the subject before I get nervous."

Suze chuckled.

"How's Bobby?"

"He's great. We're great. Six months later and I'm still madly in love."

Astrid squashed an unexpected twinge of envy, confused as to where it had come from. It certainly wasn't over Suze being in love and all the emotional messiness love entailed. It was probably just Suze's happiness, her contentment. Something that Astrid wasn't feeling right now.

"...so I was going to invite you to a party at his place tomorrow but now that you have..." Suze paused, her gaze focusing on something behind Astrid. "Well, will you look at that," she mused.

Astrid turned and looked out the window. A sleek black limo had stopped in front of The Cup.

"The Cup doesn't draw the limo crowd," Suze said.

Astrid watched a uniformed driver exit the limo. "Maybe he's lost."

Suze whistled under her breath. "Well, he can get lost in my neighborhood anytime."

"What about Bobby?"

"A girl can still look," Suze replied wistfully.

Astrid watched the uniformed hunk approach The Cup. Black clad legs, blonde hair, and blue eyes. Classic good looks that did nothing for her. Instead, coal black hair, dark eyes, and tailored slacks danced through her mind. Her pulse quickened.

"Hmmmm," she said absently.

Suze sighed loudly, dispelling her vision of Erik. Astrid turned back to Suze. "Well, maybe you should go ask him for his number."

"No. I shall remain forever true to Bobby."

Astrid laughed.

"Excuse me. Are you Astrid Thomas?"

Astrid's laughter died as she stared up into sky blue eyes. "Yes."

"I'm here on behalf of Erik Santos."

Astrid gasped. "How did you know I was here?"

"I was instructed to wait for you at your house." He shrugged a muscular shoulder. "When you left this morning, I followed you here."

Astrid's gaze shot to the limo. Tinted windows hid the inside. "Is Mr. Santos here?"

"Yes, ma'am."

Her heartbeat raced, threatening to jump right out of her chest. "I'm s-sorry. I–"

"Would you excuse us for a moment?" Suze interrupted sweetly.

"Certainly," the driver replied. "I'll wait for you by the door." A slight bow and he moved away.

"What are you doing? You can't back out of this now," Suze wailed in dismay.

"I wasn't. I'm not. He caught me by surprise, is all. I just need...to sit here a moment." Astrid closed her eyes and willed herself to relax. She drew in a shaky breath and exhaled slowly.

Tomorrow was here.

After several deep breaths, she opened her eyes. "Wish me luck," she said. She stood and slung her purse over her shoulder.

Suze grinned. "I wish you multiple orgasms, Astrid."

Astrid smiled faintly and stood. "Oh. Grumpy's been fed so he's good until tonight. Do you still have the key to my place?"

At Suze's nod, she turned to leave.

"Hey, Astrid?"

Astrid turned back towards Suze.

"You're doing the right thing, kiddo."

Astrid nodded. Yes, she was doing the right thing. Even if her legs were shaky and she felt all trembly inside.

She started towards the waiting driver. Halfway there, she ducked inside the restroom and leaned against the door, closing her eyes.

She was going to do it.

What if she couldn't do it?

You're emotionally frigid.

Astrid's lips tightened as Jeffrey's parting accusation came unbidden to her mind. Emotionally frigid. Well, if he was right, this was one time where that trait would come in handy. A weekend of sex without emotion.

Which seemed to work for Erik. His every action, from his burning glances, to his hot touch, to the hard ridge in his perfectly creased pants, proved that he found nothing frigid about her.

She pushed away from the door, dispelling unwanted thoughts of Jeffrey, and entered the restroom. At the mirror, she paused and turned a critical eye to the wide-eyed woman staring back at her. Free of makeup, her smooth, tawny skin glistened under the bright fluorescent lighting. Her sable hair flowed over her shoulders, its layered cut flat without the help of a curling iron. A snug-fitting fuchsia t-shirt hugged her breasts, and faded jeans rested comfortably on her hips.

She frowned in dismay. Of all mornings to leave the house without a thought to her appearance. The spitting image of a trophy wife she was not. More like the clean-cut housewife in one of those laundry detergent commercials. She wished for the hundredth time she'd been blessed with Suze's sensuality.

She retracted the wish and smiled. Obviously, Erik Santos preferred a trophy wife who resembled a wholesome housewife.

She hurriedly used the bathroom, washed her hands, and exited the restroom. With one last steadying breath, she stopped in front of the driver. "I'm ready," she said.

He tipped his head in acknowledgement and held the door for her to precede him. Adrenaline surged through her. She concentrated on each step that took her closer to the limo, willing her unsteady legs not to collapse. Mere feet separated her from Erik Santos. Twenty...ten...five...

She halted as the driver opened the door for her. With a quick thanks, she slid into the back seat.

Her gaze landed immediately on the man seated to her left. Muted light shining through the tinted window behind him highlighted his dark hair. His black leather jacket complemented his hair, providing a stunning contrast to his naturally bronzed skin. A gray scooped-neck shirt was tucked into midnight black pants. Pants that covered long legs, casually parted in a 'V'. Erik Santos was danger personified.

Her gaze returned to his face.

His roamed over her. Over her hair, lingering briefly on her mouth, resting languidly on her breasts, then examining her face.

"Good morning, Astrid. Did you sleep well?"

"Yes."

He smiled. The first real smile she'd seen. Astrid felt as if she'd been socked in the stomach, all the wind knocked out of her.

"Liar," he said.

She fought the urge to squirm. "Why would I lie?"

"Because you don't want to admit that you tossed and turned in your lonely bed. Imagining my mouth exploring every inch of your body."

Astrid forced her breathing to remain normal. "You're very sure of yourself, Mr. Santos."

"My livelihood depends on my being sure of myself, Astrid." He leaned forward and opened the door of a small refrigerator. He removed a pitcher and a bottle of champagne, before pouring a little of each into a crystal wineglass. He handed it to her.

"And I think it's time you started calling me Erik."

Astrid took a sip from her glass, savoring the sweetness of the freshly squeezed orange juice enlivened by the tiny champagne bubbles. She took another sip, a sip bordering on a gulp, and let the bubbles percolate through her blood, brewing courage.

She smiled, hoping her smile looked playful. "Oh, I don't know. I kind of like…Snookums."

He raised a brow. "Snookums?"

Astrid nodded. "I'm just trying to get into my role, darling."

Erik laughed, the deep rumbling sound caressed her eardrums.

She relaxed a little.

"You're a quick study, Astrid."

Astrid tipped her glass to him and cocked her head. "Thank you, Snookums."

His smile lingered. His dark eyes probed.

"So, was I right?" he asked.

"Right about what?" she asked, feigning ignorance.

"Did you spend the night alone, tangled in your sheets, wondering what I was going to do to you?"

"No."

"No?" His tone said he knew she was lying.

She smiled. "I spent the night thinking about what you'd already done," she said, surprising herself with her honesty. She'd meant to say something witty and flip.

His eyes darkened.

"Take off your shirt," he ordered softly.

Astrid's smile disappeared, her budding cockiness evaporating as if it had never existed. Her eyes darted to the glass partition separating them from the driver. Half of the driver's face was reflected in the rearview mirror.

"He can't see us," Erik said, interpreting her gaze.

Astrid turned her attention back to Erik.

Seconds passed.

Seconds became minutes.

Her heart pounded. Her face felt flushed. Slowly, she grasped the bottom of her t-shirt and lifted it over her head.

"Now, the bra."

She reached behind her, thrusting her breasts forward, drawing Erik's gaze to them. She paused, reveling in the raw desire etched on his face. His lips were parted, his eyes partly closed. The forefinger of one hand moved slowly over the seat, drawing abstract ovals over and over again.

She unhooked her bra and tossed it to the floor, her eyes never leaving his. His gaze caressed her breasts. Hunger glittered in their darkness.

Astrid's nipples hardened.

Erik's fingers froze.

Emboldened, Astrid ran splayed fingers down and over her breasts. When she reached the undersides, she cupped a breast in each palm, lifting up. Keeping her eyes locked on his glossy-eyed gaze, she bent down to one side.

Her tongue glazed a taut nipple.

His tongue glanced his lower lip.

"Come here," he rasped.

Astrid licked.

Erik's eyes flared.

"Make me," she said.

The corners of his mouth lifted slightly. From her childish challenge or the tremor in her voice?

"Make you what, Astrid?"

Her eyes widened as he slid off his seat.

"Make you...learn to be obey?"

Astrid's pulse hummed at the thought of another lesson.

"Make you...come. Here?"

She gasped as his meaning hit her.

He chuckled and knelt before her, dipping his finger in her forgotten mimosa. He dangled his finger over the swell of her breast.

Cold liquid hit her burning skin.

Astrid inhaled sharply.

The liquid trickled downward, across her aureole, to the tip of her nipple.

Her nipple puckered.

The orange drop fell onto her lap.

"You have beautiful breasts. So responsive," Erik said. His voice was hoarse.

Another drop hit. His tongue flicked her nipple, catching the droplet before it fell.

Astrid gasped and grabbed his head.

He stopped and removed her hands. "Don't move," he ordered.

She dropped her hands, fisting them against the seat.

His tongue resumed licking. Satiny flicks that teased and inflamed.

Astrid arched toward him.

Erik moved way from her.

Astrid stared blankly and then sank back against the seat.

He smiled. Hands cupped her breasts, weighing their fullness. "So perfect," he breathed, lowering his head.

She held her breath, watching, waiting, hoping…His mouth met her skin, igniting her nerve endings, transmitting shockwaves through her body.

His tongue swirled her stiff nipple while his hands kneaded her breasts. Shivers darted through her body.

A moan escaped her.

His hands moved to her jeans. The rasp of her zipper mingled with heavy breathing. Her heavy breathing.

"Lift up," Erik said, his voice muffled against her breast.

Astrid lifted. Denim and silk slid over her skin.

Erik's trail of kisses moved down, over her stomach. Soft buttery leather caressed her bottom as his hands parted her legs.

"Can you come, here, Astrid?" he mocked, his voice unsteady.

"I don't know. I've never…Oh!"

His head burrowed between her legs, his tongue questing, seeking. Fingers spread her labia, making a path for his tongue. He speared her tiny nub with the moist tip of his tongue.

She couldn't remain still.

She jerked her hips forward, pushing them toward him. "Oh, yes," she breathed.

Her hips gyrated wildly.

His tongue probed.

She panted.

He licked.

Tingles started in her feet, spreading over her ankles and up her calves. *Oh yes, oh yes. It's right there, right there. Don't stop…*

His fingers grabbed her nipples. Pinching and pulling. Pleasure spiked outward and spiraled downward, merging with the fire stoked by his tongue. Astrid grabbed his head and held it captive. Her hips bucked.

Her eyelids fluttered shut, then open. Her unfocused gaze darted aimlessly around the limo until they collided with azure eyes reflected in the rearview mirror. She imagined the driver saw her, saw the ecstasy stamped on her face...

She cried out as waves crashed through her body.

Erik's movements slowed. Licking became kissing. Pinches became caresses. Unable to remain upright, Astrid collapsed back against the seat.

The gentle sway of the limo was the only movement.

Moments later, Erik leaned back on his heels. Straightening, he took her with him as he sank back into his seat, and Astrid landed in his lap. In an attempt to get comfortable, she shifted her position. His penis jerked against her buttocks.

Erik inhaled sharply and repositioned her. Away from his cock.

Disappointment zipped through her. She looked at him.

Heat blazed in his gaze before he turned away. He reached down and picked up her bra, handing it to her.

"Get dressed."

"But—"

He tucked a strand of hair behind her ear. "We're here," he said huskily.

Astrid turned her confused gaze to the window. Tropical plants added vibrant splashes of color to the emerald green grass and the forest green shrubbery. Strategically placed palm trees lined the newly paved road. Evergreens and pine trees covered the distant hills. No building was yet in sight. Despite its beauty, the passing scenery gave no hint as to where "here" was.

She turned back to him.

He eased her off his lap as the limo slowed.

Afraid of being caught naked, she dressed quickly. Another glance out the window revealed an occasional golf cart ducking in and out of sight between rolling hills. A white stucco building sprawled amid palm trees, its orange tile roof gleaming in the sunshine. Khaki and polo shirt clad employees bustled about near the arched entrance, while a handful of expensively dressed men and women milled around. "Spa Ynez" was etched in calligraphy lettering above the arch.

Astrid cringed at the thought of leaving the limo. In her worn jeans and t-shirt, she felt like a mongrel among show dogs.

Until she saw the flickers of heat smoldering in obsidian eyes.

The limo stopped, and the back door opened suddenly.

"Hello, Mr. Santos."

"Good morning, Mr. Santos."

"It's wonderful to see you, Mr. Santos."

As they exited the limo, every staff member greeted Erik with a smile and a look of awe. Erik returned each greeting politely, amazing Astrid by calling each person by name. He steered her through the entrance and into the lobby, a proprietary hand resting on her back. A burst of heat warmed her heart at his possessive touch.

A beautiful brunette greeted them at the marbled reception desk. While Erik rattled off a list of requests that were foreign to Astrid, the woman nodded repeatedly, her emerald eyes gleaming with something more than admiration.

He turned to Astrid. "I have some business to conduct but Sierra will take excellent care of you." He leaned down, kissed her lightly, and was gone.

Astrid stared at his retreating back, stunned. Slowly, she swiveled to face Sierra. Envy shone brightly in Sierra's eyes before professionalism extinguished it. She smiled politely at Astrid. "Welcome, Ms. Thomas. Please follow me."

Chapter Three

Experienced hands kneaded her flesh. Over her shoulders, and then down, palms pressing and moving parallel to her spine. Over to the side, trailing squeezes along her bra line, and then back up. Astrid's body felt like taffy. A lifeless lump, pushed and pulled until it was reshaped into something different.

"Hmmm, that feels wonderful, Jim," she breathed.

"Thank you, Ms. Thomas." After a few moments, his hands left her. "I need to go get more oil. I'll be right back."

Astrid sighed, feeling more relaxed than she had all day. Which shouldn't be surprising since Erik had kept her in a perpetual state of arousal. Her face heated as she thought about what she'd done—and let be done to her—in little more than a day, with a man she didn't even know.

Scandalous.

And what was even more scandalous was how much she was enjoying it. And that, despite her climax in the limo, her body still felt inflamed with need. She'd never felt like this before. Oh, she'd always liked sex, and past orgasms were satisfying but...The intensity of the feeling was new. With only a look from Erik, her body throbbed; a mere touch sent her racing toward ecstasy. It didn't make sense. She'd never felt anything even close to this with Jeffrey.

The soft whoosh of the door signaled the return of the masseur. She heard the tinkle of running water, then the rustle of clothing as Jim returned to the table where she lay. Liquid dribbled on her skin moments before his hands were on her.

"Aaaaah," Astrid moaned, as the warm liquid was massaged into her shoulders. Her right arm was lifted, and strong fingers rotated and grasped her flesh, squeezing as they moved up to her shoulders. The action was repeated with the other arm before returning to her shoulders.

As thumbs dug into the fleshy part of her back, fingertips lightly grazed the sides of her breasts.

Astrid stifled a gasp. The action reminded her of Erik's hands, so recently caressing and teasing her, making her squirm inside while her body remained still. The tension had been almost unbearable.

Like now.

She shifted slightly, crossing her legs at the ankles and pressing her thighs together, trying to diffuse some of the heat that was returning between her legs. Masculine hands massaged her lower back, dipping beneath the sheet with firm squeezes to her buttocks.

The silky sheet slid off her, leaving her backside bare. Artificially cooled air wafted over her, prickling her exposed skin where it touched.

Astrid opened her eyes, focusing on the edge of the stark white sheet lying against the charcoal gray carpet. Was this supposed to happen? Wasn't there some sort of spa etiquette that said only body parts being massaged were supposed to be uncovered?

The room was silent. Outside of the tiny gusts of air that continued to tickle the nerve endings beneath her skin, nothing moved.

Astrid turned her head in Jim's direction, just as his hands slipped between her legs, guiding them apart. Fingertips glided along her inner thighs, flicking up and inward.

Her skin quivered.

She didn't have to wonder if this was a breach of spa etiquette. Nor did she have to ponder whether or not her physical response was appropriate. Had mere hours as a trophy wife turned her into a wanton woman?

Shame flooded her. She jackknifed her legs closed and jerked around, facing her assailant.

"Get your hands…!" The words died on her lips.

Ebony eyes stared back at her.

Relief whizzed through her. Her traitorous body wasn't heating up from the touch of just anyone. Only Erik's touch. His strokes and caresses.

"Get my hands where, Astrid?" His hands nestled between her thighs, once again parting them.

She stared dumbly into his burning gaze, her mind, along with every cell in her body, focused on the movement of his hands.

"Here?" His finger slipped between her slick folds, dipping in and out in short, slow, strokes.

"Yes," she panted.

His fingertips teased her, taking her thoughts back to the sinful movement of his tongue in the limo. Suddenly, she wanted him to do those same things now, only she didn't want him to use his fingers or his tongue. She pushed her hips toward him, inviting him to stroke her, to enter her.

His deep chuckle echoed softly through the room. He slapped her butt lightly. "Were you going to offer Jim a piece of this?"

"No. Only you."

He paused, most likely surprised by her answer. "Are you offering it to me now?"

"Yes."

His breath hissed through the quiet room.

As an electronic whir penetrated the silence, Astrid felt the table being lowered. She stifled a groan as Erik's fingers left her swollen lips, traveling over the rounded mounds of her bottom. Squeezes and pinches to the base of her back before the palms of his hands slid up her spine, leaving a trail of heat in their wake. He paused at the nape of her neck. Terry cloth brushed against her back as he leaned over her. Warm breath cascaded over her neck moments before his lips touched her. Nibbling, licking, searing.

Astrid moaned.

"We have five minutes," he murmured against her neck.

Five minutes or five hours made little difference to her. She'd give him whatever he wanted.

Her overheated skin lapped up the moisture made by his tongue as he drew circles on her flesh, inching over her back. Hands kneading, tongue laving, lips kissing.

He stopped.

Astrid gave a cry of dismay.

She heard the whisper of fabric falling to the floor and the sound of a foil packet ripping open moments before she felt his hard body on top of hers. The robe was gone, and his body felt like molten steel. Astrid moved, craving the feel of his skin rubbing against hers. She felt like she had waited forever for this, to feel this.

His knee parted her legs and his cock nudged against her.

Astrid whimpered.

A hand tangled in her hair, tugging her head back. His head lowered, and his mouth captured hers, moving over it ruthlessly, parting her lips, mating her tongue with his. There was nothing gentle about his kiss—it possessed her, branding her as his.

He took.

She gave.

He took more when Astrid thought she had nothing left, sapping her of all logic, of all thought. For the first time ever, she welcomed the feeling of powerlessness and reveled in it.

She felt his hand reach between their bodies, guiding him where she wanted him. She moaned into his mouth. Her moan coalesced into a cry as he thrust his hips forward, burying himself deep inside her. He ate her cry while moving within her. Thoughts of everything but him, the feel of him, instantly fled. She groaned and butted against him, meeting him, pulling away from him. Skin slapped skin.

"I…don't…need…five…minutes…," she gasped into his mouth.

Sensation pulsed through her body with every stroke.

Climbing.

Spiraling.

Rippling.

Tremors shook her. Erik swallowed her cries while quickening his movements, moving in and out in hard thrusts. His grip on her tightened, his breathing became ragged, and he plunged deeper inside her.

Astrid felt frozen in the moment, luxuriating in the feel of him moving within her.

Erik tensed.

Astrid tightened.

His groan sounded as if it was being ripped from his chest.

Power surged through her as his contractions rippled through her, his body seeming to quake for a full minute. Gently, he collapsed on top of her. Fingers stroked her hair. Light kisses rained over her cheek and neck. She could stay like this for hours, savoring the heaviness of his body, the slickness of his skin, the—

A knock at the door reminded her of where she was.

She stiffened.

Erik kissed the corner of her mouth, then withdrew and moved off of her. Saying nothing, he raised the table to its original height and replaced the discarded sheet over her hips.

She wanted to turn her head and look at him—to see if passion lingered in his eyes. Instead, she kept her head turned away, slightly embarrassed by her passionate response in such a public place.

"Ms. Thomas is ready for her bath now," Erik said as he opened the door, his voice an octave deeper than usual.

Wondering what would Jim make of that, Astrid smiled and hid her flushed cheeks in the crook of her arm.

Six hours later, Astrid found herself once again in front of a mirror. Her face glowed from cleansing, exfoliation, steam, and masque treatments. Following a delicious roasted chicken salad for lunch, her body had luxuriated amid enzymes that, as they fermented, generated heat that left her languid. The following mineral bath and blanket wrap completed the experience, leaving her as relaxed as a rag doll.

And then there was her appearance.

The salon had performed a miracle. The back of her hair was pinned up, while corkscrew curls were arranged artistically on the crown of her head and wispy tendrils framed her face. The I-just-rolled-out-of-bed hairdo and the perfectly applied make-up left her stunned. If only Suze could see her. Gone was the wholesome Astrid, and in her place was the tantalizing Astrid. No wonder wealthy women always looked so great.

Her gaze drifted lower. To the clingy ankle-length dress. The 'V' at the neck almost reaching to her navel, the slit in the front almost joining the 'V' of her bodice. This shimmery gray dress made the red one look tame.

Her lips quirked into a slight smile. At least there were no stilettos in sight.

Still, she wished the dress wasn't so…revealing. Especially since she didn't know where they were going.

Her thoughts journeyed back to the massage table. A table that she had writhed against, almost purring at the feel of his hard body moving against hers. Her pulse raced at the memory of the shudders that had rippled through her. An orgasm stronger than any she'd ever felt with Jeffrey.

Which was odd. Though she'd always kept her emotions in check, she'd thought their sex life had been good. After all, she'd reached orgasm regularly, just as Jeffrey had. That meant it was good, right? And yet, with Erik...the phrase mind-blowing sex now had meaning.

Weird.

Maybe this wasn't totally about sex.

She frowned at the thought. Of course it was! A single day with a man—even a man as arousing and intriguing as Erik Santos—could not be mistaken for any deeper meaning. A deeper meaning that she didn't even want. Her job was the only meaning she needed.

With a start, she realized she hadn't thought about her job since the weekend started. Granted, her current events were months out, so there was no valid reason for her to worry about them. But she always did anyway, jotting down things to do and people to call as they came to her.

She rummaged through her purse for her cell phone. Turning it on, she paged through the missed calls. Nothing urgent. She recalled the number of the first call but paused before pressing the dial button. Did she really want to talk to Sarah Martin about her fifth venue change? Or Donald Adams about the Chamber of Commerce block party?

Slowly, she flipped the cell phone shut and returned it to her purse, refusing to ponder the reason for her actions.

She turned at the sound of the door opening. Her breath froze at the sight of Erik. The leather jacket and black slacks had been exchanged for a black double-breasted tux. His hair, still damp from a recent shower, was mussed, as if fingers had combed through it repeatedly.

His dark eyes swept her body, lingering at her breasts, caressing them with his gaze, before moving lower, over her hips, pausing at the juncture of her thighs, and back up.

On cue, her body heated. Impulsively, she placed her hands on her hips, widening the 'V' of her top. She turned around in a slow circle. "Do you like what you see?"

His gaze branded her wherever it touched. "Yes," he said huskily. He walked to her and held out a large box.

Surprised, she raised the lid and lifted a simple black dress halfway out of the box, fingering the softest material she'd ever touched. Despite its simplicity, the designer label told her it cost more than she made in her best week.

Her confused gaze met Erik's intense stare.

He took the dress from her and held it by its spaghetti straps. "I'd like you to wear this."

"You don't like what I have on?"

"I very much like what you have on." His voice was gravelly.

The dress dangled between them.

Slowly, she took it from his hands and turned toward the bathroom. His hand on her shoulder stopped her.

"Change here," he said. He moved to the chair by the bed and folded his lean body into its plush depths.

Staring. Waiting.

Astrid looked directly into his eyes.

And drowned in the liquid fire shimmering there.

She slipped her arms out of the straps and shrugged her shoulders. The bodice drooped over her waist. She gathered the dress in her hands and shimmied her hips.

Sequins tinkled as they collided with the floor.

Once again, she stood naked in front of Erik. Last time, she'd felt nervous. This time, she felt desirable.

There was no need to ask him if he liked what he saw.

"You're not wearing the panties I bought you." Tension spiked his voice.

"I was hoping they wouldn't be necessary."

His smile was laced with eroticism.

Astrid tried to control her breathing. To slow her fluttering heart. To keep her calm, cool act of seduction in place.

"Put them on."

Inordinately pleased by the effect she was having on him, Astrid scooped the thong panties from the dresser and resumed dressing. As she slid the sleek black dress up over her hips and over her arms, she turned toward the mirror.

And gasped.

Where the clingy sequined dress had made her look glamorous, like a leading actress—or, maybe a high-class escort—the shapely black dress made her look sensuous. Elegant.

Erik came up behind her, drawing her gaze to him. A platinum pendant with a teardrop diamond dangled from his hands. He fastened the clasp of the necklace then inserted matching earrings into her pierced earlobes.

Diamonds sparkled.

Astrid's eyes glittered.

"They're beautiful," she said breathlessly.

"Yes," he said. But his eyes weren't on the jewelry. Instead, they were fixated on hers while his mouth nuzzled her neck.

Astrid swallowed. She shook off an unexpected flash of happiness, reminding herself of the reason for the gift. She was his playmate, and wealthy men bought gifts for their playmates.

It didn't mean anything.

She forced a smile before turning to him. Cupping his face between her hands, she lowered his head and touched his lips with hers. "Thank you, Snookums," she said softly, using the nickname to dispel the intensity of her feelings.

He stiffened.

She paused, then nibbled his lip lightly before drawing back.

His body still felt tense as he stared down at her, his expression unreadable. Had she done something wrong? Just as she opened her mouth to ask, his hands were on her, drawing her close, pressing her lips and body to his.

Astrid melted against him. His breath quickened against her mouth, and she opened up to him, her tongue parrying with his. His mouth moved roughly against hers before he ended the kiss.

Disoriented, she stared into his bottomless eyes. Why had he ended such a hot kiss? A kiss that had sparked such heat in both of them, rekindling the desire they'd satisfied a few short hours ago.

But instead of giving in to that desire, he slipped his arm around her and led her from the room. Was this to punish her for her rejection of the thong? If so, she could tell by the barely restrained need in his touch as well as the rigid desire imprisoned in his pants that she wasn't the only one being punished.

He wanted her. Again.

☽⟨♡⟩☾

Astrid was acutely aware of Erik's hand resting on the small of her back— and of the staff's surreptitious glances from Erik to her—as they walked through the lobby. She didn't know what to make of the looks. Was she a rarity? Or did Erik come here often, with a different woman each time? Unsettled, she forced the question from her mind.

Greetings followed them onto the terrace.

And ended once they arrived at a secluded balcony.

Erik leaned his elbow against the railing, facing her.

"You must be Spa Ynez's number one customer," she said.

"Oh?" he asked, playing with her curls.

"Or royalty. The staff pays you such homage."

His finger moved to the curve of her neck, stroking. "You sound disapproving."

"Not at all," she said quickly.

His finger drifted down, idly tracing her collarbone. She lost her train of thought, scrambling to remember what she'd been about to say. "...I just meant that you don't seem the type to frequent a spa."

"What 'type' frequents a spa?" His hand moved to the front of her dress, lightly tracing the 'V'.

"Vain, self-absorbed, narcissistic..."

He chuckled. "You must be thinking of my brother."

Astrid waited.

He didn't elaborate.

"You don't care about your appearance—"

"You find my appearance lacking?" His finger dipped between her breasts.

"No…Oh!" Astrid gripped his hand, halting its movement. "I can't think when you touch me."

"I can't help touching you."

Something inside Astrid gave way. "I like you touching me." Submissiveness be damned. She placed a fingertip against his mouth, outlining his lips. He captured her hand with his, pressing her palm against his mouth.

"You're a gorgeous man, Erik. You're not vain; however, you do use your appeal to get what you want. *If* you want it." Kisses pressed against her palm. His tongue seared her skin.

"I want you, Astrid." Desire replaced humor. "Would you give yourself to me right here if I asked?"

The turbulence in his eyes jolted her. She forced her gaze away from him, glancing around the deserted terrace and through the glass in the latticed doors towards the lobby. The nearest person was Sierra, busy helping a customer at the front desk. Given the distance, coupled with the darkness and their position on the balcony, Astrid guessed she couldn't see them.

She looked at Erik.

He dropped her hand and stepped back so that he was once again leaning against the railing.

"Take your panties off," he said quietly.

Astrid's heart skidded along her ribcage. Surely he didn't just say…

"Take my…panties off?"

His gaze was unchanged, still smoldering, waiting.

Her gaze darted again to the doors. Nobody stood nearby. But if someone came out on the balcony…

I can't do this. What's the word? her panicked brain screamed.

"Someone might see us," she said.

Dark eyes glittered in the soft moonlight.

"You like the threat of being seen, Astrid."

She wanted to deny it. To call him a liar. But she couldn't forget the excitement she'd felt in the back of the limo. As Erik's tongue had sampled the juices between her legs, each lap sending a frenzy of tremors through her body, the glimpse of the driver's eyes had sent her toppling over the edge.

But that had been within the safety of a car, with no real threat of being seen. The possibility of being seen was very real on this darkened balcony.

"Don't make me tell you again."

Don't make me…

Her breathing quickened.

No man had ever dared to threaten her. If he had, she would have leveled him, verbally or physically or both. But hearing the words—and the resolve underlying them—pass from Erik's lips made her lightheaded.

And wet. Very wet.

What if she refused? What would he do to her then? His face, his tense jaw visible despite the shadows, promised punishment. Wicked, tantalizing, erotic punishment.

She'd do what he'd asked, or rather, commanded.

Slowly, she lifted her dress and hooked her fingertips in the waistband of the thong and pulled down. She stepped out of it and held it in her hand.

"Drop it."

"Onto the patio?"

His smile rebuked her. "You didn't want it, remember?"

Fear flickered through her body.

Punishment.

She didn't have seek it out after all. He was going to give it to her anyway. For defying him when she'd dressed and skipped the underwear. Images of the last time he'd 'punished' her flashed through her mind. Him kneeling below her, sliding her clothing off her body while his hands and tongue danced over her skin. But that had been in the privacy of his bedroom. Surely he wouldn't do something so…intimate in public.

Would he?

Despite the fear, anticipation pulsed through her veins, proving that Erik was right; she did desire punishment.

She opened her hand and watched the tiny bit of material as it hit the concrete, its darkness blending in with the night.

"Now lift your dress."

Her eyes widened.

She looked away, noting that Sierra had another customer, and took a step back, trying to find more shadows.

"Would you stand in front of the door?"

"No."

Astrid bit her lower lip, letting fear and excitement war within her. The tension in Erik—from his fingers gripping the railing to his clenched jaw to his hooded eyes—told her that she wasn't the only one fighting a battle. He looked like he wanted to close the distance between them and strip the dress from her. She shivered, closed her eyes, and gathered her dress around her waist.

Cool night air ruffled the faint triangle of dark hair between her legs.

The silence drew her gaze back to Erik.

Erik's tongue moistened his lower lip, his gaze fixated on her dark triangle.

"Touch yourself for me."

Her quickened breathing dissolved into ragged pants. Stroke herself? She'd only done that while tucked into her own bed. Never in front of a lover. Never in public.

She couldn't do this.

"Imagine it's me. My hand…touching…stroking."

She wanted to do this.

"Giving you what you want…need…crave."

The thought made her dizzy with desire.

Astrid slipped a finger between her thighs, her fingers questing, finding, and then rubbing.

Erik's harsh breath joined hers.

She rubbed faster, rotating her hips, all thoughts of Sierra and spa guests growing dimmer with every stroke. The heat building in her body catapulted the heat in Erik's gaze to a raging fire, spurring her on, making her aware of nothing but him.

Erik walked forward, stopping in front of her. His hands slipped under the straps of her dress. She felt the straps slide off her shoulders, gathering at her wrists.

His gaze drifted down. To her quivering breasts.

He stared.

Her nipples peaked.

"Keep rubbing yourself," he commanded hoarsely.

Astrid obeyed, unaware that she'd stopped.

His hands moved to her breasts, stroking their rounded sides before cupping them and pushing. His thumbs flicked across her nipples.

She moaned.

Fingertips tweaked her nipples.

Heat sped to her pussy.

"Do you want me to stop?"

His tongue flicked the hollow of her throat.

"N-No!"

"But someone might see," he said, his warm breath caressing her collarbone.

"I don't care."

At this moment, it was true. A whole herd of tourists could come trampling through the lobby and out onto the balcony, and she would've ignored them. She didn't want the delicious sensations rolling through her body to stop. Unable to endure his teasing any longer, she grasped his head and guided it to her aching nipple. His mouth closed around her while his hand slipped between her legs.

Astrid choked on a shriek.

A groan gurgled deep in Erik's throat.

She wanted more. More of him, more of what he'd given her in the limo, on the massage table, and what he was giving her now. She buried her hands in his hair, pressing him close and moving his head back and forth.

He sucked, licked, and bit.

Another moan escaped her.

She arched her back, pressing closer, closer, burying her hot nipple in his mouth.

He retreated.

She pursued.

"Unzip my pants." His voice sounded like sandpaper.

Reality intruded for the briefest of seconds, reminding her that they were in public, susceptible to discovery at any moment by the staff, the hoard of tourists she'd just shrugged off, a guest, or—

Say the word!

But she didn't. Despite the logical urgings of her brain, she still didn't want it to stop.

Onyx eyes, glazed with need, stared back at her.

She dropped her hands to his pants. Her unsteady fingers fumbled for his zipper. Her knuckles brushed against his stony hardness.

He shuddered.

She dragged the zipper down.

He pulled her dress up.

"Take my cock out."

She moved her trembling hands to his belt buckle.

"No," he said.

He guided her hands back to his pants. She inserted her hand through the gaping opening and pushed aside his silky underwear. His cock sprang free and she wrapped her hand around it, stroking.

Erik shuddered.

He dipped his hand back between her legs. A groan escaped her. "Tell me what you want me to do with my cock."

He stroked his finger between her throbbing lips, discovering her wanting, her wetness.

Astrid moved her hips, pressing against his hand, inviting the scorching touch of his fingers.

"Tell me," he ordered.

Her body told him what she wanted.

"Tell me."

A frustrated sigh whooshed from her throat. "I want you to take this…"

She squeezed his cock.

He gasped.

"…and thrust it inside me."

She rubbed the swollen head of his penis against her engorged lips.

He twitched violently between her fingers.

"Do…you…understand…what…I…want?" she panted, hips thrusting forward with each pass of his penis.

Erik's breath wheezed out of him.

The click of heels clipped the pavement.

Erik cursed before untangling the straps of her dress and pulling them up over her shoulders.

"Why are you—"

"Someone's coming."

As his words sunk into Astrid's fuzzy brain, she searched frantically for the source of the sound. It was coming from the other end of the terrace. There must be another set of doors! She jerked away from Erik and quickly smoothed the dress over her hips as Erik zipped his pants.

He moved to her side, crushing the black fabric under the sole of his shoe. Astrid blushed at the realization that she'd forgotten all about the discarded underwear.

"Erik, darling, are you out here?"

Astrid jumped and took another step away. Her blush deepened at the thought that, mere seconds ago, she'd been willing to let the world see her. How close the idea had come to reality, and worse, by someone Erik knew.

Erik grabbed her waist and anchored her against him.

The terrace was flooded in light as a stunningly beautiful woman drifted toward them.

Damn!

Erik tightened his grip and pulled Astrid closer.

"What are you doing here, Natalie?"

"Tsk, Tsk. Is that any way to greet me?"

His eyes moved dispassionately over her, noting the new hairstyle. The dark, shoulder-length tresses were now honey colored and cropped close to her jaw line.

Natalie tossed her head. "Do you like it?"

"It becomes you."

Natalie chuckled. "The compliment seemed to hurt you."

The cloying scent of jasmine engulfed him with her hug. He averted his head, causing Natalie's lips to graze his cheek. She stepped back.

He smiled down at Astrid, noticing the faint flush to her cheeks. "Natalie, I'd like you to meet Astrid. Astrid, Natalie."

He wasn't smiling when he turned back to Natalie.

"It's nice to meet you," Astrid said, holding out her hand.

Erik's cock quivered at the strains of passion knotting her voice.

Natalie's smile didn't reach her eyes. "Thank you," she said, icicles hanging from her words. She swung her gaze back to him. "I love the renovations. The place looks magnificent."

"Thank you," he said tightly.

"Let's celebrate. I'll buy you dinner." Natalie smiled sweetly. "And Astrid, of course."

"I'm afraid we can't. We're eating here."

"Last I remember, the restaurant was closed for remodeling."

Erik said nothing.

Fury flared in her eyes. "How nice," she said. "I didn't realize you'd started having your *friends* here for sleepovers."

"That's enough, Natalie." Steel spiked his tone.

Natalie's lips thinned. "Well, I won't keep you. Maybe we can have dinner another time." Her slender body briefly touched his, a cloud of jasmine surrounding him once again. "See you at next month's Board meeting."

The light clip of Natalie's heels filled the silence.

"I'm sorry about that," he said finally.

"No problem," Astrid said.

The tightness in her voice told him otherwise.

She turned back to the balcony, her back ramrod straight. "It's beautiful here."

His gaze followed hers. Past downtown Santa Barbara, nestled far beneath them, to the Pacific Ocean meeting the horizon. The view never failed to calm him. And he always needed calming after a visit from Natalie.

"I don't hold sleepovers here," he found himself saying. He thought he saw her shoulders relax.

How odd that he felt the need to explain to her. First, about the bed in his office, now this.

Astrid turned around, interrupting his thoughts.

Cinnamon eyes stared up at him. While Natalie's had glimmered with artifice, innocence gleamed within Astrid's.

Lust returned, hitting him like a jackhammer. He wanted to take her in his arms, plunder her lush mouth, taste her succulent flesh, and wrap her long legs around his waist, like he'd been about to do before Natalie had appeared.

He didn't want to talk about Natalie.

With a sigh, he turned Astrid around and pulled her back against him. "Natalie was my fiancé."

Astrid leaned into him.

His cock strained forward.

"What happened?" she asked.

Visions of rumpled sheets, naked skin, and entwined limbs flitted through his mind. "I found her in bed with her business partner."

Astrid said nothing for several moments.

"I'm sorry," she said softly.

"She blamed me for putting her there." He shrugged. "Maybe she was right."

"A person can't blame someone else for their own lack of integrity."

Erik smiled at the censure in her tone. "True," he continued. "Anyway, she and her partner owned Spa Ynez, which was how I met her. At the time, it was a profitable spa, but small, with only fifteen rooms and a handful of services. But I saw its potential to become a successful luxury spa."

Astrid's chuckle reverberated through his chest. "I knew you weren't the spa type. Spa owner, yes. Spa groupie, definitely not."

Erik smiled. "I *have* used the services."

"Of course. To evaluate it for investment purposes."

Erik laughed outright. "You've figured me out."

His gaze traveled the ocean, connecting the white dots that he knew were boats. His humor faded. "I bought Spa Ynez and made Natalie a limited partner.

Spa Ynez was one of three projects I was working on at the time. I worked seven days a week—though, actually, that's the norm for me."

Astrid turned to look up at him, her hip rubbing against him. "You're not working now."

But he'd planned to. He hadn't taken a weekend off in months. Erik replaced the uncomfortable thought with action. He moved his hands to her hips and rubbed his cock against her ass.

"Mmmmmm," she purred.

She'd made that same sound in the limo. As her thighs had tightened around him, her muscles trembling with the strain of holding back. Raw excitement had raged through his body, forcing him to focus every ounce of willpower on not taking what he had wanted. Just as it still raged, stoked by her firm ass pressed against him, by her citrus scented hair, by...her.

Craving would soon overtake willpower.

He moved his hips away. Reluctantly.

And forced himself to continue. "Natalie was a workaholic, too. She had a vested interest in Spa Ynez." He shrugged. "I thought she enjoyed working together."

He watched the end of the sunset. The blinding ball of golden light shone dimly through stringy clouds, casting a deep indigo hue to the skies.

"Did you love her?"

"I admired her business sense, thought we'd make great partners. I respected her."

"That doesn't answer the question."

He paused. "It wasn't the fireworks, can't-live-without-you Hollywood fantasy. I don't know what that feels like or if that even exists."

Astrid's hand touched his, fingertips stroking, drawing circles on the back of his hand.

He glanced down at her. She stared straight ahead, a slight frown marring her brow. He ran a finger over her brow, massaging, until the frown faded. "I must not be doing a very good job of keeping you entertained."

Astrid laughed. "I can't remember ever being more entertained."

Her tone was playful but he could've sworn her voice had softened. Irrationally, her comment pleased him. He peered closer at her face. No clues there. She was still staring out towards the ocean so he couldn't see her expression.

"You were frowning."

She remained silent.

He slid his finger down the side of her face, the back of his hand caressing her jaw. He loved the way her skin felt, so smooth, so soft. He couldn't seem to stop touching her.

"I was just thinking about the existence of your 'Hollywood fantasy' type of love."

He let his hand drift over her throat.

"You've experienced it?"

He felt her swallow hard. "No. I never thought I'd want to. But...maybe I...could."

His hand paused. Was she in love with someone? If so, then what the hell was she doing here with him? He gave himself a mental shake. He didn't care. He wouldn't be seeing her after this weekend. She was simply a challenge, the ultimate turn-on.

He moved his hand, rubbing it lightly against the base of her throat.

He searched for a new topic.

And returned to the old one. "And what kind of man do you think that you 'could'?"

Her chuckle sounded forced. "Oh, the usual. Honest, trustworthy, loyal, caring, sexy, honest—"

"You already said 'honest.'"

"Oh. Well...I guess it's doubly important to me."

He let the pads of his fingers move down, to trail over the skin exposed by the neckline of her dress.

He couldn't seem to let the topic go. "Hmmm. Your description sounds intentionally vague. Does that mean you have someone in mind?"

Silence.

"Maybe," she said finally. "But it could never be."

"Then he's a fool for not snatching you up," he said, shocked to discover that he meant it. He cleared his throat, determined to change the subject.

"Was Natalie why you placed a personal ad?" she asked softly.

Erik stilled.

Tell her.

He lowered his head and nibbled her ear.

She sighed.

"It was so I could meet you," he hedged, glancing at his watch. "Come. It's time for dinner."

Chapter Four

Natalie had been half right—the main restaurant was still closed for renovations, but the kitchen was functional. The chef, who had gone out on vacation until the reopening, had gladly come in to fix dinner for two. He'd personally come out to serve their entrées, clearly in awe of serving the big boss.

Astrid was also in awe of the big boss. Never had a restaurant been opened just for her. A formal table, complete with candlelight, had been set up in the middle of a lavish lawn, and hotel staff were positioned to prevent idle guests from interrupting their privacy. Erik was right; she was being pampered and was definitely living the lifestyle to which she was not accustomed.

She sighed inwardly at the reminder of just how different their lives were. The women Erik dated were probably used to this sort of treatment, immune to the gifts and the attention, merely expecting it as their due.

On the other hand...

Astrid's pulse skittered at the direction of her thoughts.

...Maybe Erik didn't do this sort of thing for women often. If the anger in Natalie's gaze, coupled with that crack about a sleepover, was any indication, the events of this weekend were not common.

And he had said that he usually worked weekends.

Which would mean...what? That she was special? That there was more than a game of pretend going on here?

Right. And Ed McMahon was going to come sauntering across the lawn with her Publishers Clearing House Sweepstakes check in hand, too. Because that's about how likely it was that this weekend meant anything to Erik.

Still, it was a wonderful fantasy. Just like the possibility of experiencing the Hollywood type of love was a wonderful fantasy. What was *not* a wonderful fantasy was the fact that she was sitting here envisioning things she'd always dismissed in disdain.

Annoyed, Astrid sank back in her chair and pushed aside the unsettling thoughts, forcing her mind to align with her stomach, which the Niman Ranch pork loin, smothered in a wild mushroom sauce, atop creamy polenta had made euphoric. "That was delicious," she said, smiling at Erik.

"I'm glad you liked it."

For the first time, his smile was open and unguarded, which made her want to encourage more of them. Instead, she clammed up, uncharacteristically tongue-tied. Her smile faded and she looked away, searching for something clever to say.

She let her gaze skim over the scenery in front of her, to the perfectly manicured lawn, with its climbing bougainvillea and towering palm trees, to the untamed wilderness that began abruptly where the landscaping ended. The Santa Ynez Mountains towered in the background, insuring that neighbors would never encroach on the privacy of the location. She wondered how much a spa like this cost. Did Erik live as lavishly? Or were his tastes simpler?

"If you keep frowning, my ego is going to take a serious beating."

She forced another smile, letting his comment wash away questions that couldn't be asked.

"Do you have any other brothers or sisters besides Bobby?" she asked, attempting to distract her thoughts.

He smiled faintly. "No."

They sat in silence for a few moments.

"Do you and Bobby get along well?"

His smile became amused. "You weren't really thinking about me and Bobby."

True. Until she'd uttered those words, she hadn't spared his brother a single thought. Instead, these silly, dreamy musings about Erik had been swirling endlessly through her head. Astrid fingered the diamond pendant at her neck and let her gaze drift from the waiter hovering yards away to the flickering candle on the table and back to Erik's gorgeous face. "I never knew trophy wives were made to feel special."

Oh hell. Her comment was supposed to come out light-hearted and flirty. Instead, the soft, breathy quality to her tone had made it sound serious and heartfelt.

Heat flooded her face.

Erik was no longer smiling. His dark eyes stared back at her.

Of all the stupid things to say. What on earth—

"They usually aren't," he said quietly.

Abruptly, Erik turned and motioned for the waiter.

Confused, Astrid watched the waiter approach. Did Erik mean that since she was being treated special, that he didn't think of her as a trophy wife? Which would then mean that there was a glimmer of truth in what she'd presumed to be pure fantasy?

Dinnerware clinked softly as coffee and dessert were placed in front of them, bringing her attention back to the man across from her. His gaze was once again playful, as if he hadn't just uttered words that had left her reeling. Well, there was her answer. Obviously, she'd read more into the comment.

Erik dipped his fork into the bowl and held the fork out to her.

She glanced from him to the fork and back again, her mind still stuck on his last three words. Slowly, the shift of his smile from playful to purposeful and the intent glistening in his eyes penetrated her fuzzy brain.

The heat in his gaze seared his words from her mind.

Heart pounding, she leaned forward and swept the contents of the fork into her mouth. Vanilla bean ice cream, warm apples, and tangy cranberries, along with a crumbly topping, delighted her taste buds with each chew.

Erik stared at her mouth.

The flavorful dessert turned instantly tasteless, and Astrid struggled to swallow.

He held out another forkful.

The hunger spreading through her stomach had nothing to do with the cobbler.

He moved the fork closer.

Astrid closed her lips around the fork, managing to get ice cream on the corner of her mouth. As she raised her napkin, Erik's thumb stopped her mid-motion as he rubbed the ice cream along her lips and then dipped his finger inside.

Astrid's breath hung suspended in the air.

His thumb remained motionless against her lip.

She licked the pad of his finger. The sweetness of ice cream mingled with the slight saltiness of his skin, arousing her.

His nostrils flared.

She closed her lips around his thumb, swirling her tongue, and sucked lightly.

Erik muttered a curse, his eyes darkening beyond midnight.

A movement from the corner of her eye caught her attention. The waiter started toward them. A look of surprise lit his face, and he pivoted, walking back the way he'd come.

Astrid's face burned and she moved her head back.

Erik stroked her parted lips with his thumb. "Don't stop."

Flashbacks to the bar scurried through her mind. Only, this time, it was Erik's finger instead of the swizzle stick. There was no comparison between the cold stirrer and Erik's heated flesh scalding her mouth. Nor was there any comparison between the men's gazes. Whereas the barfly's gaze had been awestruck and wishful, Erik's was hot and commanding. His blazing eyes said he knew what he was going to get and when he was going to get it.

Astrid continued stroking his thumb with her tongue, adding slow back and forth head motions to the action.

His gasp caused a quiver between her legs.

Mutual need mingled in the crisp air.

He gave her lips one last caress, then picked up his fork and toyed with his dessert. Though he said nothing, his eyes continued to speak to her, promising more intimate acts to come.

As Astrid reached for her coffee, her unsteady hands caused the cup to rattle against its saucer. She took a sip, anxious to let the mellow taste of the coffee beans wash away the taste of him and restore her composure.

She felt a little calmer, more normal, until she noticed the faint sheen of her saliva on his thumbnail. A temporary mark of her possession.

The air hummed with thwarted sexuality.

"You didn't answer the question I asked earlier," she said, her voice quivering.

"What question?"

"Do you and Bobby get along?"

"Are you nervous, Astrid?"

"No."

"No?"

She shook her head. "Aroused is more accurate."

"Would you like me to satisfy your…'arousal'?"

Before she could answer, the waiter appeared with more coffee. Erik thanked him, and the waiter left.

"I don't think your extremely efficient staff would give us the chance," she said jokingly, attempting to douse the flame of need flickering beneath her skin.

He cocked an eyebrow. "I seem to remember five minutes suiting you quite well."

Astrid blushed.

Erik laughed.

"Do you have any brothers or sisters, Astrid?"

Astrid let out a shaky sigh of relief, grateful for the change in topic. "No."

"Well, you're probably fortunate. To answer your question about Bobby, we've buried our differences the last few years."

"Differences?"

"Bobby lives the carefree playboy life. I pushed him to change, he rebelled. I gave up, now we're friends."

Thankful that her pulse was once again under control, Astrid stared at his bland expression, guessing there was a lot more than he was telling. "But it still bothers you?"

"He's smart and talented, but he lives off an unrestricted trust fund so he has no incentive to work or to pursue some goal." He shrugged. "The waste. That's what bothers me."

Astrid read between the lines, gleaning the reason behind Erik's work ethic. Had he been given a trust fund, which he had turned into millions? Or had he done it all on his own?

His look turned thoughtful. "But Bobby seems to have changed the last couple of months. He's begun interviewing for jobs. Even claims to be *in love* with Suze."

Such sarcasm wrapped around the word love. Why was being in love such a hard thing for him to imagine? Granted, it was hard for *her* to imagine. For herself, anyway. Or so she'd always thought.

He'd implied he found her special.

Stop it!

"Why do you find being in love so distasteful?" she asked.

"I find it overrated, not distasteful."

She continued to stare at his bland expression, trying to see beyond it. He sounded sincere and yet…something didn't add up. Visions of Natalie, her coldness and her anger, flickered through Astrid's mind. Even if Natalie embodied his experience with women—which, by itself, was quite sad—Astrid had a hard time believing that he would place a personal ad.

"So, what's the real reason behind placing the personal ad?"

So I could meet you. At her mind's obsessive thoughts, annoyance rose within her.

Erik stared off into the mountains, his withdrawal almost tangible.

Night air twirled through the space between them.

"Women are attracted to a wealthy man's money first and him second—if he's lucky." He laughed without humor. "But more often that not, the man is unimportant. He can be easily substituted for another."

That surprised her. "You really believe that?"

"Yes," he said flatly.

"But surely there's someone you know whose relationship isn't like that."

His expression softened slightly. "My parents had the only healthy relationship I know. Despite all the ups and downs they went through."

Erik paused to take a sip of coffee. He shrugged and turned back to her, his gaze once again bleak. "The ad cut through all the bullshit. Material things for sex. Simple. Straightforward. Honest."

"Why did you advertise for a passive woman?" she persisted.

"Why not?"

"You strike me as a man who'd be bored by a woman who wouldn't stand up to you."

His gaze intensified, eyes burning into hers. "Do you really want a relationship where you're controlled or treated as a plaything? Of course not. It's exciting to you because it's the opposite of the real Astrid Thomas."

Astrid raised her chin a notch, her annoyance no longer self-directed. "And what do you know about the real Astrid Thomas?"

His gaze seemed to see right through her, and a foxy smile spread across his face. He set the cup down and leaned across the table, taking her hand in his. He turned it over so that her palm faced upward. Dusky eyelashes swept down, obscuring his expression from her. He stroked the palm of her hand lightly, tracing the faint spidery lines with a fingertip.

"You live your life always in control. Always with your head, never with your heart. But there's a part of you that yearns to do the opposite." He paused. Lush eyelashes rose, revealing his piercing eyes. Fingers continued to stroke her skin causing shivers to race down her spine.

"You're intelligent and practical. You always try to do the 'right' thing, by your own definition of right," he continued.

Astrid kept her gaze fixed on his. She forced a cocky smile, a casually arched brow, and hid the anger from her tone. "And you can tell all this by having sex with me?"

"No. I can tell that by watching you." His fingers left her palm, moving over her wrist, up the inside of her arm, burning a trail of prickling skin in their wake. "From having sex with you, I can tell that you're passionate, sensitive, and uninhibited. And that you were dying to give up control, and it took me to make you realize it."

Heat rushed to her face, kindling her fury. "A fascinating speculation. But are you sure that you're talking about *me*, Mr. Santos?" she asked, mimicking the question he had asked during the interview.

He tilted his head in inquiry. "Are you accusing me of not being in control?"

"No. I'm accusing you of always being in control. Of living 'with your head, never with your heart. But there's a part of you that yearns to do the opposite.'"

His hand stopped moving.

The reflection of the candles flickered in his unblinking eyes.

An owl hooted in the distance.

"You might be right," he said quietly.

Her eyes widened, surprise at his admission suspending her anger.

"Now why don't you tell me I'm right?"

Because he wasn't right. She didn't 'yearn' to live her life any differently, or be any different, than she already was. "You're wrong, Mr. Santos."

He laughed softly.

She sputtered.

"Prove it, Astrid."

Chapter Five

Her anger was back in full force.

She rose from her seat on unsteady legs. "Fine," she said tightly, grabbing his hand.

He let her pull him to his feet.

She led him along the stone path, ignoring the beauty of the night as she practically stomped to their room. She remained silent as they walked, fuming at the fact that he found her denial amusing.

Who did he think he was, spewing armchair psychology and being so flip about her rigid control? Was he there when her mother ran off, wiping out the savings account? Was he there when she'd had to pick up the pieces, caring for her embittered father until he'd begun drinking every meal and then died, deserting her at twelve years old? Erik didn't know her, just as Jeffrey hadn't known her. She had reason to fear emotion and no one was going to tell her any different.

And how dare he accuse her of not permitting herself to let go during sex. She let herself enjoy sex—allowed herself to feel pleasure—and it didn't take him or anyone else to give her permission to do so. The sheer fact that she was aware of these feelings proved that she let go of her control.

Then the yearning to do the opposite part...that couldn't be farther from the truth. Sure, more and more, it felt that something was missing in her life, but she knew that it had nothing to do with that kind of yearning. Sure, she'd lapsed into schoolgirlish musings about him finding her special and considered the possibility—the very slight possibility—that she could experience love. But that didn't mean that she yearned for love.

Did it?

She shut her mind to even taking that question seriously. Instead, she focused on giving Erik his proof—proof that he was the one who refused to lose control during sex, and *she* was the one to make *him* realize it. He was the one who needed to deal with his control issues, not her.

As soon as he opened the door to the room, she led him inside and stopped at the foot of the bed. Turning, she slipped his jacket from his shoulders, letting the expensive material crumple to the floor. Next, she began unbuttoning his shirt.

"Do you know what I'm going to do to you, Erik?"

"Try on my shirt?"

She smiled tightly. They'd see how long his arrogant self-confidence would last. She slid her hands through the opening in his shirt.

"No. First, I'm going to run my fingers along your chest, like I'd imagined doing during the interview," she said, entwining her fingers in the curly hair and massaging his muscled chest as she went.

"You were thinking of doing this then?"

Was that a catch in his voice she'd heard? She let a trace of victory seep into her smile. "This and a lot more. But we'll get to that later."

She smoothed her hands out, rubbing her palms over his nipples, feeling them become hard points. She stood on tiptoe and ran her tongue over the pointy tips.

"How about sooner rather than later?" he asked. His attempt at humor was ruined by the soft grunt at the end of 'later.'

While her mouth ignored his question and continued its teasing, she un-buckled and unzipped his exquisitely tailored pants. They dropped in a heap around his ankles.

She ran her hand slowly down the front of his underwear. Soft, silky boxers, which surprised her somewhat. He'd struck her as a man who'd wear briefs.

All thought as to the kind of underwear man he might be fled from her mind as her fingers passed over his straining cock.

There was nothing soft about his grunt this time.

She slid the boxers over his hips, squeezing the firm cheeks of his ass as her hands traveled down, until she felt them fall free.

She drew back slightly and looked down at him.

Erik stood at attention.

Every lovely inch of him.

Ignoring the desire spreading through her body, Astrid smiled sweetly. "For a man who likes passive women, you sure are..." She stroked the underside of his cock lightly.

He gasped.

"...hard."

"I'm trying to be accommodating," he said between gritted teeth.

Astrid chuckled, wallowing in his fleeting cockiness and her reign of control. The last vestiges of her anger faded away as she placed her hands on his chest and pushed, toppling him onto the bed.

"Scoot up. To the head of the bed," she ordered.

He obeyed.

She slid her dress off of her shoulders and shrugged out of it. He scanned her body greedily. His cock jerked, electrifying her. Made brazen by his response, she continued with her demonstration of control.

She ran her tongue slowly over her upper lip. "Do you like what you see?"

"Yes," he growled.

"Which parts?" She fondled her breasts. "These?"

"Yes." It was a groan.

His gaze was glued to her breasts, watching her hands move over them. Squeezing, massaging. She gave each nipple a brief pluck before moving on, sliding her palms down her body, over her abdomen. Lower, lower. His eyes followed her movements, as her fingers glided over the light dusting of pubic hair and dipped between her sex.

He sucked in air sharply, and his hand went to his cock.

Astrid stopped. She clucked her tongue and shook an admonishing finger at him. With a muffled oath, he let his hand fall back to the bed.

She smiled and continued, stroking herself and undulating her hips. Her eyes never left his, her sense of power growing with his fascination. With each glide of her finger, his tension grew. His jaw clenched, his hands clutched the bedspread, his thigh muscles tightened with the effort of remaining still. He looked like a man poised for action, waiting for the firing of the gun so he could rush to the finish line. The only part of him that moved was the enticingly hard muscle between his legs.

All of which told Astrid he was being pushed beyond his limits—that his control was minutes from snapping—and sent her pleasure skyward.

His cock beckoned.

Astrid forced herself to ignore its call. As she strummed her clit, moving faster, heat snaked up her legs, stealing their strength and making it a struggle to remain standing. This physical evidence of her lack of control should have scared her, for she couldn't ever remember desire this intense or need this strong. But, instead of fear, she felt giddy at the realization that Erik was not alone.

Her control was minutes from snapping, too, and never had the feeling been so exciting.

Her swollen lips throbbed.

His lips parted. He emitted a harsh sound, a cross between a groan and a curse.

"Do you like this part?"

"Yes, damn it. You know I do."

She slid her hand lower and inserted her middle finger.

In. Out. In. Out.

"Come here, Astrid."

His order sounded like a plea. Satisfaction mingled with the fire coursing through her veins.

She pouted and gyrated her hips faster. "That is no way to get what you want, Erik. What do you say?"

"...please."

"I didn't hear you. What did you say?"

"Please!"

Astrid climbed onto the bed and crawled slowly on top of him. His hands gripped her sides, hurrying her progress.

She stopped. "No hands, Erik."

Another muffled curse. His hands fell away.

Astrid resumed her journey, traveling up his body until her face was even with his. She flattened her hips against him. His cock sought her crotch.

Erik groaned.

She suppressed a gasp.

She laced her fingers through his, forcing his hands above his head and moved her hips suggestively. "What do you want me to do with your cock?"

"Stick it inside you," he panted.

She wanted to drag it out, to ignore his plea, but she wanted it, too.

Wanted it now.

Which proved Erik was right; she was dying to let go of control. Because of him, with him. By seducing him and tumbling the walls of his control, she'd brought her own crashing down, freeing her to fully feel without thought or restraint. She'd been deluding herself in thinking she'd relinquished control in the past. Before Erik, her passion had never felt so overwhelming nor had her need ever felt so uncontrollable that it bordered on obsession.

And it—she—felt terrific. Exhilarated.

Astrid freed her hand from his and caught his cock. The tip pulsed, poised at her opening. She recaptured his hand and lowered her head, claiming his lips. As her tongue plundered his mouth, she thrust her hips down, impaling him inside her.

Her gasp mingled with his moan. Their mouths froze, all attention focused on the movement between their legs.

She lifted her hips.

Erik's grip on her hands tightened.

She lowered her hips.

Erik bucked fiercely to meet her.

Hips joined hips. Thighs slapped thighs. Frantic sighs filled the air.

Suddenly, Erik jerked her hands down to her side.

"Hey," Astrid managed to get out before she was flipped onto her back. Roles reversed, Erik remained motionless on top of her. Panting. Staring.

"I'm still right," he said, dipping his mouth to hers.

Yes, he was.

"Like hell you are," she said, wishing her voice sounded a little stronger.

His laugh came from deep in his throat.

She ignored it, not caring what he thought, having no desire to win the argument. That could come later. Now, she just wanted him to continue giving her what she wanted, what her body was begging for.

He suckled her lip as he lifted his hips, leaving only the head of his erection inside. Astrid jerked out of his grasp and grabbed his ass.

She pulled.

He resisted.

"Erik, please!"

He nudged his hips forward an inch.

"Tell me I'm right," he said, giving her another inch.

"Oh...Yes," Astrid breathed.

"'Yes' you want to let go of your control?"

"Oh..."

Erik moved his hips up and down, slowly and repeatedly, never allowing more than the tip of his cock to penetrate her.

Astrid's fingers dug into his flesh. "Erik...give it to me...!"

"Give it to *me*, Astrid."

His hips plunged downward, burying every long inch inside her; a shock of ecstasy ripped her breath from her throat.

Astrid screamed.

"Tell me you want to let go, Astrid."

He rotated his hips, moving deep within her. Astrid pushed against his hips, wanting to feel him move in and out, needing the friction of him to quench the unbearable tension building within her.

He withdrew.

Astrid moaned.

He drove into her.

Astrid gasped.

"Say it."

Slowly up, slowly down.

"Oh...Oh..." Astrid chanted, grappling his hips. "...faster..."

His movements slowed even more.

Astrid whimpered. "You're...right..."

His movements quickened. "About what?"

"I'm...not..."

His thrusts deepened.

"...in...in control..."

Erik groaned, his body pumping in earnest, without restraint, driving them both to the end they sought.

Astrid's hands roamed Erik's body, in constant movement, over his hips, up his back, threading through his hair, and back down, only to start again. Urging, coaxing, guiding, demanding. She no longer thought about what she was doing, no longer used words to express what she wanted.

Words weren't necessary. As she writhed beneath him, Erik seemed to guess what she wanted, what her body needed. His lips possessed, claimed, and attacked hers. He suckled, sucked, and nipped her lips, her neck, her breasts, and every bit of skin in between.

The pleasure was overwhelming.

She wanted it to last.

She wanted it to end.

"No..." she gushed, making a feeble attempt to still Erik's hips.

"Yes," Erik said, working his hips faster and harder.

He didn't ask for her release, he took it, making every nerve ending in her body spark to life simultaneously. Time hung, her breath froze, and her body quaked. And quivered. And shuddered.

"Did you like that?" Erik asked as her last spasm faded away.

His tone said he knew the answer to the question but wanted her to admit it. Out loud. To him. "Yes."

Erik began moving again.

Astrid remained still for a moment, luxuriating in the feel of him inside her, his hardness, his strength, his desire, which she sensed he still held in check.

Why? She felt totally satiated and wanted him to experience the explosive pleasure she had felt. As she lifted her hips to meet his, to return the satisfaction he had given her, Erik lowered himself on top of her, and his hands gripped her hips, holding her still.

"Don't move," he said against her neck, his voice strained.

Astrid stopped.

Erik moved his hips away, then back, his movements languid. His lips nuzzled her neck, in synch with his hips, while his tongue swirled down her neck and back up.

Astrid shivered, a gasp escaping her.

"Were you craving that?"

Despite the haze once again clouding her brain, she knew he wasn't referring to the fire rekindling in her body, stoked by the flick of his tongue, the grasp of his hands, the movement of his hips.

"Yes," she said, finally admitting her compelling desire to give up control.

He withdrew until only a few inches of his erection remained inside her.

"Did you let go?"

"Yes." *Yes, yes, yes! Lower your hips...please...Now!*

Erik inched forward.

Astrid moaned.

"How did you feel, Astrid?" Erik gave her one more inch.

Astrid moaned louder. "Like this..." Like now, where she couldn't think about anything but him and what he was doing to her. Where she didn't want to think, didn't want to talk, just wanted to feel, to abandon herself to the sensations roiling through her.

"Erik..."

Erik withdrew, taking away the precious inches.

Astrid whimpered.

"Tell me how you felt, Astrid."

He knew how she felt. Oh God, she wanted him. She wiggled her hips, unable to lie still any longer, not caring that he'd asked her not to move.

Erik remained motionless.

"...I felt..." She couldn't think, couldn't focus. What did he want her to say? "...out of control."

"Show me."

Show him? She'd already shown him, with both her voice and her body. What more was—

Erik plunged into her, the shock of it tearing another gasp of ecstasy from her throat and stealing all thought. Mindlessly, her hands gripped his hips, desperate to set the pace. Her tongue circled his mouth, hungry for the taste of him, insatiable. Her blood soared, spiraling upward and outward, then cascading downward as his ragged breathing set off a chain of tremors through her body.

Astrid's release was silent, the air temporarily locked in her chest, her mind and body reeling from the aftermath of sensation.

Erik's grunt sounded like a shotgun in the still air.

She clung to him, clenching and gripping with her hands, her thighs, her muscles, as his body quaked.

When his body stilled, he slid out of her and settled down beside her, rolling her on top of him. His hands stroked her body lightly. Astrid lay where she was, sprawled half on him, half on the bed, unmoving.

Seconds ticked by, turning into minutes.

"My God," she said finally, her voice infused with the awe she felt. "And I'm not using God's name in vain."

Erik's chuckle rippled through her. "My feelings exactly."

She smiled, wanting to believe him, but she couldn't. Intense sexual experiences were probably a frequent occurrence for him, whereas for her...She'd never experienced anything like that in her life. That was the orgasm of all orgasms. Off the charts, the scales, the–

"Comfortable?"

She snuggled closer. "Ummm-hmmm. If I get any more comfortable, I'll be asleep."

She closed her eyes, realizing that she could, indeed, go to sleep. Her body felt heavy and lifeless, like a bowl of cooked spaghetti. With supreme effort, she nestled even closer to Erik, moving her leg toward his hip.

Her knee grazed something hard, drawing her startled gaze to his.

He stared back at her, his gaze hooded, his look intense. He traced her bottom lip with his thumb, while the pads of his fingers tilted her chin, drawing her forward, urging her toward him.

"Erik, I don't think I can do that again."

"You don't have to." And with that, he craned his neck forward, guiding her toward him. His lips moved over hers, gently and slowly, as if he had all the time in the world and wanted to spend all of it on this kiss.

Which had the opposite effect on Astrid. She slithered up his body, deepening the kiss, exploring his mouth as if she hadn't just done so minutes before. As if from nowhere, desire uncoiled in her stomach, slowly seeping into her bloodstream and infusing her muscles.

Her breathing rattled from her chest in jerky gusts. Where had this desire come from? She'd meant what she'd said. Moments ago, she really had felt tired and comfortable and satisfied. Now, the familiar restlessness was back, the longing for something unnamable that only Erik could give.

She rubbed her body against him, positioning herself on top, slipping her hand between their bodies. While her tongue plundered, her grasping hands searched blindly, instinctively finding what they sought. She placed him where she wanted him and lifted her body.

Erik's hand closed over hers, stopping her. She raised her unfocused gaze to his, confused.

"No," he said softly, his hand caressing hers. "This time, we do this the way it was meant to be done."

The way it was meant to be done. What did he mean? Before she could ask, he turned her once again onto her back. His lips skimmed her breast, and his tongue lapped at her nipple, driving all thoughts and questions from her mind. Astrid ran her hands over his back, pinching, urging.

His hands strummed her body, gliding up and down her sides, her hips, her stomach. Lips and tongue laved her body, stoking her burning skin.

Lips kissing, tongue bathing, hands kneading.

Astrid squirmed.

"Please, Erik." Only this time, she wasn't quite sure what she was asking for.

But he seemed to know. With one deep thrust, he entered her, filling her, giving himself. They moved in synch. Slowly, rhythmically. Flesh caressed flesh. Breath met breath.

Astrid cried out as lightening pulsed through her body. Erik plunged, his movements frenzied, his thrusts deepening.

Thrusts that seemed to go on and on, relighting her passion. Astrid felt her body climbing, seeking, needing again.

Her fingernails sank into his back.

His hands gripped her.

She held her breath.

His breath burst from his lips.

"Give it to me, Astrid." Urgent need flooded his whisper. Before, it had been an order, this time it was a plea. His voice sent warmth spreading over her skin, while the feel of his body sent heat searing through her body.

His hands clenched her hips, his breathing accelerated, his thrusts lengthened.

"Now, Astrid." His voice begged.

She gave.

He gave.

Astrid shrieked.

Erik swore.

She hung onto him, tingles radiating from inside her body outward, heightened by Erik's spasmodic quivers inside her.

Slowly, gently, he collapsed on top of her. This time, it was he who lay unmoving, the breath whistling through her hair the only movement. She felt his hand glide over her hip, stroking lightly.

Astrid loosened her hold on him and gently ran her hands up and down his back. Once again, she savored the feel of him on top of her, feeling oddly comforted by the weight of his body. She couldn't remember ever enjoying lying under a man like this before.

Four spectacular, but totally different, orgasms. One frantic, one frenzied, and the other two sensual and caring. None of them under her control. She'd have to think about that, and what it meant, later. Now, she just wanted to lie beneath Erik and revel in these feelings, whatever they were, whatever they meant.

Her eyes grew heavy and closed.

As he reached for his jeans, Erik glanced down at Astrid. Her cheek rested on an arm. Her dark hair flowed over her elbow, a few tendrils obscuring part of her face and spilling onto the ultra-white sheets. She looked utterly relaxed, like a woman totally and truly satiated.

Which should have filled him with masculine pride.

Instead, irritation gnawed at his stomach.

He should be knocked out like she was or better yet, rubbing up against that hot ass of hers, sliding his dick into her tight opening, waking her with gentle movements that would turn urgent as she moaned and began sinuously moving against him, with him...

His cock sprung upward, ready to act on the idea.

His hands slid his jeans over his hips, while his dick wept with dismay as he tucked it inside. His mind showed its approval by reminding him of his irritation.

Irritation whose roots had sprouted before Sunday.

He couldn't pinpoint its exact beginning. Possibly last night on the terrace when he'd broken one of his cardinal rules: Never discuss past relationships with a woman. If the subject came up, a smile or a vague self-deprecating response was fine. But a detailed confession? Totally unacceptable. What had gotten into him?

Since you're so good at confessions, why didn't you tell her the about the ad?

He should have told her, since the reason wasn't really a big deal.

Except that, to him, it was a big deal.

He prided himself on his cool-headed objectivity, on his ability to apply reason to problems and come up with a rational, logical solution. This same approach worked with relationships, too—he'd look at the pros and cons of becoming involved and make a decision accordingly. Just like he'd done with Natalie. They'd had similar backgrounds, similar goals, performed well at social functions, had infrequent and mediocre sex, rarely laughed, never—

Okay, so maybe the approach wasn't working so great with relationships.

How'd he get on the subject of relationships?

This was a weekend, not a relationship.

Well, this approach wasn't working with this weekend, either. All the more reason he could not admit that after interacting with Astrid Thomas for less than five minutes, he'd gotten caught up in the fantasy. After imagining what it would be like to make her lose that impeccable poise and control, he'd instantly decided to pretend that the personal ad was his. Logic had flown out window, and he'd made an emotional decision. Hell, he hadn't become successful by making decisions based on emotion.

How embarrassing. Definitely not something that anyone needed to know. Especially not Astrid.

And yet, she kept asking him. Why the hell was it so important?

His gaze drifted across her shoulders to the swell of a breast, with its dusky nipple poking through the sheet. His cock threatened mutiny, urging him to yank the sheet off for more of last night.

And he knew she wouldn't protest. She'd unfold her body and rub it against him like a cat while making that mewling sound in the back of her throat.

Then, if she admitted to being out of control, if her body showed him she was out of control, if she begged, pleaded, and cajoled him into thrusting inside her, his restraint would dissolve.

Like it had last night.

Like it never had before.

He turned away, disgusted by his body's weakness, and exited onto the patio. The grounds were silent, the guests either sleeping or eating or having sex.

Like he should be doing. Making the best use of time with the hours remaining before she left, free to pursue the man she imagined herself in love with.

His lips tightened.

His eyes restlessly scanned the mountain range, ignoring the sun just creeping up over a rounded peak.

This playmate thing was not going as planned.

Not going as planned? If he felt like laughing, he'd crack up over that one. How the hell did something unplanned "go as planned"?

Well, if he had *planned* on a playmate, he would have chosen a woman who really was a weekend trophy wife, someone whose one and only objective was to make him happy.

Astrid is making you happy.

He tapped his fingers impatiently against the banister, crushing the unwanted thought under his fingertips.

His eyes scoured the landscape for a distraction. A young doe, calmly foraging for breakfast, entertained him briefly. She lifted her head, chewing slowly, as her large brown eyes assessed her safety.

Expressive brown eyes that reminded him of Astrid.

Dissatisfied that Bambi had made him think of Astrid, he frowned, his thoughts returning to their prior musings.

If he had *planned* this weekend, they would have had sex upon their first meeting, on the floor, in the car, or wherever they happened to be instead of waiting for a more romantic spot. Then there were all the other little things he hadn't *planned* on enjoying. Like getting such a kick out of buying her clothes and jewelry and feeling his head swell at the suspicion that his gestures left her near tears. Or of feeling the urge to pound his chest like King Kong when he brought her to orgasm.

And what the hell was he doing here? He never brought women to properties he owned. And even if he had decided to do so, he couldn't imagine spending the night with one there. Maybe the anger he'd seen in Natalie's eyes had been justified. In the two years they'd been together, they'd always projected a business relationship to the spa's staff and had certainly never spent the night here. Yet, here he was with Astrid, orchestrating erotic activities almost made public.

And let's not forget his response to Astrid's taunt about 'yearning to do the opposite,' to live with his heart. Where the hell had that come from? He'd never once had the desire to live with his heart.

Until now. Because she was special.

Like hell.

Erik angrily surveyed the grounds, looking for a task overlooked or a repair requiring his attention. The perfectly trimmed grass and hedges, along with the healthy foliage and immaculately groomed palm trees, seemed to mock him.

He clenched his jaw with resolve.

Time he stopped acting like a sap and got this trophy wife weekend back on track.

Astrid opened her eyes and blinked, slowly recognizing her surroundings. She turned over onto her side. The bed was empty. Movement on the patio caught her attention.

Erik stood with his back to her, presumably gazing out over the rolling mountain ranges. Jeans rested snugly against his lean hips, while budding sunlight glistened off his muscular back. She could stare at his body forever and never tire of it.

She threw back the covers and slipped out of bed. Smiling, she covered her nakedness with a spa robe and padded out onto the patio.

Erik glanced at her over his shoulder, his expression almost stern.

Her smile faltered. "Hi."

"Hello," he said politely, turning back to the mountains.

Astrid wasn't sure what to do. Was something wrong or was he just grouchy when he woke up? Taking a chance, she moved behind him and wrapped her arms around his waist.

He tensed.

She froze.

Slowly, he dropped his hands to her arms and caressed them lightly.

"Is everything okay?" she asked.

"Yes. Did you sleep well?"

She rested her head against him. "Never better."

He remained silent, still tense.

"I expected to awaken to you doing a victory dance," she said, trying to lighten the mood.

"Victory dance?"

"You won."

At that, he turned and faced her, leaning against the railing. He looped his fingers in the sides of her sash and pulled her toward him.

The hardness she felt through the robe thrilled her.

"Is that what you think I feel like doing?"

The unreadable ebony eyes staring down at her puzzled her.

"In a minute, I'm going to show you exactly what I feel like doing," he said. He kissed her slowly and deeply before setting her away from him.

A shiver of anticipation trickled through her. Once again, she'd obviously misunderstood his mood. She stared longingly at his retreating body, running her eyes over his beautifully sculpted ass and back up, absently noting the neatly trimmed hair that stopped just above the collar line. His exposed neck, seen from behind, without his awareness, made him seem almost…vulnerable.

Which was silly.

Vulnerability was a word she'd never associate with Erik Santos.

She smiled, shaking her head at such sentimental rambling. As she made her way back to the bedroom, the sight of a bouquet of white orchids on the glass coffee table in the sitting room, along with a dozen—no, make that two dozen—pastel-colored boxes piled on the camel-colored sofa stopped her mid-stride.

Had those been there last night? Most likely. She'd made a beeline for the bed the minute they'd entered the room, looking neither left nor right, intent solely on the lesson she was going to teach Erik.

And who had ended up teaching whom?

She shelved that question while she bent her head towards the flowers. She inhaled their fragrant scent before removing the small envelope.

If nothing is to your liking, blame me, not Michael. Erik.

She reread the card in disbelief, feeling the tide of pleasure wash through her with its meaning. Erik had personally shopped for gifts for her instead of sending his driver. This must've been one of the 'business' items he'd had to attend to when they'd first arrived.

Flush with warm, fuzzy feelings, she set the card aside and ran her fingertips lightly over the boxes. Cliché though it might be, she was touched by the thoughtfulness of his gesture. The boxes could be filled with colored rocks and that wouldn't diminish her pleasure; what moved her was the fact that he had picked every item out himself, for her, with her likes in mind. Which could mean a lot of things...

Like, maybe he really did think she was special in the way she'd fantasized about. And maybe there was more than great—no, make that spectacular, stellar, mind-blowing—sex developing between them.

Still smiling, she returned to the bedroom, flopped onto the bed, and lay back with her hands under her head. She stared at the ceiling, listening the to faint sound of the shower running in the bathroom.

Erik was being so...nice. Actually, he'd been nice—considerate, attentive, generous—all weekend. Not once had she been treated like she imagined a trophy wife was treated. Yet another reason why she didn't understand the personal ad. If he'd really wanted to play dominant/submissive games, wouldn't he be more...selfish? Then again, if she'd really believed that, she would never have agreed to play.

And, as expected, the games hadn't been one-sided. The sheer physicality of their sex still had her reeling. And last night...well, there was no description for last night. The sex had felt different. Raw sex had transformed into something softer. If she didn't know better, she'd almost believe that they had made love.

Love.

A word synonymous with pain, suffering, and emotional chaos.

But if she was honest, love could embody good feelings. She remembered family vacations when her mom was still with them, when her dad had laughed and smiled and told corny jokes, and she and her mom had laughed with him. Or the bedtime stories, even though she was too old for them, that he would tell nightly after her mom had left. She'd loved her dad deeply and had been devastated when he'd died. Suze, who'd been her friend since before his death, was the only person she'd loved since.

The loud thump of something striking the bathtub and Erik's muffled curse made her chuckle softly, drawing her thoughts to him.

Maybe it was time to take a risk, to let someone besides Suze into her life. Maybe Erik was right about that 'yearning to do the opposite' thing. After all, he'd been right about her desire to lose control during sex. Well, at least where he was concerned.

Maybe she'd tell him he was right. Again.

Even better, maybe she'd show him.

Scared, but feeling surprisingly elated, she got off the bed and retrieved her purse. As she rooted around inside for her lip balm, her fingers brushed against her cell phone.

She smiled ruefully. Erik could be bad for her business. Still smiling, she removed her cell phone and turned it on. As she scrolled through her messages, she frowned. Six calls from Suze, four of which were within the last two hours. It was possible that Suze was being her usual nosy self, but it was also possible she'd called about Grumpy.

Concern replaced elation as she dialed Suze's number.

Chapter Six

Suze answered the phone on the first ring.

"It's about time you called, Astrid! I called you at least ten times and—"

"Is something wrong?"

"Wrong?"

"With Grumpy."

"Oh, Grumpy." Astrid could almost see her dismissive hand gesture. "No, he's fine, although I have no idea where he is at the moment."

Astrid felt a flicker of alarm. "Did he get out?"

"Of course not. He's just being difficult, as always, sulking because you're not here or some other imagined slight."

Astrid heaved a sigh of relief just as Suze sighed impatiently.

"Well, tell me about the weekend. Are you having fun?"

"I would be if you'd quit calling me."

"Oh." Her tone sounded sheepish.

Astrid laughed. "I'm just joking. My cell phone's been off most of the time."

"In that case, tell me everything," Suze's voice became instantly remorseless. "Is Erik there?"

With the mention of Erik's name, a rush of happiness sang through Astrid's veins. "He's in the shower."

"Does he rock in bed?"

Despite the dopey smile she felt taking over her face, she was not going to answer that question. "Suze, I have to go."

"No, wait!"

"Goodbye, Suze."

"Okay, just give me a hint, and I'll hang up."

Even though she couldn't see herself, she knew her smile had gone from dopey to moonstruck. "I'm having a wonderful time and…" Astrid paused as she heard the water shut off. She lowered her voice to a loud whisper. "Yes, Erik totally rocks in bed and out of it. But I have to go—"

Suze squealed. "I knew it! I knew you two would hit it off! And all because of a little mistake. Why, I couldn't have planned that better if—"

Suze's comment pierced through her goofy stupor. "What little mistake?"

"You know, the mix-up with the ad. Who would've—"

"What mix-up with the ad?"

Silence.

"Suze, what mix-up with the ad?"

"Oh...uh...I thought Erik had told you by now..."

"Told me what?"

"Well, it's no big deal, really...Oh, Grumpy's probably hungry. I better go find him and feed him. Bye."

Astrid listened to empty airspace for a few moments. Just as she snapped the cell phone closed, the bathroom door opened.

As Erik entered the room toweling his hair, her eyes roamed his body hungrily, her rapidly accelerating pulse noting the skimpy white towel casually draped around his hips. Several deep breaths and several seconds later, her pulse was back to normal, her body under control. She forced her face to remain blank as she met his gaze.

He must've seen something in her face. Or maybe it was the cell phone in her hand. His look became concerned. "Everything okay?" he asked.

She made a noncommittal sound. "That was Suze...She mentioned some mix-up with your ad."

Erik paused in the act of drying his hair.

"What did she mean?" Astrid asked.

He resumed toweling his hair.

Silence hung thick in the air between them.

The towel dropped to his neck where it curled around his shoulders. "It wasn't my ad."

"What?"

Erik didn't answer immediately.

Finally, he sighed. "There was a mix-up with my ad for an event planner. It was accidentally merged with a personal ad. When outlandish replies started coming in on everything from scented stationery to skimpy underwear, I discovered the mistake."

Well, that explained why she'd had a hard time believing he'd placed one all along.

"So you really weren't looking for a playmate." It wasn't a question, and Erik didn't seem to take it as one.

Nothing made sense.

But there had to be a reasonable explanation. "If you weren't looking for a playmate, why'd you bring me in? Or, why didn't you interview me for the event planner?"

Another long pause.

"Your letter intrigued me. It contained innuendos geared toward the personal ad, yet the resume was professional. I wanted to know why an apparently legitimate event planner would respond to a personal ad—and understand the coincidence of an event planner answering the personal ad."

"But why'd you interview me for a playmate when I got there? And why'd you continue to lie—"

He raked a hand impatiently through his hair. "Look, I pretended to place a personal ad just as you've been pretending to be a playmate." He spread his hands, palms up. "It's been a fun game, Astrid—one in which we both got what we wanted. You gave into the fantasy of being out of control, and I got to see you do it."

Astrid stared at him. While she was dismayed that he'd lied, she'd been willing to reserve judgment in hopes that he had a valid reason for doing so. But...

It's been a fun game, Astrid.

The hurt that pierced her from that statement was hard to shrug off. Stupid fantasies that had been building inside her collapsed with his words.

"You're right. It makes no difference at all," she said, forcing strength that she didn't feel into her voice and a smile that her stiff lips didn't feel like making. "Well, I'm going to go take a shower."

Astrid sank into the limo as Michael, the chauffeur, swung the door shut. The soft click sounded incredibly loud in the silent interior. She willed herself to relax, to allow her body to sink into the cottony soft leather. She ran her fingers over the crease in the seat, stroking it lightly. She let her gaze take in the interior of the limo, committing to memory what she'd neglected to notice the first time when she'd had eyes only for Erik. From the L-shaped seat, which spanned nearly the length of the limo and the width of the driver's compartment, to the lacquered mahogany cabinet. An ice bucket, napkins, and crystal glasses adorned the top of the cabinet. Probably the same glasses from which she'd sipped her mimosa before Erik had taken it from her, dribbling droplets over her breasts.

She didn't want to think about that.

It was hard to believe that hours ago she'd been in the midst of the most memorable weekend of her life. A weekend that'd ended after she'd gotten out of the shower. Though technically the weekend wasn't yet over, these weren't the memories she'd expected to be left with.

She avoided letting her gaze stray to Erik. She'd already noted that he looked gorgeous, as usual. She'd never seen a man who could pull off a burgundy silk shirt with such panache, but Erik did. His bronzed skin and black hair were the perfect contrast. All this, heaped on top of everything that she had shared with him this weekend, made her painfully aware that she'd be hard pressed to meet another man like him.

Her fingers drummed the armrest, accidentally pressing a button. The television came on. A financial analyst predicted economic stability while stock symbols scrolled along the bottom of the screen. Another flick of her finger and the analyst disappeared.

"Sorry."

"That's okay," Erik murmured, taking her hand.

No, it wasn't. Nothing felt okay. Before Suze had called, she'd been floating on the tide of her feelings, about to step off into the unknown and admit feelings she hadn't known she was capable of feeling. Thank God she hadn't. The humiliation of having Erik look at her with sadness or impatience or disgust would have been beyond endurance.

How could she have been stupid enough to believe that Erik might actually care for her? He was so far out of her league, she didn't stand one iota of a chance in keeping his interest, let alone capturing his heart.

It's been a fun game, Astrid.

Well, she should be thankful that her budding feelings had been clipped before they'd gone any farther.

"I'm glad we did this," Erik said. His fingers caressed the back of her hand.

She wanted to snatch her hand away.

"Me, too. Thank you."

"We should do it again."

Her frozen lips formed what she hoped passed for a smile.

Erik smiled—the boyish one that did funny things to her pulse. "We could try a different game next time. How about a weekend trophy husband?"

Astrid concentrated on keeping the smile on her face. "That sounds…fun but I don't want to do it again." She leaned her head back, closed her eyes, and hoped that he'd think she was going to sleep.

Frowning, Erik stared at Astrid's closed eyes, at her body pressed up against the door like it'd been the whole trip. What the hell did she mean, she didn't want to do it again? Granted, their last conversation hadn't gone well. His mind had been like a carousel, going round and round on thoughts he hadn't wanted to think about, right when she had asked him a question he hadn't wanted to answer. But that was hardly reason enough to forgo another weekend.

He should ask her what was really going on here, but he knew what was really going on. Erik glanced out the window, ignoring the scenery that many paid millions to enjoy, his mind calculating ways to rectify the botched conversation. As the miles left to travel dwindled, he decided that he only had one option.

He turned his gaze back to Astrid. Her eyes were still closed, her head against the seat, giving off an easy to interpret 'Do Not Disturb' vibe, so different from the passionate woman who'd lain beneath him, digging her perfectly manicured fingernails into his back.

His cock tightened.

He grimaced at his body's bad timing.

Just as it was not the time for sex, it was not the time to continue their conversation. They needed to discuss this where there would be no distractions. Just as soon as they arrived at her place, he'd tell her the truth about the ad.

Chapter Seven

Astrid sat in the waiting room. She picked up the latest copy of *Santa Barbara Magazine*, absently thumbing through it. Her hand stilled as she came across an ad for Spa Ynez.

She snapped the magazine closed and returned it to the coffee table. She refused the think about Erik now. When she'd jumped out of the limo, slamming the door on his request to come with her, she'd slammed the door on her thoughts of him and that weekend three weeks ago. She'd escaped to the Bahamas for exactly that reason—to put that weekend out of her mind. That glorious, wonderful, heart-stopping weekend...

"Ms. Thomas?"

She looked up.

"Dr. Weimer will see you now."

She picked up her briefcase and followed the receptionist into the doctor's office.

"Please have a seat. Dr. Weimer will be right in. Can I get you anything while you wait?"

She declined politely and the receptionist left the room, closing the door quietly behind her.

Astrid glanced around the office, noticing the framed certificates on the wall, noting his specialization in Obstetrics and Gynecology. She looked away, tapping her fingers against the armchair.

The door opened suddenly, causing her to jump. She turned, her lips automatically forming a pleasant smile for Dr. Weimer.

Only it wasn't Dr. Weimer.

Smile forgotten, her mouth dropped open.

"Good morning, Astrid."

Against her will, her pulse raced at the sight of Erik. His dark suit reminded her of their first meeting, when she'd innocently assumed he'd wanted her to help him with an event. His absence hadn't dulled her memory to just how good he could look. Or how dangerous.

Barely concealed anger radiated from him.

Catching herself, she closed her mouth. "What are you doing here?"

"Remember my calls? The ones you haven't returned?"

Yeah, she remembered. He'd said he felt bad about the way their conversation had gone, that he wanted to explain about the ad. But she hadn't wanted to hear his explanations. Since it'd all been a game, his reasons were irrelevant.

"Don't remember? Well, surely you remember me standing on your doorstep, ringing your doorbell?"

She remembered that, too. How hard it had been not to go to the door, invite him in, and settle for another weekend.

"I was on vacation."

His glare told her he knew she was lying.

"How did you know I'd be here?"

"I gather you didn't read the letter, either."

An image of his unopened letter flashed in her mind. The letter that she'd repeatedly thrown away and then immediately retrieved from the garbage.

She didn't answer. Just stared at him, at the thick black hair that she'd buried her hands in. The eyes that'd devoured her body, burning her skin with their desire. The lips that she'd kissed, that had kissed her back.

A lump formed in her throat.

She had to get away. Now.

She whisked her briefcase from the floor and jumped to her feet.

"Sit down, Astrid."

Astrid stiffened. Her blood pressure skyrocketed. "You lost the privilege to issue orders three weeks ago."

"Please."

She paused, surprised by the weariness in his tone as well as the defeat that flickered in his eyes.

Never did she expect to see that expression on his face. Why was he here, just as she was finally making progress in putting him out of her mind? Not much progress, but every bit counted.

He blocked the doorway, legs akimbo, arms folded.

"You've got..." she looked at her watch "...three minutes, and I'm not sitting."

Amusement shone briefly on his face before bleakness obliterated it.

"Is there really a Dr. Weimer?" she asked, unable to wait for him to begin.

"Yes. I was originally going to see you afterwards. After he was done. But he's been called to the hospital for a medical emergency."

"Why were you going to see me? I'm not here for a personal ad."

"I'm on the board for A Caring Hand clinics," he said, ignoring her sarcasm just as she'd ignored his. "I knew they were looking for someone to plan and organize their fund-raising events, so I sent your resume to Dr. Weimer."

How dare he meddle in her life! First Suze, now him. Her anger returned. She was leaving.

He grabbed her arms.

"Please let me explain, Astrid. This is not a game." His grasp on her arms became a caress, scorching her flesh through the linen suit.

Damn him.

She stepped out of his embrace.

"Thank you," he said quietly. "I'd passed your resume on to Dr. Weimer to make up for misleading you. Since you refused to answer my phone calls or answer the door, I sent you a letter to apologize and to inform you of this interview."

"I'll find my own contracts, so thanks but no thanks."

She tried to push past him.

"It wasn't a game," he said quickly.

Astrid stopped. "W-what?"

"I wasn't playing a game," he said.

Her breath came out in one loud whoosh. She stared into his face, stunned by his expression. It reminded her of her absurd thought about his vulnerability when she'd admired the back of his neck. Only the idea didn't seem so absurd now, since that's exactly what she saw when she looked into his eyes. A gorgeous hunk of a man exuding strength and vulnerability at the same time.

"Well, it started out as one," he continued. "Which is why I insisted I was still playing the day that we talked." He laughed self-consciously. "Hell, until that moment, I didn't even know that it had stopped being a game."

Astrid simply stared at him, unable to believe what she was hearing. The elation returned, the feeling she'd experienced that day at the spa, before the call from Suze. She tried to squash it, along with her hope. It was possible that Erik was only here to explain his actions.

"I'd like the chance to prove it to you. No games this time."

He paused.

His words echoed through her brain as her eyes roamed over him, lapping up the details she'd missed over the weeks and thought she'd never see again. His dark hair, which was thoroughly mussed, the light shadows beneath his piercing eyes—eyes that were softened by emotion—his crisp, white shirt that she would love to strip off of him.

No games this time.

"But first…" he exhaled heavily. "About the ad. I've always relied on logic and objectivity when making decisions. But when you walked into my office, I instantly decided to pretend I'd placed the ad."

He stuffed his hands in his pockets, directing a wry smile her way. "One look at you, in your demure little suit, with your soulful brown eyes that even your professionalism couldn't hide and…"

As Erik appeared to struggle to find the right words, Astrid struggled to hold back a smile. She'd never seen him awkward and uncomfortable. Not only was it stunning, it was…endearing.

Erik's smile faded. "For the first time in my adult life, logic had nothing to do with anything. I'd made a spontaneous, emotional decision. Something both you and Natalie seemed to feel I was incapable of."

Astrid frowned, disliking being cast in the same light as Natalie. "I never told you I thought you were incapable of spontaneity."

"At the interview, as well as throughout the weekend, you were so incredulous at the thought of me placing the ad and—"

How could he be so dense? "I didn't believe that someone as gorgeous, sexy, intelligent, interesting, successful..."

Erik's smoldering gaze stopped her.

"Um, what I mean is, I couldn't believe that a man who could have women fighting each other to be with him would place a personal ad."

Erik walked toward her and took her hands in his, rubbing his thumbs across the backs of her hands. He lifted one to his mouth, his lips brushing against it in a light caress.

Astrid's stomach fluttered, the passion she'd tried to keep at bay since she'd left Erik surfacing.

"After I'd caught Natalie in bed with her partner, she had accused me of being dull and lacking spontaneity, thereby forcing her to seek excitement elsewhere."

Astrid felt again the disbelief that she'd experienced on the balcony at Spa Ynez when Erik had told her that Natalie'd said he'd driven her to bed with another man. But for a different reason this time. How could a woman possibly find Erik dull? Forceful, driven, pigheaded—

"Why are you smiling?"

"I was just thinking how wrong Natalie was and how happy I am that she was."

The smile he gave her was dazzling, making her feel like the luckiest woman in the world, as if she'd just done some great deed, instead of making a simple statement.

His smile faded and his expression turned pensive.

"I think a part of me believed that Natalie was right and then when I thought you felt the same thing, well, I guess that was the last straw. My ego was determined to prove you both, as well as myself, wrong."

He remained silent.

"I don't understand," Astrid prompted. "After you proved everyone wrong by spontaneously giving in to the ad, why did you still refuse to tell me?"

"Because, rather than feeling empowered by my ability to discard the reason that I've lived my life by, I felt...embarrassed. Humiliated. So I didn't want you to know."

He paused, the look of vulnerability returning, tugging at Astrid's heart.

"Astrid, I'm not always–"

Before he could finish his sentence, Astrid threw her arms around his neck. Her mouth met his, sparking the need that'd refused to go away. The need to touch him, to feel him, to be with him. As her lips nibbled, his lips parted, his tongue seeking, tasting, possessing. Desire spiraled through her body while euphoria snaked through her heart. He wanted her, mind and body. When she was able to catch her breath, she chuckled against his mouth. "I know, Erik. You're not always in control. I understand all about that."

His chuckle joined hers. "That's not what I was going to say."

She had a feeling she knew what he was going to say. Something silly like he lacked spontaneity. "I don't want to hear what you were going to say."

"Then you don't want to hear me say I'd like for us to start over?"

She drew back. "Oh, no. On the contrary, I do want to hear you say that."

He pulled her toward him, but she resisted.

She raised an eyebrow. "Well?"

His frown gave way to realization. He gave an exaggerated sigh. "I'd like to start over."

"On one condition."

Erik groaned.

"That we get to play games...often."

His eyes sparkled. "I think I can manage that," he said, drawing her back into his arms.

About the Author:

As a teenager, Rachelle Chase composed stories in her head for hours while lying in bed, reworking her favorite scenes over and over before falling asleep. Many years later, not much has changed. Except now, she writes them down. Out of Control is her first published work. You can visit her at www.rachellechase.com.

Hawkmoor

by Amber Green

To My Reader:

What's a good man to do when his options narrow down to the possible destruction of his entire society or the certain destruction of his true heart?

Darien Hawkmoor's world is under control—his control—and he likes it that way. Then his long-lost child-bride surfaces, a lusciously curved adult with no memory of the shape-shifters' Hidden World and no understanding of the precarious balance of power among the Families. Darien's carefully built peace shatters as the various Families vie for power and position. With people dying, and the moon swelling toward full, he faces the most painful of decisions. He must bring Lady Hawkmoor under control, or he must sacrifice her to rebuild the peace.

Chapter One

"You were right, O Mighty Lord of the Hidden World!"

Darien rolled his eyes at the interruption and kept his hands moving, pulling lines of ink across the paper. He was in the flow now, easily balancing the details of a suspension bridge, calculating the precise alloy of titanium—

"I have the data," Ajax went on, lisping around his fangs.

Stop the presses! Ajax has data. Darien kept drawing. Immersed in the tensions and balances of the bridge, he had almost grasped an answer to the Pereira dispute. He did his best work this way, letting the Families recede from his consciousness while he designed. He could lighten those cables with—

"Darien, it's her. It has to be her." Ajax was serious. Darien frowned, trying to remember his calculations. But Ajax being serious? "Mary Alison Hawkmoor is alive."

The bridge evaporated. Darien looked up from his drawing.

Ajax grinned, fangs fully extruded in his excitement, and handed over a printout.

The digitized photo showed an unsmiling young woman with chin-length soft brown hair. A heart-shaped face and a pug nose. Spare makeup, if any. No visible jewelry. She stared past the camera impatiently. "Driver's license photo?"

"Nope. Mary Alice Enhog-Moore has applied for a permit to carry a concealed weapon in the state of New York."

Darien frowned again at the mangling of the name, but that must have saved her life. He was far from the only shapeshifter who'd been searching among the nation's vast population of Does, Roes, and Smiths, in transient camps, labor camps and telephone books, for the past nineteen years.

He closed his eyes and recalled the scent of the little girl at their bonding ceremony, two months before the Atlanta Massacre. Ivory Soap. She'd smelled of Ivory Soap and grape candy.

She had spit at him. He remembered that vividly, with a seven-year-old's disgust. He opened the drawer of his side desk and looked at the gold-framed photo. His own tight face. The grape smear on the collar of his starched white shirt. Mary Alison grinning mischievously at his side, the sun glowing in her chin-length hair. The still-white ceremonial bandages on her left arm and his right arm. The wrought-iron arch of his corner of Central Park rising behind them both.

Why New York? Had she come looking for him? Usually the bond should pull her to him, but she'd only been four years old. Too young, they said, for bonding to fully take. But she'd come.

And she wanted a weapon? "Was the permit issued?"

"She applied only this morning."

"You have her address."

"I *have* the data." Ajax handed him a summary and an aerial map. Mary Alison ran a martial arts studio in a basement not five miles from here. Two blocks from the loft he and Lia had shared that one summer. Mary Alison had come onto his turf. He knew every corner and balcony there, every tree, bench and rooftop.

Lia knew them too. The thought launched him from his seat, snapping orders.

"Put everyone you can in the chopper, armed to the teeth. Put Jay in charge. Have them land on the hospital helipad here, and converge from here, here, and here. Stealth is—" *Stealth is the first law of the Hidden World.* "—secondary. Assume Lia is closing in. Keep her away from my wife."

He threw open the door to the stairs, unwilling to wait for the elevator, and raised his voice. "Kent! Jesús! Meet me at the van!"

༏ೱഄ൬ഄൣ

Once in Mary Alison's neighborhood, he left his lieutenants around the corner with the van. Four shifters together generated enough energy to make some humans shiver and look over their shoulders. Mary Alison would certainly feel their massed power, and after so long on her own, she might well take that as a threat.

He paused at the entryway of her building and examined the doorbell signs. A bookkeeping service. An insurance office. Two law offices. The basement was listed as "For Rent" with a "NOT" marked over it and the phone number marked out.

He climbed down the stairs cautiously, and entered a tiny reception area. The cinderblock walls had been painted glossy white and hung with a trio of needlepoint landscapes in shades of gray. He examined one, a precisely rendered view from the floor of a massive conifer forest, and grinned. Most shifters lost their color vision on all fours, but wolves and bears also lost clarity of vision. From the detail here, Mary Alison must see with cat eyes.

What kind of cat? Lions, being pack animals, predominated among felines. Every so often they got careless and made the tabloids. Or would she be a tiger like her mother?

No. He knew those beasts. Had Mary Alison been any of them, he would've taken that cat instead of the lynx as his secondary Shape. Possibly a cougar? In some counties, sheriffs still paid bounty on all nonindigenous species.

A woman's voice echoed from the back room. "You got him off balance, Joey, but where's your own center?"

So that was a real Southern accent. It sounded different on television.

She continued calmly, an expert in her element. "Put your knee in his butt and push forward hard so he can't get his weight back on his hips. Keep hold of his left arm; pull it up under him. Right. Now shove forward with your hips and ride him down."

"Cripes!" That was a New Yorker. Male. Darien's fangs reacted, startling him.

"It feels like I'm trying to do him doggy style!"

"Then y'all got it right," she responded with no trace of humor. "Sex isn't all that different from any other grapple."

Dead silence fell. Then a cough echoed. The male voice muttered, "I don't need a pile of citizen complaints."

"Let them complain. Who—" The woman's voice sharpened. "Who's out there?"

He pulled in his fangs. "Darien Hawkmoor."

He licked his teeth; they felt human. He smoothed any wrinkle from his coat with his hands and stepped around the partition wall to a gym half the size of a basketball court. Under the piercing scent of liniment, he smelled fresh sweat and bleach and old socks.

Mary Alison stood between two big men who radiated the assured control of law enforcement officers. One man wore a black orthopedic girdle. Both wore gray sweatpants and sweaty undershirts; they stood protectively, flanking her.

She was small, and looked smaller between those men. She wore a gray sweatshirt with the sleeves hacked off at her elbows. Gray sweatpants. White sneakers that barely dimpled the padding on the floor.

She gave him a bright smile. "I'll be happy to speak to you in about fifteen minutes, sir, but I only work with two students at a time. Please wait out front."

Darien shoved his hands in his pockets. "We might not have fifteen minutes, Mary Alison. Dismiss your students."

The men bristled. Mary Alison raised her hands to stay them and took one step forward, into the margin of his extended aura. Astonishment splashed through her face. She flushed and snatched in her margins, like a woman snatching a long skirt out of a puddle, and broke the contact.

"I'm Darien," he said again.

"Gentlemen," she murmured, her accent very Southern now, "may we pick this up another day?"

"You sure? I don't like—"

"Please," she said, still staring at Darien.

The men exchanged unhappy looks, but reached for their bags without further protest. Mary Alison seemed to have them both eating from her hand. She looked Darien up and down, assessing him, but didn't speak again until the men had stepped through the far door to the showers. "What did you call yourself?"

"Darien Hawkmoor. Your husband."

"I don't recall getting married, Darien Hawkmoor."

"You weren't quite five at the time. The scars on your arm must have faded long ago, but you might remember having them."

"You care to say something that makes sense, Mr. Darien Hawkmoor? Some one little thing?"

He sighed. *Kindly tear off those ugly rags so we can make mad doggie love on this wrestling mat* made excellent sense at a testicular level, but she probably wouldn't stand there and listen to it. "You've been missing for nineteen years."

"I've known exactly where I was. How hard were you looking?"

That stung. He'd dedicated resources, especially in the past year. "Until today, everyone thought you died in Atlanta."

"Umm hmm. I have work to do, Mr. Hogmore—"

"Hawkmoor," he interrupted. She'd said it properly before. Was she playing with the sound? "Not Hogmore and not Enhog-Moore. You transferred the "en" sound from Alison to Hawkmoor." He heard the men talking in the showers. "Come outside with me."

"I don't think so. I don't know you."

"You will." He seized her arm.

She seized his, and with a jerk and twist she threw him flat on his back. She knelt with one knee on his throat, the pressure light but the threat real.

"When I let you up," she growled, "you gon' need to leave."

He inhaled deeply. *Not* the most intelligent thing he'd ever done. His cock pulsed from hard to painfully hard.

But the bond went both ways. Her pupils dilated and her aroused scent filled the air like a haze.

His fangs reacted. He coughed to hide them, and forced them back to human teeth. "Do you often become sexually stimulated by the scent of a stranger? Come walk with me, and I'll explain."

The showerheads in the next room turned off. In minutes she would have backup. He had to get her out of here now. He poured a torrent of adrenaline through her system and filled her with a terror of something in the shower, something coming out.

She sprang away from him and fled.

He followed, hampered by his office clothes. Outside, the wind drowned him in street-vendor grease and spices and car exhaust and the collective body odor of strangers.

He closed his eyes and swung toward her like a magnet points north. There, behind the falafel vendor's cart. Just downwind.

He strolled toward her. She stepped around the cart and faced him, her arms crossed. "That was some trick, flushing me from my own place. I don't appreciate that."

He grinned. "How long would it have taken to sweet-talk you out of your den?"

"You'd have to start talking sweet before I could time it."

"Should I tell you how many nights I've lain awake wondering what you looked like, how you spent your time? Whether you had a lover or a husband in the human sense?"

"Human sense?"

She thought herself human? Of course. If she'd known otherwise she would've surfaced years ago. "You were born to the Hidden World, Mary Alison. When your parents died, you became holder of the oaths. As your bondmate—your husband—I have exercised your authority and fulfilled your obligations for nineteen years."

"Most people don't marry in kindergarten."

He shrugged. "You grew up in a culture where people pair up too casually and divorce as casually. We seldom choose our initial mates and never divorce." Was it too soon to warn her? "We may add a third person to the bond if the pair can't—"

"Okay!" she snapped. "I really need to shortchange my students to get curbside sociology lessons. You got a point?"

Yes, but she wasn't ready to hear it. No shifter would sell life insurance to a pair taking a third, or a triad taking a fourth. The amenable image he'd cultivated to conceal his expanding influence might become a liability now. He could name several Families that would pounce on the chance to join him as Hawkmoor, ready to persuade or force the senior pair under the will of a dominant Third.

Lia would be the first contender.

While he considered what she needed to know, Mary Alison sidled away. He grinned again. She might think herself human, but she moved like a shifter. She darted out of sight. He followed.

Chapter Two

MA jogged down the sidewalk, forcing rational thought through the hormone rush. She turned north and west, then north again, not letting traffic stop her, anxiously aware that the buildings around her were becoming less familiar. This pace would put no distance between her and that long-legged man, but she could think of no refuge close enough to expend her strength in a flat run. She had no taxi fare, no bus fare, no tokens or cards or money of any kind.

In movies, people being chased could board a bus, or jump the subway turnstiles and push through a door and get away. *No.* The thought of going underground with so many strangers packed around her provoked a wave of nausea.

Nor could she bully her way onto a bus. Bus drivers here were hard-eyed and outspoken; she'd never once ridden a bus in New York without witnessing an incident that would've kept the gossips of Poetry, Georgia, busy for months.

That man knew way too much. How? Once, at a second-grade sleepover, she'd told the girls about her crazy dreams, about being Mary Alison instead of Mary Alice, about a Prince Darien who would someday come for her. Her social worker had come for her instead. The months of "play therapy" that followed had taught her to keep her mouth shut.

Evening traffic—cars, joggers, and bikers—increasingly clogged the road and sidewalks. She skirted the edge of a mob trying to force itself down the throat of a subway entrance.

Something came up fast and quiet behind her. She jumped aside and spun to straight arm—a bicyclist. He went down swearing, in a tangle of hardware and shiny tights.

She bit her lip at the names he called her and jogged on. *I don't just attack people! Don't you know what that stupid bell is for?* And didn't he know that nobody outside a comic book looked decent in tighty-tights that showed everything? Oh, Jerusalem! She was looking at a stranger's bulges.

She needed out of here. *Got to get off the street.* She kicked up her pace a notch until she hit the next corner. Where, really? Where?

A whiff of fresh bread decided her. She pivoted west and sprinted toward the Chelsea Market. An enclosed city block full of people and confusion. She could lose anyone there.

An hour later she saw him talking to several men in suits. She hid herself in the sensory clutter of the crowd and studied him. He looked tall by himself, but the men around him were taller. Maybe that swimmer's build just made him look tall. He had high cheekbones and deep, fierce eyes under thick, bronze-lit hair.

A voice rumbled in her memory. "Darien Berenov. Today he becomes Darien Hawkmoor; your bondmate, the other half of you."

The hell he was. He roused things inside her that needed to stay buried. She faded further into the bustle around her. But she couldn't resist tailing him for a little way.

Men came to him at a quicker pace, and she caught a sense of agitation communicated from them to him. Something was up.

He shoved his hands deep in his pockets and looked around. Looking for her. She stood behind a giant fudge kettle and waited for his attention to pass, but when she stepped out, he locked gazes with her. He shouted something and fought his way through a tour group toward her.

She bolted.

Evening met her outside the Market. Neon and headlights, and reflections of both, glared and reflected everywhere. She flew down sidewalks that had largely emptied for one of those lulls when people seemed to already be where they wanted to be. In Poetry, those lulls lasted hours. Here, twenty minutes was rare.

One good thing about a city: it had hidey-holes everywhere. She found a bar just big enough for six stools and a booth, and climbed onto a stool to catch her breath. She couldn't keep rushing around at random. She needed a plan.

"What'll it be, sister?" A greasy-looking man looked up from something he was doing in a sink, and studied her through a mirror cluttered with beer emblems.

"Sorry. I just need a minute, sir. Is that okay?"

The greasy man half-turned and stared at her over one shoulder. She looked down at her fists on the bar. She hated being examined.

The man ran some water and thunked a glass of it in front of her. She gulped the first half, then sipped more politely. When it was gone, she wiped a stray droplet from her bottom lip and took a shuddering breath. "Bless you. That was wonderful."

"There's good cops close by, sister. You want I should call one?"

She had numbers for her own pet cops, but her numbers and her phone were in her studio. She rolled the glass between her hands, trying to figure out what to say. *I am being followed by a guy, maybe a hypnotist, who knows the secret name I gave myself when I was a little kid. He also knows the name of my "invisible friend" and insists he is that friend. Yes, he is visible now. No, he hasn't threatened me. He chased me at a slow jog for a few miles. And oh, Jerusalem! He makes me terribly horny.*

Um, no.

"I appreciate the thought, sir, but what I really need is a back door. Do you have one, please?"

Her bug-out kit, pills and cash and all, was in her studio. The man knew where her place was, but would he expect her to circle back there? Maybe not. The studio might be a lousy objective, but she didn't have a better one.

She ducked into the bathroom to turn her sweatshirt inside out. The navy lining would blend with the deepening dusk.

She slipped through the back door and struck a power-walk pose, elbows out and chin up and butt slinging side to side like a whitetail deer's flag.

Within a quarter mile of home, she felt his lurking presence. His voice rode the twilight air, sultry with promise, slowing her steps to a halt.

"You never could control your temper on the night of the full moon, Mary Alison."

She couldn't hear his footfall, or the brush of cloth on cloth as he walked. Only that dark voice. Rich and smoky and earthy. Closer. She tasted a hint of sweetness too. Like in the smoke of pecan wood.

She snapped alert. She'd lost track of what he was saying, and he was barely ten feet away now. Hypnotized? She gritted her teeth and fought the urge to reach out to him.

"You ovulate on the full moon. You only cry on the full moon."

"I never cry." Certainly not on the full moon. Not with the heavy meds she needed on those nights. She gave him her shoulder and put the width of the street between them.

His voice warmed her like a towel from the dryer. "Never?"

He was teasing. That oddly affectionate dimension to his voice made it worse. She should run. She was no distance runner but she could out-sprint most weekend athletes.

She stepped into the street instead, reaching out. Trying to feel who and what he was.

She saw her hand groping the air. How stupid did that look? She put her hands behind her back. No, that poked her tits at him. Might look inviting. She dropped her arms. Exactly who was he?

"Come to me, Mary Alison, and know who I am."

"That has to be one of the lamest come-ons ever." She moved a step closer. *There.* He colored and flavored and added texture to the air, yards further than even a cop usually reached. She felt more than his personality, his force of will. He had her trick of actively reaching out to sense what was there. Her insides tightened again. *No one can do that but me!*

"None but us," he whispered, easing toward her.

His air surrounded her, filled her when she breathed in. She felt slow, heavy, soft. She felt drunk. Medicated to the gills, when she hadn't taken the first pill. She stood still, letting him come; she could not run.

He stopped close enough she could see the deep glitter in his eyes. She felt him gather his energy, preparing to do something.

"I don't like people making me do stuff I don't want to do!" Her voice was shrill and childish. Helpless. She closed her eyes, loathing the sound, trying with everything she had to break free. He touched her face.

With that touch, she broke free and she ran.

Vaulted a bus bench and then a bum in the gutter. Ducked under a ladder carried by two men. Leapt a broken section of sidewalk, orange warning ribbons and all. Dodged left and right through a fleet of taxis, their horns blaring a signal to everyone in half a mile. *Crazy Woman Here! Crazy! Crazy!*

She darted along the edge of a crowd that conveniently spilled from a building just then, stirring the pattern so the people would spread out and riling them so they would vent their annoyance on the man behind her.

She couldn't hear him, but she felt him. Like she was a hound-dog on a fifty-foot leash and he was letting her run, maintaining only a light pressure on the lead so she would know he was there.

She ran faster, cutting through one of the tiny parks that littered this city. The green space was choked with obstacles, but they slowed her pursuer no more than they did her. She needed real woods. She cut toward the green expanse of Central Park.

"No!" he called from behind her. "Central Park is a trap!"

She bounded over a waist-high wrought-iron fence and found the other side much further down. Ten feet down, or more, and sloping hard. She tumbled through weeds and old bottles and thick leaf mould and pieces of broken cinderblock, banging against the trunks of trees, smelling dogwood and two kinds of pines and a beech and something she didn't know.

She fell dazed against the trunk of a young oak. While she lay there, blinking and trying to catch her breath, the moon nudged its upper edge over a row of rooftops to her left. Fat and yellow and nearly full.

She lifted both hands to touch the moonlight, as she had since earliest childhood. Whatever hurt, moonlight made it better.

Except when the full moon rose to torment her with the seizures, the twisted dreams and more twisted memories.

She dropped her hands. Was all this a hallucination? Couldn't be. The moon wasn't even full yet. And here in the heart of the metropolis, the protective orange glare of mercury lights drowned out the moonlight. Mostly.

She rested against the oak tree and focused her attention on her lungs, forcing them to slow enough to actually use the air they were hauling in and heaving out. The man walked down the slope toward her.

He stopped right between her feet. His hair was ruffled, but he hadn't so much as loosened that expensive-looking tie of his. At least he was breathing hard. That was something. He put his hands on his hips and stared at her.

"What do you want, man?" Her voice was wheezy, but it had lost that whine.

"You're bleeding."

No shit, dumbass. I just found all the trash the mayor missed on his last inspection tour. There ain't no part of me but what has a cut or a scratch or a bruise.

"Thank you for not going to the Park," he said conversationally. "I would anticipate ambush there." He paused, and his voice again took on that tangible affection. "Have you been there recently, Mary Alison? The day we met, I gathered a double handful of cornel-cherries for you. All the aunts cooed and said 'how sweet' but you wouldn't touch them."

"How sweet. Tell you what. You go crawl back up under your crazy-man rock, and I'll go crawl back up under my crazy-woman rock, and we'll each live happily ever after. How's that sound?"

"Sounds miserable," he said promptly. "How can we fulfill our biological imperative to engender numerous maddening offspring unless we spend time curled up under the same rock?"

"I can't have kids. I'm on medication."

"You haven't even had aspirin recently."

"I need it when I need it." When the moon hung full in the sky. "I have hormonally triggered epilepsy, and the seizures give me hallucinations." She was babbling, but he hadn't come closer since she'd started, so she kept on babbling. "I take two kinds of pills, when I can get them. It's pretty mix-and-match. If they're too strong, I walk into walls."

If they weren't strong enough, she might prowl the night fighting urges to hump anything with three legs. Right now she needed them bad, because this man definitely had the third leg, and it was definitely calling her, making her hips want to curl up from the ground and waft a little female come-hither scent his way. She pulled her gaze away from his crotch.

He stepped over her leg and came up by her waist. She felt questions sliding along her skin, like she was naked and being examined by a man who had all his clothes on.

She mentally crossed her arms and legs to hide everything. Her breathing had just about recovered. In another minute, if she could get to her feet and get him off his, she would run again.

"No," he said, "please don't run. It wouldn't do any good, you know. Chasing you would be no challenge, with your body scent up as it is, and in the last half hour this city has become dangerous." He crouched beside her.

She propped herself on her elbows. "Did you just say I stink?"

"I suspect any answer would have adverse consequences. May I help you stand?"

"Touch me, bubba, and you'll get consequences."

"Hmm. The way you put me on the floor in there showed an intriguing grasp of applied physics. How in the world did Lady Hawkmoor get a job teaching wrestling to police officers?"

"I didn't get the job. I made it. I'm self-employed." How weird was this conversation? This rich Yankee talking lords and ladies and infant marriage and personal safety to a hill girl who wanted no more than ten minutes' private time to get nekkid and bump peepees. She gathered her balance.

"I suppose it pays better than waiting tables."

Did he mean that as condescending as it sounded? Her face heated. Then she laughed. "Not really, but I didn't steal two years of movement science at the Vo-Tech to wait tables." She hitched her legs around and sat up. "You mind? I'll get a crick—"

His head rose and his hand touched her shoulder, a warning to silence and stillness clearer than any words said aloud. He pulled his force of will in to a smaller circle, smothering her sphere of awareness, walling the pair of them off from the world. The mercury lights dimmed along with the sound of traffic.

A woman sang out nearby. "Come out! Come out, wherever you are!"

Chapter Three

MA heard the taunting laughter from every direction and knew she was screwed. She'd either been caught in a gang war or in one of those Vigilante TV productions.

Had to be VTV. Neither a gang-banger nor a militiaman would know what this guy knew. And Darien, or the actor playing him, was just too good-looking to be real. He must've poured a whole bottle of pheromones in his shorts to get her to react like this, four nights ahead of the full moon. Microphones and cameras must be everywhere. Well, anybody knew how to get out of a VTV hunt.

She sprang away from him, kicking away his hand and ignoring his urgent growl. She ran to the nearest street, hands spread, and called, "Sanctuary! Sanctuary!"

They laughed at her. Coming from the shadows, from between parked cars, from alleyways and doorways, a dozen men and women laughed at her. *Screwed.*

She dropped her arms and ran.

They flowed over the ground at her heels, now closer and now further back. Herding her, she realized. Turning her north and east, north again, then east again. She tried to picture the terrain ahead, but she'd left familiar territory blocks behind.

Something whistled past her and bounced off a shop window. Ducking, she backtracked the trajectory and saw Darien flaring his coat to catch more darts. His hand closed on her wrist. "Come!"

Sirens wailed in the distance, promising help soon. She twisted against Darien's thumb to free her wrist. His grip held. What did the man have for tendons, steel cable?

Her leg cocked for attack, but—*I can't hurt Darien!* She scowled. Where had that come from? He lifted her until her face was on level with his, her sneakers swinging in the air, and pressed her back against rough bricks.

She opened her mouth to speak, to distract him while she kicked his balls to Jericho, but his will slammed into her. Gray shadows dimmed her vision. She fought them back. She heard him say "I'm sorry," and he slammed into her again.

She deflected the pressure as she would a punch; mental *tan sao*. His force slid by. He frowned, and her knee shot home.

At the same moment, brick shards flew off the building by her ear. The sound of yelling and gunfire followed. Darien jerked and started falling, but a big black guy with lots of hair caught him, sliding under his arm and holding him up while Darien's weight still pinned her to the brick wall.

The big guy spoke into Darien's neck. "Not to be stepping out of my place, most puissant lord, but we need to vacate the vicinity posthaste." He met MA's eyes. His voice went cold. "You will please follow me, Lady Hawkmoor."

She nodded to fool him, and he made the mistake of turning his back on her. She hit her feet and slid away, but within ten steps two other guys boxed her against a car. She yelled at the top of her lungs to draw attention, but people screamed en masse around the corner, over and over again, and another fusillade of bullets ricocheted all around with a popcorn-popper effect.

The big guy carrying Darien ducked around a corner. A car skidded after them, spitting gunfire. Sirens wailed.

One of the guys crowding her, a tall Viking of a guy, grabbed her. She threw him hard to the gutter. The other guy, a Hispanic not much bigger than she was, body-slammed her on top of the Viking, driving the wind out of her.

She twisted from between the men and got on one knee. Both men held her, dragging her down, but neither seemed willing to hit her. She kicked hard into the nearest armpit, but the Viking caught her foot and rolled with it, and she went down again.

A pair of men in suits ran past, holding oversized aluminum briefcases as shields.

She yelled, "Help me!"

One of them looked at her, his face twisting in misery, but he kept running. She aimed at him a hard and pure hope that he never got it up, ever again.

The Hispanic tried for a wristlock, but he wasn't fast enough. She snapped two of his fingers and rammed her head into his chest, feeling ribs crack free of his sternum. The blond guy picked her up and swung her away from the road and threw her to the sidewalk.

She tucked and rolled and came up running, but they tackled her together just as another car came by, spewing gunfire.

Bullets and flakes of cement and square crumbles of car glass ricocheted overhead. She covered her eyes against the shrapnel and felt-*felt* bullets pound into the guys who lay plastered over her. Secondary explosions erupted inside them. *God Almighty, Maker of Heaven and Earth! Nothing like that is legal. No bullets like that should exist.*

Bloody smells choked her. Grit from the sidewalk dug into her face. Maybe three times her weight in what had once been prime male flesh lay across her head and shoulders. She held still, feeling hot blood run over her neck and shoulder and her left arm, hoping the shooters would think her dead.

Brakes screeched, and metal tore screaming through metal. A man shrieked, made animal sounds that should never come from a human throat. Gunfire erupted again.

Both of the men who lay across her moved. One rolled off her. The other convulsed in huge, spastic jerks. She couldn't see a damned thing but sidewalk and brick wall, both splashed with wet red. Still she played possum, fighting the instinct to run. *Can't outrun a bullet.*

She heard car doors, and more gunfire. A dog howled right behind her. She hoped the dog made it through this.

Pain spiked into her left leg, above the knee, and the lower leg died. The dog sprawled on top of her, as if to shield her. She heaved the weight off her back, but she'd lost feeling for her entire leg, from the butt down. The dead feeling pulsed higher, across her back like cold water, and she lost the other leg just like that.

A man's hand clamped on her forearm. She wrenched around, and got an eyeful of the Viking. Blood bubbled at his mouth. Jerusalem! He was stark naked and bleeding like fury!

He tossed her like a bag of laundry through the back door of a van. A huge, shaggy dog was thrown in behind her. It gave a gurgling cough and bent in terrible ways. Another dog scrambled in and collapsed. She blinked, and things went away.

Chapter Four

Darien looked through the polycarbonate roof of the van. He saw moonlight, then Orion, and thousands upon thousands of other gleaming stars in a velvet-black sky. Too many stars. Seatbelts pinned his shoulders; the full six-point combat harness. He smelled blood. Tense voices hissed from both radios. "What happened?"

Voicing the question brought part of the answer. The attack on his main building. Machine guns downtown. He'd put out word that some television show had asked permission to use his building to film an episode, but the mayor still would never forgive him. "How bad did it get?"

Ajax answered from the driver's seat. "Our city buildings were both leveled. So was Lia's. Aaron reports fending off an attack."

Darien struggled to sit up. His head rewarded the movement with shooting pain and roiling nausea. Aaron ruled Boston with silvered claws and a closed mouth. For him to report trouble was ominous. Even more ominous was Ajax giving information flatly, with no teasing or mock honorifics. "Jessie? Amy? Denise? Mike's baby?"

"You told them to stay north this year, remember? Ramon bought it. Jojo's hurt and on the run, headed west with that human of his. The Tejas girl was missing, but Lia's people picked her up. Kent and 'Sús should live, though neither will enjoy it for a while. Lady Hawkmoor caught a tranquilizer dart; she's probably awake now."

Ajax grinned, himself suddenly. "Not to be giving a Hawkmoor advice, but some handsome prince or other might want to check that his Lady Fair isn't trying to unlock the back door and jump out in the road. You got a scrapper there."

Yes, I do. The ache in his groin made him exceedingly glad to have slept through the first hours after her kick. He pulled his attention back to the situation. "Evacuate the Finger Lakes cabins."

"Done. They should land in Timmins any moment now."

Good. Ontario was the traditional safe haven.

Ajax flicked him anther look. "We're sixteen miles from the Canton airstrip, and your plane is waiting to take off. You have a few hours before you'll need to pick up the pieces."

A few hours could be too long. He'd have to spend the flight contacting anyone he could. Making his Hawkmoor voice heard. He rubbed his eyes and found a bandage on his forehead. Some of the blood he smelled was his. "How bad is my head?"

"Shrapnel cuts. Concussion. I put in ten stitches. If the moon stays out, you'll be fine by morning."

The driver had stopped to stitch him? Darien unclipped his belts and went back to check on Kent and Jesús.

As soon as he opened the curtain, bad smells hit him. A timber wolf lay stretched across the floor in the moonlight. New skin, hairless and baby-pink, covered much of his exposed side. He raised his head weakly as Darien crouched.

Darien caressed the thin new skin, sharing the comfort of touch so badly needed by a wolf, while he assessed the damage. No internal ruptures or bleeding, but Kent's vital force was drawn thin from too many rapid shifts. Each Shape would be closer to whole, but the more powerful the shifter, the less damage he "forgot" in each shift. Kent had exhausted himself. Darien could shape him, but doing so right now might leave behind some crucial element of what made him Kent.

Darien stroked the new skin again. "Tomorrow," he promised. "Reach tomorrow and be whole."

Jesús huddled on a bench seat, naked and in human form. He'd bled heavily, with the added stink of damaged organs, but the blood was wolf-blood. The human had a whole skin, although what it wrapped was broken in many places. Jesús was too young to have another Shape; he had only the broken human and what had to have been a shattered wolf.

Sitting by him, Darien leaned his aching head against the back of the seat. Jesús sighed, and tried to shift. Darien shut it down. "Not yet, my wolf. An hour or two."

As he spoke, he looked around the van. Mary Alison lay strapped in the top bunk opposite, moonlight glittering in the whites of her eyes. She reeked of fear.

Jesús moaned. He didn't have hours. Darien probed the ruptured organs, shaping what he could make sound, sealing or shriveling the rest to cut blood loss and blunt the pain. A man didn't need a whole liver or both lungs to get through a few hours. Let the moonlight work its passive healing for a little while and then he would nudge Jesús through a healing shift.

Darien leaned back, but pain still hummed under his hands. He ran his hands along the damaged spine. The bony structure was a fragile, malformed mess. He dug deep, reshaping the essential ridges and arches, fusing bone to bone. He'd never been very successful at shaping joints, but he found which nerves were singing their danger warning, and he quieted them.

Jesús slumped unconscious. Darien moved him to the floor beside Kent. Losing Ramon, the healer, would be bad in normal times. Losing him in the opening shots of a war would be catastrophic. Darien was a shaper, not a true healer. But tonight's rioting required his other abilities. Open war would follow unless Hawkmoor could enforce the peace.

He turned to the top bunk. Mary Alison glared at him. Aside from the bunk's safety straps, cloth strips bound her wrists and ankles. One wrist-loop bit into her knuckles. In five minutes she would've worked that hand free.

The road curved, and his moon-shadow spilled over her shoulders and face. He closed his eyes, fighting dizziness. The scents of blood and of fear called to his need to bite, to tear and to eat. When he fought down those instincts, nausea and dizziness from his own injury swamped him. He leaned against the edge of the bunk, actually raising one hand to cover his fangs as he hadn't needed to do since school. When he regained control, he unbuckled the straps. "Come," he said. "We have work to do."

She curled away from him, working her hands in their binding. He tried again. "Give me your hands. Let me untie you."

She extended her hands, hesitantly and not all the way, as if expecting a trick.

He pulled the loops over her knuckles and rubbed her cold hands. He needed to touch her, to focus on her as a person and not as prey. She relaxed fractionally.

"Thank you, Darien." Even those few words held her Southern accent. And something else. A tentative warmth.

"You know my name," he guessed. "You were too young to remember it all, but my name means something to you."

She pulled away and curled between the bunk and the roof of the van. "You're a hypnotist. You don't need to play games like this to put stuff in my head. Why don't you go back to cuddling with that naked Mexican guy?"

He stroked her ankle. "The naked guy's Jesús. The wolf is Kent."

"Wolf. Ri-i-ight. What's the real game? What do you want? What would get you to go away and leave me alone?"

"You are Lady Hawkmoor. We are your people. We will never go away. We will never leave you alone. Get used to the idea."

She recoiled to the far corner of the bunk. He saw her field of vision, felt her muscles gather and prepare. For what? He reached for her thoughts. She planned it in detail. A two-footed kick to the head. Hard enough to break his neck. He felt her regret, her wavering, and her final decision to do whatever it took to get away.

Here came the feet. He stepped back and yanked her by the ankle out of the bunk. He belatedly thought of the wounded on the floor and jerked upward, slamming the sole of her sneaker against the poly-glass roof of the van and pinning it there.

She squalled with surprise, a wholly feline sound, and writhed in his grip. He dropped her on the seat he and Jesús had just vacated. Onto the drying blood. She recoiled, jumping off the seat and into his arms.

He staggered under the impact, and grinned like an idiot. "Hellooo." She'd come to him. Her instinctive reaction had sent her to him. She stared, her eyes huge and black in the moonlight. The workings of her mind eluded him now, but his eyes and his nose told him what he needed to know.

She swallowed. Her skin heated against his.

He lowered his face until her warm breath caressed his lips. "May I kiss you now?"

She grabbed fistfuls of his hair and kissed him as if not kissing him meant that the world around them would explode and burn to a gray, crunchy cinder. She rose on her toes and raised one leg to hook about his waist. He propped against the back of the bench seat and let her climb him.

The floor of the van lifted and twisted under his feet, and the world around them exploded in searing light.

Chapter Five

Darien woke, alone, hanging by his arms. He struggled to get his weight on his feet so he could breathe. *Okay, good. Now to shift.*

Lightning shot down his arms. He thrashed like a fish on two lines until the pain forced him to shut down the shifter energy. When the electric flow trickled to a stop, he stood swaying, his arms now mercifully numb.

He'd been hung to face an electronic door. Next to it, he saw a stone fireplace. The room was decorated as the den of a hunting lodge. Lia's scents, human and jaguar, surrounded him.

He closed his eyes. Jaguar. Solitary, regal and powerful. He could imagine no other Shape for Lia.

Darien had been raised from birth to expect a wolf as his first Shape. At the onset of puberty, he'd gone to live with the WolfRunners and immediately gravitated to the huge timber wolves. News of his first shift, to timber wolf, had been transmitted in code throughout the globe before he'd even stopped throwing up.

The itching dissatisfaction with his wolf Shape had begun last fall. He'd studied tigers and jaguars, but their Shapes eluded him. He'd just moved on to the possibility of a bear when the snow moon had twisted his bones with agonizing ferocity, compacting him to a size he would not have believed possible. He'd lurched to the mirror and seen a lynx.

A forty-pound lynx.

In the year since then he'd kept his lynx Shape secret from everyone but Ajax. They'd discussed two explanations. The more prosaic one went back to a she-lynx that had, long ago, caught him too near her cub and had cut herself a place in his memory. The other was too tantalizing to ignore; that Mary Alison was alive and was a cat. If her cat-Shape was not one he'd studied, he could've defaulted to the form of the lynx.

A forty-pound lynx.

Lia, 300 pounds of dense bone and jaguar meat, would never stop laughing.

He could ignore the singularly unimpressive lynx; his wolf Shape was certainly dominant enough. He couldn't ignore the idea of Mary Alison reaching out to him. As a boy, he'd dreamed of her picking vegetables under hot sun, eating something salty that he suspected was bacon, and taking flying leaps from a swing. He'd been told that these were simply dreams, that the ceremony had taken place too early, that so young a girl couldn't bond fully. By the time he had power to act on his own, the dreams had subsided and the search for Lady Hawkmoor had become form without substance. He had not publicized his order to renew a real search.

But he had found her. And, effectively, had delivered her to Lia.

The window shades glowed with daylight. By now Kent and Jesús needed to have shifted again. Unless healed quickly, wounds like theirs might linger for months.

His men might be dead. Mary Alison? Most likely, Lia was at this moment trying to decide how much fun playing with Mary Alison could be.

No, Lia had had hours to make that decision. He'd lost the whole night. This would be her Ontario lodge. He'd cut a new road to his compound to avoid sight of it. Now he was here.

Although his linen shirt hung in charred tatters, he felt no burns at all. He'd also lost his head injury. A healer had touched him. Who? He inhaled scents of burnt linen and Lia and some bear she'd been rutting with until a fine and sweet tobacco reached him. Bear and tobacco and healing. Five Bears McGuire.

Five Bears occasionally liked the taste of a female partner. That's what had come between him and Kent. Although Lia could pirate just about any man's bed, McGuire ought to be too kinky even for her.

He remembered Lia at sixteen, the youngest student at Yale, her very existence in his territory a challenge. His father had said to kill her or seduce her. Killing her would've been simpler.

The door in front of him emitted a series of clicks. When it hissed open, Lia struck a backlit pose, framed in the doorway. Her glossy, black hair curled along the collar of her white blouse. The light behind her rendered the blouse translucent; she wore nothing under it, and probably nothing under that brief white skirt. Strappy sandals with high heels emphasized her long legs.

She carried a glass jar with a red cap. When she stepped into the room, the door swished shut behind her and gave another complicated series of clicks.

"You have put me off long enough, Darien."

"Have we had this conversation before, Lia? Your only road to advancement is over my dead body."

"Over your dead body or at your side, as your bondmate."

"We most definitely have had this conversation before."

He tried to move the dead weight of his arms. From the stink of silver on bare skin, he supposed he should be glad for the numbness. But Lia's undulating approach and erect nipples indicated salacious intent. "Don't you think that by the time you've hurt me or drugged me enough to break my will, you will also have impaired my hydraulic function?"

"Oh, my darling, I have no intention of drugging or injuring you." She smiled her secretive smile, and raised the red-capped jar. He saw scraps of dirty-white cloth with a yellowish melted spot. She snapped open the red lid and thrust the opening at his face.

Mary Alison's scent, metallic with fear, washed through his senses. His fangs extended, his pants tightened, and even more alarms rang through his head. He forced words around his fangs. "Where is she?"

Lia capped the jar and set it aside. She stalked in a circle around him, her white leather skirt opening along the side with each step. The precision and the power in those long strides mesmerized him. Would Mary Alison's compact build have any of that moving poetry?

"I find the little one insignificant. She will never love me, but she will obey me." Lia's knowing fingers caressed his far-too-tight fly. "Show me that you are man enough to keep us both, Darien, and I will allow her to live. Make me very happy and I will not send her to the punishment cage with a few of my more deprived cats."

"She is Hawkmoor, Lia. You can't treat her like some impertinent spare female."

She brushed against his chest, filling him with her scent and Mary Alison's. "Watch me."

"How many laws do you think you can break before the humans notice more than random chaos?"

"I have broken no laws of the Hidden. You are legitimate captives. If it were not such a waste I might geld you—"

"You never used to make idle threats. Nor did you lie." As captives of another Family, he and Mary Alison would lose their status as Hawkmoor and would be unable to confer it on Lia.

Lia frowned, and he caught a hint of uneasiness. "I have not lied, Darien. The daylight attacks on humans are not my doing."

"Who but you would cry havoc, and let slip the dogs of war?"

The memory softened her face. Shakespeare In The Park. They'd recited lines to each other for days afterward. "Many would. Perhaps only I could." She went cold again. "In that sense, perhaps the attacks are my doing, although I did not plan them."

"You've openly challenged Hawkmoor. No oaths govern the other Families until the challenge is resolved. I should've killed you when you first came."

"Yes, you should have. But you were trapped by your insistence that Mary Alison was alive, and that it was her job to defend her borders against a female." She smiled briefly. "Currently, your choices are to please me or to die in a manner of my choosing."

"Release me," he growled.

Lia smiled again. "No, I think not." Her nails curved, arching out to needle-tipped razors. He'd taught her that trick during long, sweet, sweaty afternoons in her loft. But that had been before he understood the damage he was doing. Before he understood conflicting obligations. Before he fully understood the price of being Hawkmoor.

Lia's claws sliced his burnt shirt to broad ribbons. The charred cloth flaked away, and her claws left fine whispers of scratches in his skin. Chill-bumps raised the hairs on his skin. She hooked claws in his belt and tilted her head to look sideways at him. "If I leave you your belt, will you promise to use it on me?"

Was Five Bears fool enough to rise to that bait? He smiled back, careful to conceal his fangs. A man with fangs is a man without control. He could barely form words. "No promises, Lia."

She sliced through the belt and in a second swipe cut open his waistband. She stepped back and crossed her arms under her pert breasts. Waiting. Her scent oozed around him.

Darien shifted the bones of his hands and wrists within the double ring of the activated-silver handcuffs. Electric pain shimmered up and down, fingertip to elbow, the cuffs punishing the flow of flesh and bone. He clenched his teeth. Letting Lia watch him fail was more impossible than shaping his hands, even with the burning silver and the surges of electricity. Finally, long and narrow and tipped with claws, his hands dropped free.

Returning circulation throbbed down his arms. His vision shifted to the low-color, motion-sensitive precision of cat vision. He forced it back to human and reshaped his hands, taking his time so she could watch. She'd once sculpted his hands for a bronze casting. They were, she'd said, perfect male hands. Perfectly sized and shaped. She meant to knead the cheeks of her ass and hold her lovely violet labiae open with both thumbs while he nuzzled and licked—

Lia's pink tongue flicked out. "You have a cat Shape now. How verrry interesting. Are we compatible, or have you chosen the tiger? Not a lion. Lions are so ordinary."

"Neither." He jumped forward. She twisted away. She stopped by the couch, scraping her now-human nails delicately over the white leather and bowing teasingly over it.

He shed the remaining scraps of his clothes, pretending not to watch her. When she pouted, he lunged. She whirled away.

He hooked his fingers in the waistband of her skirt, lifted her and slung her around over the back of the couch. Grinning, she tumbled to the other side and landed on her hands and knees.

He vaulted the couch. She flowed to her feet and ran. He came up behind her and pinned her against the wall. She struck his burned wrists. He growled, pain bringing the wolf even with her cat-scent, and pressed her harder against the wall. He bit the side of her neck until she squirmed and rocked back on his cock.

He slid a hand up under that little skirt. The touch of lace under it surprised him. "When did you start wearing underpants?"

"When Bear told me how much fun they are to tear off."

"Bear has some worthwhile ideas." Darien ripped away the bit of lace. Lia's scent redoubled, clouding his head.

"Yes!" she hissed, "Yes! Oh, yes!"

For a second he forgot the world around him, forgot his burned wrists and how they'd been burned, forgot everyone depending on him to be the sanity and the balance for the Hidden World. For that instant he was only male, and Lia's scent brought his fangs fully erect, twisting and cutting his lips. The blood intensified Lia's scent, but another scent threaded through it. *Mary Alison.* "Where is she?"

Lia went rigid. "You have me, and you can think of her?"

He held her pinned against the wall, letting that be his answer.

After a moment she slumped. She tried to turn, but he held her. She spoke earnestly, "It will all work out, Darien. Now that we have the kitten, we can bond as a triad or just kill her. Either way, she can never again hold us apart."

His stomach clenched. Mary Alison's right to refuse a triad bond had been his excuse, not the reason he'd refused. But now, if Mary Alison agreed, if things worked out just exactly right, forming a triad would convert Lia from rival to ally. Minor ally, in theory. The trick would be making the reality match the theory. He had Lia in his hands, but until he had Mary Alison out of her control, he remained a prisoner. He relaxed his muscles deliberately. "Kitten?"

"Bear says her father called her that." She ducked under his arm and pressed a single sensor on the table. The door cycled though its clicks and hissed open.

Mary Alison stumbled through the doorway. She fell to her knees and remained there, blank-faced and waiting, while the door shut behind her. She wore white cotton underpants. Nothing else.

His vision locked on her breasts; they were fuller than he'd guessed, nearly twice the size of Lia's perfect teacups. She'd lost the scratches and bruises from her downhill tumble; either she'd shifted or Five Bears had spent time with her.

Then he looked—really looked—at those empty eyes. They drew him. Mary Alison's nostrils flared as he neared, and her nipples tightened to point at him. Lia's aura intensified around them, and Mary Alison's face relaxed again to utter blankness.

He took her hand. She didn't react. He could not feel her aura at all. "Lia, what have you done?"

Lia chuckled. "Come to me, Kitten."

Mary Alison rose to her feet and stepped around him to go to Lia. Her back had more visible muscles than a human, and she moved with a shifter's grace.

Lia pulled the smaller woman close and chin-stroked her hair. "What do you think, Darien? I could hold her while you fucked her, and you could kiss me over her head."

Mary Alison did not react. She'd been cut. Everything that made her an individual had been cut away. "What've you done?"

"I have not brought in the surgeon. Not yet. Bear and I just deactivated her frontal lobes. Initially I planned to take off that defiant edge, but she kept fighting me. We had to strip her this far just to tame her, and even so I was not sure I could hold her if you—ah—distracted me. Think of that, Darien. With the right touch you might have freed her."

He looked in Mary Alison's incurious face and wrestled his boiling fury, forced his fangs back to human contours.

Lia's voice sharpened. "If you wanted her, you would have found her years ago. But you wanted a conveniently absent mate far more than you ever wanted this little body here."

The little body stood tiredly in Lia's arms, not seeming to notice the elegant hands cupping her lush round breasts.

Lia tugged at Mary Alison's underpants. "Kitten, take these off."

Mary Alison hesitated. Lia's aura concentrated about her. Darien had never felt Lia so readily. He must still have a link with Mary Alison, however occluded, to feel Lia through her.

Mary Alison exhaled and obeyed. When she stood naked, his gaze riveted on the tawny puff of genital hair. His mouth went dry and his cock surged back up to thump the skin under his navel.

Lia slipped an arm around Mary Alison's waist. "I and my kitten need to shower. Would you care to join us, Darien?"

He remembered her shower games. "She's my wife, Lia."

"Right now, she is my property. Yet I offer to share. Am I not most generous? Should you not thank me?"

Mary Alison was here, and helpless, because he'd failed to protect her. He had to get her through today with no more damage. He could call his wolves when the moon rose, and matters would change then. He rubbed his burned wrists, healing them. "Thank you, Lia. I most ardently desire to share your shower."

"Good. Come, Kitten."

Darien memorized the codes as Lia keyed open the door. She looked back at him, one eyebrow lifting as she saw his focus. Then her gaze settled on Mary Alison and went thoughtful.

"If we stand together, Darien, exerting the authority of Hawkmoor, we can stop these raids before they become full warfare. She must be shown as utterly under control. Otherwise Boston will concentrate on attempts to press her to authorize more advantageous deals against Philadelphia, and Chicago will watch Quebec and Detroit to see which of them is bribing her, and Raleigh will think *Fresh Meat* and become deaf to you."

Lia was too intelligent to underestimate, he reminded himself. Too much of what she said made sense. Mary Alison couldn't know the Families, their entangled histories, or the fragile alliances he maintained among them. She couldn't know what to believe, who to rely on, how to appeal to any one of them. Letting her speak as Hawkmoor would invite chaos and destruction.

After a deep lobotomy, a new personality grew in the regenerating brain. A quieter, less confident person. She would never be the same Mary Alison.

The lesser cut so popular for teenagers would merely subdue her for a few months.

In the context of a lifetime, two months wasn't so long.

But when Lia had ordered that pesky sister of hers cut, the surgeon had left a silver needle behind. It had burned away the girl's brain faster than moonlight could heal, and no one had known what was wrong until the autopsy.

Chapter Six

Darien braced his arms against one wall of the shower. Lia crouched between his legs, her fingers digging into his buttocks while she licked and sucked maddeningly at his cock. He groaned. She growled and took what she wanted, licking up one side and down the other, then swallowing the head while her palms worked the shaft.

Lia used Mary Alison's soapy hands to massage his back. He did his best to hold still. This wasn't showering with two women so much as showering with one four-armed woman. The soap smelled of tropical fruits and coconut. Lia assured him it was quite edible. He didn't see how, but she was the one with suds in her mouth.

Mary Alison bit his shoulder, a special favorite move. His balls tightened and his head went back, but Lia pressed her thumb firmly against the base of his cock.

"Don't you dare come yet. I have something special planned for that hard-on."

That, he thought dully, shouldn't sound so wonderful.

He couldn't look at Mary Alison. The fruity soap and rushing water kept her scent from teasing him, but catching a view of that body, ripe and lush as a fertility goddess, torqued his breeding drive just as hard. What held him back was the dead calm in her face, the sign that she was Lia's marionette.

Lia smiled, her lips reddened and her eyelids heavy. "Turn around and do her, Darien. I want to feel it through her."

"No." It came out as another groan.

"She wants it."

"You want it, Lia. She wants what you make her want."

"Are you feeling particularly dense, darling? She needs no push in that direction. I tasted her longing in every bite."

"A mind that cannot refuse cannot give consent."

"She could kneel on the shower stool and be just the right height for you to slide that cock up her cleavage. Think of it—slicked up and warm and so very soft. She could hold her breasts together and you could pump—"

"No," he repeated.

Mary Alison leaned against his back, indeed warm and soft. Lia went around behind him, sliding her soapy wet skin against his. "She wants it, Darien. Just as you want her."

He leaned his head against the tile, trying to think of something besides two naked women and the fullness of the moon. His cock leered rebelliously up at him. *Oh, go to sleep*, he ordered. It twitched, aching hard. If he didn't get to sink it somewhere warm and wet very soon, it was going to explode on him.

He turned to press his back to the shockingly cold tile and took a deep breath of the steamy air. Lia massaged shampoo through Mary Alison's hair, working up a rich creamy lather that drifted down her neck, collecting on her shoulders and between her breasts. That could not, by any means, be an accident of gravity.

A white driblet slid down over Mary Alison's brow; he wiped it off before it could sting her eyes. A flicker of expression crossed her face. Was some part of her struggling against Lia's control? Or had she been beaten down too far?

Long ago, Lia had said that a prisoner becomes a slave the moment she relaxes and gives up. Mary Alison had not relaxed in Lia's grasp. He had to free her before that happened.

He slid a finger down the energy path behind Mary Alison's ear and down her neck. No response. He looked over her head at Lia. "You need to loosen control if you want me to get anywhere. I never saw the charm of necrophilia."

Lia frowned, but something altered, so that he felt less of her. He tilted Mary Alison's face up, cupping it in both hands, and brushed his thumbs over her bottom lip. Her pupils dilated, and her lids dropped over them.

He slid his hands down through the suds on her shoulders and then reached past her to stroke Lia's soapy shoulders. He could snap that neck, but even with a true healer in attendance, killing the controller often killed the controlled. Or damaged her so deeply she could never recover.

He played in the fragrant suds, sliding his cock against Mary Alison's abdomen while fingerpainting Lia's breasts and upper chest, moving up to massage her scalp. As Lia purred, he probed their combined auras, trying to see what might weaken their link.

Mary Alison's pulse-rate rose with Lia's. He closed his eyes and held both women against him in a languid, teasing dance. Without warning, something opened and he sank down into them.

Lia welcomed him with surprised delight, sweeping complex plans by him so fast he caught only fragments of financial calculations and political/psychological analyses of the Families.

Beneath Lia's calculations, he found Mary Alison's distaste for the greasy-rich soap, and her fierce resistance to the blazing need to copulate, the urge to grab his hard cock and mount it while trusting him to hold her up.

Yes, I will hold you, he assured her. She snarled at him.

Below her mating instinct, ready to erupt, seethed unquenchable rage.

Lia paused in her computations to comb through Mary Alison's nerves and shoot a pre-orgasmic twinge through her.

Mary Alison gasped, and Lia laughed at her.

Darien seized the chance, fueling Mary Alison's outrage with his own until she exploded. She wrenched free of them and slammed into the shower door, but it was not glass and it didn't shatter. She bounced back. Lia tripped her and she fell, splashing the ankle-deep water in a frothy wave up the walls.

Darien pushed between the women. Mary Alison snarled at them both, oblivious to the hot spray in her face. When he reached for her, she knocked his hand aside and scrambled as far away as she could get in the tiled enclosure.

Without Lia's presence to block him, Darien flooded through Mary Alison, washing out the rage so she could think, could comprehend her situation and react in a way that would not get them both killed or cut. *You are my bondmate. You must trust me!*

Mary Alison raised a shaking hand to rake wet hair out of her eyes, and glared defiance at them both.

Lia, excluded as Darien had been a moment ago, spat out a phrase in Spanish, stepped around Darien, and snapped a kick at Mary Alison. Mary Alison danced out of the arc of the kick and jerked the door open.

Darien felt the ceramic curves of the handle against his palm, against her palm. He clenched his fists. No ceramic. He'd felt that through her. Full sensory sharing without physical contact. This was the stuff of legend.

Cold air displaced the steam. He felt Lia's power build, and lash out. He caught her wrists, absorbing the sensation of acid pouring through his veins, but he shielded Mary Alison as she ran out into the den.

Seeing the room through her eyes, he forced her gaze to the silver mesh at the windows, the electronic door with its winking lights.

Get out of my head, man!

Just as well she'd had no defense training, because even as he was thinking it, she thrust him out with dizzying force. He released Lia and slapped an arm to the wall to orient himself.

Mary Alison abruptly sucked in her rage, as he might suck in his fangs. Stark naked, dripping wet, and quivering with leftover adrenaline, she systematically prowled the den, examining each window, each nook and corner in turn.

Lia stood in the bathroom doorway, pulling on a thick crimson bathrobe with vicious jerks. Her lips barely moved when she spoke. "You should take note that I contacted Dr. Kelly early this morning."

Dr. Kelly specialized in the deepest cuts. He might balk at cutting Lady Hawkmoor, but then he made a point never to ask who lay under the surgical drapes. Darien weighed his alternatives. None was pleasant.

"Come back and face the music, Kitten," he said. "Cooperate, or you could face a surgeon before moonrise. Have you ever known anyone with a frontal lobotomy?"

She spun to face him, wild-eyed, slinging drops of water and whipping strings of hair across her face. As quickly, she spun away. Her back muscles clenched and relaxed before she spoke.

"You sure changed your tune, man," she said. "Tall, dark and skinny there must be one hell of a lay."

She used to be. He took a slow breath. Mary Alison paused under the silver cuffs, scowling up at them a moment before she moved on to test another window's lock. If she dangled from those cuffs, her feet would not touch the floor. She would suffocate in slow stages, or burn her hands off at the wrist.

"You don't know the forces at work, Mary Alison Hawkmoor." He came toward her until she took a step back. "Don't call me 'man' again. In our culture it implies that 'man' is rather more than what I am. It challenges me to prove myself. You might not quite be ready for that."

Hands clapped. Lia applauded in slow motion, the wide cuffs of the plush robe swinging under her wrists. Mary Alison's fear licked along the edges of his mind, stinging like a taste of sour-apple candy.

Lia smiled her thinnest smile at him and spoke past him. "By moonrise, Kitten, you might plead for a lobotomy. Your bondmate, here, is about to assure that you hurt—"

"What do you want, Lia? Theatrics aside, what do you really want?" Lia wanted power, Mary Alison's status as Hawkmoor. If Lia said that out loud, he would have a position from which to negotiate.

"For now?" She laughed shortly. "I want blood. Do you think both of you can turn up your noses at me? I want your cock rammed up her ass. I want that undersized mouth of hers screaming and sobbing and drooling. When she breaks, I want to be there to comfort her and to bond with her."

"You don't want her pain," he said. "You want her power. You want to be Hawkmoor. You can get the legal triad without breaking her. I will agree. She will agree. Let the bonds form over time. Let—"

"Did you just tell this bitch I would marry her? Man, you are out of your mind!"

"If you don't believe in the validity of any of this, Mary Alison, you ought not care what I promise. I am, in a very real sense, trying to save your ass. Cooperate if you can. If you can't, at least stop interfering."

He poured the full force of his will through her bond. Any of his wolves would've hunkered down under that rush of power. Instead, Mary Alison did something impossible, effectively turning sidewise to let his power flow past her. She crossed her arms and scowled at him.

Chapter Seven

"I want to be Hawkmoor," Lia agreed. Darien turned to face the tall bitch, and Lia smiled her Supermodel smile at him. "I want you, too. Luckily you and she and the name come as a package."

"The hell we do," she muttered, not caring if they heard. The room was too cold for standing naked, with water puddling around her feet. She tried the last window. Locked. Sealed at every edge. She saw no way to open it.

Darien spoke. "Do we agree to the standard one-year trial?"

"No," Lia objected. "Only the full union will make me Hawkmoor."

"Agreed," he said quickly. "Mary Alison, say you agree."

She felt him pushing at her again, and she let the power slip by. This was getting easier. She rubbed her arms briskly. Darien pushed harder. Like hell she would trust him. "That kind of agreement ought to be more than saying words."

She squinted at the higher windows again. Each had a winking LED in the upper corner, and each had metal mesh over or in it. Supermodel-Lia moved. MA swiveled to watch her.

"Agreement is much more than words." Lia took a few steps, shaking her feet delicately like a wet cat. Water beaded on the polished wood floor in her wake. She stopped at Darien's side, and the two-timing bastard put an arm around her. "But the words are all I require of you right now."

"How nice," she snarled.

"Say you agree." Darien's voice was smooth but his shadowed gaze fixed on her as if she just might be good to eat.

I'm naked and locked in a room with two crazy people. I'll say anything you want. Her skin puckered all over.

"Say the words," he prompted.

She glared at him. "I agree!"

He grinned at her, unabashedly triumphant.

Just exactly what all had she agreed to? And why wasn't she madder about it? *Because Darien wants it.* And because if she didn't agree, they would dispose of her. Supermodel had made that clear.

"I need my pills," she muttered, really thinking out loud. Darien looked too good even without the impressive hard-on he'd had in the shower. He still had soap on him too, like a lace doily over one shoulder and frothing down to his—

Don't look, she reminded herself. *Don't look and don't think and don't lose control*. He looked too good, too much like a kid's dream of Prince Darien. But he was, after all, soapy from washing that supermodel off him. "You got another robe?"

Supermodel smiled coldly. "Take this one, Kitten."

Yeah, she would take the only robe. They'd hypnotized her and made her a puppet. She was rude enough to take the only robe and leave them naked to tease each other up.

Darien stood behind her and the woman stood in front of her and together they dressed her. As if she needed any help. Darien's hard-on prodded her back. She couldn't move away from him without rubbing up on the woman, though, and she'd had just about enough of that. *Oh, Jerusalem!* He smelled good, and his arms fit around her just right. The woman smiled down at her. Not coldly. The woman was aroused too.

The air was too thick; she couldn't get away from the smell of sex and piña colada shampoo. She turned to Darien to get her face out of Supermodel's cleavage. "Who plans to get my pills?"

"What pills do you need, Kitten?" Supermodel spoke into her wet hair. "I can send someone to the pharmacy."

"Gabapentin and Quetiapine," she said carefully. Every time a student had tried to get too friendly she'd brandished those words like garlic at a vampire. No one wanted a woman who took strong anticonvulsant and antipsychotic medication.

"Why do you need medication?" Darien asked in his smoky, intoxicating voice.

She huddled in the robe, hoping they detected less of her arousal than she did of theirs. She tried to step out from between them, but they had linked arms around her. She would have to hurt one to get free. And after she actually hit one of them, what room would she have left to negotiate in?

That sounded like Darien's thinking. It made sense, but she had to have breathing room soon or she was going to hit somebody anyway. "Look, if you two want to get it on again, feel free. I'll take some clothes and leave you to it."

"Why do you need medication?" Lia asked, her lips way too close.

"Are you offering to make a drugstore run or not? If you just want to poke into my business, you might ought pay attention to your own. No disrespect intended, but—"

Darien pressed his ridge against her, derailing her train of thought. All she wanted in the world right then was to jump him. And for him to make the Supermodel go away. And for it to be forever. *And-and-and,* she taunted herself. And if frogs had wings they wouldn't be slapping their butts in the mud.

Darien rested one hand on her hip, pulling her slightly toward him; his other hand stroked her sleeve as if the red plush might be fur that needed petting.

As if showing how deliciously his hands could move on her. But she'd have to stand in line. He belonged to Lia. Before those hands smelled of soap, they had smelled of Lia.

"Every thing about you is our business," he said. "Especially since you said you can't have children because of the medication. Why do you need such medicine?"

"I told you I get seizures! The stuff stops the seizures! Lady, your fella here is too close. Can you back him off some?"

"I am Lia. You are the lady here."

"Whatever. I don't need your horny dog on my back. Get him off before I damage him."

He leaned close to her plush collar, inhaling deeply. "Damage me, Kitten? You are in heat, and I am here for you."

"Yes," purred the woman. "Here for you."

Miss Lia, playing threesies might turn you on, but not me. And I drop my drawers only when I want to.

She shivered. When she wanted to or when Lia made her. She resolutely shut that door. She would deal with those memories later. Darien touched her face. *So what about you? Hero or villain?* "Make her go away," she said.

"He can't," said Lia, giving a shimmy that rubbed everywhere. MA's fist moved faster than any human could block, but Darien caught her wrist. As if he'd expected exactly that move, in exactly that instant.

"You forget, Lia," he said, "I can invoke the two moons."

"You can't!" Lia stood up straight. "No one does that anymore."

"I just did." Gently, with small motions, he pulled MA to his side, under his arm.

"What about me?" Lia made fists in the red cloth, trying to pull MA back toward her. "You agreed! Does Hawkmoor retract?"

"We agreed," he said solemnly, and opened Lia's hands.

MA waited tensely. Darien knew this Lia, knew how to bluff her and how to work her. If he was picking sides for real, or if he was a bad guy, might as well know it here and now.

The arm around her tightened in a brief hug. He spoke over her head to Lia. "You may prepare the declaration. You are legally a Hawkmoor. But Mary Alison and I, as initial pair, have exclusive rights to procreation attempts for two full moons."

Procreation attempts, she thought dizzily. Darien surrounded her with his heat. Traces of his scent emerged from the soap. He might never have had a woman who knew the names of each of her abdominal muscles and who could clench them in order, who could milk that cock of his with the adductors high on her inner thighs, the iliopsoas deep inside—

"You planned this!" Lia sounded ready to spit. "You set me up as your teaser pony!"

MA felt a swing coming, but Darien stopped it with a look.

Instead Lia leaned close and snarled, "It will not work, Darien. She has no Shape."

The hell I don't, Miss Skinny-Lou Don't-need-a-bra!

"Be that as it may," Darien responded calmly, "we have rights, and your senior wife has asked that you absent yourself."

"If you think—if either of you thinks—that this 'senior wife' shit will make me subordinate to this kitten, you are mistaken."

"Lia," he said patiently, "it's done. You can go find one of your cats or you can go wedge yourself between the bears, but you must go. For two months no one can touch me or Mary Alison except as an act of petit treason."

Lia hissed in reply, not bothering to form words. MA turned in Darien's arms and watched her stalk away.

Darien let out a long, slow breath. "I propose, Kitten—"

"My name's not Kitten. You can call me Mary Alison, but I'm nobody's kitten."

"I meant it affectionately!"

"*She* didn't."

"Point taken." He kissed the top of her head.

"Now, *look*, you condescending son of a bitch—" She took in a breath, and the scent of the man hit her. Her vision hazed over, and her knees lost strength. She wanted him, wanted him bad and wanted him now.

She hooked a foot behind his ankle and pushed him over backward. As he fell, grinning hugely, she dropped on top of him. The red robe flared open, spreading out to both sides. She wriggled his big, beautiful cock into position and tried to squeeze it inside by main force. It wouldn't fit. His foreskin was rough and dry and in the way.

He caught her by the elbows. "Slow down, Ki—Mary Alison!"

"The hell you say. *Do* something!"

He laughed a slow, deep laugh and reached down, one thumb circling her clit and sliding open the lips. She gasped and then felt him, smooth and sleek and powerful, sliding inside and Oh, Jerusalem! He would hit that stupid freak-of-nature hymen that kept growing back!

"Don't stop," she pleaded.

"Not to worry," he murmured. He hit the barrier and paused. "Been a while, has it?" He slid deeper, the barrier giving way with no more than a pinch, but all too soon he ran out of room.

She moaned and rocked. His thumb circled her clit again, around and around and then across, roughly. A shock pierced up through her navel. She arched hard. When she came down, he fit all the way in; her hips met his.

She clutched at his shoulders, disoriented by a rush of emotions and images she couldn't begin to sort out. She saw the dream-forest, its overwhelming detail and lack of color. A stunning variety of life streamed past as she leaped and ran through the dappled moonlight, relishing the springing energy in her muscles. *Running, searching, wanting! Wanting—*

Wanting Darien. She opened her eyes. He looked as dazed as she felt. Muscles corded his shoulders. She knew every one of them as a clinical entity, but now they presented themselves as a perfect whole. Strength incarnate. Hunger washed through her, and she moved her hips on him. "Do it, man."

He rolled her under him, and then quickly rolled them both all the way over again. This time she landed with her back to a thick, wooly rug. He paused over her, his chest and shoulders blocking out the light, and some tension let go inside her.

She felt, in this moment, safe from anything. Safe from anyone, in this powerful man's shadow. Tears burned at her eyelids. She closed her eyes and made them swallow back the tears.

Darien lowered his weight onto her and took up a majestic, deep thrusting rhythm. Filling her, but not battering her. She joined his rhythm, luxuriating in the feel of this perfect man inside, above, all around her. He couldn't fit better if he'd been born and bred for her.

Another measure of tension flowed away. *If this is lunacy, sign the papers and throw away the key.* Darien had come for her. Finally, he'd come.

She spread her fingers across his biceps, enjoying the taut skin and hard muscle, bracing against the sinewy pressure from below. He slipped one hand under her fanny, lifting her to a better angle. His warm breath stirred her hair while his lips traced her hairline. His heavy breathing and heartbeat called hers to match tempo. This is what it should be like, and never had been.

She clenched her pelvic muscles around his shaft, and felt his reaction from inside him. She jerked back.

"Don't be afraid," he whispered, stopping on the in-stroke and then sinking on in, filling her body entirely. "You're my bondmate. You're supposed to feel what I feel, and right now I feel wonderful. Open—please open to me, Mary Alison."

Her hands slid over the heated skin of his arms and chest. *Darien.* She'd opened her body to him, but her mind? He'd broken into that by force. She turned her hands to cover her breasts.

His dark eyes went sad. "Once a door has been kicked in, the simple matter of opening or closing it is never again simple, is it?"

She felt his galloping pulse, the corded muscles so tightly controlled, but his tone remained mellow, soothing. What could be scarier than a man who tried that hard not to be scary?

"It doesn't have to be all or nothing, Mary Alison. Feel what I feel. You can do that, while keeping everything else safe behind another door." He smiled faintly. "Don't you want to know what it feels like for the guy? Haven't you wondered? Open to me; let me share this with you."

He wasn't asking for all her secrets. He was asking for—and offering—right now. She turned her hands to him. Cautiously, she let go some of the plates of her emotional armor.

His awareness flowed through her and then eased back inside him, bringing her along.

He resumed the slow, deep thrusting, moving higher and a bit to the side so his pubic bone pressed against her clit with each stroke. Once again, she had to hold his upper arms to anchor herself against the driving force from below. He opened his eyes, and she saw her own face, looking up from under too-pale brows. A wave of self-consciousness washed her back into her own body.

Darien closed his eyes and coaxed her back, murmuring things she couldn't make out but that erased the embarrassment. Now his sensations blended with her own, like feeling her tongue against the roof of her mouth.

"Relax," he said. The word radiated warmth through her, and her insides melted. Darien clutched her tighter, and his pace doubled, the strokes coming short and hard.

A different tension wound her tight. His pulse pounded in her ears, faster and harder. Heat poured from her body into his, from his into hers. She tumbled in the vortex, hearing short, sharp cries and not knowing if they were hers or his.

Then everything crushed together and everything burst apart and sent her soaring like a flat stone slung out over the water. She skipped over the surface of reality and finally sank into herself, feeling the aftershocks stuttering through her and her harsh panting in time with his. Her heartbeat changed with his to a deep, slow pounding.

His weight pressed on her, hot and sweating and so heavy, making her intimately aware of his hand under her bottom and his arm under her shoulders. When she opened her mouth, she tasted the salt on his chest. He couldn't have melted into her for a more thorough union. By this act Darien had marked her as part of him forever. And oh, was it good.

Chapter Eight

"Wake up, Sleeping Beauty. I assume you do want to clean up before I introduce you to the Families?"

She reluctantly patted at the drying shampoo in her hair. *Ick.* "I need to wash before I meet anybody."

"So do I. Can you stand yet?"

Her hand dropped. "What families?"

"The ones who owe you fealty, and that means everyone for a thousand miles in any direction except west."

"Get real."

He leaned so close she could see only one eye looking at her. Then he licked quickly between her brows. "How much reality can you take, Mary Alison? Were you awake when McGuire healed all those cuts and scratches you had?"

McGuire? Healed? She vaguely remembered falling, and getting plenty of skin-level damage. Then a street skirmish. Getting knocked down and waking up tied to a bunk in a minibus with some kind of glass top. Kissing Darien. An explosion—a bearded man pulling her out of it. A long helicopter ride made chaotic by zoo smells and zoo noises. Healed? Hypnotized was more like it.

Darien sighed. "Humans need voices, but you and I communicate more directly. Is that the limit of what you can accept?"

"A couple of people in the town I grew up in could read minds. A little." She paused. "They were not the kind of people you wanted knowing your business."

"You learned to hide your...business."

The hard way. She shuddered.

"You asked about the Families. Think of city-states. We have a Family in each major city, and in some moderate-sized cities. Some Families occupy two or three cities, with all the area between them. Scattered pairs and triads live with their children away from the cities, but report to the nearest Family and are considered part of that Family."

She sat up and stretched experimentally. Darien settled behind her and massaged her back. Oh, he was good at that. She leaned into the pressure of those magic hands.

"A century and a half ago," he continued, "the Families were autonomous. After the humans got through slaughtering each other and us in the 1860s, we held a conference and agreed to something like a feudal system, with individuals accountable to Families and Families accountable to their heads, and the heads of the Families having some obligation to consult Hawkmoor before taking territory or vengeance. Taking advantage of rapid transportation and instant communication, your ancestors increasingly enforced the obligation to consult Hawkmoor. More kinds of disputes come to us now. We find ways to give one Family what it needs without screwing over another too badly. A few months ago, Birmingham asked to annex a town from Mobile. They debated transportation facilities and room to hunt, the French traditions in Mobile versus the English traditions in Birmingham. But what Birmingham really wanted was access to a new water park. Birmingham got access in groups of ten, with a week's advance notice, and everyone is happy."

A water park? Was that what they considered worth fighting for?

Darien went on. "Since Atlanta, Hawkmoor can declare a Family outlaw. Anyone can raid in outlaw territory without fear of repercussion. We alone draw the line, and we alone can say when the killing stops. Theoretically. Nearly all of us are, by nature, predators. Stopping the killing is not nearly as easy as letting it happen."

She picked up the red robe. If that was true, it was scary as hell. "The Los Angeles riot last July? You did that?"

"No. California is outside our jurisdiction. My grandmother Berenov has title to it, but I hear she cringes at the sound of a Southern California accent. We have the Mississippi valley and everything east of it, except the free ports of Miami and New Orleans. Boston was autonomous until a few years ago, and Quebec wants autonomy. We have some influence in the Northern Great Plains, the Prairie Provinces, Greenland and Siberia."

"You're saying you really are a prince."

"Please don't use that term."

She tried to stand but he was in her way, holding out his hand. She looked at the man's face, his deep eyes, and let him lift her to her feet. His face softened. He hadn't expected her to accept that little courtesy. She stretched again, and blushed when she saw how intently he watched her. Like the thick robe was some gauzy nothing. "Um, I really do need to wash. Can you talk over the sound of running water?"

"I could, but I need to wash very quickly and join Lia for the announcements. She's in a hurry to tell everyone that you've been sec—found—and that we three have bonded. Some Families will believe it only if they see us together. You have a few more minutes before you'll need to join us for the announcements we expect to be most difficult."

What did you almost say, Darien? That I've been secured? Second-somethinged? Sexually consummated? Not consummated. Consumed. Yeah, definitely consumed.

She moved blindly toward the shower. *Consumed.* She stopped and turned. He was right there; his arms came around her. She buried her face against his chest.

"Don't—" She stopped. What could she say? *Don't hurt me? Don't let those people hurt me? Yeah, right.* Whining like a helpless fluff-brain would make her a whole lot safer. She pressed against Darien, taking what comfort was offered. If it was only physical, it was still better than nothing.

Between them, Mr. Happy perked up and nudged her belly button. *Gomer! that's not my belly button! It ain't my finger neither, Louann.* Her laugh came out thin and brittle, edged with hysteria.

Darien's arms tightened around her, and his willpower probed at her, trying to get back inside her head. She pulled away.

"You wash first," she said. "Then while I'm in there, you and Supermodel can scare up some real clothes. I don't plan on meeting anybody with you all nudist-camp and Mr. Happy there advertising some kind of honeymoon."

His face went through several expressions but he kept his reply to the point. "You're what, about a size ten-petite?"

"Men's extra-small or a ladies' medium. I need a medium-large sports bra with extra-firm support and some briefs—none of that butt-floss—in medium-small. In shoes I wear a 4 and one-half EEEE boys' or a 6 WW women's."

"A bra that doesn't come with numbers and letters?"

Had his brain turned off at the first mention of a bra? *Men!* "And I'm gonna need my pills before tonight."

A bandy legged, heavily muscled man led her to a room where Lia and Darien, both wearing exquisitely tailored CEO suits, sat on a couch facing wall-mounted TV screens. No, computer screens. Darien saw her and killed the light from the screens. He and Lia rose and turned to face her.

The way they looked at her, she ought to be wearing a sweeping gown and a crown, not an old-lady-in-church dress in wild-azalea shades of pink. The dress fit better than she'd hoped, but her feet scuffed the floor in an oversized pair of white moccasins.

Lia waved her forward.

Darien's brows crunched together the slightest bit, and MA stayed where she was. Darien smiled and came to meet her. He led her to the couch, to the spot in the middle with a discreet footstool in front of it. Lia and Darien sat flanking her while the two large computer screens flickered with static.

"Don't say any more than you have to," Darien muttered.

One screen filled with half a dozen faces, adults of mixed ages and races. The other screen broke into jagged stripes, then resolved to the faces of three middle-aged men who looked like brothers. She was, she realized with a sliding, nauseated feeling, the center of attention.

One of the three middle-aged men barked out a laugh. "You caught them. You caught them both!"

He was speaking to Lia, clearly. MA spun a cotton-candy smile. "Yes, sir. I did. Not that you all come here to listen to me to brag about it."

She felt a spurt of approval from Darien, a muted echo from Lia.

"You have your mother's eyes, Lady Hawkmoor," one of the women from the crowded panel spoke. MA fixed on her. She looked around thirty-five and like the sort of person who would call her violet-and-beige suit an 'aubergine and ecru ensemble.'

Another woman nodded. "I was about to say the same. I took your mother's classes at Eastgate, getting further and further lost, until she gave me precisely that look of yours and suggested I drop any thoughts of a science major."

Tell me more, MA begged silently, but they didn't.

A man between the women cleared his throat. "Lady Hawkmoor, your father and his sisters led the Northern Territorial Initiative. Will you take up that initiative again?"

The what? Something from TV news echoed in memory. "If you have a position paper I would be glad to read it."

Everyone looked at her. She worked not to fidget under so many probing eyes. Darien's approval swirled around her, buffering the pressure. Finally an older man leaned forward. "It will be on your printer in 48 hours."

"Thank you."

One of the three men from the other screen spoke. "Have you a preliminary position, Lady Hawkmoor?"

"Not one I am willing to share," she retorted, and blushed, thinking of a front-to-front position with Darien.

Lia laughed softly, running cold water along her nerves to quench the blush.

Darien sat forward, commanding attention. "Lady Hawkmoor is not subject to questioning until she's had time to adjust to the Families' ways. Have you a question for Lia or me?"

Another of the three men leaned forward. "Yes, Lord High Prince Darien the Shaper." He spat the words like an insult; Darien's irritation tickled unpleasantly. "When will we again freely hunt the vast woodlands of the South?"

When the southerner who owns the woodland in question gives you permission, MA thought derisively. *Not that permission's easy to get. Land's precious. A Landowner's ID is a man's best protection against a bus trip to a transient camp or boot camp, and everyone knows about adverse possession.*

"Freely hunt?" Darien's eyes narrowed. "Never. Free hunting brought Atlanta. At least one hundred seven of us and ninety allies and over four thousand strangers died that night. Dover, the Pillar of Memory was your idea, wasn't it? Those people are *gone*. Eastgate School is *gone*. The teachers are *gone*. Mary Alison's mother was the last Caspian tiger this world will ever see. Our gene-crafting algorithm died with her, as did our entire genetic database. Our science is *gone*. We don't know a quarter of the lineages or the legends we knew twenty years ago. Our history is *gone*. The price of free hunting is too high."

My mother was a tiger? Like an Elk or a Shriner or the old ladies who sit on parade floats decked in red and white carnations?

The interview ended, but another started and it was more of the same. So were the next several. They went on for hours. When lunch came, she had to eat her soup and sandwich in front of the screens, painfully conscious of people watching her while Darien talked politics from some eco-nutzoid secret society where the officers' titles were different kinds of large predators.

She snorted. *Save the wolves. Save the squirrels they eat and the trees the squirrels live in. Keep people clustered together. Keep the open spaces open and the big tracts of land big. Watch for old ladies to die and raze their homes to enlarge the big parks.*

She'd periodically searched for Memaw's old homesite, for the stone cellar and the tree-house, but every year things faded more into the forest. *Gotta save them trees. Save trees for the wolves to piss on and to fertilize with little piles of wolf poop that used to be squirrels.*

The discussion continued around her. The status quo got mentioned a lot, but they couldn't agree on what the status quo was. *Goody for the people who have lodges like this,* she thought. *Regular folk like me get to stand in buses so crowded that the bead of sweat trickling down my arm might be mine or from the guy crammed next to me, but gotta keep them open lands open.*

She tried to maintain an interested expression, but the talks got worse than a day-long revival. At least a revival had times to stand and sing once in a while, not just sit and listen, and sit and listen, and sit and pretend to listen.

Dinner was more soup and sandwiches eaten on the couch with a dozen people watching her and Darien fielding questions. The next interview was split-screen; she had to look at four bunches of old ladies, maybe twenty of them in all. Darien addressed them as Aunt this and Aunt that. Growing up on the edges of other people's families had honed her sense of who ranked where, and these old ladies ranked. She held her spine straight and told the truth when asked about her health, her schooling, her studio, and her needlepoint.

They didn't seem to like her answers, but she was too tired to really care. Besides, the moon would be rising soon, and she needed her pills. She tried to communicate her growing agitation to Darien, but he just pressed his hand on hers. When the aunts left the screen, she stood. "I'll take my pills now."

Lia, still seated, smiled at her. "No."

That smile. Lia had used that same smile when doing her hypnotism thing last night. The refusal itself took a moment to settle in. Panic stirred. No pills? A nearly full moon was ready to rise, and she didn't have pills to protect her from the convulsions, or from the hallucinations that would follow.

She put iron in her voice. "I need them. Now."

"We have decided you do not. You appear to be in fine health, and we want to see precisely what the moon does to you."

You want to watch? Darien too? He was trying to reach out to her, but the impression she got was sympathy. She didn't need sympathy. She needed concrete help. She shrugged him off.

"Do I understand that no one can touch me?" she asked. "So I can walk to town and find a drugstore myself?" She had no money, but if she had to pick a lock or blow a pharmacy clerk, it wouldn't be the first time.

"You misunderstand," Lia smiled as she said it. "No one can touch you in a sexual manner, but you will be restrained if you attempt to leave. If safety were the only consideration, it would be enough. Town is fifteen kilometers away, and the woods will be alive. We need to see if you have a Shape that could survive whatever you might encounter before we set you loose. The medications you specified would suppress your nature and render you unconscious for the night."

You'd have to be an Olympian to be in better shape than I am! She routinely threw and pinned professional athletes. As for unconsciousness, that was what nights were for; her nature was nothing lovely when the moon dominated a clear sky.

"I think," Lia drew out the words as if they tasted good, "you should go to the cage now."

Darien stirred. "Your reasoning, Lia?"

"Not counting the bears or you, nineteen adult males occupy the premises. Only four of them are in exclusive bonds, and only two of the unattached males are wolves you could control. Meanwhile, all but three of my females are either unreceptive or in exclusive bonds. Count the odds, Darien. The fighting and fucking will begin in less than half an hour. The children will need to be locked in their dorms until sunrise."

MA rubbed her eyes. Was she talking about a private zoo, or ranks in this secret society of theirs? Either way, an orgy ought to provide plenty of chances to escape.

Darien touched her shoulder. "A locked bedroom would provide sufficient protection."

Talk onnnn, Princey! A bedroom would have a vast array of items she could use as lock-picks. A toenail clipper could cut wire. Or she could bust a window.

Darien's arm draped around her. She leaned in, absorbing his strength and the irony of wanting it. *A strong guy can protect you against the world, but relying on him leaves you defenseless against the guy and whatever sick whim strikes him.* She'd seen the results; they were never pretty. She stood straight, armoring her mind so she couldn't feel whether he was probing.

Lia insisted that the cage was safer, and Darien assured her he had every confidence in the security of any bedroom Lia would design into her home. In the end, Darien won.

The bedroom had four windows. One window faced north, where an indigo-and-gold cloudbank retreated on the wind. The other three bedroom windows faced west. Bars of orange sunlight filtered through the blinds to tiger-stripe the beige bedspread, overwhelming the delicate blue floral pattern.

A pair of kids brought in laundry baskets of clean clothes. The girl brought pink clothes and the boy brought dark colors. Guy colors. Sexist as hell. The bandy-legged guy brought suits on hangers and hung them in the closet, shoving aside somebody else's clothes to make room. When the kids and the guy left, the door locked noisily behind them.

MA sorted through the pink stuff. Socks, sweats, tee-shirts, slacks, and a brand-new package of lacy pink briefs. No sneakers. They'd bought new undies but left her in shoes that didn't fit. "What happened to my own shoes?" She remembered having them on during the helicopter flight up here.

"I'll ask tomorrow."

"I'll remind you." She checked the dresser drawers for a manicure kit, pawing through a stranger's things like a burglar.

"What are you looking for?"

"Just looking." She shoved the drawer shut and turned. He lay stretched out on the blue-flowered bedspread, watching her.

She looked away, hoping her face didn't show the desire curling low in her abdomen. The air around her heated. Through the ornate mirror, she watched him unknot and unwind his navy silk tie, his darkening eyes fixed on her through the mirror in a way that made his action as riveting as a striptease. She broke a fine sweat.

He opened one button, watching her, smiling a small and knowing smile. A wolf howled. Several others answered it.

"Uh-oh," Darien muttered, swinging upright to face the window.

Chapter Nine

Darien stood at the north window, his hands pressed to the window frame, picking out his wolves in the gloom. Dammit, there was Jesús and behind him Denise, big as a male and twice as bitchy. The white ones had to be Rich, Mike, and Zach.

Mary Alison came up behind him. "What?"

"Those are my wolves! I reached Ajax too late. He'd already called the others."

"Are your 'wolves' going to fight with Lia's?"

"Of course they will. Even once they know a truce is in effect, they'll add to the chaos. If they go home now, though, Lia's wolves will follow them, and I don't have enough unattached females to keep them all from fighting there."

"Sounds like poor planning," she said, turning away.

"It's planning for normal times," he snapped. "Most of my people here are attached. I keep unattached females at the Finger Lakes, and unattached males in larger cities, where the ambient light level stays high. Unfortunately, my guys know to head north when trouble hits, and when the city boys come out here where nothing competes with the moon, they can go crazy."

He heard Ajax in the howls. Finally! Someone who could hear him despite the distance and different Shapes. *Ajax! We've bonded with Lia. Get home when you can, without taking Lia's males with you. We will follow when possible.*

Ajax howled in frustration, his howl swallowed by the sound of too many others.

Ajax, take a more commanding Shape.

Ajax shifted, losing contact, but a lion's cough promptly identified him. Unless Lia kept a tiger around, Ajax was now the baddest beast in the woods.

Darien turned to Mary Alison.

She sat on the edge of the bed and gave a little bounce. "You said my mother died in the Atlanta riots. You said it like you knew it for a fact."

If she were anywhere near as blasé as she looked, she wouldn't have asked. He kept his voice as neutral as hers. "Your parents and your brothers were among the first bodies identified in Atlanta on October first, the morning after the massacre. My mother was there to visit. She survived the first wave of killing. My father found her trail, and yours with it. The two of you covered nearly fifteen miles; she carried you a mile and walked you a mile. The two of you split up at a highway. You disappeared. She was trapped in a hospital and died there."

He came closer to breathe in her scent. Wide-eyed, she scuttled back against the padded blue headboard.

"I'm told I showed up near Poetry the day before Halloween," she said in a rush. "That's a good long way from Atlanta."

"Told?" He slid over beside her and threw an arm around her so she couldn't gracefully retreat. "What do you recall?" Did she have any image of his mother? Anything he could turn over and over in his mind and fit in with his own few memories?

She was afraid of him. He forced himself to relax and rubbed her arm and back until she curled up under his arm, against his side.

"I remember being cold," she said distantly. "Being hungry. Being scared. Hiding in dark, dirty places. I remember getting in a police car. The cop gave me a fuzzy blanket and a thermos of soup. They sent me to a foster home at the edge of the National Forest. Memaw raised me there until I was 13."

He watched the warmth fill her face, and loved this Memaw person without ever having met her. In that moment of remembered happiness, Mary Alison was beautiful. Her hair had the soft in-between color that was light brown on a woman and blond on a man. Delicate freckles dappled her cheeks, and a gold undertone lit her skin, as if she stood perpetually in the slanting rays of an autumn twilight.

"Memaw never let me miss a day of school," she said. "I got attendance awards every year. Honor roll too. After fourth grade, I knew I had to stay on top of the class or pay tuition, and there wasn't any money for that. When Memaw died—" She stopped.

He held her close. "Please go on."

"I went through some other foster homes, then I turned fourteen and the state washed its hands of me. I got my first wage-earner's ID at a shoe store; he kept me in shoes and let me sleep in the stockroom." The look on her face was anything but warm.

"Eventually," she went on, "I hopped the bus to Atlanta. Then Chattanooga. Attended the Vo-Tech there on a fake ID. Got caught in an ID sweep, but jumped fence at the camp before they even shaved my head. Went back to Atlanta for a while, and even here to Ontario for a year. I kept wanting to see Central Park, though, and once I got there, I couldn't seem to leave."

She shrugged. "Where've you been all these years?"

"New York," he said quietly. She felt right, leaning against him. He could imagine her listening to his heart. "Both downtown and upstate. I trained near Chattanooga for two summers. Now I usually summer here in Ontario. My mother's people keep a lodge and hunting grounds outside Timmins."

"Timmins—that's here?"

"I believe so. If I'm right, we could see the roof of this place from my fire-tower."

"I was in Iroquois Falls. I went through Timmins a couple of times. We might've passed each other on the road."

"I would've known if we had." He heard Lia's spiteful voice. *If you wanted her, you would have found her years ago.* The truth in that was what made it hurt. He'd been told over and over through the years that he clung to a fantasy; Mary Alison could not have survived. Even if she'd survived, the ceremony had been moved up two years for political expediency, and she'd been too young for the bond to take. Yet she'd trailed him, city to city and past the Great Lakes. No one should be able to do that.

Ajax roared, a shattering thunderclap of noise that sounded like a signal for all the frustrated males outside to tear into one another, screaming and snarling.

Mary Alison bit her lip. Darien snuggled closer to her. His bondmate. "Relax," he said into the fine hair at the crown of her head. "We're on the third floor. None of them could get in."

She opened her mouth, and he felt she wanted to say something, but she closed her mouth without speaking.

He leaned down and kissed that trembling lip. Her breath caught.

He brushed his lips over hers again, lingeringly, and cupped her cheek in his hand. Her lashes, the color of oak-tanned doeskin, dropped over her eyes and lay thickly against the top line of her cheekbones. Warm and giving lips parted for him. He tasted the wet inner edge of her lips, and she clutched at his shirt. His world contracted to the precise texture of her eyebrow against his bottom lip, the taste of fine-grained skin around her eye.

She hummed and pulled him over her with little tugs, then opened his belt, along with the button and zipper under it. He kept his weight on his elbows and knees to give those nimble hands room to work. She pulled his shirt free of his slacks and kneaded at his hips and waist while he used his mouth to examine the texture, taste and scent of every hollow and curve of her face.

He tasted her throat; smooth skin with the rushing pulse of blood just underneath. She ran her hands over his chest; she'd opened all his buttons, just like that. As he shrugged out of his clothes, she made a sound halfway between a purr and a chuckle. He heard the cat in it, and growled against the skin of her throat.

"Tell me now, Mary Alison, what kind of cat are you?"

"You already said it. I'm a cat in heat. Now burn me down."

"I thought 'burn me down' was an invitation to dance."

"Undo my zipper and I'll show you dance."

She turned to present that long pink zipper running the length of her spine. He opened a narrow vee at the nape of her neck and tasted the skin there, nipping lightly and then pressing with his chin to mute the sting. He chinned open the zipper to open a deeper and deeper vee, pressing kisses to her spine as he went.

She mewled and wriggled under him, breaking into a fine misting of sweat that tasted wonderfully female. He nipped at her butt and she jumped. A breathless cry of wanting teased at his nerves.

His vision lost color. He forced it back to human norm. He had to hold this Shape until Mary Alison shifted.

He swallowed his fangs and sat up. He was The Shaper; he'd excelled in the toughest training the Hidden World offered. If he really had to, and if he stayed out of direct moonlight, he might be able to hold his human form all through the night.

Between his knees, Mary Alison wriggled out of her sleeves and out of her girdle-like elastic bra. She turned over inside the dress, so that deep end of the pink zipper now opened to a tantalizing frame for her navel.

She ducked under his arm and flicked her tongue across his nipple. He jumped and she grinned. "Afraid I'd bite, man?"

He grinned back, a grin that said he was up for as much as she could dole out and then some, and watched uncertainty creep into the corners of her eyes. He cupped her face in both his hands and tasted his way around it again, eye to eye to mouth.

"Get out of Mrs. Henderson's Legion Hall dress. I don't want to hear for the next ten years how it got ruined."

She flushed, her skin warming. "Thanks for the sweet talk."

A new flurry of snarls and growls erupted outside. She pouted at him, but her eyes flicked toward the bank of windows. To distract her from the fights outside, Darien grasped her by the elbows and lifted her in the air.

She laughed and kicked free of the dress, managing to flap it in his face. Then she lifted her arms like a diver and leaned to the side. He let her fall that way, and bounced with her on the flowered bedspread. Her surprised laugh bubbled up again, and he laughed with her. She stopped laughing, and looked puzzled.

"What?" he asked.

"Why am I not sore?" She blushed. "I mean—"

"Hmmm?" He drew out the question, nuzzling through her hair to her heated neck.

"Well—" Her blush intensified, and her gaze slid away from him.

He cupped her face in his hands again. "If you won't open to me, you need to say out loud what you're thinking."

She mumbled something, and cleared her throat and looked at his shoulder. "Lia said you always leave her real sore."

He tilted her face and kissed her thoroughly, but without teeth. When he broke away, she looked gratifyingly dazed.

"Lia," he said, "would be disappointed in a sexual encounter that didn't leave her limping."

"Yeah, I sorta figured but—"

"Sweetheart, you have the most fascinating variety of blushes. Have I seen them all yet?"

No, he hadn't. A deeper one rose up her breasts and upper chest, paused, and then flooded her neck and face.

"But what?" he prompted.

"If you want me to talk, you might stop interrupting."

He stretched out and laced his fingers behind his head. The morning's activities had given him enough relief that he could think past the breeding urge, but he was evidently still missing some element of the conversation. His dick twitched. He waved it experimentally. Mr. Happy?

Mary Alison got up and draped the pink dress carefully across the back of a chair. She spoke over her shoulder. "Do you want the left or the right side of the bed? If you don't have a preference, I'll sleep on this side."

He looked at her incredulously. "You don't intend to actually *sleep*?" A feline mating squall curdled the air.

Mary Alison lay down and jerked the blankets up over her.

He leaned over her, planting a fist on either side of her shoulders. She looked fixedly at a large, ornate wall mirror.

"Mary Alison, look at me."

She wouldn't.

"I won't force you in this."

She kept her gaze on the mirror. "My, my. That'd be a novelty. Do you figure you don't have to, that eventually my base animal nature will emerge, and I'll jump your bones again?"

He felt the heat rise in his own face.

She gave him a quick sidelong look. "Thought so."

He didn't back down. "Mary Alison, look at me. What do you see?"

She looked at him. Sadness lined her face like an old woman's. Outside, wolves howled in chorus. "You're Darien."

He waited. She looked away again. She sighed and looked back. "You're Darien, but you're...not..."

"Not the white knight your imagination painted me to be?"

Another blush. But she looked steadily at him.

"You aren't dreaming, Mary Alison. This is what I really am." He leaned closer, immersing himself in her scent. "I took your blood and your soul and your name when I was seven years old. In return I gave you everything I am. But for all these years, I was told you were gone. I became the Hawkmoor you were supposed to have been, and Lia became part of me. You don't have to like those facts, but you must deal with them. I will protect you to the limits of my power, but I will not let you destroy my people."

She touched his cheekbone. "Do you honestly want me bad enough to keep your hands off that Supermodel for two months?"

He turned and kissed her fingertip. "I want you bad enough I'd swear off Lia for a lifetime, if she'd let it happen that way."

"Then come under the covers, man, and show me what you can do."

The taunt—or promise—in her voice erected his fangs. Ducking his head, he snatched the blankets down and buried his face between her full, round breasts. No one saw his fangs. Ever.

He slid under the covers, in with her body heat. In with her scent. He suckled at her breast, drawing the nipple in over his tongue and holding it against the roof of his mouth as he stroked the roughness of his tongue over the eyelid-fine skin of her areola. She gasped and kneaded at his shoulders, but the reaction was too tame. He wanted her wild.

He passed a hand over her ribs, touching lightly to leave a tingling trail that made her squirm. He lingered at her waist, and then drew his palm lower to the furred juncture of her legs. He heard her first moan through his mouth as much as his ears.

He moved lower under the covers, kissing and suckling his unhurried way over her abdomen, drowning in her scent, stroking the smooth skin of her flanks while she moved under him as the sea moves under a boat.

He settled lower still, shouldering under her legs and nuzzling the inner surface of her thigh. She said his name over and over, "Dariendariendarien…" Calling it like a mourning dove calls in the evening.

"Hold your breasts, Mary Alison," he said, her dampened curls tickling his lips. "Play with your nipples as I would."

He inhaled deeply, her aroma piercing him to the core, and fought back to his human Shape. She stopped moving against him.

Her voice became tentative. "Darien? Hey, it's okay-you don't really have to—"

"Hush, sweetheart." He inhaled her musk-flavored warmth again. With his thumbs he stroked her outer labial folds until she squirmed helplessly, and then he opened them and trickled his breath over her bared inner lips in a long, leisurely stream. "Hold your breasts for me."

He felt his way with kisses in the dark, exploring the tiny valentine shape of her. A valentine, he thought, with only a hint of ruffling. A sweet pea blossom.

He kissed one side and then the other, holding her hips with both hands and riding her as she lifted and fell under him. Moaning helplessly, she twisted her fingers in his hair and locked her ankles behind his shoulders, urging him on. He roughened his tongue and lashed her with it until she went rigid under him, her thighs trembling. Her back arched.

Now! He dug in his toes and lunged forward, entering her in one deep stroke.

Mary Alison climaxed. *Darrriennn!*

He held her in that incandescent high for a long moment. Then he poured shaping energy over and through her. It slid off her skin at first, like rain off a slicker. He kept pouring it over her, saturating the air she breathed.

Her eyes widened, and she pushed at his chest. Her feet twisted, seeking a purchase she could use to throw him off.

He slid a hand between them, finding her clitoris and holding it between his two longest fingers. He thrust into the wet, inner flesh, fighting the muscles that clinched around him over and over, taking her higher. Her eyes rolled back and she opened her mouth with a wail of raw sexual exultation, and stuttering spasms shook her legs.

Through it all he poured the shifter energy through her, skin to skin, inside and outside, wherever they touched.

Suddenly, her shifter aura burned over his skin. *Cat.*

Cramps wracked her, and she shrank. Her bones bent and broke under him. Nerves imbedded in shaping flesh tore, and re-formed, and tore again. Her pain seared through them both. She screamed; his ears rang from it.

He rode her convulsions for endless agonizing minutes; healing, shaping, straining to keep her body from tearing itself apart in a process she should've learned to control years ago. He cut off the blaze of pain at spinal level, but that wasn't something he could do long or often.

Her bones shaped and shattered and reshaped themselves, cat and human and cat and human, as she fought to keep her human Shape. In a fury of remorse, he diverted all the essences of her cat nature, poured his power into her, and Shaped her human.

When it was over, human arms and human legs locked around him, and she sobbed against his chest.

He stroked her hair with a shaking hand. "I'm so sorry. I didn't know it would be that bad."

"Worse. It gets worse."

"No," he said, thinking through the lectures and the drills he'd memorized fifteen years ago. "I can help. I can take some of the pain, ease the cramping. I can teach you some exercises, too. Breathing, muscle relaxation, imagery."

She took a noisy, hiccupping breath. "I've tried yoga. It helps, but I need my pills. Promise me, Darien. Promise I'll get my pills before tomorrow night."

He shook loose a pillowcase to towel the sweat off her. She shivered, and he tucked the blankets gently under her chin.

"Promise me," she repeated, her voice gone dull.

He cupped his hand behind her head. "I can't lie to you, Mary Alison. I will help in other ways, but I can't promise to dope you out of your mind."

She pinched his fingertips and peeled them away from her. Then she turned to the wall. "Tell you what," she said, the bitterness galling like a taste of green walnuts. "Sell tickets and give me a cut of the take, and I'll buy my own pills."

"Cost is not an issue—"

"Shut up. I've heard all I want to hear and then some."

He cuddled against her back anyway. He was too tall to spoon perfectly with her, but he wrapped around her and pulled her in as close as human forms could get. After a long time, she relaxed in his arms.

He awoke as a lynx, over-heated among the blankets. He stretched cat-tight muscles, reveling in the compressed power.

Mary Alison? He sat up and looked for her. Something seemed strange about the room. He shifted to human to look again.

The bedspread had been draped over the bank of windows to the west and the ornate wall mirror was missing. A line of yellowish light marked the bottom edge of the bathroom door.

He tried the knob. Locked. "Mary Alison?"

"Go away."

Her voice sounded alarmingly hoarse. From shifting? He smelled sickness, and all his Shapes recoiled.

"Open the door, Mary Alison. I want to help you."

Weight settled against the other side of the door.

"Mary Alison, move away from the door."

"Fuck off and die." Tired and ill, the voice had none of the rancor the words would suggest.

Her shadow darkened the knob side of the door. He kicked the hinge side, the impact slamming from heel to hip, and the door burst open to a sound of shattering glass. Too late he remembered the full-length mirror on the inside of the door.

Bright light blinded him as the smell of blood and of sickness triggered his shift. He stopped it; reversed it. He needed to be human to connect with Mary Alison and assess her condition.

She moaned. He squinted and saw her in a glittering bed of curved glass triangles. Between his kick and her fall, they'd managed to shatter both the mirror from the bathroom door and the mirror she'd taken from the bedroom.

The bedside lamp, the reading lamp, makeup lights, and the bathroom lights glared from every angle, glistening on her bare, sweating skin and on clinging flakes of glass like a mermaid's scales. Shards spangled her hair. Specks and fine lines of blood seeped around the sparkling flakes of glass.

"Don't look at me," she rasped.

He thickened the soles of his feet against the broken glass and crouched beside her. Her swollen bottom lip had the puncture marks of fangs as well as the bruised slits human teeth make.

"You're fighting it? Alone? Why, Mary Alison? You have to know tomorrow will be worse."

"Tomorrow I'll have my pills." Her puffy, bloodshot eyes opened. "I never killed for them yet, but there's a first time for everything."

She was serious. He reached for her, to heal that bloody lip first, but she scrambled away from him. The glass tinkled as it broke into smaller shards under her hands and feet. The surge of blood-scent twisted his insides, shaping him from the inside out. He swallowed the power. He was Hawkmoor; Darien the Shaper. Instinct alone could not force him through the shift.

Mary Alison huddled in the tub, eyes closed, humming a high-pitched sound on the very edge of audibility.

He stepped gingerly across the glass and pulled a long sliver out of her lacerated foot. When he tried to close the cuts, though, his power washed over her without sinking in.

He turned on the water without comment, yanking the shower curtain down off the rod so it would cast no shadow. She'd paid dearly for the light; he couldn't deprive her of it.

While waiting for the water to warm, he picked glass from her hands and feet, and then her back. She flinched with each touch, but said nothing. Still his power slid past her without effect.

He clenched his teeth against a comment he might regret later. Healing was shaping, and he'd already shaped her once. With Mary Alison, that first free shot was the only free shot. Overpowering her a second time would take someone as strong as Five Bears himself. If Five Bears could do it.

When the water warmed, he aimed the spray on her and combed her short hair with his fingers, catching tiny shards in his skin and rinsing them off. She moaned again, lost in her misery as the slices opened and closed along his fingers.

He soaped her to loosen the last flakes of glass, and poured warm water over her by the doubled-handful.

She sagged, losing consciousness for the barest moment and waking as he caught her in his arms. In that unguarded moment his power sank in, shaping her skin to a smooth and perfect surface. Before he could go deeper, she recoiled; again his power slid off her.

She licked her healed bottom lip and touched it with her fingertips. She frowned. "I need my pills."

"You need me. You need to trust me to take care of you."

"Yeah, right." Water drops clumped her lashes and ran down her face like tears. "It's morning," she said.

He looked out the broken door. The spectrum of light in the bedroom ran more blue than it had minutes ago. "You're right. Stay here. I'll get the bedspread to cover that glass."

"The glass was real," she said wonderingly.

"All of it was real, Mary Alison."

Her lip curled. "Does being a *real* prince make you judge of what all is real?"

He crouched in front of her and caught up both her hands. "I am your bondmate. That is real. We are shapeshifters, Mary Alison. Not humans. If we were all to drug ourselves insensible on the full moon, we would still be shifters. We smell like shifters, not like humans. When we crossbreed with humans, the children are mules—more than human but less than shifter. We act and think like shifters. Our laws are our own, ingrained in us, and they supersede the humans' laws. *That's* reality, Mary Alison, and your refusal to accept it does not make it any less real. As irrational as I consider your attitude to be, it's real too. Why *don't* you let me be the judge when I am sure what is real and you are not?"

"You got a clue how arrogant that sounds, Prince Darien?"

He tossed her hands down and turned away. "I liked it better when you called me 'man.'"

She spoke again. "Would you please hand me that roll of floss? I can't borrow somebody's toothbrush."

He could argue until the moon changed phase, and she would continue to ignore any fact that nudged the boundaries of her comfort zone. If his bones and flesh flowed to a cat-shape, she would no doubt cover her eyes and moan for her pills.

He dressed casually for breakfast, surreptitiously admiring Mary Alison's contortions as she squeezed into that elastic brassiere. Those pills had kept her from having to acknowledge her Shape until now. Tonight he would keep watch. When the moon overwhelmed her, he would catch her. He would make her see.

But before moonrise he had to contact the rest of the Families. He also had to find where yesterday's contacts had stopped the chaos and where he needed to bring more pressure to bear. Showing their collective teeth, using the reasoned voices of daylight, the Hawkmoor triad just might stop the destruction today.

"If I wear sweats, will I still get breakfast?" Mary Alison asked.

He started. "Oh, yes. We won't try more interviews until just before noon, and we'll probably nap before then. Be glad we showered early. I doubt many people will get hot water."

She nodded shortly and worked a third pair of socks onto her feet.

"Are your feet that cold, Mary Alison?"

"No," she snapped. "But my shoes don't fit, do they?"

No, and they wouldn't. Not when she stared at every window as if staring would open it and set her free.

A knock came at the door, along with electronic clicks, and then the butler's voice. "Breakfast in five minutes, sir."

"Thank you," he called back. "We'll be there."

"Does he think my name is Sir?" Mary Alison glowered at the closed door.

"Bigley won't address you directly until he's told he can."

She yanked the door open. "Hey, you! Bigley! Address me directly when you got something to say! Got that?"

"Yes, madam," the butler drawled in his pseudo-Brit accent. "I got that."

During breakfast, she palmed a knife. Darien thought of letting her keep it. She was small, outnumbered, and surrounded. But she had to have some martial competence to pay rent on a studio. He relieved her of the blade.

Chapter Ten

After breakfast, when Mary Alison was yawning so hard he could count her molars, Lia advised her to catch up on her sleep while Darien caught up on the news. Mary Alison gave her a poisonous look, which was spoiled by another jaw-popping yawn, and said she'd find her own way to bed, thank you very kindly.

Lia's amusement brushed like a silk scarf over Darien's skin. He declined to share it. Mary Alison would be followed whether she knew it or not, and would be intercepted if she approached an exit. Surveillance was necessary, but gloating was not.

The headlines were bad: Riots and looting. Drive-bys and bombings. Militia and gang skirmishes. The shifters had started the chaos, but they were now a minority of the participants.

The perimeter walls of the infamous Georgia Labor Camp IV and two transient camps had been breached from the outside, and the denizens freed to swarm over the countryside, as the commentator put it, like a plague of rats.

A pair of cheetahs had been doused with gasoline on a Baltimore street and burned alive. Zoos in Toronto, Boston, Indianapolis, Shreveport and Chicago reported raids on their large mammal habitats. Elephant steak and barbecued dik-dik had appeared on the menus of certain exotic restaurants.

Militias and Guards from Hartford to Miami to Austin to Ottawa had declared curfew and promised emergency food distributions. Schools were closed.

Vigilante Television blamed *The Bounty Hunter Show* for starting it; *Bounty Hunter* blamed the Militia Coalition; and various militias blamed VTV, *Bounty Hunter*, Federals, and each other in a mad, tail-chasing, yapping spree.

Lia snuggled under his arm and sipped coffee. "How did she do?"

"She has a Shape," he said reluctantly, "but she doesn't know how to get there. She has doped herself out of shifting for so many years that she breaks, tears and dislocates like a fourteen-year-old. I will need time today to teach her."

"Words will not be enough; you will need to reach inside her. But for the bond, I do not see how you could hope to succeed. Two nights back, she hid from me even the fact she could shift, and her shielding becomes stronger at every turn."

The TV screen filled with shouting, sooty firefighters, and a line of print that said "deadly back-draft." He turned it off.

Lia's deliberate voice sounded loud in the silence. "If you can't control her, she must be cut, and sooner is better than too late. I can fly in Dr. Kelly this afternoon."

"I know," he said. "Give me today to bring her under control. Just today."

"It is not permanent, Darien," she said, very softly.

He shook his head. Over the months following the cut, the brain grew back. But so did a new personality, one partly defined by the memory of being cut. Now that he knew her, he couldn't permit so much of Mary Alison to be cut away.

He'd expected to be home by now. He and Mary Alison would have to find some chance to break out in the next couple of hours, while Lia and her beasts slept.

"I need a good nap," he said.

"Me, too. I envy her; you wear her scent like fine perfume."

"Cologne, Lia." The old affection rushed through him, and he gave her a quick hug. "Guys wear cologne."

He opened the door, and stopped. He put up a hand to keep Lia from stirring the air. A female scent. Mary Alison. With that too-familiar tang of fear. "She was here, Lia. She heard us."

Lia reached for a keyboard on the wall, but the screen lit before she touched it. "Broken window," she said, then added a command tone to her voice. "Retrieval Sigma, Lady Hawkmoor."

Darien put a hand on her shoulder. "Tell me that 'sigma' means alive and unhurt."

"Alive if possible."

His wolves' noses should find her quicker than Lia's cats' eyes. He needed to remove the bears from Lia's team. McGuire would be chief bear. Had he and Kent reconciled yet? "Change your order, Lia. Tell them to retrieve her unhurt."

Lia laughed her musical laugh. "We have never drilled 'retrieve unhurt.' Bear can put her back together if necessary." A long alphanumeric message scrolled over the screen. She frowned. "Bigley tried to stop her. He has a ruptured testicle, a broken knee, a crushed trachea, and burst eardrums. She could not do that to him. Who helped her?"

"Tell your people not to hurt her."

"I cannot promise, Darien. Whoever helped her knocked out one of my best men."

Chapter Eleven

MA trotted through the misty woods, concentrating on placing her feet where they would leave no mark. The oversized moccasins with their thick layers of socks felt odd, but the padding helped conceal her track.

Darien intruded on her thoughts. She crouched on a stump and filled her mind with the mist until she could see nothing but the glowing pale gray of it, could taste nothing but the chill, mushroomy, dead-leaf damp of it. Her heartbeat and breathing slowed to the controlled rhythms she taught her students.

Aching exhaustion weighed her down. She blocked it. *Later.* She could rest when she was safe. Or when she absolutely had to.

Something approaching stirred the mist. She held still, filling herself with the essence of the forest, becoming part of it.

Vague bulks took shape, and oh, Jerusalem, it was too late for the pills. She couldn't possibly be seeing a tiger in this Canadian forest. Tigers belonged in Asia, in sweaty jungles full of screaming monkeys and flowers big enough to wear as hats.

Another cat followed the tiger. That one had no stripes; it might be a small lioness or the world's biggest cougar. Something larger snorted behind them.

The cats craned their necks all about, scanning for motion as cats do, and padded off into the mist. MA held still, maintaining the concealing veil of mist around her.

The third thing shuffled forward, its breath billowing out clouds of steam, until she picked out the shape of a bear. She thought, *oh my!* and stifled a giggle that threatened to take her over.

The bear, a grizzly, rose on his hind legs, put his back to a pine tree, and scratched like a huge man. Pine needles and cones rained between them.

The bear curled up, closed his little piggy eyes, and huffed another cloud of steam that drifted away behind him.

If he was going to sleep, she could run at the first snore. Until then she would wait. No one ever beat her at hide and seek.

A breeze tickled her skin. The cold, which hadn't bothered her before, reached damp claws into her muscles. She shivered to generate warmth and relaxed muscle by muscle, flushing out the lactic acid buildup.

The sun burned through enough of the fog to ignite a golden glow like a Georgia dawn, although it must be well after 8 a.m. The best part of her morning run in Poetry had always been along the west edge of the Shadwells' catfish ponds, where the dawn light tinted spirals of rising mist with lavender, pink, and coral.

She caught herself dozing and jerked awake, letting the adrenaline shock drive out any trace of sleepiness.

The bear yawned, showing fangs as big as her fingers. His broad tongue unfurled from between those fangs and slopped over the end of his black nose before slurping back in. *Ick.* At least she couldn't smell him. He probably stank to high heaven.

In the distance another bear coughed. MA flinched, and flinched again when the grizz rocked to his feet, nose in the air. He rose on his hind legs, as if trying to see over the roof of a house, and coughed a response. The hair rose on her neck as the cough-cloud drifted behind him to dissipate. *Oh, Jerusalem!* Bears see through their noses, and she was upwind of this one. *Screwed.*

The bear settled back on his haunches until another cough sounded in the woods behind her. The grizz rocked to his feet and shook all over. Then he lifted his right front paw, pointed it at her, and jabbed toward the north, where the other bear was. *What the hell?* The bear stepped toward her and repeated the gesture.

Fear hammered at her ribs. What kind of circus act was this? How did he expect her to react?

He swiped his paw theatrically over his face, rolled his eyes at the sky, and jabbed the paw toward her. Then he jabbed it toward the north.

She slid off the tree stump, stretching her legs before they could clench up, and backed away, toward the north. The bear scrubbed his chin all over the stump where she'd touched it, and put his huge pawprint over a footprint she'd left.

Pass the pills and find the room with soft walls, MA. Reality is out of reach. She backed a few more steps and the bear followed her, putting his paws exactly where she'd stepped.

She turned and ran. The bear huffed behind her, enveloping her in his stinking warm cloud. Her vision hazed and her throat cramped with swallowed screams. She threw herself through the woods, ducking branches and jumping deadfalls and leaving tangled strands of her hair in twiggy tree-claws.

Chased-by-a-bear stories yammered together in her head. *Run downhill-his front legs are shorter than his back legs! Pass by a carcass and climb a tree! Throw a box of black pepper!*

The other bear rose like smoke from a thicket. A black bear. Half the size of the grizzly but still a bear. She hooked one hand on a thin tree and whipped around it to stop. The bark dug painfully into her palm and fingers, sensitized as they were by the cold.

The tame grizz skidded, his back feet sliding around in front of him and throwing up a rooster-tail of leaves and loam. She backed toward the west and he growled, a gutturally menacing ripple of sound that stopped her dead. But would one more step north intrude on the black bear's space? She looked over her shoulder. The black bear turned his butt toward her—definitely a guy bear there—and lazily clawed a tree.

Heads or tails? Go with the nutty logic of a bear escort? Or run for it? Both bears growled.

She followed the smaller bear, since he let her do that, and picked up her pace as the grizz pressed closer from behind. Soon they had her running full-tilt in the cold air, not able to think of anything but the mechanics of movement, and of protecting her face from numberless jabbing twigs. She ran and ran, and the bears seemed tireless.

Finally, stumbling and wheezing, she tripped and plunged into a drift of frost-struck leaves. Mice exploded out of the depths of the leaf-mound and streaked toward whatever other cover they might find. She heard a bear shuffle up to her. Oh, *shit.*

The first rule is never to let a carnivore or a scavenger know you're helpless. Too late there. Second rule is never run. Ri-i-ight. Third rule is protect your face and neck.

She locked her arms about her face and neck. A warm cloud of bear-breath drifted over her back and head.

She peeked. The grizz stared back, so close to her shoulder that she could see only muzzle and one eye. A scream clawed at her throat. The bear huffed his stinking, steamy breath at her and backed away. *Did you just laugh at me, bear?*

The black bear ambled over to the grizz and scrubbed the top of his head under the grizzly's chin. The grizz closed his eyes and chin-stroked the black. "Oh, man!" she wheezed. "You ought not do that. You're both guys!"

They both looked at her. She'd spoken aloud. And oh, Jerusalem! She knew that look. They'd understood her words. Not any circus command nor any psycho-emotional bullshit. These two bears understood her words and were sneering at her.

She sat up, brushing crumbled leaves off her face and neck. "You *are* guys. Not bears. Guys."

She remembered the campfire stories. The early European settlers had heard drumming at night, had searched the woods for that sound and found bear footprints mingled with human prints around the remains of a bonfire. Little girls of Memaw's generation were warned not to enter the forest alone or at night, lest bear dancers get them and they grow up in the forest as bear-wives, with husbands who wore human skin by day and bear fur by night.

She remembered dreams of wandering through the woods at night, calling for bears, but had never quite made the decision to actually do something so fundamentally silly.

Could Darien's ravings have any connection to those old stories? She'd always been smart enough to follow most conversations, even among highly educated people, but so much of what Darien said was so steeped in metaphor she really couldn't be sure.

Both of them whuffed at her.

"Okay, you're bears too. But you're also guys. Human guys."

The grizz leaned toward her a little, his muzzle wrinkling. She held her ground. She could not possibly outrun them. The grizz lowered his head to her level. Something pressed at her insides, and one thought came through. *Not human.*

Jerusalem! "Stop that right now. I can take the idea you're skinwalkers, or shifters, whether that makes sense or not, but if you think you're going to climb inside my head like Darien, you got another think coming!"

She was breathing too fast. She worked on slowing down, taking control. At some point, up had to be up; down had to be down; real had to be real.

If some small segment of the populace has skinwalking ability, those portions of the population who know about that ability would probably revere it. Legends would expand on the reality. Secret societies would grow up around the legendry. That's where Darien and his "wolves" fit in.

The grizz backed away to where the black bear sat. They waited while she pulled her feet up under her and stood, not bothering to brush at the bits of leaves and bark clinging to her clothes. The bears walked her long enough to catch her breath before they pushed her to jog again. They crossed three blacktops, but she didn't see or hear any cars to flag down.

Over an hour later they hit a deer-fence and turned to follow it to a cattle-gate and a driveway. She stopped there and planted her fists on her knees, gasping out clouds in the chill air.

An electronic keyboard with glowing numbers and letters on the keys decorated the post at the end of the fence. She glared at it. If one of these bears started punching codes on those keys, she would break for the woods. She'd hit her limit on freakiness for the day. The year. Just about a lifetime, although it was probably bad luck to go that far.

But they were not bears. They were skinwalkers—shapeshifters—straight out of the old stories. If they could change to human, they probably did know what keys to hit, and in what order. So why did they seem to be waiting for her to act?

The black bear padded over to beside the grizz, which nuzzled him with obvious affection. She blushed. Maybe they just had other plans for the rest of the day.

She crossed the cattle gate and a bear coughed approvingly. Sighing, she stared up the drive. She could obediently walk up that drive until she got to a house. The way today was going, it would probably be made of gingerbread. Or she could leave the driveway, cross the fence, and take her chances in the woods.

Dear Darien and his supermodel were ten or twelve miles south now. Whatever lay at the end of this driveway had to be something different, at least.

A low hum approached. She stopped and watched a golf-cart with oversized tires come around the bend. Two women rode in it. They looked like sisters, in sizes medium-large and large.

The cart rolled right to her and both women jumped out. Medium-Large spoke hurriedly. "Welcome home, Lady Hawkmoor. Do you prefer to ride in the front or the back?"

MA crossed her arms. "I'd love a ride home, whether front seat or back, but I don't get the idea you're heading my way."

"Darien apologizes for not meeting you personally. He's uplinked right now, trying to calm the Hidden. He needs you at his back, my lady. He needs you this minute, if possible."

Calm the hidden what? Never mind, Darien's a ways away. "I hear words, ma'am, and they sound like English, but communication is just not happening."

The bigger woman leaned toward her from the far side of the cart. "Try this. Get in. Now."

"Or what?" she challenged.

"Or I shoot you," the woman said, opening her coat. "That would make a mess, but we have five bears to take care of it."

Five? The two she'd seen and three more? She pictured them beating drums and dancing around a campfire.

She scrubbed her face with the palms of her hands. *Why is a pack of bear-men dancing in the woods scarier than a gun ten feet away?* How long had it been since she'd slept? Was all this part of some long, detailed hallucination? Did she need her pills, or had she found some and overdosed?

She got in the cart.

None of the cluster of cabins they came to was made of gingerbread. They left the cart for at the rustic front porch of the biggest one. A clamoring pack of kids pelted around the corner and surrounded them, yapping for permission to park the cart. One was picked to drive, and every one of the others piled in or on the cart as it drove off.

Once inside, in a foyer of polished wood, the women sighed deeply and turned to MA with friendlier expressions.

"I'm Jessie," one said. "Would you like some tea? Some beef stew? I can bring you and Darien some as soon as you like."

MA blinked, feeling stupid. "Darien and Lia are here?"

The other woman turned quickly and left the area. Jessie smiled a plastic smile. "Darien wants to see you now. This way, please."

MA crossed her arms again. "According to your high and mighty Darien, I'm Lady Hawkmoor. He wants to pull a string and watch me dance? He can wait until I'm ready to play. Right now I want something to eat and someplace to rest."

The woman's eyes had grown round. She swallowed. "This way, my lady. I'll bring the soup right in."

That was a pretty easy win, MA thought, yawning behind her hand. Then she followed the woman through a door and found Darien talking urgently to a three-panel computer screen. *Darien.* All her bravado ran out of her spine and down the back of her legs and puddled on the floor, leaving her weak and breathless.

Darien. *Oh, Jerusalem. Can I just watch him a minute?*

He was arguing the same argument he'd gone through on Lia's computer, only with different sets of faces. She wanted to tune out the words and just bask in the sound of his voice and his salty, pecan-smoke scent. Stinging twinges shot down from her navel, and she felt the wetness come. If only she could fill herself with that thick cock and ride it forever, and never wake up to what would follow.

Long before the minute was up, he turned to her. His harried face opened in a broad, warm smile.

Something cold solidified in her. *Lie to me if you have to, but not with that smile.* She backed a step, but behind her the door shut with a definite *k-snick*.

Darien's look cooled. He darkened the screens and came to her. "You must sit with me, Mary Alison. You needn't agree with me or even look happy, but it's come down to female versus female, so if I am to be heard, at least one of you must be seen with me."

"Supermodel won't sit quietly and let you talk? So you need to show at least one of us is under your control? At what point do you cut slices out of my brain to make it real and permanent?"

"You would eventually recover."

How stupid do you think I am? She didn't want to ask that. He might answer. She floundered for another question. "What idiot told you somebody recovers from a frontal lobotomy?"

He started to speak, and stopped. Instead he dipped his head and kissed her, his mouth hungry and as honest in that hunger as anything she'd ever encountered. In response, a terrible wanting poured through her. She rose up on her toes and gave him her mouth.

He locked a fist at the nape of her neck and, with his other hand at the small of her back he lifted her and pressed her hard against his body. She locked her legs about his waist and swirled her tongue around his and—*fangs? No.* Monsters in the woods she could take, but not Darien as a monster. *Not Darien.* No, they were teeth. She checked again. Teeth.

He broke away, panting, and let her slide slowly down him until her shaking legs held her. But his tone was businesslike. "Come now, we can't delay this conference."

Oh, can't we? But she was on his turf and past tired and sliding in and out of skinwalker hallucinations. Or maybe inside one long hallucination. Her realistic chances of escape hovered near zero. A wave of exhaustion washed through her, blurring her vision and clouding her mind.

She let him propel her toward the bank of computer screens. He sat, one arm hooked around her waist all snuggly-cozy like any beau, and reactivated the screens.

People peered like over-aged psychology interns at her. She looked past the screens, trying not to yawn, and folded her hands to keep from reaching up to fool with her messy hair. Darien and the people talked about her as if she weren't there. She hated that. But now she was too tired to think. And with Darien here she was safe. Safe? That was an alien thought.

Tired. Pure tired.

The voices fuzzed into the background. Darien pulled her to sit on his lap and nestled her head in that comfortable hollow in his shoulder. She didn't have to see his treacherous smile from here. Sleep dragged her under.

Chapter Twelve

Mary Alison's sleeping face filled him with satisfaction. Had she tasted him in that insidious command to sleep, she would've fought him off, as impossible as that ought to be. She'd been raised human, and still she resisted his command where none of his wolves could.

No wolf would try; if Hawkmoor said a wolf needed sleep, the wolf slept.

But she was Hawkmoor. All the power he and his father had built over the years would become hers the moment she exerted her authority. Before she understood power, or obligation. She could not be allowed to make decisions until she understood what was at stake. Too much depended on stability of leadership, on bone-deep knowledge of what Hawkmoor stood for.

Bruise-colored shadows surrounded her eyes, and lines framed her mouth. He wanted to soothe away those lines, that tiredness, the anxiety. The giggling snub-nosed child had to have left some trace of herself behind. Somewhere.

He propped his elbow to let the armchair support her weight. For such a little thing, she weighed rather a lot. Density. So much life pressed into one small package.

He touched the hollow space cupped by the crest of her hip. She was bursting with fertility. She would never be a mother, though, unless she mated with a male who shared a majority of her Shapes. Whatever Shape she had or found, he had to match it. He could not deprive her of children, if she wanted them. Nor could he stand the thought of another man fathering them for her.

She would shift tonight. He would have to teach her to flow with the moon-light, to think of the coming Shape instead of the actual process of changing.

Jesús announced the Austin connection and stood behind him to translate. Darien moved to display Mary Alison's face. Her pink lips pursed, and she made a small protesting noise. His insides tightened in answer. He tried to reach her, but even in sleep her emotional armor held.

Young Anita answered in Austin. A child answering always startled him, but Anita lived for the fun of breaking rules. She lit up to see him and called over her shoulder in a rapid spatter of Spanish. "Don't translate that, cousin," she added in English, grinning impishly up at Jesús.

Darien grinned back. "Dearest little queen of the night, I know my wives would never let me near you without a blindfold, earplugs, and incense all around, lest your charms make me insensible to their own."

Two younger girls appeared, jostling for space at the screen and cooing "Ooooh! Oh!" as Jesús translated in his serious voice.

Anita shushed the younger ones with slaps and shoves. "You are *good*." She said to him. "Repeat, please, so I can write it down."

"No, my sweet dove at twilight. The charm of a compliment, like that of a red rose, lies half in its ephemeral nature."

The younger girls sighed gustily while Anita preened. Their Aunt Lopez came in then and shooed them all away, but Anita called out that she hoped her Family chose someone just like him for her—only maybe not so very old.

Clara Lopez shut the door on the girls. "Austin is under control," she said, her firm voice contrasting with her haggard face. "No more incidents will be reported from here. Is that Mary Alison? Have you two bonded with Lia?"

He nodded again.

"If she is not hard enough to best Lia, I pity her. If she is hard enough, I pity you, caught between the two of them."

Darien grinned ruefully, and said more than he'd said to anyone else. "We don't yet know her capabilities."

"Then you do not yet know who will sit in that throne you have stood behind all these years. These are the days in which history is made, Darien Berenov Hawkmoor. You might have married years ago, and let another Lady fight off Lia and the other ambitious women. Instead you held up this one as the invisible icon of all Hawkmoor is, and now you ask everyone to acknowledge her before even you know anything about her."

He picked a bit of leaf out of Mary Alison's fawn-colored hair. "Austin, I greatly value your habit of telling the uncomfortable truth. Please spread this message: Hawkmoor is whole now, and as of noon today, Hawkmoor has declared peace. Any who defy us now must expect blood and ashes in greater quantity than our parents saw in the sixties, or their grandparents saw in the Great Slaughter." He lifted his eyes to the screen, watching her reaction. "We are Hawkmoor, and we have spoken."

Lopez nodded, and turned the conversations to the pleasantries. She swore her undying appreciation for the aid he'd rushed in after last year's tornadoes, and he assured her of Hawkmoor's steadfast readiness to support and succor Austin. Lopez answered to both Hawkmoor and Tlazepocatl, but she was far enough from the center of either's attention to enjoy vast independence. Keeping on her good side was well worth an extra minute here and there.

Cutting the connection, he heard the whup-whup of helicopter blades. That would be Lia. What had taken her so long? He shifted Mary Alison's weight to free one arm and told Jesús to continue with the schedule.

Lia stalked into the room ten minutes later, nodding a greeting to the seniors of Dayton. They watched her with glittering eyes as she dropped casual kisses on Darien's cheek and Mary Alison's forehead, leaving rosettes of waxy lipstick as ownership brands. Darien smiled at her. "Enjoy your flight?"

"Always. When will you let me teach you to fly?"

He shook his head. He'd studied the physics of helicopters. The oddity was not how many fell; it was that any flew at all.

Boston called before Dayton was done, and he had to wrap up the Ohio connection without seeming to. He'd already missed two connections with Boston; whether Aaron was in trouble or not, he did not want intervention. For any other city that would be worrisome, but Boston was Boston.

Aaron's weather-beaten face filled the screen. "So she's there," he said in his nasal voice. "That's all I need to see." He clicked off.

Darien laughed shortly. "Which of you did he mean?"

"Does it matter? His timing is perfect, however. Has everyone seen her?"

"Enough of them for now." He rolled his head and shrugged with exaggerated motions to loosen his neck and shoulder muscles, and sighed when Lia's fingers dug in just at the right place.

"Good," she said. "Dr. Kelly is preparing your infirmary. He says he can start in five minutes."

His arm tightened on Mary Alison. "I've decided against the cut."

"You said today, Darien. I hold you to that."

"Today isn't over."

"Yet you have decided," she pointed out, deadly calm.

Mary Alison stirred. He pushed her deeper. She stirred again, fighting him. He covered her eyes. "I have all day to bring her under control, and it occurs that I am the one who decides what that means."

Her eyes narrowed. "You exceed your bounds, Darien."

"Do I?" He smiled, showing no fangs. A man in control. "I have nullified your political challenge by announcing the triad and by adopting your peace plan as Hawkmoor's. You cannot challenge our stance without undermining yourself. Now that you are in triad, you cannot force the cut without either personal combat or my permission. I will not give permission. Nor will I allow combat."

"Interfering in female contests for dominance is not within your rights, my darling."

"A contest for dominance implies a doubt as to the outcome. In such a contest a male has no place. But protecting the helpless is my duty, and Mary Alison is helpless against you."

The hell I am, he heard clearly. Mary Alison. He'd lost the battle to keep her unconscious.

Scowling, MA climbed off Darien's lap. "What's this? Dominance? You even kinkier than I thought?"

Lia laughed, a sound like ice breaking. MA gave her a look that had made gang-bangers seek easier meat.

Darien stood between them. "Mary Alison, I give you protection. That includes protection against Lia."

"How *nice*. You want to protect me from what I'm least scared of. Tell you what, man. I don't want your protection. All I ask of you—that you haven't already refused—is for you to stay the hell out of my way."

Lia smiled icily. "I challenge you."

"Shit," said the big guy who'd carried Darien out of the Manhattan war zone. Six-no, eight-people had crowded into the room in that many seconds. None looked happy. They blocked the exit. She backed to the wall to keep them all in sight.

Darien put up a hand. "Mary Alison, promise me you will not attack first, and you will not raise a weapon. By law the challenger can use a weapon only if the challenged does. Promise me, Mary Alison."

His voice, his smoky, intoxicating voice. He was pushing her. Pushing a different way, but still pushing. "You want a promise, man?" She heard the hysteria in her voice, and that made it worse. "I promise you this; I will *never* forget last night."

In an instant he loomed over her, blocking out the light. Fury and frustration shimmered in the air around him. His mouth worked, and he spoke as if it were full of rocks.

"When you remember last night, *Kitten*, remember all of it!"

MA stopped at the door of a gymnasium. Basketball hoops hung from each wall. Two shrieking girls double-bounced on a trampoline, and nine plastic-armored kids played roller-hockey.

She moved on. She was pacing, really, and checking out the cabins while she did it. Ajax, the big guy who talked like an escapee from Camelot, trailed her so close she expected him to step on her heels. Darien said he had to follow her, even into the can, in case Lia cheated.

Lia was gunning for her; that sounded just fine. Got things nicely out in the open.

The ban on weapons should work to her advantage. She'd scrapped in the street as long as she could remember, whether for lunch money or just for the right to walk home without sucking dick behind Herb Mabry's place. Lia looked like the type who would study something artsy, like Aikido.

So why was Lia so cheerful? Could she kill barehanded? Did she have reason to think she might not have to?

Was she a skinwalker, too? What else made sense?

MA stopped so quick that Ajax did bump her. He fell back, apologizing all over himself. She seized the moment. "Two questions: Does Lia have claws she can use, and is there a doctor around that she's in tight with?"

"Claws are weapons, Lady. If you feel ill, you should consult Darien or

McGuire. The doctor Lia brought is—" His black eyes snapped side to side, trying not to see her. "—a surgeon."

She said it for him. "A brain surgeon." *And Lia brought him.* "Is he loyal to Lia, or to the highest bidder, or what?"

"I am unaware of any ongoing arrangement between the two of them. He goes from family to family as called."

A freelance. A freelancer could not afford enemies. How much had Lia told him, and how much might he believe from another source? It might be time to find out whether Lady Hawkmoor for real outranked Lia, who was now Lia Hawkmoor.

Of course, he might be waiting for her. A freelance brain-cutter would be used to unwilling patients, and would know tricks to subdue them. Something like a dart gun to drop her before she got close enough to fight. She cut her eyes to the big guy. "Would you protect me from him?"

The hesitation before he said yes reassured her. This was not the day for easy answers. "Then I want to meet this doctor while Lia's with Darien. Take me there now."

Chapter Thirteen

She recognized the surgeon by his antiseptic smell and the air of a stranger. A privileged guest, but still a stranger. She approached him with the assured self-confidence she would use at an ID checkpoint. *Sure, I'm a land-owner. See my ID?*

"Hello," she said. "Dr. Kelly? I'm Mary Alison Hawkmoor." Saying her name out loud for the first time did something to her. Left her dizzy. She remembered what she was doing and stuck out her hand. He raised it to just below his chin.

"Lady Hawkmoor," he said, and she pegged him as Coastal Georgia; Savannah or the barrier islands. A long way from home. But then, how many lobotomists could a country support? He smiled warmly. "You have your dear mother's eyes."

Heat rose in her cheeks, but it was a good heat. The doctor had practically kissed her hand. "I am so sorry you've been left to wait, Doctor. You do realize that we must be absolutely certain before we take such a step?"

"I only wish more families would consider the ramifications of the procedure. Too often I am called to cut a teenager with no more wrong with him than severe testosterone poisoning."

Startled, she laughed out loud. He laughed freely with her, without any trace of either the gentleness or the wariness people used with someone who might not be quite normal. *Time to take a chance.* "Do you forgive us for maintaining the mystery?"

"Yes, Lady," he said, all sober. "Especially with Lia involved."

"Lia," she said, carefully, maintaining an awareness of each of his hands, and how best to break it, "is your patient."

He stared at her in frank astonishment. Then he laughed again, hard guffaws that tapered off to wheezing gasps as he leaned against the doorway.

He blinked, and only the red patches on his cheeks and the wet rims of his eyes remained to show he'd been helpless with laughter a moment before. "I understand, Lady." His voice was deeper, the words distinct, like the words of an oath. "I comprehend the trust you place in me, and I will not disappoint."

"Thank you. Our final preparations might conclude quite abruptly."

His nod echoed hers. "I will be ready."

Back outside, she looked up at the autumn sky. The wind tasted heavy and wet. Snow coming.

She turned abruptly, and Ajax skipped back to his preferred distance. That distance said he was a slugger, not a grappler. She deliberately stepped closer, inside his striking range. "You don't like Lia," she said quietly. "You're scared of her."

Ajax looked anywhere but at her. He wanted to back away. She rose slightly on her toes, ready to crowd him even worse if he moved.

"Wariness of Lia, Lady, signifies good sense."

"Do you have the balls to back me against her?"

"My duty is to keep the contest fair."

"But if she beat me, you'd carry me straight to this surgeon for her, wouldn't you?"

He looked at her then. "No. Darien has forbidden it."

Yeah, ri-i-ight. Okay, we'll leave that one alone for a minute. "Say I win. Would you take Lia to the surgeon for me?"

He smiled. "Do you have what it takes to best Lia?"

"That ain't a yes, big boy, and it ain't a no. Speak."

"I have no explicit orders. I'm free to obey your will."

"When I win, don't stop to cheer. Get her in there fast."

"I will." His voice went deep, like the surgeon's had. If that was the sound of swallowed laughter, she was screwed. If it was the sound of an oath, she just might come out of this whole.

≈⟩(☉)⟨≈

Opening the inner door to the last cabin, she smelled fresh bread, and something spicy with tomatoes, and Lia's perfume.

She threw herself forward into the dark entryway, low and hard, and felt the kick go over. She sprang up under it. Locking the leg on her shoulder with her forearms braced on either side of the lower shin, she wrenched through a sideways torque that no knee was built to take. With a wet pop, the knee gave. Lia screamed.

Mary Alison dropped the leg and plunged past the falling woman, moving inside so she would not remain backlit in the doorway. Someone hit a switch; the light spilled over Lia on the floor. Her knee could not possibly be realigning itself. That just did not happen.

And bears don't dance. She's a skinwalker—a shapeshifter—too.

Lia stood up, scowling, using both legs. That could not happen either, but disbelief would get her nowhere except to that center cabin, under the knife of the kindly Dr. Kelly. *Okay, it can happen! Okay! I do believe in fairies; I do! I do! The hell I do, but something's going on. Something that lets her reshape her body. The middle of a fight's a bad time to be thinking about the nature of reality, gal. Think later. Fight now.*

Making a spear of her body, Mary Alison lunged in under Lia's guard. Lia grabbed her and folded, bringing her to the ground. *Jerusalem!* Not Aikido, but something with a strong grappling component.

Long legs locked around her waist. Lia braced one hand on the ground. With all her weight and all her power, Mary Alison drove her elbow into that elegant hand. The hand broke with several sharp cracks, and the leg-lock loosened just enough.

She burst free and got her own legs under her. No way could she let Lia get her down again.

She whirled and kicked hard into Lia's exposed armpit. Who knew how long the damage would last? Maybe it depended on what was damaged, and how bad?

Mary Alison went for the throat. Batting aside Lia's good hand, she put her fist through the cricoid and on through the larynx, feeling the tiny bones crush like chicken ribs.

She sprang away. *Shape-shift that, bitch!*

Lia flopped and writhed like a snake under a shovel, her face going purple. Ajax shouldered between her and Mary Alison. He looked down at Lia, purple-faced and sweaty and bulgy-eyed on the floor, and spoke calmly. "It is over, Lia. You are down. You will stay down."

Lia snarled. Her face went from purple to red, taking on a monstrous shape, and the crushed hand reformed with two-inch, black, shiny claws. She had claws coming out of her hand. Not a Halloween glove. Real claws.

Mary Alison fell back. Ajax and the thing wearing Lia's white mini-dress blocked the exit. The big guy's hair rose out like a lion's mane, and he roared. If he'd had a lion's lungs, that explosion of noise might've brought down the ceiling.

Mary Alison turned, and saw a door open at the far end of the hall. *Daylight.* Ignoring the screams, she ran. Something like a brick hit her shoulder, spinning her to face Lia, who had a human face but meaty cat breath.

Mary Alison hit her as hard as she'd ever hit anyone in her life. Lia staggered, and swiped her under the chin with those claws. As the blood sprayed out, a black-maned lion attacked Lia from the back.

Mary Alison stumbled away from the monsters, holding her throat. Hot red bubbled over her hands, between her fingers. People screamed, and the lion roared, and she was going to throw up right here with strangers all around her.

The corridor slid sideways and up. She was falling. In six to ten seconds, she would be unconscious. Six or eight minutes later, she would be dead.

A woman in a cook's jacket caught her by the elbows. "Shift! Shift, or you will die!"

Lia, held by a now-naked Ajax, giggled like a little girl and covered her mouth with a blood-smeared hand.

"No one can help her," Lia giggled. "She won't let anyone help."

"Lia to doctor," she mouthed, trying to press the thought into the big guy's head, but Ajax was not Darien. She might as well scream underwater. She pushed harder. *LIA. Doctor. Now!*

Ajax lifted Lia, still giggling, and carried her out of sight.

Lia had claws. Everyone knew what Lia was. Ajax was a shifter, too. What if they all were?

Dog-breath slopped through the raw-liver smell of the blood. A dog half-wearing a turquoise sweatshirt nosed under her neck and lapped noisily. She tried to shove the dog away, and it tripped in its flopping turquoise sleeves.

The light dimmed to a brownish mark, and went out. Darien called her name, his voice all thin and buzzy.

"Let me in," he begged, holding her tight to the heat of his bare skin. She huddled against him, craving his warmth. "I am your bondmate." His words echoed all through her; they tasted of pecan-wood smoke on an autumn evening.

But if she let him inside her head, she would be his puppet, as she'd been Lia's.

No. If she had to die, she would die as herself.

"Please, Mary Alison! Let me help you."

He was real; he was solid. Where he touched, she could feel solid too. It was not a matter of opening herself to him. She just stopped fighting.

He poured hot energy through her. Too hot and too much! It filled her and overfilled her and threatened to burst her apart, but it tasted like the oxygen her body craved. She soaked it in through her skin, until she tasted someone else-that loathsome bearded man who'd broken open her mind to let Lia in.

Yesterday? Only yesterday? But never again. *Never!*

The heat gave her strength, and with that strength she knew how to do one thing. She dove into the mazes inside her mind, and pulled shut a new seal at every turn until the energy poured over her, but could no longer flood through her. She was safe. Safe for a few minutes, and after that nothing would matter any more.

Mary Alison!

She drifted through random memories. Needlepoint. Peanut butter. Chi sao. Sitting in Memaw's dogwood tree, looking up at the moon. Looking up at it past city lights and calling in her mind for him. *Darien? Where are you?*

Mary Alison!

She was lost, and he was her only beacon. She swam toward his voice, his warm and living voice, and he wrapped around her. When he had her securely tied to him, he gave her a bare instant's warning. *Don't fight-just let it happen, and it won't hurt so much.*

Noooo!

Too late! He tore her apart from the inside. Her spine broke like a string of firecrackers, and her pelvis shattered. The pain ignited a lightning storm in her head. She barely noticed the tearing of muscles and the strangled sounds she could abruptly make.

She heaved a breath—her first in how long?—and fought, her teeth and claws ripping into Darien as his hands grew huge on her face.

Claws?

She was a bobcat again, like in the dreams. The men had grown to giant size, and the clothes she'd worn entangled her paws. Her inhuman squall of despair rang in her ears. She writhed free of the clothes, clawing wildly. Darien swore and bled, but still he held her. She raked him open and leaped away, skidding on the tile floor until she found enough traction to skitter down the hallway.

Behind her rose a squall that reverberated through her, singing out everything she was in one long, feline cry. Stunned by recognition, she slid against a wall. Before she could get her feet under her, a weight pounced on her. Darien.

Only he was a cat, a bobcat like she was but twice as big and with tufts of hair that made his ears look like horns. She twisted, getting her paws under her. His fangs pinched the back of her neck, holding rather than biting, and all her strength poured out of her. He bore her down to the floor.

She screamed with frustration. She screamed again with the inexplicably powerful longing to meld with Darien. To find, in him, the missing half of herself. Her throat split open along Lia's clawmarks.

Darien flowed out of his cat form, growing to human size and human shape. At the same time, he pinned her in the angle between floor and wall and closed the slices in her throat. Then he poured that scalding energy through her again, bringing her back. She could be human again, real again, unless she drowned in the pain. This time Darien pushed her in the right direction. She was almost there.

The slashes reopened across her throat. She gagged. Her human shape had multiple deep lacerations to the jugular veins, the carotid arteries, the larynx, the pharynx—

That doesn't help, Mary Alison! Darien's annoyance startled her. "Picture yourself whole and undamaged. I can help you if you let me!" She felt his hammering heart, his raging frustration as he sculpted the artery. Bear was so much faster, could do so much more! Bear? The bearded man who'd held her down for Lia. *Nooo!*

"She's blocking me," the bearded man said indistinctly, through a buzzing hum. She wasn't sure he was really there.

Lia screamed through Darien's mind, and hers. *Darien! Darien, help me! Darien, they—*

Darien cut her off, deliberately and permanently. His voice echoed through Mary Alison. "There's no time left, Kitten. You have to trust me now."

The world folded down to that one thought, to his arms tight about her shoulders; she sensed that when this moment faded, nothing would remain. If nothing followed, she wanted Darien's face as her last sight. She tried to see him, but got only a blurry impression of his deep, sad eyes. "Don't think. Just trust me. Just let it happen."

She closed her eyes and clung to him, letting his ability to mend be as real as Lia's ability to slash. *It's all real, isn't it? But you're real too. I always knew you'd come for me. I'm cold.*

I know you are. You'll be warm soon.

Okay.

His face blurred more, and he shrank against her. Her bones bent and broke as she followed, but the pain was distant, muted.

She could breathe! She extended her claws, marveling at them, and let them back in. Her head fell back; she was too weak to do more than drink in his masculine scent.

You are whole. Stay whole; stay healed.

He curled about her, and again he dragged her through layers of pain and change. "You are whole," he whispered, and held her hand in his, brushing her human fingers over the smooth surface of her throat.

Her heart cramped, a deep pain like a kick, and stopped.

"Blood loss," someone said. "Get the IVs in."

"One more shift first," Darien said. "I want to get the pooled blood out of her lungs and back in her veins. Have the needles ready when I bring her back."

He would bring her back.

He pushed her down into that small furry shape again, and this time her bones slid instead of snapping, and her muscles did not tear. But somewhere during the process, it all faded away.

Chapter Fourteen

Darien woke hours later, in lynx form. Bitterly cold air in his face made him sneeze. He licked his sharp cat-fangs and padded to the open window. The moon hovered behind the treetops to the east. Cat paws half the size of his had left prints in the white dust over the roof under the window. He followed them. Below, his wolves cavorted between the cabins, marking up the fresh snowfall.

Jesús howled the intruder-call. The pack gathered beneath him, snarling threats of unspeakable harm. He shifted, shivering in his thin human skin on the rooftop, and the mortified wolves hunkered down below.

"Should I assume that all of you noticed Lady Hawkmoor going this way before me?"

They rolled in the thin snow, groveling. None of them had noticed her. He shrank back down into his cat-fur. He could see only one tree branch in jumping reach. It did not look strong enough to hold his forty pounds.

Tinkling sub-vocal laughter tickled his nerves. A small bobcat-face peered between clumps of needles. Laughing. Inviting him to a chase. The face disappeared and snow fell as she leaped away.

His pack watched from below. He jumped.

The branch dipped alarmingly as he leaped to a thicker one, spilling snow onto to the uplifted faces of his pack. They surrounded the tree trunk, their breath rising in white steam clouds.

He followed her, feeling oversized and clumsy, making longer leaps than she could but having to choose heavier boughs than she did. When she dropped to the ground, he crouched on his branch to watch her roll in the snow.

You look all serious, Darien. Can't you just play?

He dropped beside her. She stopped and looked at him from upside down, her whiskers twitching. The tufts of fur decorating her ears were too short, and made her face seem rounder than it should be. He laughed at himself. By lynx standards, she was no beauty. But she was no lynx, either.

He stepped toward her. She streaked away through the underbrush. He chased her, willing to learn the rules of her game, here in his forest.

Eventually, he treed her again. She looked down at him, panting dainty, pearl-colored clouds in the cold air.

Come down, Mary Alison. That branch won't hold my weight.

She looked at him, her cat face tilted.

He put one paw on the trunk of her tree. She tensed. *Don't run, Mary Alison. My legs are half again as long as yours.*

Her short tail lashed side to side. Her tufted ears swiveled out to the sides and folded to a fighting position.

He laughed, the cold air sliding over his cat-tongue and filling his mouth. *You can't fight me, Mary Alison. I have twice your mass.*

Everyone has twice my mass. Or he's not worth fighting.

He wanted to pace, but he held his position, one paw pushing the space she'd claimed as her own. *Most of us have many times your mass. A shifter is conditioned to accord respect to size and to fighting prowess on an absolute standard. No matter how mean a bobcat you are, being a bobcat is not enough.*

It will have to be. It's what I am.

You are about old enough to take a second Shape. I will inform the WolfRunners to make space for you, unless you prefer to try a tiger or other large cat.

Her fur spread out, maximizing her size. *Have I ever mentioned my interest in fluffy baby bunnies and duckies?*

He dropped off the trunk. *As an appetizer, I hope!*

Cat laughter again. She folded down and watched him, her eyes dilated to pools of black within thin bright rings. He fluffed his fur, sending more warm scent rising to her in the cold air. How much did the cat's heat influence her?

Her ears cupped attentively. *How much do you weigh, cat-Darien?*

Forty-one pounds, seven point two ounces, before eating.

Just roughly, right? How much you do think I weigh?

He reached higher and ruffled his fur to release more scent. *Twenty pounds, give or take half a pound.*

She paced, her tail lashing. Receptive as hell, and possibly the only bobcat this side of the Great Lakes.

He stretched toward her again. *Are you wondering whether we're sexually compatible in these Shapes, or if we'd have to get bare-assed in the snow to do it? You do realize that my human Shape also has almost twice the mass of yours?*

They had to be compatible. If it didn't fit, he could shift until it did. But that would mean finessing a new Shape when he wanted to explode in the most primitive manner possible.

Bare-assed? Mr. Harvard says "bare-assed"?

I went to Yale. Bare-assed is a vocabulary word we learned in order to develop our sexual prowess with the pink-collar workers of the area. Cross-cultural sexual exploration is so much more fun with a little dirty talking thrown in.

You're teasing me. She turned away and looked back over her shoulder at him. *Aren't you?*

I confess my guilt.

You almost sound apologetic. Almost.

Yes, well. One cannot really apologize for something one neither truly regrets nor intends to cease doing. Apologizing in such circumstances would be hypocritical.

She showed him the tip of her tongue.

Come down, Mary Alison. Let's find a drink of water and then a leaf cave just big enough for the two of us.

Catch me! Laughing, she launched herself at him.

He shifted, human arms and human mass, and damned cold human toes in the snow. She landed hard against his chest, knocking him back a step. She laughed again, bumping her cat-head under his chin and scrubbing her jaw along his. Her rough purr seemed to startle her. She leaped away from him and high-stepped along a log about three feet away.

He shifted again, her bobcat summoning his lynx. She pounced on him, and they tumbled together to the snow. He instinctively did an extra twist and roll to obliterate his human footprints. She skittered away, bouncing sideways. An invitation to chase.

The wind shifted just then, and her scent slammed through him. He pounced on her, knocking her sliding across the snow, and wrapped about her securely, locking on her neck with jaws that ached to bite in earnest. And oh, yes, they fit. Her triumphant squall echoed through the snowy woods.

About the Author:

Amber Green is the pseudonym for a professional paper-pusher who shares her house with one husband, two sons, five cats, a perma-puppy, and a geriatric dog. The poultry is supposed to stay out of the house and usually does, but one black hen occasionally sneaks through the cat door to perch atop the terrarium/iguana tank, somehow balancing upside-down to hold staring contests with the lizard. When not writing, tending to her day job, or taking a broom to marauding opossums, the author can normally be found watering her plants or reading with her sons while giving thanks for the invention of the air conditioner.

Lessons in Pleasure

by Charlotte Featherstone

To My Reader:

What could be sexier than an immoral Regency rake that uses his extensive skills to draw the one woman he could never have into his bed and his heart?

I give you Saint, a deliciously wicked bad boy who will stop at nothing to claim the woman he loves. Enjoy the fantasy...

This book is dedicated to my hero of a husband and my daughter. Without them I wouldn't be living my fantasy—publication. Thank you for your patience, understanding, and willingness to exist on take out and Kraft dinners.

And to the three best writing friends an author could ever have. Kristina, for always being the voice of reason, the perpetual cheerleader and my Fairy Punctuation Mother. Thank you for encouraging me to take this path and for having faith in my abilities when I couldn't see them. Kathi, for her continued support, her belief in my talent, and for encouraging me to keep Saint as wicked as he wanted to be. Thank you for helping me believe in myself. I love having you as a fan. And Amy, who has struggled through all my 'bad' writing attempts to get me here. Who is an indispensable font of wisdom, knowledge and advice—thank you so much for your support. Thank you all. I could never have done it without you! Your support and encouragement and understanding are what have gotten me here.

Chapter One

Tunbridge Wells
Kent, England
1802

"*Saint*, you wicked, wicked man."

"Is that not why you sought me out this evening, Octavia?" Damian Wester-ham, the Earl of St. Croix, chuckled before playfully slapping Octavia Rawdon's delightfully curved derriere, eliciting a small gasp of pleasure. "You like my particular brand of wickedness, do you not?"

"Indeed," she purred, arching her back as his fingers glided expertly along her spine. "Your brand is very exciting," she whimpered when he rolled her straining nipple between his thumb and finger.

"*Milord*," Sheffield mumbled discreetly from behind the closed door. "I must speak with you at once."

"Go away," he growled before nipping Octavia's neck.

"Milord." This time the knock was more insistent. With a sigh, Damian extricated himself from Octavia's long limbs and reached for his dressing gown.

"Give me a moment, my dear."

"I'll be waiting right where you left me."

He looked into Octavia's glistening eyes that had been rendered far too bright by too many bottles of his excellent claret. She was a pretty creature he supposed, and enough to make desire course within him, but she was still not what he needed to appease the ache in his body. The constant search for sexual fulfillment was something that had haunted him for years. The more he drank from the illicit cup, the more he thirsted for the tonic to quench his craving.

"Milord?"

"A moment," he bit out, savagely tying the belt around his waist.

Without a backward glance at the woman sprawled in his bed, Damian strolled to the door and opened it with more than a touch of irritation.

"What is it that can't wait, Sheffield?"

"Pardon the interruption, my lord," his butler murmured, signaling him with his rheumy eyes to close the door. "But there is a lady downstairs."

"Is there, indeed?" he asked, wondering if Octavia had invited one of her stage friends for an evening of sport. "Send her up, then."

When he was about to re-enter the room, Sheffield reached for the door and shut it before Damian's face.

"The lady is Miss Farrington, milord."

Miss Farrington. His body tensed at the mere sound of her name. Lily Farrington, here. In his house after all these years?

"You weren't..." Sheffield trailed off, suddenly unable to look him in the eye. "That is to say, were you expecting Miss Farrington?"

Suppressing a smug grin, Damian schooled his features, pretending he hadn't an inkling of why the starched Lily Farrington would be risking her impeccable reputation by coming to the home of a rake. A rakehell who was known far and wide for his proclivities, not to mention his penchant for voluptuous beauties.

Carefully, he hid his self-satisfaction behind a blank expression. Studying his nails he murmured, "Not even me and my wicked mind could conjure up such a scenario involving the virtuous Miss Farrington, Sheffield."

Something that might have been relief flashed in the butler's face before he shielded it with proper servitude.

"She is awaiting you in your study, milord."

"Fine," he muttered, strolling to his dressing room for a pair of trousers and a shirt. There was no way in hell he was going to meet the virginal Lily Farrington in nothing but his silk dressing gown. Good God, the chit would have a fit of apoplexy if she caught sight of him in such a garment. His cock would no doubt rear to attention, as it always did whenever he was in her presence. Bloody hell, he'd not give Lily Farrington that type of leverage. She needn't know that the mere glimpse or sniff of her sent him into pained hardness.

"What shall I do with the creature in your room?" Sheffield muttered.

Shrugging, Damian opened the door of his dressing room. "I'll leave that to you. Do with her what you think is best."

"Aye, milord."

Struggling into his trousers, Damian fought to clear the fuzziness in his head. Too much damned claret, he thought with disgust. That was the reason he couldn't manage to put his feet in his trousers. On the third attempt, he successfully pulled on the garment, sliding the last button home before shrugging into a shirt, which he did not even bother to button.

Exiting the room, he strolled past his bedchamber, listening to the protests of Octavia as Sheffield attempted to make her give up her hold on his bed. Not giving her a second thought, he rounded the corner, caught a glimpse of his disheveled appearance in a mirror, and immediately smoothed his hair back.

His gaze scoured his face, searching for any signs of lingering dissoluteness. It was regrettable that he hadn't the time to shave, but then, how was he to know the pure and innocent Lily would arrive so quickly? He grinned, thinking of how Miss Farrington must have all but raced from her house when she heard the news. Surely she could not have learned of his dawn appointment much more than an hour ago. She was indeed a dutiful little creature. Dutiful, stunning and possessed of a body that could tempt a man in his dotage. What more could an immoral wastrel ask for?

With one last cursory glance in the mirror, he strolled down the marble staircase, arriving at his study. With a deep, calming breath, he opened the door and took in the majestic sight of Lily Farrington. His breath caught, and his traitorous cock did stir and straighten in his trousers. Just one look at her in her silver and white gown was enough to make him hard as iron.

She was a fetching little thing, all innocent and lovely with her long golden curls and pale blue eyes. Her skin was like flawless alabaster, and her lips reminded him of the soft coral inside a conch shell. She was the very epitome of a Celestial Virgin. But he knew beneath her fine gown and pure façade was a minx with a body that could tempt the devil. One only had to look deeply at Lily Farrington to see the wanton beneath the lace.

He shut the door, and she whirled around and faced him. Her silver skirt, made of the finest shimmering gauze, was rendered translucent by the firelight, outlining her lush thighs and rounded hips in vivid detail. There was a lovely triangle of space where her thighs grazed together that captured his attention, a space where his finger would fit nicely while he was drawing the honey out of her body.

"Saint," she gasped, then steadied herself. "I'm sorry to disturb you."

Damian reluctantly tore his gaze from her plump thighs and met her face. That guileless, innocent face he'd dreamed of for years. She looked the same as she had that fateful night seven years ago, all innocence and freshness.

"And what would you say if I were to tell you that you are indeed disturbing me."

"I would admonish you for lack of decorum, sir," she lectured, her blue eyes flashing at him with indignation. "It is the Sabbath, after all."

"Ah yes, the Sabbath. Well, my friend and I were just communing together. Would you care to join us?"

Her eyes widened a fraction, and her lip trembled. "That would be like getting into bed with the devil, and I would never, ever allow myself to be consumed by your lascivious tendencies."

"Never, ever, is an awfully long time, wouldn't you say? But as it is, I have no need to worry. I have a willing disciple, you see. She's more than eager to find herself consumed by my particular brand of sin."

"From the smell of you, you've already been consumed. You reek of debauchery and cheap perfume. Your lady is obviously not of the Quality."

"Whether she is of the Quality or not is moot," he said, taking a step toward her, intimidating her with his insolent gaze. "You all look the same with your legs spread, ready for a man."

Damn her! She goaded him far too easily. He didn't like what she did to him, how she made him feel dirty and vile with one sweep of her golden lashes. There once was a time when she looked at him with adoration, not the contempt she was now showing him.

"I shall let you get back to your cheap harlot," she sniffed haughtily. "You'll no doubt want your money's worth tonight."

She lifted her pretty chin in a thoroughly arrogant manner and his damnable erection surged with her insolence. She was a saucy-mouthed creature and numerous scenarios ran through his mind as he imagined himself showing the virginal Lily what she could do with her impertinent mouth.

"Are you suggesting," he asked, his temper barely tethered, "that I have to buy my pleasure?"

"I've heard you frequent the Pantiles at night. Everyone in Tunbridge Wells knows that it turns into a veritable meat market when the sun goes down. I should never have come. It was a mistake," she muttered, making to pass him in a flurry of silver gauze. "I'll leave you to your activities."

"She's already leaving," he murmured, catching her about the waist. "Do you not hear the carriage?"

Her eyes went round, and her tongue darted out to wet her lip, leaving her lips to glisten in the firelight. "But why?"

"Why?" he asked, arching his brow knowingly. "Because tonight, I plan to avail myself of a much finer and tastier morsel."

Oh, he was positively scandalous! Lily took in the sight of him, his whiskered face so close to hers. She could smell the claret on his breath, and the perfume on his skin that was bared to her beneath his open shirt. He brought her against his chest and her hand inadvertently raked over his taut belly, the muscles flinching and tightening beneath her fingers. Desire and jealously flared inside her, confusing her, making her think things she'd refused to think of since she'd been seventeen years old.

"So," he said, his lips perilously close to hers. "Why have you come here? I assume it's not to further our explorations."

Her face flushed furiously then. Damn him for being a heartless bastard. How could he have brought up that bit of business? They had been but youths, discovering their bodies when they explored each other. It had been innocent curiosity, a few meaningless sessions of discovery, no matter what the rogue said to the contrary.

"Charles Hewitt. I want you to withdraw your challenge."

He stared at her for minute, before furling his strong, full lips in a frustratingly arrogant half smile. "No."

"His wife is with child. Penelope is beyond herself with worry. For Heaven's sake, Saint, he's going to be a father."

"He should have thought of that before *he* challenged *me*."

Lily watched as he poured himself a glass of claret. He motioned to an empty glass, which she refused with a shake of her head. With a shrug he emptied his goblet, then refilled it.

"You cannot mean to go through with this. You cannot want to kill him."

"It is not up to me to withdraw. I'm afraid you'll have to talk to him."

"I have, damn you, and he won't do it."

He looked her over with his blue gaze, before grinning his rogue's smile.

"Well, then, you've come to make a deal with the devil, have you?"

"Yes," she blurted, before shaking her head. "I mean, no."

"Come now, Miss Farrington, you cannot expect to ask such a thing of me without compensation. It just isn't done. They might call me *Saint*, but I assure you, I have very little of the actual virtues of the sainted."

"You needn't remind me," she mumbled to herself.

"No?" he crooned, obviously hearing her. "You seem to have some misguided notion that I might do you this favor without one in return."

"What do you want of me in exchange for withdrawing from this duel?"

"It will have to be substantial," he said, looking into his glass as he swirled the crimson liquid around the crystal. "My reputation, you know."

"Hang your reputation, sir. You're known far and wide as a devil. Your reputation can take a bit of a blow."

"Is that what you think of me?" He gazed at her through thick black lashes. "There was a time when you murmured Saint as a benediction, not a blasphemy."

"I was seventeen, and I knew nothing of your wickedness. I'm not here to discuss what was once between us that day in the meadow. I'm here tonight on business that affects the future. A child's future. Tell me what you want for withdrawing from this challenge."

"It is a dilemma," he murmured before sipping his claret. "I'm quite eaten up by dissipation. I'm not sure what sort of payment I could extract from you to assuage my appetite."

"Tell me, and be done with it," she commanded as if she were a martyr waiting to hear the method of her execution.

"I will think about my terms and get back with you. Is that agreeable?"

"No, it is not. The duel is at dawn, if you will recall. Tell me what you want."

"What I want, my dearest Lily is for you to go home and await my decision. If I so choose to end this duel, I'll send you word, along with my stipulations."

"And how do I know you'll think on all I've said?"

"You have my word as a gentleman." His eyes darkened and narrowed when she snorted disdainfully. "Perhaps you require my signature in blood, then?"

"Nothing as gruesome as that, my lord."

"Perhaps a drink?"

She nodded, watching as Saint sipped from his glass then offered her a taste from the very spot his lips had just touched. She drank a small portion, refusing to acknowledge the frisson of awareness that snaked through her veins when her lips met the warmth left from his mouth. Swallowing deeply, she went to lick a drop that crept out of the corner of her mouth. With lightening speed, Saint's finger reached out and caught the liquid. He stared at the crimson drop a long while before meeting her gaze and sliding his finger into his mouth. "Our bargain is sealed, Miss Farrington. Run along and await my answer."

Damian couldn't conceal his grin as he watched Lily all but fly from the room. He had the little vixen right where he wanted her. His scheme had been uncomplicated, enjoyable and infinitely successful. Reaching into his desk, he scrawled a few lines then sealed two missives with his signet ring. He looked down at the familiar griffin clutching a sword and smiled. It was all coming together. When he'd plotted to get the elusive Lily Farrington back into his life he had counted on her goodness and kindness to see the plan through. She had not disappointed him. Many things had changed over the years, but one thing had not—Lily Farrington was the same as she ever was, and he was as much ensnared in her coils as he had been seven years ago.

Thanks to Lily's spotless reputation and the fact the citizens of Tunbridge Wells adored her, it had been mere child's play to execute his plan. It had taken only two bold looks at her from his rakish, knowing eyes to have the over-bearing and pompous twit, Charles Hewitt, wishing to champion her. One more overt glance and the lingering of his impudent gaze on the tempting mounds of her breasts along with a raised brow was all that was required to have Hewitt confronting him after the service. Hewitt had come barreling after him, tossing out a challenge with nary a thought for the pregnant wife he might leave behind.

He'd been more than pleased to accommodate the fool. As expected, Lily had come to bargain her soul to save another's. How fitting then, that she should come to the devil who had betrayed her seven years before. He had no regrets for what he was about to do. He would willingly take her soul and body in this devil's agreement. But what he wanted the most, what he would gain from this bargain, was her love.

Gazing once more at the missives sitting atop his desk, a feeling of supreme satisfaction coursed through his veins. His plan would work. He had spent too many years without her in his life to let this opportunity slip through his fingers. He'd let her go too easily the last time. But he was older now, seasoned, and he would fight for what he wanted. He'd regain her trust and her love—or die trying.

It was a miracle that she had never married. He had followed her life, wondering at the fact she'd not accepted any offers throughout the years. And there had been offers. He was certain of that.

As perplexing as her desire was to remain a spinster, one thing was obvious, this was his chance to win her back. If his plans failed, if he failed to gain her love, perhaps he would be successful at least in exorcising her from his mind and body. Three nights with Lily might just be enough to make him forget her.

Bloody hell. He'd never be able to banish her from his blood. He was as dependent upon Lily Farrington to sustain him as he was on air to make him breathe.

He picked up the letters and strolled to the door. "Sheffield," he called, stepping out into the hall, nearly running the butler down as the servant emerged from the shadows. "Make certain that this reaches Miss Farrington's house by five this morning. She is to get it directly." Handing the missives to the butler, he instructed him on how to proceed.

"You understand what you're to do?"

"Of course, milord. And your appointment, shall you wish to eat prior to traveling to Billings Farm?"

"I believe, Sheffield, that my early morning plans have changed. Have cook prepare a hearty breakfast, to be served at ten. I have a feeling that I'm going to need quite a bit a nourishment for the days ahead."

"As you wish, milord."

Damian smiled, well satisfied with the night's business. *Oh yes, Lily, I've got you exactly where I want you, and I will not take no for an answer this time.*

"Damnable man," Lily ranted as she padded across her bedroom floor. Where the devil could he be? What could he be doing? Preparing for death, or worse, the killing of an innocent.

Oh why, she thought, wringing her hands. Why had Penelope's husband issued a challenge to Saint? He'd only looked at her, for heaven's sake. It wasn't as if Saint had been devouring her, right there in the church for all to see. She'd tried to tell Mr. Hewitt that his protection was misguided, that Saint didn't care about her and couldn't have been looking at her with anything but contempt, but Penelope's husband had flatly refused to listen to reason. And now he was going to get himself killed. Saint would have no qualms about killing a man in cold blood. He had no moral convictions whatsoever.

A soft thud echoed in the quiet room. On the window seat, illuminated by moonlight sat a small rock with a letter tied to it. Beastly man! Leave it to Saint to leave her guessing till an hour before the dawn appointment.

Very well, Madam, you shall have what you seek. Send this missive back out the window; it will be taken as confirmation of your acceptance.

But where were the terms? What did he want of her? The ticking of the clock echoed in her ears, reminding her of the precious little time that remained before dawn. Penelope would be devastated if Saint succeeded in murdering her husband. Oh God, she had to agree to Saint's terms. What else could she do? She could not allow her pregnant friend to be widowed because of her. It was *her* responsibility to set things right. After all, Charles was fighting to avenge her honor. She had to save Charles for the sake of Penelope.

Closing her eyes, Lily tossed the missive out of the window, half expecting the devil himself to appear in a fireball of sin and lust. Instead, another letter landed unceremoniously on the floor beside her bare feet.

With tremulous hands she opened it, Saint's bold handwriting illuminated by the moonlight.

"As payment for my generosity, you will grant to me three nights. You will meet me tomorrow evening at the Temple on the west ground. Do not disappoint me."

Lily let the paper slip between her fingers, only to land atop her feet. She'd made a deal with the devil, and he was coming for his due—three nights of sinful delight. Three nights with Saint. Lily shivered at the thought. He would ruin her, in more ways than one.

Seven years ago, she had let Saint do things to her that no woman conscious of her reputation would ever allow. She had given him access to her body and her heart. She had loved him, and he had betrayed her with another.

He would betray her again; she was certain of it. He was a dissolute rogue who wanted nothing from her except what pleasure he could take of her body. She must live up to her end of this accord; she must give him what he wanted. But she would not be foolish like the last time. She would not make the mistake of falling in love with Saint.

Chapter Two

Oh, the gall of the man, Lily thought as she maneuvered her mare through the dark paths leading to St. Croix's property. Had she known what he would ask for she would never have stepped foot in his den of deceit.

As soon as she thought it, she knew she was lying to herself. She would have done anything to prevent the duel. Not because she cared so very much for Charles Hewitt, but because she couldn't allow Penelope to lose the husband she adored all because of her. Damn Saint. Why could he have not kept his lecherous eyes to himself? Why had he chosen that particular Sunday to arise from his bed, seeking to repent his sins and carnal appetites? What epiphany had struck him to make him take up his family pew as if it were a weekly occurrence after an absence of seven years?

And what was left for her to do but give the devil his reward? He had honored their bargain, and now she had to give herself up to his wickedness, no matter the consequences to her reputation, her heart, or her soul.

A part of her had known all along what Saint would require for sparing Mr. Hewitt's life. But she had put those thoughts out of her mind, refusing to believe he would be so wicked as to demand her surrender. But he was so very depraved. So immoral that the rogue had probably purposely set out to prick Mr. Hewitt's notoriously quick temper.

With a large sigh, Lily forced her thoughts aside. It would not do to dwell on Saint's motives. Her time would be much better spent formulating a plan to prevent the rake from touching her heart.

Her mare continued on, seemingly heedless of the inherent risk of traversing the rocky paths in the dark. It seemed as if something drew Daisy to St. Croix's grounds. Indeed, Lily barely had to hold the reins as Daisy mindlessly trotted deeper into the blackness of night. The Devil was luring the mare, Lily thought with a shiver. Just as he had lured her that fateful night. She could still hear his murmured words, deep and seductive and utterly enthralling. She would have followed Saint to the ends of the earth if he had asked. She certainly had been dangerously close to giving him her virginity, but God's hand had come down, hard and heavy, and very displeased with their illicit activities.

'*There are fornicators amongst us*,' the vicar had cried with zeal from his pulpit the very next morning. "*They enjoy the pleasures of the flesh without benefit of marriage or for the purpose of procreation."*

Lily could still feel the cold, mutinous glare of Reverend Dewey's rheumy eyes. She'd squirmed beneath that menacing gaze, but Saint had been beside her, gently squeezing her hand, silently telling her she had naught to fear.

"They shall copulate no more," Reverend Dewey had proclaimed, slamming his fist against the holy book. *"Their licentiousness shall not go unpunished. They shall not corrupt the honest folk of Tunbridge Wells with their illicit and gratuitous carnal appetites. They shall pay,"* he'd announced, his lips curved in malicious enjoyment, *"and they shall be parted. God will see to their punishment. No man,"* he said, boldly raking Saint with his condemnation, *"no man is above the law of God."*

He'd known about her and Saint, had seen them, he informed her at the end of the service. His words still had the power to make her skin crawl with revulsion. *'I saw you atop the grassy hill, wanton and hedonistic with St. Croix's member in your hand.* She had wanted to vomit knowing that he had watched them, concealed by the darkness and the forest. Lily could almost feel the vicar's bony hand encased in hers as she remembered how the virulent evilness of him seeped through her kid leather gloves. He'd known all about what they had done to each other. Lily had never been more frightened of the consequences than she had at that moment, standing on the steps of King Charles the Martyr church, the vicar's evil eyes staring through her, letting her glimpse the punishment the Lord had in store for her.

Saint, like a typical arrogant aristocrat, had flatly refused to put credence in the vicar's ramblings. He even went so far as to suggest the vicar harbored secret fantasies about her, and was only perturbed with Saint for "getting the prize before he could lay claim to it."

Lily had doubted everything—doubted herself for letting Saint talk her into allowing him to fondle her breasts and the place between her legs, doubted Saint for telling her that what they were doing was perfectly natural and ordained by God for their enjoyment. *'He wouldn't make a woman as lovely as you,'* he'd murmured in her ear as she lay beneath him, *'if he did not wish for me to savor her.'*

She'd learned the hard way what illicit desires and forbidden touches could do to one's life, and then she learned the consequences of impetuously giving her heart to someone who didn't love her. After Saint's betrayal, she had gone to live with her aunt in London. Needing to be away from him and mend her broken heart, she escaped to the city where she thought she could begin a new life. Unfortunately, her entrance into Society only forced her to bear witness as Saint succumbed to one vice after another.

The path widened and Daisy increased her pace, trotting to where the moon hung low in the sky, its silver glow reflecting off the water of St. Croix's pond. Beyond it lay the Temple. Their treasured hiding place as children, and then their sanctum for privacy when their feelings for one another had grown beyond friendly childhood affection. The Temple had been the place of their first kiss, where she first experienced the feel of Saint's hand on her breast. The Temple had been where Saint had initiated her descent into sinful pleasures.

And here she was, seven years later back at the temple with its yellowed sandstone walls and domed roof. Back at the place where she'd fallen in love with Saint.

She would not let him master her as he had all those longs years ago. She could not let her heart or body win out over her mind. She'd suffered most cruelly under Saint's callous actions. She'd loved him and he had tossed her love aside for another. He'd broken her heart, and as a consequence she hadn't allowed herself to give it to another again. She would not allow herself to be tortured in the same fashion again.

Saint hadn't cared a fig for her. If he had, he would have pursued her in London. He would never have thrown himself wholeheartedly into the vocation of dissipated wastrel. Had he returned her feelings, she would not have had to spend the last years trying to forget him and sheltering her fragile heart.

No, Saint could have whatever he wished from her in these three nights, but he would never have her heart.

Daisy came to a halt before the Temple, and Lily felt a tremor of nervousness race along her spine and into her neck. Hearing the creaking of hinges, Lily turned her head to see a pale shaft of golden light which was immediately blocked by the menacing shadow that stood in the doorway. Saint was here, waiting for her.

"'Bout time," he drawled, a hint of danger beneath his words. "I thought perhaps I might have to drag you kicking and screaming from the sanctity of your house."

She stiffened at his tone and lowered herself to the ground. "I vowed to uphold this bargain, and I will," she said, catching her breath at the sight of him looming in the doorway, his long arms raised above his head as he rested his hands against the doorframe.

"If you will recall, my missive clearly said *evening*. Not bloody midnight."

"How was I to know what time you meant? I supposed midnight would be evening to you. You do, after all, rise rather late in the day."

Lily thought she saw him narrow his eyes, but since his features were cast in darkness and shadow she couldn't be sure. All she was certain of was the fact that Saint looked utterly devilish, and very masculine wearing nothing but black trousers and a white linen shirt that was opened at the throat.

"You will not make the same mistake tomorrow night, or I shall tack on another day, just to punish you for your insolence."

The rogue might have been able to persuade her to do his bidding at seventeen, but as a woman who was four and twenty, she would no longer allow herself to fall in line with his demands.

"Well?" she said, once assured her composure and cool demeanor were firmly in place. "We've wasted enough time on the pleasantries. Shall we not get this business finished so that I may return home, and you—" she turned and gazed at him, refusing to admit how her heart raced when she looked at him. "You may then return to whatever it is you do in the middle of the night."

Damian stared at her, surprised his mouth wasn't hanging open in astonishment. She was an insolent little baggage, so full of self-righteousness and haughty assurance. What did she take him for, some green lad who wished for nothing more than a tumble? Had she thought she'd glide in here with the bearing of a queen so he could bed her and send her on her way?

He looked her over once more, taking in her prim dress and demure shawl. She'd done her hair in a severe bun, the strands stretched so tightly that the corners of her eyes were tugged upwards. She looked like a spinsterish prude. She'd done it on purpose, of course, just to vex him. To make him hurry up and get on with the business of fulfilling the rest of their bargain. But what the little minx didn't understand was that her spinsterish façade combined with her saucy tongue made him wish for many things other than a perfunctory bedding. He had no intention of spreading her legs and filling her body with his cock, spending his seed, then sending her home. He did wish to take her, but not in the way she imagined. This wasn't about a quick rut. What he wanted to do to Lily Farrington was far beyond rudimentary bed sport. This was about pleasure—his and hers, and nothing less would do. He would have her complete surrender; he would hear her begging him to fill her before the three nights were over.

"What?" she asked, her hands fisted on her hips as she tilted her chin to look at him. "Perhaps you feel this bargain is no longer suited to your taste?"

"I assure you, Miss Farrington," he drawled, pushing himself away from the frame and shutting the door behind them. "This bargain more than suits me. It's very much to my taste, and my current fetish is for viper-tongued virgins who need to be taught a thing or two about keeping a man waiting when he's rock hard and searching for release."

"I see," she murmured, her innocent eyes round with shock.

"No," he drawled, reaching for her hand and bringing her further into his den of pleasure. "But I'm certain that by the time I'm finished with you, you'll see the truth clear enough."

Chapter Three

Lily gasped when saw the transformation inside the temple. It had been nothing but a stone outbuilding, housing gardening supplies and a bench when they were children. Now it very much resembled a Sultan's tented Harem.

"I take it you approve?"

She nodded, stunned by the beauty of the crimson and gold fabrics that covered a canopy day bed and the numerous pillows strewn about a red silk coverlet. A hearth had been installed, and large logs cracked and flared as the flames flickered in the soft light. A clock rested on the mantle, its gold pendulum gently swaying in a rhythmic, hypnotic motion.

"What do you think of the bath?"

Lily followed the trail of candles lining a path to a large circle cut out of the flagstone floor. From deep inside, steam billowed out in smoking tendrils.

"It looks like a Turkish bath," she murmured, awed at the beauty and the magical change in the temple. It looked cozy and intimate with the candles and the smell of wood burning, and yet it was a sensual feast for the eyes with dramatic colors and sumptuous fabrics. Beside the bath, a table sat, filled with bowls and an epergne piled high with fruit and other delicacies.

"It is a hot bath." Saint's fingers slowly crept along her neck, pulling thin strands of hair from the confines of her bun. "When I discovered in the course of my studies of the landscape that the Chalybeate Spring runs beneath my property, I endeavored to design my own hot spring bath."

"Geology, Saint? Who would have thought you would take such an interest?"

"I have many interests, Miss Farrington," he whispered against her neck before pulling the pins from her hair, "and tonight I plan to acquaint you with a few." She shivered despite herself, and immediately stiffened when she heard Saint's amused chuckle.

"Do you like words, Lily? Do they arouse you? I will indulge you in that, my innocent beauty. I, too, like to hear words uttered in passion."

The shivering continued, working its way up her spine as Saint kneaded her nape, his long fingers working to loosen the tense muscles.

"I suppose you'll want me on the daybed," she whimpered, feeling his finger trail down her spine, his touch feather light, barely discernable through her thin chemise before he slowly unfastened the buttons of her gown.

"No." His lips brushed her shoulder. "Tonight is not about a quick rut, my lovely Lily. The nights you have granted me are to be more than the mere taking of your virginity and copulation. I'm going to give you lessons, my sweet. Lessons you are sorely in need of."

The gown slipped over her arms and breasts, then slowly Saint pushed it along her waist, sliding it down her belly and over her hips. All the while, she could feel his breath whispering against her hair, her neck, her spine.

"Tonight's lesson is the pleasure of self."

"I don't need a lesson," she announced as her dress pooled around her feet and Saint's fingers danced lightly up her thighs and over her hips.

"Oh, I think you do. You've forgotten what it is to feel desire, to be wanton and free. You've hidden your charms beneath propriety and prudery for too many years, Lily, and tonight I mean to re-awaken you to those charms."

He left her then, trembling and needy, her nipples grazing painfully against her chemise. The inside of her thighs were already damp with only the barest touch of his hands and his words.

"Come," he commanded stepping out from behind her and taking her hand in his. "It is time to bathe."

Lily followed him to the hot spring, forcing her legs to carry her the short distance. Saint's tactic had been most unexpected. She hadn't thought Saint would make her deflowering intimate and romantic. She'd been prepared for him to toss her on any available surface, lift her skirts and take his pleasure of her. She had thought to be taken of her virginity, not seduced into giving it to him.

"Into the water, Lily."

She looked at him then, meeting his dark blue gaze. "Are you coming in?"

"No. I want to watch you. This is your lesson. I'm awakening *you* to passion."

"I don't think...that is I shouldn't. It's not proper."

Saint reached out and grazed his thumb along her lower lip, his eyes darkening as he stared at her mouth. "A lady always behaves in a manner befitting the occasion, and the behavior for foreplay, my sweet Lily, is unbridled passion."

"But this is—"

He kissed her then, a soft touching of mouths, stopping her protests with the touch of his tongue against the spot on her lips where his thumb had been. "Indulge yourself, Lily, let yourself be free to feel."

She wanted to, but she knew it was wrong to feel such things. She was supposed to be a lady—a polite lady, not a wanton bargaining her body for the pleasures of a rogue who wouldn't think twice of betraying her.

"We made a bargain, Lily, I have kept my promise; are you now backing out of the agreement?"

"No," she said, feeling somehow dishonorable. She had agreed and there was no place for further protests.

"Then lower yourself into the water and enjoy the feel of it against your skin. Let me watch you."

She nodded, self conscious and afraid as Saint helped her into the warm mineral-rich water. She couldn't help but moan when the water engulfed her body, making her shiver with its heat, with the feel of the foam as it clung to her skin.

"You like it," Saint announced, stretching out on a cushion near the edge of the bath. "I heard your appreciative whimper."

"It's warm," Lily agreed, widening her arms and swishing the water around her.

"And yet your nipples are hard, are they not?"

With a gasp, Lily peered into the water to see her nipples hard and erect, straining against her transparent chemise.

"Obviously the water gives you pleasure other than warmth."

She covered herself then, fearing Saint understood the thoughts coursing through her mind. She didn't want him to know that the feel of the warm water reminded her of the times that his large, warm palm engulfed her breasts, making her nipples pebble hard.

"Would you care for a fig?"

She nodded and swam over to him, reaching for one of the sugared figs that lay in a bowl beside him. Motioning her hand aside, Saint picked out a large, plump fig and dipped it into golden honey before holding it out to her, the liquid trailing slowly down the fruit and onto his finger.

He held it out to her, and she took it, delighting in the sweetness of the honey combined with the rich taste of the fig. With a sweep of his finger, he drenched her lips with the honey, telling her in a deep command to lick it from his finger.

She obliged him, meeting his gaze as her tongue moved along her lips, then his finger, licking the stickiness from his skin. Uneasiness turned to satisfaction as his eyes widened then narrowed as he watched her tongue glide along his finger.

"It is still in you, isn't it, Lily? The good reverend Dewey wasn't able to banish all the passion from you, was he?"

Lily said nothing, but instead pushed herself back into the bath, this time floating on her back, perfectly aware that her breasts were bobbing in the water, her pink nipples painfully erect in the chill air as they clung to her chemise. Her wanton display should be enough of an answer she thought, sighing as she relaxed, allowing herself to float in the water's heated warmth. Saint needn't know how she longed for him, and what they had shared. She'd tried to forget him in the long seven years they had been apart but never could.

Damian took in the sight of Lily's ripe body, her firm breasts buoyed by the water, her thatch of golden hair outlined by her chemise. Jesus, he hadn't been this aroused by merely looking since he had been a calf-eyed youth stumbling upon her bathing. His cock swelled, the blood engorging it to an almost painful size as he watched Lily's lovely tits rock in the water. Damian quelled the urge to stroke himself. He had given in to temptation that long ago day as he watched her lather her body, but he was no longer an impatient youth. He was a sophisticated lover, and no matter how much he yearned to take his throbbing cock in his hand and pleasure himself as he watched the innocent minx display her charms for him, he wouldn't. Tonight was a lesson for Lily. She was to be awakened to her own desires. He was already fully and painfully aware of his.

"Mmmm," she purred, as she moved her arms up and down, the water slicing over her pale limbs. "This is quite the most decadent thing, is it not?"

"You've only just begun to learn the meaning of decadence." Damian sat up and reached for her. "Come, let me dry you."

"But it's so delightfully warm in here, Saint."

"Come," he whispered, shackling her wrists in his hands and pulling her up. "Feel what the cool air will do to you."

Lily sucked in a breath as Saint pulled her from the warm water, her chemise clinging to every curve and indentation of her body. Cool air met her, chilling her, making her nipples harden once more. She felt restless with longing, for the touch of Saint's hands to ease the tightening stiffness of her aching nipples. It was madness to feel anything for the man. She should be cold and aloof. She should certainly not be wishing for things that would only bring about her ruin.

Holding up a towel, Saint encouraged her to remove her chemise. Lily did as he asked, squirming as the cold, wet material slid up her body and over her head. Long arms wrapped around her as Saint proceeded to cover her with the towel and lead her to the hearth. He dried her, gently rubbing the cotton along her limbs and back, then swiped it across her breasts, stiffening and firming them further.

The heat from the fire enveloped her, and she felt a languid warmth infuse her veins, as if she had drunk too many glasses of wine.

"You've lovely skin, Lily," Saint murmured behind her ear as he reached for a brush, raking it through her wet curls. "I remember it very well, the way it felt like silk beneath my hands. The way it used to pucker beneath my tongue."

His voice was hypnotic and low. The feel of the brush as he stroked it through her hair lulled her further, made her forget she stood completely naked, her front warmed by the fire, and her back by Saint's heated body.

"Do you ever think of us, Lily? Of what we did and what we meant to each other?"

"Hmm," she murmured, letting her head tip back and rest against Saint's chest. "We were naughty, Saint. The vicar told us so. We should never have given in to our curiosity."

"Even now you believe him?" he asked, kissing her forehead and slowly moving his lips to cover her eyelids then her nose. "You're a woman now, Lily. Have you never thought of what it would have been like for us had you given in to your desires?"

The warmth enveloped her and the soothing sound of Saint's heart made her eyes flutter closed. "What we did was forbidden."

"We kissed and explored each other's bodies, Lily. We shared intimate moments of discovery, moments that some people never experience in their life."

"God punished us, Saint."

She felt him stiffen and wished she hadn't said it, if only to keep him touching her.

"There was no punishment by God. The only retribution was delivered by you, when you ran from me and shut me out of your life."

"You betrayed me. What of Molly Simms?" she asked, barely able to get the woman's name out of her mouth.

He turned her to him then, his long, hard arms bringing her roughly up against him. "You must understand that I never intended for it to happen."

She sucked in her breath when she felt his hands cup her buttocks, his chiseled chest flattening her breasts.

"I was on fire for you, Lily, surely you remember that. I was so hot for you. You'd finally agreed to be mine, to give me what I had been begging for—for months. But you ran from it, you let the vicar put fear in you. You ran from me, not listening to a word I said. Molly," he said, gripping her harder, drawing her tightly against his tense body. "Molly just happened upon me. Jesus, Lily, I wanted you so badly. I was near to exploding with desire for you. And then Molly found me, and she took me into her mouth, just as I'd fantasized you would. I hadn't intended—"

"But you didn't stop it." Lily shuddered inwardly at the memory. He'd found a more willing participant to see to his needs. She'd been crushed, utterly devastated to find Saint and Molly, the tavern wench, together, in the exact spot where she and Saint had lain only a short time before. The sight of them together had forever tarnished what Lily had once treasured. "Nor did you seek me out to explain your actions."

"You ran to London," he exclaimed, then checked himself, his hands loosening their hold on her. "Let us not talk of this," he whispered, nuzzling her hair from her face and kissing a path down to her lips. "This night is for loving, not remembering past hurts. I promise that I shall not hurt you. Trust me, Lily. If only for tonight."

Reluctantly she nodded and parted her lips, allowing Saint entrance, quickly meeting his seeking tongue. He tasted of spice and claret, of man and lust. It was astonishing how familiar his lips and tongue felt.

It had been seven years since they'd last kissed. In the ensuing years they had done nothing but utter frightfully polite comments to one another, each giving the other wide berth to go their own way. Lily had watched from afar as Saint indulged himself in wicked pleasures, clearly forgetting her as he succumbed to vice. Despite her every attempt, she'd never stopped loving him or wanting him. Never stopped gazing at him across the fashionable ballrooms of London or stealing quick peeks of him when he returned home to Tunbridge Wells. She had never felt this way about another man, and she feared she never would. Her attraction to him was dangerous. His mouth, his very taste felt so right, so perfect. Her heart, which had never completely healed after his betrayal was already beginning to shatter, knowing after these three nights were over she would have nothing left of him.

"Forget the past, Lily. Come to bed." Saint picked her up and carried her to the daybed before the fire. "It is time to begin your first lesson."

Chapter Four

Damian slid onto the bed alongside Lily, her spine, elegantly curved, faced him. She was more beautiful then he recalled. It wasn't surprising though. The Lily he had fallen in love with had been but a girl beginning to blossom. Her breasts had been nothing but taut, firm buds—more nipple and areole than flesh. Her stomach had been flat and straight, her hips conveying only the faintest hint of flaring. She had been lovely then, but as he looked upon Lily laying before him, her porcelain skin, large full breasts and ample hips and thighs, Damian realized that the girl had grown into a voluptuous, enticing beauty who still had the ability to make his jaded heart beat with longing and hope.

Sighing, she snuggled further onto her side, inching closer to the edge of the bed, seeking the warmth of the firelight. He followed her, letting his fingers flick the ends of her hair over her shoulder before sliding his fingertips down her neck and along her shoulder blade.

"Mmm," she purred appreciatively. His fingers were at her waist, and the urge to cup her heart shaped derriere called to him. "Your fingers still feel so wonderful, Saint. Your touch was always magical to me."

There was something in her words that stopped him from rushing, that made him wish to take his time, to pleasure her as he knew he could. She obviously remembered the feel of his hands along her body. It had been seven years since he'd laid one finger on her, and yet she recalled the sensation immediately. He decided then to use his fingers along her skin to reawaken her to him, to remind her of how she had once cared for him. Once wanted him and loved him.

"Saint," she murmured, sliding her plump bottom along the bed till it rested in the juncture of his thighs. "Touch me."

And he did, running the tips of his fingers along her neck and shoulders, and down the length of her arms. He swept his fingers, feather light along her back, delighting in her moans and the gooseflesh that arose on her skin. Each time coming a little closer to the swells of her breast, a little lower along her hip, letting a finger trace a small portion of one plump cheek of her bottom until she became more restless.

He teased her with each stroke until she positioned herself onto her back, provoking him to touch her where she wanted, but where she would not ask him to. He purposely traced the edge of her breast, smiling as she arched her back, grazing her impudent nipple against his knuckle. He slid his hand away, letting it rest against her hip. She sighed and raised her leg, bending it so that it was draped over his thighs, exposing her mound of golden curls.

"Please," she whimpered, her voice husky with need, the gooseflesh spreading along her belly and thighs, crinkling her areoles and filling her nipples with blood so that they were no longer a light pink but a dark rose.

"Are you not satisfied?" he asked against her ear, his fingers tracing over her knee before slowly and lightly gliding up the inside of her thigh, stopping just before her wet curls. She arched against his hand and he slid his fingers away from her, fearing that if he touched her all would be lost.

"Saint." It was a plea for surcease. "Please."

"Pleasure yourself," he commanded, placing her hand on her breast. "Learn your body and give it the pleasure it craves."

"I can't…it isn't—"

"It is," he crooned against her temple, his fingers once again soothing her into restless longing. "Take your breasts and your nipples between your fingers and show me what you would have me do to you."

She paused, her breathing heavy before she cupped them in her hands, bringing the peaks together, her thumbs coaxing her nipples into strained pebbles. Her eyes were tightly shut, but he watched as her lips parted on a silent pant.

"How does it feel?" A husky moan was all she managed. Damian smiled as she worked her breasts faster and harder between her hands, his own need stirring unruly in his trousers. "Put your hand on your mound."

He saw the hesitation in her face, heard her hushed breathing, but she let him take her hand in his, and together they placed their fingers on her wet lips. His cock leapt at the provocative sight of his long fingers lying atop hers, her fingers buried between her folds, stroking and probing and swirling around in her glistening honey.

The urge to take and plunder, to bury his mouth inside her, to taste what had always been denied him coursed violently through him. She was writhing now, her hips arching slowly, seductively as her finger swirled around her glistening sex. "So damn beautiful," he growled against her throat, his gaze fixated on her alabaster fingers immersed in pink silk.

"You're watching?" she panted between breaths. "Like that time you were spying on me in the bath?"

His belly tightened as memories of that day flooded his brain, and he stroked himself through his trousers. "Yes."

"Does watching bring you pleasure?"

"Yes."

"Did you," she licked her lips and cried out as her fingers swirled faster around the pink nubbin of flesh. "Did you touch yourself as you watched me?"

"Yes."

Damian ripped open the flap of his trousers and gripped his cock, pumping his hand up and down, watching her pleasure herself, reveling in his own self-pleasuring. He'd never masturbated before anyone before, preferring his conquests to do the task for him. But there was something about stroking himself before Lily that stirred his senses. Something that heated his blood and made his rod throb painfully, knowing she was watching and listening to his sounds of pleasure.

"Saint," she huffed, spiraling towards her climax. "Have you...have you ever done that since, and thought of me?"

"Yes," he gritted between his teeth, his hand now furiously pumping up and down, watching her escalate her own passion. Memories of the way he'd spied on her soaping her breasts, remembrances of the way he'd freed himself, coming in his hand as he watched her lather her sex, sprung into his head, making him feel hotter and more sexually needy then he had in years.

"Lily," he whispered, working himself into complete abandon. "Tell me," he growled, looking into her face, seeing her teetering on the edge of her climax. "Have you ever wanted to reach between your legs and pleasure yourself, pretending it was my fingers giving you release?"

"*Yes!*" she cried, her hips bucking wildly, her breathing coming in short rasps. He growled, reaching for her, pumping himself onto her lush bottom, then sinking back onto the bed with Lily in his arms, the scent of their arousal mingling together in the quiet room.

"Lily?"

"Hmm," she purred, sounding very close to sleep.

"When you next see me, your body will respond to me. I won't have to touch you in order for you to feel the need."

She nodded slowly and yawned against him. "Yes, Saint."

"Tomorrow night, Lily, I'll not deny myself. You realize that, don't you? Tomorrow night you'll belong to me in every sense of the word."

When no response came, Damian peeked down at the angelic and sleeping face of Lily. Her blond curls fanned over the black hair covering his chest. He liked the contrast of it, liked the possessive way her hair covered him. Feeling more content and satiated than he had in a long while, Damian reached for the silk coverlet and covered them, drifting off to peaceful slumber with the woman he never thought he'd have, lying gloriously naked beside him.

Chapter Five

Lily strolled along the manicured paths of Lady Carmichael's perennial beds, fanning herself against the heat of the afternoon sun. The garden was hot and sticky, the paths full of elegantly dressed couples, the cream of Tunbridge Wells society, all turned out for the Carmichael's annual garden party.

The scent of roses and lavender assailed her senses, and she stopped to inhale the heady fragrance of a blush-pink damask rose. Smoothing her finger over the velvety petals, Lily flushed, remembering the feel of Saint's manhood, just as soft and as velvety as the rose she was stroking, when he'd rubbed it along her buttocks, his seed slowly and evocatively trickling down her flesh.

Lily shivered despite the warmth of the air. She'd acted wantonly last night—more than wanton, she'd been sinful. What had provoked her to touch herself in such a manner, and before Saint, for Heaven's sake? She still couldn't fathom what had made her admit to him that she had wished to pleasure herself, and to fantasize of him while doing so. The man truly was a devil for being able to cozen that sort of information out of her.

He'd said nothing to her while she'd done it, but she had felt his breathing, harsh and fast against her neck. Had felt the heat of his dark blue eyes on her fingers as she played in her folds. That knowledge, that he was watching her and deriving pleasure of it had emboldened her, had pushed her on, only to enjoy the experience more then she ever thought she could. In truth, she had never really pleasured herself, preferring to indulge in the pressing together of her thighs rather than actually touching herself. She had thought just that little bit had been decadent and sinful; she had no idea the true exquisiteness that could arise from touching oneself, especially when the person she'd always dreamed of was lying beside her, watching her and encouraging her to succumb to her body's craving.

Feeling restless and warm, and just a touch unsteady, Lily slipped behind an enormous oak tree, resting against its cool, rough trunk. Why was it that Saint was the only man to arouse her thus? What was it about his wickedness that called to her carefully suppressed wantonness? Closing her eyes, Lily let herself relive those moments in Saint's arms, the feel of her climax crashing down upon her, Saint's strong arms holding her against him, the faint stirring of his breath caressing her hair. It had been Heaven, the most exquisite feeling she'd ever experienced—and he hadn't even taken her virginity.

He had desired her, been unbelievably tender with her, yet he had refused to discuss their past. He hadn't told her why he did not come after her once she'd discovered him with Molly. What little he had said last night was the most he'd ever said about the matter. She must have meant very little to him to not even bother to attempt to explain himself. He couldn't have loved her. He had just been using her body for his lust—a convenient body to service him. She was being a fool to believe anything might have changed. He was still using her for his own needs.

How would she ever survive his lessons, she wondered, continuing to fan herself, letting her fingertips graze the exposed skin of her breasts? How could she keep from falling in love with the rogue when he made her feel like this?

The sound of gravel crunching alerted Lily that the others were making their way back to the lawn for tea and cakes. Relieved to be truly alone at last, Lily let her fingers move the air before her, cooling her neck and bosom. How would she wait till tonight? How could she resist the urge to touch her swollen breasts and aching nipples? Just the memory of the way Saint had greeted her, lounging rakishly in the doorway of the Temple was enough to make her burn and yearn for his touch.

She pushed the image aside. She must remember his betrayal. It was the only thing that would save her. He had made her feel this way before—desired and beautiful. He was skilled at making her want him, but she had to be strong, had to resist his allure—to come away from these three nights with her pride and her heart intact.

A twig snapped, and her eyes flew open, greeting the dark blue eyes of Saint.

"Saint," she whispered, blushing furiously, her skin instantly alive with prickles of heat and awareness—just as he said it would.

"Are you warm, Miss Farrington?"

His voice was dark and sensual, fully in command. But his eyes, they belied his cool demeanor. Those beautiful cobalt eyes mirrored her own desire.

"Care for a drink?" he asked, raising a crystal flute filled with water. Tiny rivulets of liquid ran along the outside of the glass, trickling down the stem and onto his bronzed finger. Lily followed the water as it trailed down his finger and along the top of his hand where it rolled off his skin and into the grass. "Allow me," he murmured, raising the glass to her mouth and pressing the rim of the crystal against her lip. She gasped as cool water met her skin, gasped again as a drop rolled from her lip, slowing descending to her chin where Saint caught it with a flick of his tongue.

"You're warm," he drawled, reaching into the water and picking out a shard of ice, which he held between his thumb and forefinger. "Should I cool you, do you think? One would hate for you to become overheated."

Lily's lips parted on a silent breath as he traced the line of her neck, dipping low to edge her bodice, and then boldly sliding the melting ice up between her breasts. Her breathing became rapid despite the cooling liquid; her breasts were heaving, begging to be freed from of the confines of her bodice.

As if aware of her torment, Saint pulled one sleeve of her sky blue muslin gown, baring one breast to the air—and his gaze. Without a sound he circled her nipple with the shard, hardening it with the delightful coolness of the ice. His gaze searched her face, and Lily felt a disconcerting urge to shut her eyes. He would want to see the desire in her eyes, to see what effect he was having on her.

He traced the underside of her breast, his finger softly and almost imperceptibly grazing her skin, swelling her breasts further, making her thrust forward in order to feel more of his hand against her. Finally, he tore his gaze from hers and stared at her erect nipple, a fat drop of water dangled precariously from it. Lily stiffened as he bent his head, silently begging him to put his mouth to her and suck the water off. Wetness pooled between her thighs as she waited for him to touch her—with his hands, his mouth, with whatever he would, but he did not. Instead, he waited until the water tippled over the pink crest before expertly sipping the glistening drop between his lips. The only contact was the barest hint of his hot breath against her skin.

"Saint," she whimpered, her hands fisting in the folds of her skirt. *"Please."*

He grinned then, and saluted her with his glass. "Good day, Miss Farrington. Do enjoy the weather."

"Saint," she cried, reaching for him, but it was too late. He'd already slipped away, into the shrubbery of Lady Carmichael's garden.

"Miss Farrington?"

With a silent oath, Lily struggled to put herself back together, furiously trying to shove her breast back into her bodice. Thankfully, she had regained some of her composure, and corrected her dishabille before meeting the friendly smile of Jared Ponsonby.

"Are you well, Miss Farrington? You're looking rather flushed."

"Indeed," Lily huffed, struggling to breath, fighting for control over her trembling and needy body. "I was just a trifle overheated, Mr. Ponsonby."

"Then let us get you something in which to cool you down, Miss Farrington."

Jared offered her his arm, but before she took it, she chanced a quick glance over her shoulder and met Saint's wicked blue gaze. With a roguish grin, he slipped what was left of the ice into his mouth and winked at her, sending her thoughts flying and her heart hammering out of control.

Damian watched as Lily strolled arm in arm with Jared Ponsonby. For some inexplicable reason the sight angered him—more than angered, really. It actually made him feel violent, in a frightening, possessive, consuming sort of way. He'd felt jealousy before when he'd seen some of the village pups and local landowner's sons pay her court, but he'd dismissed the notion, vowing it was his pride that was pricked, nothing more.

While he had given her wide berth to go her own way, he had taken meticulous steps to keep himself informed—at all times of Lily Farrington's activities and suitors. He'd vowed to himself that he would step in if the need ever arose. It really had been an unnecessary promise, for she'd relegated all the others to hell, along with him.

But there was something about the way she walked beside Ponsonby that set off the alarms in his head. The predator in him stirred, began to stretch, to smell the hint of danger. There was something between them, a comfortable closeness that he felt deep in his gut. He didn't like how Lily smiled at the bastard, and liked the way Ponsonby looked at her even less.

Chilling fear once again gripped him, the feeling unpleasant, reminding him of the hell he'd suffered when he lost her the first time. He'd made a hash out of it. In his inexperienced youth, he'd tossed away the one relationship, the one person whom he'd truly loved. She had allowed the vicar to turn her away from him, then catching him with Molly had ended their relationship.

A part of him had been destroyed when she'd left him to live with her aunt. After she'd run from him he'd forced himself to stay away from her. For seven years he'd sought solace with other women, attempting to purge her from his mind—all to no avail. He had still been so desperate for her and yet, she'd barely spoken with him, hadn't even glanced his way in the ensuing years. He'd been the one pining away for her, gazing at her like a simpleton. He'd taken legions of women to his bed, all of them beautiful, all of them clamoring for his attention and his cock, and he hadn't been able to get her out of his mind, his heart—his bloody soul.

And that was the damnable reason for the knife-like fear gripping his insides. He wouldn't lose her again. Not to Ponsonby, or anyone. Lily Farrington was going to be his. She belonged to him since he'd been twenty, hell, much longer than that if he were honest. There had been no other in his life that made him feel, that made him care. It had only ever been Lily he loved. Only Lily he could envision as the Countess of St. Croix. This time he would succeed. The predator in him was too hungry, too needy to let her slip through his fingers. And if his 'lessons' went according to plan, Lily's own hunger would keep her bound to him. Forever.

Chapter Six

Lily searched the star-lit sky and sighed, delighting in the fragrant air around her. Surrounding her was the village green, its paths lit with flickering lanterns, the heat from the candles sending up the aromatic and pungent scent of rosemary, lavender and catmint. The hum of anticipation pulsed through the air, sending currents of excitement through her. Before her stood the limestone building of St. Charles the Martyr church, its arched door decorated with flowers and garland bows, as couples, dressed in their finery, languished on the steps, waiting for the outdoor musicale to begin.

It was a yearly event for the church's choir and musicians to play in the night air. All of Tunbridge Wells society, and even those adventurous patrons from London turned out to listen to the beautiful sounds of the choir. Lily sighed again, anxious for the festivities to begin. It was nearly nine o'clock, and at last the moon had appeared, bringing with it a smattering of twinkling stars.

"You're impatient, my dear," Jared teased, passing her a champagne flute from a servant's tray. "You've been a jittery, twittery mess since we arrived."

Lily grinned at Jared's teasing rebuke. "I'm quite certain, sir, that I'm not a twittery mess."

"Well, perhaps not twittery, but certainly out of sorts."

Lily kept her smiled composed, refusing to let Jared know that inside she was nothing but a mass of nerves. She didn't want him to think it had anything to do with the fact that he had hinted at marriage that very afternoon, during the serving of Lady Carmichael's famed plum cake, nor did she want him to suspect the true reasons behind her flightiness—her secret meetings with the notorious and very bad Earl of St. Croix.

Jared Ponsonby really was a nice man. A large estate owner and widower these past five years, Jared had made it clear that he was in search of a wife and a surrogate mother to his six-year-old daughter. Lily liked little Allison, and she liked Jared, too. She took pleasure in visiting Ashcroft, Jared's manor which lay only minutes from her own home. She enjoyed the games of backgammon and chess that they shared. Jared would make an infinitely suitable husband. Both kind and handsome, the type of man who would make many a female heart flutter. Unfortunately, Jared and his suggestion that they might suit did nothing to make her heart beat with longing. It hadn't come as a complete shock to hear him give voice to his desire for their union, but perhaps she wouldn't have been as unsettled to hear it, if not a rogue with beautiful blue eyes and brilliant black hair hadn't returned to the village, tempting her with his wickedness.

She had been tempted last night by Saint, but with the dawn her reasoning returned. She could not risk her heart again. She would not marry Jared, or any other man, and she most certainly would not fall in love with the Earl of St. Croix.

"Should we not find ourselves a seat, my dear?" Jared asked, offering her his arm. They strolled through the crowds, casually picking their way through people in order to make their way to where a great many chairs had been set up. Noticing a patch of grass where a number of couples had settled themselves on blankets, Lily allowed Jared to steer her over and help her to sit on the rugs that Jared's servant had placed on the ground only seconds before.

"Thank you," she murmured, arranging her skirts and carefully tucking them beneath her shoes so that not even a glimpse of her sheer stockings were evident. "You seem to have thought of everything this evening."

"Of course," he smiled, patting her hand. "It is a gentleman's duty to see to the needs of his lady. My man should be returning any moment now with a basket of delicacies and champagne."

She smiled and gazed at Jared's hand lying atop hers. In an instant, the vision of Saint's beautiful fingers on hers sliced through her mind. She remembered how they looked, bronzed and elegant, twining with hers, resting teasingly against her sex.

"Lily," Jared said, reaching for her hand, and bringing it to his lips, the same hand that she had used to pleasure herself, the same hand that Saint had held in his as he coaxed her into temptation. "Have I told you how lovely you look tonight?"

"Thank you," she said shyly, trying to cover how uncomfortable she felt under Jared's close appraisal.

"Have you had a chance to think on my offer, my dear?"

"I…I…" Lily licked her lips nervously and fought to find the words to soften the blow of her refusal.

"Take your time, Lily. I only thought that you might have arrived at your answer." He kissed her knuckles and peered into her eyes. "I will not press you."

A shiver raced down her spine, and Lily was unable to hide it. It wasn't elicited from the touch of Jared's hand, or his lips upon her skin, or the strained conversation they were now having, but rather something different. Something that compelled her to search over Jared's shoulder, to the group of oak trees that flanked the makeshift stage. And then she saw him. Leaning negligently against the tree, his feet crossed, a glass of champagne dangling from his fingers. Their eyes met, the heat from his met hers filling her veins with a sensual warmth. He looked dangerous, she thought with a slight gasp as he arched one brow. There was something about him that she'd never seen before. Something dark, almost brooding.

"Lily?" Jared asked, sensing her discomfort. "Are you well?"

"Fine," she smiled vacantly, struggling to break Saint's hypnotic gaze. She was relieved when the violinist put his bow to the strings, striking a sorrowful note into the air. It was a reprieve from Jared's probing questions, but it did not relieve her from feeling Saint's questioning gaze. She could still feel his eyes on her, burning through her. She knew when his gaze settled on her breasts; her nipples tingled and tightened against her embroidered silk bodice. Liquid warmth flooded her thighs and she knew then that the rogue was scouring every inch of her. Lily swallowed hard, forcing her eyes not to stray to him.

She knew when he left. A keen sense of emptiness invaded her, making her yearn, making her feel hungry and restless. She was utterly confused by her reaction to the man. She should not feel anything of the kind for the rogue and yet she couldn't help herself. Her emotions were a tempest swirling inside her.

"Perhaps I should fetch the champagne myself. You look much too flushed."

"Please," Lily whispered, grateful for a few minutes alone with her thoughts and free of Jared's perceptive gaze. Stretching back, Lily leaned on her wrists, trying to cool her heated flesh that seemed to come alive whenever Saint looked upon her. She forced her breathing to slow, trying to put the anticipation—the excitement of the upcoming hours with Saint out of her mind. She was just feeling composed when something sharp hit her hand. Glancing back over her shoulder, she saw a folded piece of paper, its crisp fold poking into her skin. With a rush of excitement, she opened the missive and stared at the evocative command.

By midnight. Hair down, no chemise, and his scent washed from you.

Her head came up, and Lily met the penetrating gaze of Saint across the lawn. With a haughty lift of his brow, he raised his champagne flute to her, mouthing the word *tonight* before disappearing behind the tree.

"I see you finally extricated yourself from Ponsonby's side."

Lily jumped at the sound of the deep growl behind her. Whirling around, she found Saint sprawled on the day bed, naked to the waist. The top button of his fall front trousers lay open, revealing a dark, silky line of hair that disappeared below his waistband. He looked at her, his glittering gaze dark and brooding—almost threatening in its intensity. "You're late," he stated, before tossing the book he'd been reading onto the stone flags. "It's well past midnight."

"I had to wait for Aunt Millie to retire." she mumbled, shutting the door of the Temple behind her.

"Can't have your auntie know what you're about, hmm? She would no doubt have a fit of apoplexy if she were to discover that her pure and virginal niece was sneaking about in the middle of the night in order to meet with the wicked Earl of St. Croix."

"You're in a difficult mood this evening."

"And you're in a precarious situation, my dear. You forget that I command you. I specifically told you in my missive to be here by midnight."

"You would have me drop everything in order to meet you? To not have a care for my own reputation? A reputation you nearly destroyed."

His eyes narrowed, and the muscles of his hard chest flickered beneath bronze skin. She was provoking him, and Lily felt satisfied in the knowledge. He was being unnecessarily high-handed and she would not stand for it. "You seem to forget, my dear, that you are in my debt."

"I'm here, am I not? I have not forgotten my end of this agreement."

"So, you've come here tonight to be ravished, have you? To let the wicked Earl of St. Croix have his way with you?"

His soft but dark tone thrilled her as much as his words did. There was something about the idea of Saint ravishing her that made her skin tingle and her pulse quicken. Despite her best attempts to forget, her hunger for him had only increased. Even his black mood wasn't enough to dampen her spirits. It intrigued her, made her wonder at the reason behind it. There was something very dark about him, yet it called to her, and the dangerous aura radiating from him excited her.

"Take off your cloak."

With wary eyes, Lily watched him put his arms behind his head. The effect made his sculpted chest flare at the sides, showing her the feathering muscles of his ribs, and the taut strength of his belly. He studied her, his insolent gaze penetrating—exposing her as if he could see straight through her cloak.

She undid the gold clasp, letting the black velvet slide off her shoulders, pooling to the floor. She smiled when his eyes widened and his breath hitched. Giddy elation swept through her as he looked her over, his experienced eyes scouring her from head to toe, satisfaction flickering in his gaze.

"Very nice," he growled appreciatively, yet he did not so much as flick one muscle in response. "Whatever possessed you to play the wanton for me, my sweet?"

"You said no chemise." Suddenly she felt shy and insecure. She thought to be daring, thought to tempt him as he tempted her. That's why she'd worn her French dressing gown that covered her bottom by scant inches and her breasts hardly at all. She'd bought it years ago in London when she and Penelope were shopping for Penelope's trousseau. The pale pink hue and the sheer softness of the silk had captivated her, and the silver filigree lace had conjured up visions of Saint's hands tracing the intricate swirls.

"I see you wore your hair down," he grinned, his cobalt eyes assessing her once more. "Push your hair back, Lily. It's hiding your lovely breasts."

She obeyed him, feeling some satisfaction when his manhood thickened further beneath his trousers.

"And my last request? Did you honor that as well?"

"He has not touched me."

He quirked a brow before motioning her to him. She stood beside the bed, her breasts rising and falling much too rapidly, making the lace rub abrasively against her already aching nipples. "I'll ask you once more, my sweet. Did you wash his touch from you?"

Lily shivered as Saint reached out and trailed one long finger down her throat, and between her breasts, stopping when he reached her navel. Their eyes met and held, and Lily swore she saw something like apprehension flicker in his gaze, but he masked it before she had a chance to interpret what it meant.

"You belong to me, Lily,"

"For three nights," she reminded him. Her legs trembled, and she feared she might disgrace herself when his thumb rested in her curls. The thin silk of her gown was no barrier against the sensual heat of Saint's touch.

"You're an impudent little baggage, do you know that? I'm afraid I'm going to have to put that saucy mouth of yours to good use, Lily."

Blood rushed to her skin, making her flush. She liked his words, the boldness of them, the assurance, the mastery she heard in his voice. But she tempered her excitement. This was simply a bargain to him. She meant nothing to him. She was just a body to slake his needs.

"Tonight's lesson is about giving and taking." He reached out then, capturing her wrist in his hand and bringing her down to straddle him. She gasped at the intimacy of it, at the strange feeling of Saint's muscular thighs beneath her bottom, the hardness of his erection as it throbbed and stirred atop her curls. The feeling was vivid, intimate despite the barrier of his wool trousers.

"Tonight, Lily," he grinned, gliding his hands up her sides till they reached just below her breasts. "You're going to be doing all the giving, and I'll be taking. Do you understand?"

She nodded, losing her inner battle to stay cool and aloof. Instead, she allowed herself to melt in the heated desire of his eyes.

"I'm taking everything you'll give me, Lily. Then more."

She gasped as he clasped his hand behind her head, bringing her mouth to his. She'd been prepared to be devoured, but Saint surprised her with his gentleness. Instead of demanding her tongue, commanding her to kiss him, he coaxed her, teased her into submissiveness until she was the one to seek entrance into his mouth. Their tongues touched, gently at first, then Saint growled low in his throat and threading his fingers into her unbound hair, he ravished her, biting and licking, stroking and sucking. When he finally released her mouth, she was panting, her hands curling into the silky hair of his chest, reveling in the feel of hard muscle beneath her fingers.

"You're an apt pupil, Lily Farrington," he said, playfully slapping her bottom before sliding her silk gown up her body and over her head. "Let us see just how adept you are at pleasing a man."

Chapter Seven

Damian couldn't help but growl when he felt Lily's beautiful tits graze his chin. He was delighting in stroking the vein of her neck with his tongue and she was delighting in torturing him with her pert nipples, teasing him into suckling her. But he would resist. He would ignore the predator within that was clamoring to devour the delightful morsel in his arms.

It wasn't enough to fling her onto her back and imbed himself within her. It might have satisfied his craving if she'd been one of the courtesans or opera dancers he frequented. But this was Lily—the woman he wanted above all others, the woman he had taken elaborate steps in order to seduce.

He wanted to awaken her, to make her mindless with need, to slowly satisfy her. He didn't want their first time to be a quick rut, and by the way his cock was swelling and filling, he knew it would be too quick. No, he wanted the re-awakening of Lily to be slow and sensual. He wanted to feel her tight against him, then slowly stretch to accommodate him. Unfortunately, if she didn't quit writhing in his arms, brushing her tits against his face and rubbing her mound against his trousers, he was going to grab her hips and take her in an act of raw possession.

The vision took hold, and in an impulsive but highly satisfying act, he took her breasts in his hands, pushing them together and burying his face between them, inhaling the sweet and innocent floral scent of her, his thumbs coaxing her nipples to harden further for him.

"Saint."

The sound was a guttural cry from deep in her throat. The need, the desire he heard pushed him on. He squeezed, then tugged and pinched at her nipples, while his mouth continued to suck the milky flesh of her breasts. Her fingers were on his shoulders, tightening, as he took one straining nipple into his mouth, slipping it between his lips before suckling, pulling the flesh into his mouth, drinking in her passion with increasing need. She moaned while he sucked, his other hand kneaded a path down to her belly.

She arched beautifully into his mouth as he increased his suckling, his tongue flicking out to soothe and lave the reddened nipple. When he grasped it between his teeth and gently bit, she shivered, her stomach quivering beneath his fingers. He never felt that before, the quivering of a woman as desire and need swept through her. He'd been aware of the need in his conquests from the tightening of their breasts, the scent and wetness of their arousal, but he'd never taken the time to study them, to run his fingers along their bodies and discover where else they might feel desire.

"Oh God, Saint," Lily moaned, unable to stem the shaking of her limbs as his fingers swept over her belly and along her sides. If he would only touch her *there*. If she could just feel his fingers buried deep within her she could be rid of this escalating desire, a pleasure almost painful in its intensity.

Gooseflesh flickered down her spine and along her bottom as Saint's wickedly sensual fingers swept down her back, tickling her buttocks and trailing down the back of her thighs. Unable to control the need, refusing to wait, Lily tore the last of the buttons from Saint's trousers and freed him into her hand.

"An apt pupil," he growled before clasping her breast in his hand and teasing his lips with her erect nipple. "That's it, Lily. Stroke me. You haven't forgotten, have you? You haven't forgotten what to do with my cock."

No, she hadn't forgotten what Saint's manhood felt like in her hand. He was still as soft as velvet, the tip as fine as any French silk, but he was larger, so much harder then he'd been when they had shared their illicit sessions of discovery.

"You feel so big," she purred, delighting in the wetness that seeped out of her folds. She liked his words, the baseness of him. It reminded her of the illicitness of what they were doing. She swirled the drop of fluid around the tip and along the ridge of his penis, doing it again as he groaned appreciatively against her breast.

"I taught you well, didn't I? Very well, indeed."

"Touch me, Saint…like before," she whispered, frantic to feel his fingers in her wetness.

"I'm not sure what you mean." He brought her breasts together again, his eyes challenging her, daring her to say the words.

"Saint, please," she whimpered, silently telling him by rubbing her wet curls against him. "You know where."

"That was long ago, Lily. And I touched you in many places."

"*There*," she cried, tightening her hand against him.

"Tell me."

She groaned, shutting her eyes, refusing to look at his eyes which were shining and seductive as he teased her. She didn't want to show him her desire, but she was so needy for him. Never had she felt so empty without his hands on her.

"Lily?" She opened her eyes and met his. "Ask me."

"Please?"

"No. That's begging. Ask me. Say, 'Saint, will you feel me? Will you bury your fingers in me?'"

"No," she cried, aghast at the thought and embarrassed by her arousal at his words.

"Give me the words, and I'll give you what you want."

He tickled her then, his fingers slowly grazing the top of her mound, his fingers curling in her hair, tempting her, making her wish to beg for his touch. She remembered how his fingers had felt on her. Remembered those days, hidden on the hill and the words he'd whispered in hair, the way he'd teased her, then satisfied her.

"The words, Lily. Give me what I want."

"Stroke me."

"Even better," he growled.

Lily felt the warmth pool inside her as Saint slid one finger along her wetness. He parted her, slipping one finger, then another deep inside her. Her thighs quivered and she trembled at his touch, whimpered in embarrassment over her common talk and the way she melted around him.

"Do you know what you do to me?" Saint asked, meeting her eyes through the fringe of his sable lashes. "So pure and innocent to look at, but I get one hand on you and you're wanton and hot. You're every man's fantasy, Lily."

"Every man's?"

"Yes," he groaned, probing her deeper. "Including mine. Now, come for me, Lily. It's been too long since I had you, since I felt you on my hand."

Jesus, it wasn't supposed to be happening this way. Damian tried to think through the thick cloud of lust. Her deflowering was supposed to be gentle, romantic, soft as a dove's feather. He was supposed to take her into the bath, kiss her, stroke her, murmur words of love before laying her on the bed and slowly, carefully sliding inside her. It damn well wasn't part of his plan to have her straddling him, his cock in her hand, poised at her entrance, her tits bobbing in his mouth, and base words being uttered between the two of them.

Dammit, if she wouldn't have presented herself to him in that scandalous gown he might have had a fighting chance. But the minute she dropped her cloak revealing large breasts that were barely concealed by the bodice, and a hem, if it could be called such, which just barely concealed her mound; he'd been well on his way. On his way to taking, consuming and going off far too early for either his or her pleasure.

"Mmm, Saint," she purred against him, her lips pouting in ecstasy, her fingers running wildly through his hair, her hips moving up and down to the rhythm of his fingers. "This feels so good. So right," she sighed.

He looked at her and wondered how he'd endured the many years spent apart from her. How had he been content with his dreams, with imagining her face on the women he bedded? And the answer hit him as she tossed her head back on a silent cry, her body tightening around his fingers as her arousal engulfed him. He hadn't been content. He'd always been restless. Waiting, searching for the opportunity to make her his. And this was it. He had only to slide himself into her quivering sheath and she would be his.

But he didn't want to take her like this. He didn't know what the hell he wanted. He wanted her to ride him. He wanted to watch her bend before him as he slid into her in an act of raw possession. He wanted to make love to her, watching the wonder in her eyes. He wanted to hear her guttural cries of release when he thrust himself into her, making her realize that she was his, and only his.

Slow and loving. Hard and needy. He wanted it all, everything she would give him. Hell, he hadn't shown her a fraction of what he wanted. He'd planned to lick her, to pleasure her with his mouth, and taste her as he made her come. He wanted to watch her learn him, to see her luscious mouth around his cock before he claimed her body. And yet, he could think of nothing more than making her his before anything could happen to stop it.

"Saint," she cried, surprised to find herself on her back with him bent between her legs.

"I told you that I'd make you mine."

"Yes, I know."

"You understand what that will mean, don't you, Lily?'

"That I will no longer be a virgin."

"No, that you will belong to me. Only me."

Lily gasped, then moaned, feeling the unforgiving hardness of Saint slide into her body. Slowly, inexorably penetrating her. His breathing was harsh, short pants, almost groans escaping his lips as he filled her.

"Jesus, you're tight. So wonderfully snug."

"You feel," Lily squirmed beneath his weight, delighting in his husky moan. "You feel rather large." She skimmed her hands over Saint's muscled back and down to his bottom which was rock hard between her thighs. Instinctively she put her legs around his waist, letting him go deeper, penetrating her further.

"Beautiful," he whispered, straightening from her, cupping her bottom in his hands while his gaze focused on where their bodies were joined. He stroked her a few times, letting her stretch, letting her grow wetter around him, all the while watching as he filled her.

"Lily?" he asked, his voice hoarse, every muscle in his chest and arms taut with tension and virile strength. "I want you to look at me as I make you mine."

She met his gaze, her heart skipping a beat. His eyes were a deep dark blue, and his lips were furled in a devastating grin. With one quick, deep thrust he impaled her, quickly moaning then covering her with his body, slowly moving, allowing her to accustom herself to his size and the feel of him atop her.

The pain wasn't as bad as she feared. It was a brief pinching, burning sensation that quickly gave way to a delicious feeling of being consumed by Saint.

"Move with me," he encouraged, taking her hands in his and raising them above her head so that he covered the whole length of her body, his chest rubbing against her breasts, the silky hairs covering her nipples, tickling and sensitizing them. The bed creaked, and Saint's breathing became sharper, harsher than she'd ever heard. With every stroke he thrust deeper inside her, making her moan as she matched his rhythm. Suddenly his body shook and he cried out her name before shuddering atop her.

"Just give me a few minutes," he breathed against her throat. "I'll make it better for you."

"Saint," she murmured, snuggling against him, threading her fingers in and out of his hair. "That was wonderful."

He raised his head and looked down at her. "It was?"

"It was."

"Well, then," he smiled, "wait till I have you again. If you think this was good, the next time will have you begging."

"You had me begging this time," she whispered against his lips.

He tilted her chin with his finger and met her eyes. "Not nearly enough, Lily."

✽≋⊱✬⊰≋✽

Saint stirred in bed, smiling when he felt the soft, warm body of Lily pressed tightly against him. The candles had burned low, and the tick of the mantel clock reminded him that he'd fallen asleep. Damn, he'd never been so satiated that he'd fallen asleep after the first round. But he had with Lily. The thought made him grin. Lily the virgin had sapped him so completely that he'd fallen asleep like a babe in her arms. He hoped he at least had the decency to slide into the abyss after sleep had claimed the innocent lying next to him.

Stretching his legs, he yawned, raking a hand through his hair. How long had he slept? Glancing at the clock, he saw that it was nearly three in the morning. Plenty of time left, he mused, brushing an errant curl from Lily's alabaster cheek. A fierce possessiveness stole over him as he watched her sleeping. She was his, now. In every sense of the word. Whatever Ponsonby meant to her, she hadn't given him her virginity. No, she'd given that to him.

He smiled as she snuggled closer to him, pressing her full breasts against him. He immediately grew hard, his damnable cock searching blindly beneath the covers for Lily's softness. With a muffled oath, he slipped from beneath the coverlet and stared down at Lily. He wanted her again, but he knew that it was likely too soon for her.

With a frustrated sigh, he covered her up and strolled over to the bath. That's what he needed, the heat of the water to soothe his need and clear his head. In the heady steam of the mineral water he could close his eyes and contemplate where this night's business had got him.

Plunging into the depths, he came up for air, shaking his hair and wiping the water from his eyes. He waded over to the wooden plank he had installed against the stone, and sat upon it, luxuriating in the heat and the meditative ambiance of the room. His thoughts strayed to Lily and what they had shared. She'd given him what no other man would ever possess—her virginity.

Why had she never married? She was beautiful and desirable. Her family was well connected and wealthy. Hell, he'd heard more than one rake making plans to marry her, and yet she had spurned all of them. The only man she had ever shared time with was Ponsonby. What did Ponsonby mean to her? And if the bastard meant anything to her, what were her reasons for agreeing to this outrageous bargain?

How long he had sat there, he didn't know, but the unmistakable feeling of Lily's eyes on his flesh awakened him from his contemplation.

"How long have you been awake?"

"Not long."

"Care to join me?"

With a shy smile, she drew the blanket around her and walked towards him, the crimson silk covering her from her throat to her toes.

"I have a very vivid memory, you know. It supplies me with every little detail of your body. You needn't hide it from me."

"Oh," she murmured, staring at her toes.

"Come," he whispered, smiling as she reluctantly lowered the coverlet. He helped her into the water, and unable to stop himself, he brought her to his chest, hugging and holding her. He closed his eyes. How good it felt to simply hold her in his arms.

"Saint," she said against his neck.

"Mmm," he replied, kissing her throat while he brought her legs around his waist.

"I should be going."

"It's not dawn yet."

"But my father—"

"Will be stumbling in drunker than a sailor. He won't know if you're in bed or not."

"Aunt Millie—"

"Imbibed at least three glasses of sherry before retiring. Isn't that so?"

"Saint—"

"Kiss me," he mumbled, hating the need he heard in his voice. Did Lily hear it also? Did she know what she did to him, what thoughts coursed through his brain?

She met his mouth, her tongue tracing the outline of his lower lip before sliding slowly, evocatively inside. It was a tender kiss, the type of kiss that lovers used to arouse and lull. Her hands found a way into his hair, weaving in and out in soothing strokes. His fingers trailed down her spine and along her legs, as their mouths slanted over each other in a slow, trancelike motion.

He groaned when she brushed against his swelling cock. He wanted her again, more desperately then he had earlier, if it was at all possible. He would not allow himself to take her, he reminded himself as his cock stirred against her soft belly. What honor he had left would not allow him to take her twice in the same night she'd relinquished her virginity.

"Saint," she purred against him, her fingers deftly finding him beneath the water and stroking him into pained arousal.

"You're too tender."

"I feel rather fit," she smiled into his neck. "Don't I?"

She felt a damn bit more than 'fit' and a sight more then 'all right'. She was perfect, and his need for her was consuming him, making him forget that with her he wanted to be a gentleman. He had been one once, a long time ago, before he'd betrayed her with his raging lust and deceitful cock. Seven years ago he'd played by society's rules and did the pretty as the *ton* dictated. But after Lily had left him, he'd turned to avarice, submerging himself in vice. Soon he was as dissipated as any old roué. He despised how he lived his life. He hated the fact that he had been too much of a coward to right the wrong he'd done to Lily. Hated standing on the edge of the ballroom watching her being wooed by proper young men. Seven years ago no one in Tunbridge Wells would have batted an eye at seeing them together. They'd been raised as babes in arms, their mothers the very best of friends. Now, if he were to be seen in her company he'd bring nothing but speculation upon her. He'd tarnish her good name, and he had no wish to harm her further. And that was why all these years he had carefully hidden himself amongst the crowds, watching as she danced beautifully and smiled cheerfully at her suitors, a small piece of him dying every time he saw her in another's arms.

"Lily, do you need release, my sweet?" he asked, feeling her hand tighten on him, her hips gliding against his in the water . "I can give you what you want, you know." He could give her pleasure, but would she allow him any other favors? Would she let him into her heart?

"Open for me," he commanded as he lifted her out of the bath and sat her on the cool, wet stones.

"Saint," she cried as he raised her knees, then pulled them apart, exposing her slick wetness. He looked up at her then, her eyes wide and luminous in the dim candlelight, the bath water running in rivulets down her throat and breasts, teetering on her hard nipples only to trickle along her belly.

"I want to taste you, Lily."

She moaned then clasped her hand to his head as he set her lips to her, kissing the swollen folds before parting her with his thumbs and running the flat of his tongue up the length of her.

"Saint, this is so very wicked."

Flicking his tongue up to the nubbin of flesh, Damian looked up at her, her eyes squeezed tightly shut. "Does it give you pleasure, Lily?"

"Y...yes." She thrust her hips toward him. He rewarded her with a stroke of his finger along her wetness before circling her once more.

"Then it is not wicked. Enjoy it, Lily. Learn to take pleasure in pleasure given. And I would have you know, I freely give you this pleasure."

She tilted her head and rested it against her shoulder, her hair shielding her face, hiding her expression from him. He wanted her to watch him loving her but he knew that lesson would come tomorrow night. For now, he contented himself with laving her with his tongue, tasting the musky scent of her, watching as she swelled and glistened beneath his mouth.

Lily thought she was surely going to die from pleasure. Saint was slowly building her up where she was in reach of finding fulfillment before sliding his mouth down, nuzzling her entrance with his tongue and finger, only to flick his way up again to the magic spot at the crest of her mound. She moaned as he retreated from her for the third time, leaving her panting and wanting and searching for release.

"Why are you rushing this?" he whispered against her thigh, teasing her by tracing her opening with one long wet finger. "We have hours yet till dawn."

"I can't wait."

"Ah." She refused to look at him, but she knew he would be grinning. She refused to see the wickedness of his black head, his hair wet and clinging to his neck as he buried his mouth inside her. It was beyond wanton, even more than sinful. Good God, what sort of person had she become to be enjoying such lasciviousness? He was actually pleasuring her with his mouth down *there*.

And then he began to lick her in earnest, his tongue moving firmer, faster than it had before. When she feared he would pull away, she clasped his hair, wet and silky beneath her fingers and held him to her, forcing him not to pull away, leaving her unfulfilled.

"That's it. Just let it come over you, Lily."

And it did. Wave after wave of pleasure. She felt as if she were floating, disembodied and weightless. She caught a glimpse of Saint between her thighs, watching her, and she watched him, his tongue moving slowly, seductively along her as her body shook. The sight of him pleasuring her pushed her over the edge. She felt the rush of liquid between her thighs and fought to pull away from him but he held her still, his hands planted firmly along her hips as he drank all the pleasure from her body.

She was just returning to earth when he pulled her into the water, resting her against his chest, holding her until the last of the pleasure left her body, and she began to drift into a satiated sleep.

"Lily," he murmured, stroking her back and kissing her temple. "You still haven't sufficiently begged me, you know."

"I know," she sighed, snuggling closer to him, squeezing him to her. "I will, Saint."

"Yes, you will," he vowed. "And I shall take great pleasure in it."

Chapter Eight

Palming his cock, Damian lounged against the pillows of his daybed and watched his fingers curl around his thick shaft. He'd come three times last night. He should have been more then satiated, hell, he should be drained, but he couldn't get the vision of Lily on her knees, his thighs caging her, his voice, hard and encouraging, instructing her how to suck him.

He groaned, feeling himself thicken and giving into temptation and natural inclination, he slowly pumped himself, reliving the vision of Lily, his hand holding her hair back, watching her take his cock into her mouth.

'Like this?' she'd asked, looking up at him with her luminous blue eyes, the swollen cap of his shaft rubbing against her lips. *'Yes,'* he'd said, holding his cock so it was erect, directly touching her lips. *'Open your mouth, Lily, and take all of me.'*

Lust, white and hot coursed through him as he recalled the vision of his hands in her hair, guiding her head down to him. He felt the burning heat of her wet mouth engulf him, sucking on him, torturing him in her untutored exuberance as he watched her. He had let her pleasure him for what seemed liked forever. Her touch was gentle, the flicks of her tongue exciting him as he watched the pinkness of it glistening against his flushed cock. He'd studied her body, glowing alabaster in the firelight, and grew harder as her lush tits swayed with her movements. He hadn't been able to stop himself from running his hand along them, groaning and throbbing as they swayed faster, making him think of the way they could capture his cock, and the way he could release himself on them, branding them, and her as his own.

His own hand began to pump furiously with the surging heat in his blood. How damn beautiful she had looked bent before him with his cock in her mouth. He remembered tracing the outline of it along her cheek, as it filled her mouth, feeling supreme satisfaction. It had been powerful and exciting, the best he'd ever had. She had made him lose all reason, blind to any thought other than pleasure and fulfillment. Surely that had been the reason he'd pulled out of her mouth only to splash his seed along her breasts, watching and glorying in it. Her eyes had been wide with wonder, and he thought his climax would never end, or that he wouldn't be able to stop coming all over her lush tits.

Release came fast and quick as he recalled the way she had looked, at the way he'd branded her. Spilling himself into the sheet, Damian let himself sink back into slumber.

He was in love. There was no other reason for it, this cursed lust, this inability to quench his thirst for Lily Farrington. He loved her, just as he had the summer he'd been twenty. And she was his. He smiled into the pillow. He'd taken her, marked her with his own essence. Yes, she belonged to him, just as he had always belonged to her.

�֎℈⟲℈֎

Shielding her eyes from the bright afternoon sun, Lily peered up at the hanging sign. "Shall we go into Mr. Trent's, Penelope?"

"Oh," Penelope exclaimed, pointing to a rose colored damask. "This would be perfect for a gown for the baby's christening."

Lily's eyes dropped to the softly curved mound of her friend's belly. Her covetous eyes scoured her friend's figure, envying the fact that Penelope was with child. At twenty-four, Lily had thought her dreams for a husband and child were long forgotten, shattered when she'd witnessed Saint's unfaithfulness, but it seemed the hope had not dissipated.

She had thought of nothing else as she traveled home in the silent dawn after leaving a slumbering Saint at the Temple. Her quiet ways and days filled with solitude no longer comforted her as they once did. Since agreeing to Saint's bargain she hadn't been the same. She felt restless—empty. The hours away from Saint had been filled with visions of her ensconced in his home as his countess, heavy with his babe. She imagined passing her days with him in much the same fashion as they had as children. Riding and playing games, carriage rides into the villages and surrounding countryside. And their nights would be filled with the same exquisite pleasures he'd introduced her to these past nights .

The daydreams had been idyllic, juvenile almost, for the Saint she had known no longer existed. The Saint she'd given her heart to would never have betrayed her. And yet, she had glimpsed some of the old Saint last night, in the way he held her and soothed her. The way he'd seen to her comfort.

It was all an act, Lily told herself. It was the rogue's way of getting what he wanted from her. She knew Saint's true goal was not to take his pleasure from her, but for her to willingly give it to him. She had bargained with him, after all. Her body for his pleasure in return for the sparing of Penelope's husband's life.

"Well," Penelope asked, her hazel eyes peeking out from behind her bonnet. "Shall we go in?"

"Of course," Lily said, refusing to contemplate the matter of Saint any further. It simply did not signify what he wanted from her. Their bargain stipulated three nights, and three nights he would have. What should it matter that the rogue would turn her loose after tonight? Why should she care? She'd known that would happen when she'd accepted his offer. And he won't have a care for her, she thought as she followed Penelope. He hadn't even cared enough to employ precautions in preventing a babe. The daydream of carrying Saint's son or daughter quickly died when she realized the shame that would befall her and the child.

Lily stepped into the shop. There was only one thing to be done. She must not submit her heart to him. Tonight it had to be the joining of bodies, nothing more. She couldn't allow it to be more. She had to find a way to protect her heart and her soul. She would give him her body, but never her love. Giving her love to Saint was a luxury she couldn't afford.

Penelope immediately demanded Mr. Trent's attention, discussing the price and other estimable qualities of the rose damask. Trying to push thoughts of Saint aside, Lily contented herself with studying a bolt of cream silk.

"Good morning, beautiful."

She straightened, her spine snapping to attention. She knew that voice, surely as she knew her own. To her chagrin, she realized her body knew it too. Already her skin was heating, flushing with blood, liquefying in all the places that made her long for him.

"You left my bed before I awoke," he murmured in her ear while his hand carefully and discreetly touched her gloved fingers. "I wanted to tell you how much you pleased me last night."

Schooling her features into a mask of restraint, Lily fought the urge to meet his cobalt gaze. She couldn't look into those eyes and not melt. She didn't want to see him in the daytime and be reminded of the fact that his interest in her was nothing short of carnal.

"Good afternoon, Lord St. Croix"

She felt him stiffen beside her.

"Lord St. Croix is rather formal considering what we did to each other, wouldn't you agree?"

Her stomach clenched as she recalled just how informal she had been with him. She would pay for her exuberance; despite her brave plans, her heart would pay the price. It was impossible to stand beside him and not feel the traitorous organ begin to bleed. She wanted so much more than to be another conquest for Saint. She wanted a respectable life with him, wanted his love, but Saint offered only illicit pleasure.

Mr. Trent glanced over his shoulder and peered at them with poorly concealed interest. Not wanting the draper to think anything other than their meeting was by sheerest chance, she started to move away from Saint. Cool and distant, that is the way she needed to be. Behind her mask of aloofness, Saint would never learn of her foolish dreams or how difficult it was to face the truth of their bargain in the light of day.

"Look at me," Saint demanded, his breath blowing the errant curls escaping her bonnet along her neck, making her shiver.

She couldn't look at him and stay indifferent. Even his voice was wreaking havoc with her self-control. Her heart squeezed painfully in her chest, her eyes burned with tears she would never shed before him. She refused to let him glimpse her pain or learn that she desired more than stolen evenings with Saint. She wanted a life with him. A life of love and passion and daytime duties that married couples shared together. But Saint hadn't offered what she wanted.

"Why are you doing this?" His finger tightened against hers, forcing her to look at him. She saw Penelope send her a questioning glance before turning to Mr. Trent in an attempt to draw his attention away from her and Saint. "Dammit Lily, why are you being so cold?"

Because I must. Because if I don't, I'll find myself suffering from the loss of you for the rest of my life and that is a pain I cannot bear.

When she refused to look at him or answer his question, he tightened his grip on her fingers. "You forget you belong to me, Lily."

"Our bargain was for three nights," she whispered.

"Obviously you're much too lofty for my company this morning. I daresay I'm rather surprised considering the way you clamored for my attentions last night."

She wasn't being cruel or lofty. It was self-preservation, nothing more. If she did not distance herself from Saint and her true desires, she would be destroyed. "Someone will hear you," she hissed, continuing to avoid his gaze.

"Damn you," he growled. "Look at me, then."

Despair and longing filled her, and his looming presence behind her threatened her fortitude. She must not weaken. She saw Mr. Trent look their way once again, and Lily was reminded of the fact that more than just her heart was in jeopardy at the hands of Saint. "You're inviting unwanted interest, sir. Kindly remove your hand."

He dropped his hand as if he'd been burned, but his gaze pierced her, confirming he was furious with her. "That's not what you said last night when I was buried deep inside you. You didn't mind my touch then. In fact, you didn't mind having my mouth between your thighs, either."

She sucked in her breath, taken aback by the vehemence of his words. "Your talk is scandalous, my lord."

"It got you hot and wet last night, as I recall."

What did he expect? Did he think she would fawn all over him in the light of day with the townsfolk to bear witness to it? Did he think she would allow her reputation to lie in tatters simply because he thought he owned her, that she was his to command as he pleased? She would not submit to this, no matter how her heart thumped and pulse leapt at his crude words.

Reaching for another bolt of fabric, Lily pretended to be in control of her whirling emotions. "Our bargain was for three nights. There was no stipulation in regards to our meeting in the daytime."

His eyes narrowed and he lips curled in a near snarl. "Do I shame you?"

No, she wasn't ashamed of Saint or what they had done together. She didn't want to hurt him by being aloof, but she didn't want to be the other of the injured party, either. "My nighttime duties to you do not extend to the daytime hours. And it is quite obviously daytime, my lord."

"Quite," he nodded, reassembling his mask, acting as distant and aloof as she was. "Enjoy the day, Miss Farrington. You'll no doubt come to rue the night."

With a suppressed shudder, Lily watched Saint stalk to the door, flinging it wide and letting it crash closed. He met her gaze as he stood outside. She watched him for a minute from the window, refusing to give in to the urge to follow him, then fought the tears that filled her eyes when one of the most notorious opera-dancers, Octavia Rawdon met Saint right outside the window, obviously propositioning him. Lily watched as Octavia brushed her more than ample bosom against the sleeve of his jacket, her smile more than suggestive.

And then he turned to face Lily, as if he'd known all along that she had been watching him. With a tilt of his hat, he nodded, his lips furling in a predatory grin before placing Octavia's hand in the crook of his arm and led her down the street towards the Pantiles and most likely Octavia's lodgings.

A tear trickled from Lily's eye, landing on the cream silk. As she watched Saint stroll down the street with Octavia she was reminded of Molly and the way he'd deceived her seven years ago. She'd been a fool to dream she could have anything more of Saint than what he had bargained for. He truly did feel nothing for her, for if he had, he would not have callously taken Octavia's arm in his and walked off with her.

"What awful thing did he say to you?" Penelope asked, handing her a handkerchief.

"It was nothing, Penelope."

"Beast," her friend muttered, taking her by the arm and strolling out into the sunlight. "I don't know why you insisted on meeting with that man. I'm certain Charles could have held his own against the blackheart. Oh, dear," Penelope said, juggling the bolt of fabric under one arm while rifling through her reticule. "You mustn't let him bother you, Lily. He's an inconsiderate rake who only wants what he can get, and he won't be getting what he wants, will he? Come, don't let whatever he said disturb you. Think of something much more agreeable. Like Mr. Ponsonby, perhaps."

And then Lily truly started to sob all over Penelope's new rose colored damask cloth.

Damian gritted his teeth as he looked around the Duchess Heysham's drawing room. Numerous members of the nobility as well as landed gentry stood conversing, awaiting for the signal to be called in to supper. He hated these sorts of events, and he couldn't for the life of him remember why he'd allowed his friend to talk him into coming tonight.

"You're scaring away all the prospective ladies," Hillings mumbled. "That scowl is rather threatening."

Hillings was one of his oldest friends and confidants. They'd been bosom bows at Eton and at Cambridge, and then as young-bloods, running wild in London. Hillings knew everything there was to know about him, even his unfortunate affair with Lily Farrington.

"Ponsonby should be arriving any moment," Hillings murmured, sipping his claret. "I hear he's been begging for Her Grace to sell him the plot of land that corners his estate."

"What the devil does Ponsonby need with more land?"

Hillings shrugged and looked about the room. "I heard he intended to give it to his betrothed. I understand the plot surrounds her family's estate."

Saint froze as the word 'betrothed' registered in his brain. Lily's home bordered part of Ponsonby's lands as well as the Duchess of Heysham's. Could it be anyone other than Lily who was Ponsonby's intended?

"And who is the fortunate lady to be bestowed such a gift?"

"Don't know," Hillings mumbled, smiling at a girl who was much too young. "Didn't hear that bit. I confess what I did hear was at the Cock 'n Hen—last night, while I was waiting for you to drag your sorry carcass away from your mistress."

"I don't have a mistress," Damian spat, scouring the room for Ponsonby.

"Really? Not like you not to have someone handy in every village."

He didn't need any reminders of his past, nor did he particularly desire to confront the level of his dissipation. Lily had more than sufficiently confronted him with that, and for once he was thoroughly and heartily sickened by the depth of it.

"Well," Hillings whistled. "Look at the lovely on Ponsonby's arm. I'd say she's worth any begging or pleading, wouldn't you, Saint?"

Every thought in Damian's mind froze when he saw Lily glide into the room wearing a demure, pale pink dress, the bodice covered in sparkling crystals, the skirts clinging enticingly to her rounded hips and shapely thighs. His gaze leapt to her neck, his fingers tightening around the stem of his glass when he saw that the St. Croix diamonds were not around her throat.

He'd sent them around that morning, before their encounter at the draper's, with a note—a demand really, that she oblige him and wear them tonight. She had blatantly ignored his request, and the knowledge stung as well as angered him. She was going to be his wife, whether she knew it or not. He was not going to lose her this time.

"Lovely," Hillings murmured, a devilish gleam in his eyes as he appraised Lily. "Fabulous tits."

"Shut up, Hillings," Damian growled, slamming his glass on the nearest table.

"Aw c'mon, Saint," Hillings whined. "You haven't gone all soft on me, now, have you?"

Damian followed Ponsonby's path like a panther stalking its prey. "Two words, Hillings—Lily Farrington."

"Ooh," Hillings, nodded, gulping his claret. "Sorry, old chap. Quite a blow."

"He hasn't won. He merely thinks he has."

"Oh?"

"Indeed. And I do believe that is the bell for supper. Do follow Her Grace, Hillings. She's been looking at me as though she were a Cheshire kitten and I a bowl of cream."

"Afraid, Saint? You?"

"Not interested. Now, lead the way."

When they were all settled at the table, Damian flicked open his napkin and decided that God truly was punishing him for his years spent as a dissipated wastrel. Far away, at the opposite end of the table sat Lily with Hillings on one side of her and Ponsonby on the other. On this end, Her Grace had snuggled herself beside him, along with Annabella Duckworth, a notorious and decidedly libidinous widow.

"My Lord," Anabella began as the footman started to fill their plates. "Are you going to the theatre tonight?"

"I haven't decided," he mumbled, motioning for the footman to add another half of chicken to his plate. He was ravenous, and he had the feeling he was going to need something substantial to see him through the night.

"My," the duchess purred, brushing her breast against him while her hand found his crotch beneath the table. "Such large helpings."

He moved his hand atop hers, forcing her to release her grip on him, but not before Lily looked his way, her smile melting away to a grimace of distaste. "I'm afraid, Your Grace, that I am a man of large appetites."

"So I've heard," she purred, almost licking her lips.

Damian forced himself to ignore the less than subtle innuendo and pointed gazes of the women seated beside him and concentrated instead on eating and studying Lily.

She really was a beauty. Proud, regal, and elegant in her address and manners. The very picture of genteel innocence. Who would imagine that just last night she was lying in his den of pleasure, her legs spread wide with his mouth buried in her luscious folds?

He watched her drink the wine, the tip of her tongue licking a drop of it away from the glass, reminding him of the way her tongue had flicked along his cock. The memory of it made him instantly hard. Her Grace picked that damnable time to cup him again.

"My Lord," she grinned, "I believe you should have more chicken. It seems to be doing you a world of good."

The food turned to dust in Lily's mouth as she heard a thinly veiled offer from the man-eating dowager duchess to Saint. Forcing herself to swallow, Lily tried to appear as though naught were amiss, when in fact she was furious inside.

The duchess was a beautiful lady, in her early forties with a fit and robust figure, and rumored to have lusty appetites to match her voluptuousness. Lily couldn't blame the duchess for setting her sights on Saint. What woman with a heart still beating in her chest could look at him, his black hair shining in the light, his dark blue eyes laughing at a jest, and not feel a stirring of need?

She let her eyes skim lower, over the bronzed skin of Saint's throat, the simple knot of his cravat, and the excellent cut of his jacket that needed no padding in the shoulder or chest. His waistcoat was the softest blue, of fine silk embroidered with silver thread in a chinoiserie pattern. Her eyes followed the length of his arm to where his long fingers stroked the stem of the glass, his signet ring the only jewelry he wore.

"Shall we not leave the gentleman to their port?" the duchess murmured, rising elegantly from her chair. "Of course, if some would rather, they could meet us outside, for a private tour of the garden."

It was a blatant invitation to Saint, and Lily felt like throttling the duchess. She looked down the length of the table and found Saint staring at her, his brow raised in silent question or perhaps challenge.

"I'd be happy to accompany you, Your Grace," Jared announced. "I'll be with you shortly, my dear," he whispered to Lily from across the table. "I wish to have a word with the duchess."

"Of course," she nodded, refusing to look once more at Saint, despite the fact she could still feel him staring at her. "I believe I might also take a stroll outside. The room has become rather stuffy." And with as much grace as she could summon, she swept from the room with the other ladies, keenly aware of a pair of cobalt eyes studying her backside.

Chapter Nine

Waving away the attentions of an amorous Cyprian in the box next to him, Damian focused his hunter's instincts in Lily's direction. Caution was quickly slipping away, replaced with a reckless, hungry need to devour and consume. He'd been aware of it stirring within him through supper, then awakening and rearing its head when he saw Lily and Ponsonby return to the salon after being absent for a shockingly inappropriate length of time. The predator in him wished to lash out, to tear Ponsonby from her.

Damn it to hell, he was suffering. He'd thought the pain of watching Lily slip through his fingers before was agony enough; however he had been gravely mistaken. Sitting here, in his box, watching Ponsonby fawn over Lily, watching as she in turn smiled and settled herself in her seat beside Ponsonby ignited a fire within him he'd thought impossible. Anger, dark and seething started in the pit of his gut, working its way into his brain before flooding his veins.

The longer he watched her, the blacker his mood became. Noticing once more her naked throat, the bitterness he felt swelled, threatening to consume him. There was nothing to let him know she had even thought of him. No mark to signify that she had lain with him, that she belonged to him. She'd blatantly ignored his request that she wear the St. Croix diamonds. If she had, perhaps he wouldn't now be feeling so adrift, lost at sea without a safe port. If only he could look at her wearing his diamonds, some mark of his possession, he would feel, however faintly, that she still belonged to him.

"My lord," a footman whispered behind him. "Some messages."

Without taking his eyes from Lily, Damian removed two folded missives from the footman's silver salver. With a curt nod, he excused the servant. Unfolding the first missive, Damian struggled to read Octavia's awkward grammar and poor penmanship. He wouldn't meet her tonight or any other night, he thought, ripping the message into tiny pieces and flinging it over the side of his box to the pit below.

With another glance at Lily, he tore open the last note, scanning the elegant and very feminine penmanship. The duchess wished a quick rut with him in a concealed alcove. Her Grace was rather accommodating, but he much preferred the hard-won favors of the dubious innocent seated across the theatre.

Damian consigned the duchess' generous offer to the same fate as Octavia's.

A roar of appreciated claps and shrieks rose up from the pits, and Damian glanced at the stage, where Octavia, dressed in a gaudy red silk gown, her nipples clearly edging above the bodice, danced and pranced about the stage, her lovely soprano voice echoing throughout the theatre.

Feeling the hair at the nape of his neck stirring, he turned his attention to the only possible source of his discomfort. Lily's clear gaze met his, her eyes full of mistrust, and perhaps pain, fixed on him, making him wince, knowing she was remembering how he'd escorted Octavia home that afternoon.

With a haughty tilt of her chin, she looked away from him, her fan, edged in glittering ermine, waved slowly, seductively before her.

The chit was jealous.

The thought hit him like a blow to his middle. The little minx would not have looked at him in such a way if she hadn't cared about him and what he might have possibly done with Octavia Rawdon that afternoon.

The crowd roared their appreciation once more, but Damian didn't bother to look at the stage. His eyes were fixed firmly on his quarry who was effectively making him succumb to his own healthy measure of jealousy and male possessiveness. She was his, and he didn't give a damn what Lily Farrington thought of the matter.

Damian fought against the fresh flush of anger that flooded his veins as he watched Lily raise her fan, waving it effortlessly before her face, concealing both Ponsonby and her from his gaze. He swore that he could almost feel the tickle of the ermine along his lips and cheeks, just as surely as Ponsonby was feeling it right now.

She was going to pay for this. He was indulgent only to a point, and Miss Farrington had most certainly passed the point of no return. She was going to be his, no matter how he managed to achieve it. She might have thought she could waylay him with her scathing tongue and saucy mouth, but as he warned her when he'd left her in the shop that afternoon, come the darkness, she would rue the night.

It was time to make the lady pay.

Lily strolled down the candlelit corridor, grateful for the short reprieve from the sounds of the theatre and Jared's increasingly brazen attentions. Slipping her reticule along her wrist, Lily fought to clear her mind of the sight of Saint, sprawled in a chair, looking darkly handsome and mysteriously dangerous.

"In here. Now."

A vice-like grip encased her wrist, pulling her towards an alcove concealed by red velvet curtains. Inside she came face to face with Saint's glittering cobalt gaze.

"Good evening, Miss Farrington, I trust this is nighttime enough for you."

"Saint," she gasped.

"The very one," he grinned, the mirth clearly not reflected in his eyes. He reached for her waist and brought her hard against him. He kissed her hard, sliding his tongue in her mouth, ruthlessly mating with hers before pulling away, only to raise a haughty brow while he looked at her.

"What do you mean by this? Anyone could stumble upon us, for Heaven's sake. Have you no care?"

"What care have I?" he drawled, reaching for her and bringing her against him once again, ignoring her struggles. "The only care I have, dearest Lily is getting good value out of our bargain. So far I've had you but once, and that's hardly compensation enough for risking *my* reputation."

"Your reputation can withstand any talk your withdrawal from the duel might cause. Everyone knows you're a blackguard."

"And everyone thinks you're an innocent virgin. Appearances are so deceiving, aren't they?"

She slapped his hand away from her breast, and with a muffled oath, he pulled the bodice from her shoulders, exposing both breasts to his gaze.

"What are you about?" she panted. Lily didn't know whether to be outraged or aroused by his domineering action.

"Availing myself of a very tasty morsel. Why venture into the Pantiles for a costly bit of beef that proves too old and tasteless when I can have something infinitely fresher and much more tender here, now, for free."

Lily gasped despite her desire not to. The man was wicked beyond belief. She would not put up with it, no matter how much his dangerous aura beckoned to her.

"I'm going—"

Saint caught her about the waist and brought her back against his chest. His hands fondled her breasts, cupping and squeezing, his fingers pinching her nipples, making her wet between her thighs. "If you go now, Lily, I promise you'll regret it. Now," he breathed against her hair before turning her in his arms. "On your knees."

The air left her lungs, and Lily was left feeling breathless and uncomfortably warm as she thought what Saint wanted her to do. "You can't possibly—"

"I want you on your knees, Lily, and my cock in your mouth."

He pushed her to her knees, needing only one hand on her shoulder while his other one freed his hugely engorged shaft from his trousers. Without so much as a word, he reached for her and guided himself into her mouth. A primal groan, long and deep came from him, spurring her into recklessness.

There was something about Saint like this that made her wish to follow him wherever he would lead. He was dangerous—virile, utterly male, and she was helpless to resist him, despite the warnings in her head.

He groaned again as she took him in her hand and sucked him, fast, furiously hard. Lily knew he was watching. She could feel his eyes studying her, and the knowledge emboldened her, making her wish to give him a performance he would never forget.

"You'll have to do better than that, Miss Farrington, Octavia did a much better job this afternoon."

With an anguished cry, she took all of him into her mouth and sucked—hard. She felt him swell inside her, felt his fingers shaking against her jaw and her throat. His words were scathing, unnecessarily painful. He was trying to hurt her, and yet he was trembling; she could feel it coursing through him, and she knew that he hadn't been with the opera dancer. He'd said it to punish her, to hurt her. What had he said?

She'd rue the night.

Damian groaned again, his lust clearly beyond him. He watched Lily consume him, and all he could think of was more…more…more. She was an enigma. Dressed like a bloody princess in her ethereal pink gown. Her demure curls were piled high with innocent little flowers tucked in amongst pearls, contrasting sensually as her position before him, on her knees, her tits, firm and large, grazing his thighs as she sucked him, up and down, the sounds of her mouth on him driving him to the brink. She was as skilled as any courtesan, and far more satisfying.

The innocent wanton, he thought as she took him in her hand and licked the length of him, sipping the drop of him on the tip of his cock, and licking her lips after. The vision made him reckless, and far from gentlemanly.

"I'd say you're proving your mettle, Miss Farrington," he grunted, feeling his climax upon him. "You've nearly sucked the life out me."

"Better than your little opera dancer, I'll wager," she shot back before taking him inside her mouth again.

"Perhaps," he growled, tweaking her nipple and loving that it was already hard and straining. "Octavia was quite exuberant this afternoon. She let me do all sorts of very wicked things to her."

"And yet you're here with me. How interesting."

Resting his head against the cool wall, Damian fought for control, fought to keep his eyes open. Was there anything more powerful to a man than to see a beautiful woman on her knees, his throbbing cock in her mouth—and loving it? She *was* loving it, reveling in teasing him and calling his bluff. The little minx knew he hadn't been with Octavia, and yet he didn't want to give up the sham. He liked the unbridled response Lily gave him when he taunted her with the possibilities that he might have bedded Octavia.

"Enough," he commanded, pulling out of her mouth. "Lift your skirts."

She did, showing him her wet curls between her milk white thighs. In the small confines of the alcove he could smell her arousal, and it stirred in him a hunger so great he thought he'd never survive it.

"Saint?" she asked, her voice concerned for the first time.

"Lift your skirts higher," he demanded walking behind her, bending, reaching for her wet sheath. "It seems that you like this, Miss Farrington."

She moaned when he fingered her and tried to shift her hips so that he could enter her. "Not yet, but soon."

"Saint, hurry. Someone might find us."

"We have till dawn, isn't that right, Lily?"

"But not *here*," she cried, and whimpered as he sunk his finger deep inside her. It was very strange to feel him behind her, his fingers sliding along her, making her ache for something far more solid inside her.

"You want this, don't you, Lily? Don't bother to deny it. All the evidence I need is here, displayed wantonly and most charmingly before me."

Lily couldn't help but lean back against him, hoping he'd give her more of what she needed, but instead he removed his hand. "Face me."

She willingly obeyed him, and he surprised her by lifting her onto his thighs, wrapping her legs around his waist. "Does Ponsonby do this to you?" he asked, cupping her heat with his palm.

"No."

"No?" he asked, kneading her while he flicked his tongue along her nipple, circling it until it tightened painfully, before looking up at her and letting it slide slowly from his lips. "Are you rutting with him, Lily and if you are, are you enjoying it as much?"

"No," she cried, caging his face in her hands, trailing his lips and chin with soft kisses. "I just want you," she whispered.

"Ride me, Lily," he moaned, fitting himself inside her, showing her how to move atop him, moving her up and down, the slide fast and urgent. His thighs felt hard and relentless beneath her. His hands at her waist were just as hard, and his lips just as demanding. He was panting against her, urgently pushing up inside, lifting her off his lap. When she felt his hands steal down her buttocks, spreading them, letting his fingers stroke her entrance where he was joined inside her body, Lily began to tremble. It was so terribly wicked for Saint to want to feel himself inside her as he made love to her. It was deliciously wicked.

Saint groaned against her throat, while skimming his wet finger around the rim of her while he filled her. "Tell me, Lily, how does it feel to be stretched with my cock?"

On a soft moan, she found her own rhythm, riding him as he asked, encouraged and emboldened by his touch.

"Touch yourself," he mumbled against her lips.

She put her hands on her breasts and cupped them as he had done for her. "That's lovely, Miss Farrington," he grunted, his strokes coming faster and harder, "but I wanted to see them on your wet lips."

"*Saint*," she exclaimed, wanton eagerness making her heart race at the very thought of doing such a thing in a place such as this.

'Put your hands over your mound and pleasure yourself, Lily. I want to watch."

And she did, nearly exploding with desire and excitement. It was almost too much, feeling Saint inside her, his fingers teasing the stretched entrance of her body while her fingers furiously worked to pleasure herself. There was nothing soft and romantic about their coupling. It was frantic, furious, hard and unyielding, and Lily took it all in, reveling in the strength, the raw power of Saint in a full-blooded lust.

With a deep groan, he rocked against her, splashing his seed into her while he buried his face between her breasts, panting harshly against her skin. She cradled him then, rocking slowly against him till his breathing slowed and quieted.

She felt him fishing around his pocket, producing a handkerchief, and pulling himself from her, he covered her with the linen, drying her before lowering her skirts.

"I trust, Miss Farrington, that this interlude far transcends any enjoyment you might have gotten out of your private daylight hours."

"Perhaps," she mumbled, readjusting her bodice and refusing to meet his eyes. "But then, this will be the last night for such interludes. One never can tell what will bring pleasure from one week to the next."

"You can rely on me to always bring you pleasure, Miss Farrington," he growled before swooping down and kissing her with surprising hunger and vigor.

When Lily finally managed to set herself to rights, she ventured back to her box, ignoring the stares of Penelope and her husband, along with Jared's pointed glare, and concentrated her attention on the stage. She smiled secretly, almost in wonder as she recalled what she'd done with Saint. He'd needed her. She knew that. He had shown far more of what lurked inside him than he had in the past days. There was a hunger inside him searching for more than sexual appeasement. It might be possible to make Saint feel something more than carnal desire for her.

"Dear me," Aunt Millie hiccupped, her glass of sherry teetering in her hand. "You've been gone a while, m'dear."

"I'm afraid there was a rather long line at the withdrawing room," Lily explained, sending Penelope nodding in understanding and her aunt sipping more of her sherry.

"I think I'll stay where I am," Aunt Millie grinned. "No sense missing the performance."

"Indeed," Jared scowled. "I'm sure there's nothing of interest in the halls."

"Assuredly not," Lily smiled, straightening her very wrinkled skirts. "Not a soul in sight, I'm afraid."

"Miss Farrington," an unfamiliar voice called from the curtains. "A message for you, madam,"

"Thank you," Lily smiled, taking the note from the footman and sliding it into her reticule. When she was certain everyone had forgotten the note, Lily slipped it out of her bag and read it in the dim lights.

Midnight. Wearing nothing but my diamonds and my scent.

Oh, the rogue. He knew precisely how to infuriate her, yet make her melt in all the right places. It was time to admit it. Despite her best attempts, she was succumbing to the devil's lure.

Chapter Ten

Badly done. Very badly done.

Damian cursed himself as a devil while prowling about the dimly lit Temple. What had he been about to take Lily in such a fashion? He was a debauched rakehell for using her in a such a way, yet he'd been helpless to stop himself. The hungry predator inside him had reared its head, and he hadn't been able to control the hunger for her. He desperately wanted her; her body, her heart. Her love.

And there was where the problem lay. He wanted her total submission. He wanted her to feel the exquisite yet torturous pain of being in love. Replaying the events of the night, the vision of her on his lap, the feel of his cock filling her body, he realized the need to hear the words. It infuriated him to think that for Lily, what they shared was the mere melding of bodies. But he knew the heat and lust that fueled her response to him was only just that, lust. And that had been the reason behind his cruel words and the force that he'd taken her with.

She didn't love him.

There had been nothing in her face except passion and fulfillment. She had moaned for him, got wet and smiled seductively for him, as all of his other conquests had, but nothing more. Nothing to tell him that he was special to her. Nothing to show him that he was the only one she wanted. It was a bloody bargain to her and nothing else.

With an oath, he snatched an apple from a bowl and stalked to the door, flinging it open and stared at the moon hanging low in the sky.

Where the hell was she? Was she still with Ponsonby? Did the bastard have his hands all over her? Was Ponsonby touching her in the same manner as he had done earlier?

He viciously bit into the red apple, forcing himself to remain calm. To remember he still had one more night with Lily. One more chance to make her his.

A horse and rider came into view, and he bit off another chunk of apple, squelching the sudden thudding of his heart. As the mare neared, Damian got a good glimpse of Lily—the very essence of a seductive Celestial Virgin in a white cloak, golden locks flowing behind her. A Virgin indeed, he thought, remembering how she'd been with him only hours before.

The mare stopped and Damian watched as Lily gracefully dismounted, revealing an astonishing and scandalous amount of bare flesh. His breath hitched, and he thought for a second he might choke on the apple currently lodged in his throat.

"Good evening, My Lord," she said, standing proudly before him. "I see you're anxiously awaiting my arrival."

Striving for nonchalance, he leaned against the doorframe and bit off more of the apple. "I see you've violated the first dictate of my orders. What of the others?"

Pale hands came up to unclasp her cape. He wheezed then, taking in the sight of the St. Croix diamonds around her neck, the large tear-shaped pendant nestled between the cleft of her breasts, breasts that were gloriously naked.

His eyes scanned her body, her abundant curves illuminated in the moonlight, a naked supplicant before him. He tossed the apple core carelessly to the ground.

Leaning forward he put his nose to the crook of her neck, inhaling softly as he nuzzled her skin, nearly drowning in the scent of her, in the way her floral scent mixed with his musky one.

"I suppose one cannot be unhappy with two out of three, can one?" he murmured, tracing the diamond pendant as it rested between her breasts.

"I was quite certain you wouldn't want me completely submissive."

He grinned. She was utterly and enchantingly naïve. "Well, then, Miss Farrington, you thought wrong."

Swooping her up into his arms he carried her into the Temple and set her on the carpet before the hearth. He made short work of his shirt and trousers, refusing to feel any regret that he had just cheated himself out of the very great pleasure of having Lily undress him.

She watched him undress, her breathing quickening as he reached for the buttons of his trousers. He looked down at her, on her knees, submissive and willing. He was going to demand her complete surrender tonight. He'd have her begging him, even if the waiting killed him.

"Spread your legs," he commanded tossing his shirt to the floor. She obeyed him, her thighs slightly open so that he could see a sliver of blond curls.

"More."

"Enough?" she asked, a fine flush covering her chest as she opened her legs completely to his gaze.

He nodded, and swallowed hard, trying to curb the impulse to just take her. He had to remind himself that this was the last lesson. She must learn to submit to him, to give up her fears and her need to control and trust him. Once she trusted him with her body, she would naturally trust him with her heart—or so he hoped and prayed.

"Do you see what you do me?" he asked. His erection, full and heavy sprung free of his trousers. Already a drop of essence seeped out, trickling down his shaft. His cock reared skywards as he noticed Lily following the drop with her eyes. Patience, his mind screamed.

"Tonight is a feast for the senses, Lily. I want to watch you do all sorts of wicked things, and I want to watch you as you watch me do them to you. But first," he whispered, refusing to give in to the predator's desire to pounce. "First you must do something for me."

"Yes?"

"Tell me, Lily," Saint began, walking behind her, then tilting her chin up so that he could gaze into her eyes while letting his long fingers stroke the line of her throat down to the diamond pendant glistening between her perfect tits. "Four nights ago you found me at home with another. Did you wish to be that woman?"

"No," Lily whispered, mesmerized by the heat in his blue eyes, the way his face exuded strength and mastery.

"No?" he asked, taking his erect penis in his hand, and teasing her mouth with its wet tip. "I think you lie, Lily. I think you wanted to be that woman. You were jealous, admit it."

"No," she repeated, feeling the wetness on her hand as Saint placed her fingers on her swollen sex. He then returned to teasing her lips with his penis. He looked commanding towering above her, his manhood in his hand as he swirled the tip around her mouth, down her chin and along her neck. She ached to take him into her mouth and suck him, but she refused to beg, to be at his mercy.

"So proud, aren't you, Lily? You refuse to give in, not even an inch."

"You want my surrender."

"Perhaps."

"You want me at your mercy."

"I want you to let me be in control, Lily. For once, just feel, stop thinking, and wondering and worrying. Show me you can be free in my arms."

"I...I don't know." For so long she'd refused to give thought to her deep desires. Her pulse leapt with the very thought of letting Saint have his wicked way with her, yet the part of her mind that found safety and comfort behind a cloak of restraint warned her that Saint was asking her to do something far more dangerous than any of his previous requests.

He dropped to his knees behind her, his soft lips nuzzling her neck while his thumbs grazed her aching nipples. "Trust me," he breathed, rolling her nipples then tugging on them till she moved her hips restlessly. "Trust me to take care of you. To pleasure you."

She moaned when his hands cupped her breasts and pressed them together. His tongue flicked along her neck then, his breath, warm and soft, whispered along her skin. His hands skimmed down her belly until his fingers rested on her mons, before slowly playing in her curls. "Well, Lily?" he asked, "what shall it be? Will you submit to me?"

Unable to stop herself, she nodded her head, only to gasp as he reached for her wrists, bringing them behind her, and binding them with his cravat.

"You're mine, Lily, and I promise I shall have you. In every way imaginable during this night."

"Saint," she cried, struggling to pull herself free of the cravat. "Untie me at once."

"You agreed to submit to me, Lily, and submit you will. You promised to be at my mercy, and I promised to keep you safe. And I will."

"I didn't agree to be tied up," she hissed.

He grinned then, a devilish smile that made her wetter, yet irritated her at the same time. "You'll like it. Before long, you'll be moaning and writhing, pleading with me to take you. No?" he asked when she shook her head. "Well, now, I think that is clearly a challenge. And do you know, Lily, I always rise to the challenge."

"You arrogant, self-serving—"

"Close your eyes, Lily."

"What?" she shrieked, still struggling. "And not know what you're about? Absolutely not."

"Close your eyes," he said again, his fingers tracing her brows, then he closed her lids with his thumbs. She smelled the maleness of him as it washed over her. His mouth was so very close to hers now, she could feel the warmth of his breath as it caressed her lips.

"So beautiful," he murmured, his finger tracing her mouth. "So perfect."

"Saint," she whimpered, nervousness combined with sexual excitement coursed within her veins. "I don't like this."

"You will," he said, his words almost a command. "Give up the control, Lily. Let me decide the course of the night. See what it will be like to be pleasured, to not have to always be thinking, always hiding."

"Saint?"

"Shh," he crooned against her lips, "you're safe, Lily, I won't hurt you. I just want to please you. Dear God, you don't how badly I want to please you."

And then his lips were against hers, his tongue boldly seeking entrance into her mouth, his hands roamed possessively over her body as he brought her closer to him, his tongue searching, and swirling with hers.

"Saint," she cried as he tore his mouth from hers, only to moan as his teeth nibbled at her nipples.

"Such beautiful tits," he said, his voice husky with desire. "Beautiful, made just for a man's pleasure."

Lily moaned again, thrusting her breasts upward, filling Saint's mouth with them.

"You like words, don't you, Lily? You like what they do to you."

She nodded and squeezed her eyes shut, delighting in the heightened sensation of having Saint's tongue swirl and flick around her nipple.

"Do you know what I want to do with your tits, Lily? I want to suck them, to lie beside you and do nothing but suck and lave. I want to slide my cock in and out of them, watching as they take me, watching as I bath them with my cream."

She cried out, feeling the building desire between her legs.

"You like to hear the words, do you not, Lily? They make you hot and wet, don't they?"

She nodded, not caring that she was admitting that she really was wanton. It was true. It was erotic to hear what Saint wanted to do to her. There was something about the baseness of his words that thrilled her, that titillated the wanton in her.

"I bet if I stroked you, I'd find your cunny wet. Is it wet for me, love?"

She wanted to scream, she was practically drowning in desire.

"I can see it's already glistening," he murmured, his tongue flicking her lip in between the words. "I won't have to stroke it after all."

She whimpered then, silently pleading with him to touch her, to put his tongue to her.

"What a pretty picture you make, Lily. Your beautiful tits flushed and hard, your nipples sticking out, begging for the touch of my hand and tongue. I haven't even put a hand on you, and already you're searching for release, begging me to fill you."

"Please," she moaned, not caring any more that she was submitting to her desires, and his wicked mouth.

"Oh, I expect to do so," he purred, raking one long finger down the length of her. "But I intend to do so in my own way, Lily. The only thing you shall do is obey me. Is that clear?" She nodded, almost frantically. "Very good. Now then, I shall untie your wrists, and you will go to the bed and await me."

Chapter Eleven

She was on her knees in the middle of the bed, trembling with need, with the desire to have Saint imbedded deep within her. She watched him arrange the pillows against the headboard, then he beckoned her with his fingers. Once she was settled on the pillows, her hips and hair arranged as he wished, he knelt before her, his manhood engorged and throbbing.

"Now, Lily, I shall expect you to keep your eyes open at all times. It will give me pleasure to have you watching me love you."

She nodded, swallowing hard, the beating of her heart and the rushing of her blood drowning out all other sounds.

"Open for me."

Parting her knees, she exposed herself to him.

"Very nice," he murmured, his gaze fixed on her sex. "Now, take your fingers and spread your sex."

His command sent a thrill through her, but she obeyed him.

"Open your eyes. I want you see what I'm doing to you."

Her eyes flew open and she looked into Saint's dark blue gaze. The slide of cool cloth trailed up her thigh, and she glanced down to see Saint's white cravat between his fingers. He slid the linen up, inch by glorious inch until it reached her heated sex. Slowly he began to move the cravat in a slow circular motion, his thumb adding delicious pressure.

"You like this, do you?"

"Mmm," she moaned, resting her head against the pillows. "It feels good, yet it isn't enough."

"Isn't enough?" he grinned wickedly. "Do you mean it won't make you come for me?"

She felt her cheeks flush, but nodded, liking the way his fingers pressed against her thighs. "Then perhaps this will suffice."

Lily nearly came apart as Saint pulled her towards him, his mouth and tongue settling against her. Her back arched, and she closed her eyes.

"Open your eyes, Lily. I want you see who is doing this to you. Who is responsible for making you feel alive."

Raising her head, Lily lowered her gaze to Saint's and sucked in her breath as his tongue came out to slowly rake along her pink folds, his gaze steadily watching her.

"I would have you watch me, Lily. It gives me pleasure. And if you will allow yourself, you'll find it will give you greater pleasure, too."

"It's more wicked watching," she whimpered, seeing how he grinned before flicking her slowly with his tongue.

"Perhaps," he agreed. "But we are lovers, are we not? Nothing that we do together is wicked, Lily. Agreed?"

"Yes." And then she watched him lower his head, his black hair contrasting sharply with her pale skin. She watched his head move in slow circular motions, heard the gentle slurping and licking sounds of his tongue on her, parting her, drenching her with desire. When her fingers raked through his hair, he shifted on the bed, moving further from her so that she could now see his lips on her flesh, his tongue coming out in short, purposeful flicks. He had grasped his manhood, his fingers slowly sliding up the length of his shaft. The sight of him pleasuring himself as he was pleasuring her aroused her further.

"Lily," he groaned as he continued to lick and swirl his thumb against her. "Do you trust me?"

"Yes," she whimpered, feeling her climax upon her. "I trust you Saint."

"Lily," he moaned, burying his face between her thighs, his tongue furiously stroking her.

"Saint," she screamed, exploding in his mouth. But he wouldn't stop, wouldn't let her float back down to earth. Instead he slid up her body, nuzzling her belly then wetting her breasts before bringing them together and sandwiching his hard phallus between them.

Jesus, he was hot. Damian began to stroke, his cock sliding in and out, in and out of her tits. It looked sexy, just as he dreamed it would, watching his cock between the milky mounds, the St. Croix diamonds scraping the tip.

"Squeeze for me, my love," he whispered, placing her hands on her breasts so that he could reach behind and lose himself in her slickness. She moaned as he filled her with his fingers. "Soon," he grunted, grinding his hips, watching his cock moving between her breasts. And then with a triumphant shout, he pulled out from between them, bathing her in his cream, just as he told her would.

Instead of softening, his cock stiffened as he took in the sight of his seed trickling down her breasts and onto her belly. She was his—now and forever.

"Please," she begged him, rubbing her mound against his hand. "Please," He smiled then, a wicked smile as he heard her pleading for him. "Already begging?" And then he filled her in one swift movement, watching as he joined with her. He looked up, and saw that she, too, was watching as she took him in, swallowing his cock in her heated silk.

"Beautiful, isn't it?" he asked, shaking as she reached out and stroked a finger down his shaft before he plunged into her again.

"Yes," she whispered, angling her hips so that she could see more of his penetration.

He hooked her legs over his arms, raising her hips so that she could see all of him, as he stroked and filled her.

"Saint." Her voice trembled and shook as she met his eyes. "I have to…that is…"

"You have to come?"

She nodded and closed her eyes. "I want it faster and harder."

"Say the words," he whispered, pulling out of her tight sheath and teasing her with his cock as he circled her entrance.

"What do you want to hear?" she gasped, trying to reach for him. "What do you want?"

He kissed her jaw, then grazed his lips along the sensitive lobe of her ear. "I want to make love," he whispered.

"Yes," she cried and then he filled her as fast and as hard as she would allow. She arched for him, her sheath quivering around him as he stroked her and loved her until she found her release.

He fell upon her, nuzzling her as his own body trembled in climax. "You have to know that I've never felt this, Lily," he murmured into her hair. "No other woman has ever made me lose control like you do. It's never been like this."

He wanted to say the words, he wanted to speak of his love, but he was afraid. While she received his attentions, even begged for them, she had not uttered one word of love.

Perhaps it was too soon. Perhaps he needed to take her again, to show her that he would never give her up. And he wouldn't. Even if she didn't love him she would be bound to him—forever. He'd see to it.

The early morning sun streamed through the small window as Lily turned the yellowed page and stared in amazement at yet another of Saint's drawings. She had felt restless in bed beside Saint, worrying over the approaching dawn, fearing the sun's arrival and with it the loss of Saint. She'd been stewing ever since he'd fallen asleep in her arms. She loved him. She had done the unmentionable and given her heart to him without thinking of the pain it would cause when their nights were over. She had finally admitted it to herself when she was preparing to come to the Temple. She loved him. Had always loved him and would forever love him.

Unable to bear the thought of losing him yet again, she'd quietly gotten out of bed and strolled over to a small bookcase, thinking to calm herself with a book. Instead she'd discovered his sketches. They were beautiful, evocative, and more than accomplished. And they were all of her.

She looked at the sketch for a long while, studying the way he'd captured her dress, the way the white silk had floated along her body. It had been her debut. She'd been eighteen then, a full summer since she'd even spoken with Saint, and yet he had drawn her. Had obviously been there at her debut, watching her, admiring her.

Her gaze skimmed to the velvet pouch that had been hidden inside the sketchbook. Stealing a glance at the bed and seeing that Saint was still soundly asleep, she opened the bag. Her breath left her in a silent whoosh.

It was a keepsake bag, and everything in it belonged to her. The sprig of heather she'd given him years ago was tied with a white ribbon that had obviously come from her presentation dress. A ribbon that she'd worn around her throat to the opening of Romeo and Juliet was there, as well as a string of pearls that had fallen from her hair at last year's Billingsworth ball.

A hard lump formed in her throat as she looked once more at the book. He'd drawn her over the years, as if he had been admiring her from afar. Flipping through the pages she saw that many sketches were of her from balls and soirees that she had attended. Others were more risqué. One was of her lounging on a daybed, very much resembling the one in the temple. In another, she was naked, with the exception of the St. Croix diamonds circling her neck. Her belly was rounded, but far more prominent than it actually was. And then she looked closer and saw that he had sketched her rounded with child. His child.

She looked up, and saw Saint watching her from the bed, his eyes unreadable and guarded.

"Do you understand now?"

Lily swallowed hard, forcing her mind to slow down. It didn't mean he loved her. It may only mean he harbored illicit fantasies about her. Dare she hope for more?

"What would you have me understand?" she asked, wishing to hear the words from his own lips.

His brow raised, but he kept his gaze pinned on her. She could feel the heat from it burning through his shirt that she donned when she'd gotten out of bed. "I believe you know the answer to that, my sweet."

"Do I?"

"I've been living for you for years, Lily. I've watched you and wanted you from afar for so long that I feel I'm part of you."

"You wanted me?"

"More than wanted," he murmured, coming up on his side and resting his weight on his elbow. "I love you. I've loved you since I was twenty. Hell even before that, and I'm afraid I've only managed to fall deeper in love with you these past years."

Her eyes began to fill with moisture, and she looked down at the sketches before her, blinking the tears away and then looking up at Saint.

"I know I hurt you, but I promise you, my love, I'll never hurt you again. It's only been you I wanted, Lily. It will forever only be you. I'll remain faithful. I swear it. I'll love and honor you till my dying day."

"Saint," she cried, giddy with relief. She rushed to him and threw her arms around his neck. "I love you, too. I tried not to. I thought you would only hurt me and I couldn't bear that again."

"I'll never hurt you again, my sweet. I only want the chance to love you and make you happy."

"And this bargain. When you planned this, what did you want from me?"

"You," he whispered against her mouth. "All of you. Your mind, your body, your heart."

"You have it," she smiled against his mouth, her lips grazing his before she took his mouth in hers and kissed him with all the desire she had kept hidden. As their tongues mated and danced, Saint grew restless beneath her. Pulling away from her mouth, he kissed her jaw then her throat.

"Show me, Lily. Make love to me and show me what is in your heart."

"I'd like that," she whispered against his neck, twining her hands about his wrists. "I'd like to pleasure you as you've pleasured me. To give you lessons as you've given me."

"Indeed," he growled, letting her raise his arms over his head so that he was grasping the spindles of the headboard.

"And do you trust me, my lord?"

"Completely, my sweet."

With lightening speed, she tied his wrists with the cravat lying atop her pillow, and smiled at the shock in his face.

"What the devil is the meaning of this, Miss Farrington?"

"When I'm done, I'll have you begging," she said, stroking his already erect phallus. "Give up the control Saint, and learn what it is like to be pleasured."

"I already know what it is liked to be pleasured, madam. I prefer you show me what it is like to be loved."

"As you wish. I'm an apt pupil, my lord. Are you ready?"

"I've been ready for your love for seven years, Lily. I fear I cannot wait another minute to receive it."

"Then I shall make you wait no more."

He groaned when she kissed him again, and she loved the thrill of him squirming beneath her. The morning light was just beginning to stream through the window when Lily settled her body onto Saint's rampant arousal.

Three nights of lessons had ended, but the true pleasure just was beginning.

About the Author:

Charlotte Featherstone lives in Ontario, Canada with her husband, daughter and a very large Golden Retriever named after one of her rakish heroes.

When not at her paying job, Charlotte is busy writing, surfing the net under the guise of research, chatting incessantly with her critique partners and generally avoiding any duties attributed to those of domestic goddesses. To keep Charlotte busy and out of the kitchen she would love to hear from her readers at romancewriter@charlottefeatherstone.com *or visit her website at* www.charlottefeatherstone.com.

In the Heat of the Night

by Calista Fox

To My Reader:

I hope you enjoy Nick and Molina's story as much as I enjoyed writing it. Thanks to Ms. Pich and Ms. Kendall for letting me share this story with other romance addicts.

Chapter One

As Molina Toscano breezed through the opulent marbled lobby of The Plaza Hotel, she left in her wake the faintest hint of the rich, sensual aroma of her signature perfume, *Bella*. The scent followed her like an invisible cloud, enveloping everyone around her in the intoxicating fragrance—a dark, exotic scent that was as unique and enticing as the woman who wore it.

As she passed by, the tantalizing aroma wafted under Nick Moretti's nose, instantly conjuring up the most intimate of memories. He closed his eyes for a moment and inhaled deeply. God, he loved that scent... and the erotic sensations it evoked.

Tossing aside the magazine he was absently scanning, he settled more comfortably into the plush chair he'd occupied in the lobby for the past half-hour. With great interest, Nick watched as Molina instructed the bellhop to take her two bags to the limo waiting out front for her. The manager of The Plaza was at her elbow, thanking her for her patronage and telling her how wonderful it had been to see her again.

An amused smile touched Nick's lips. Molina Toscano, like her father, Frank, held the world on a string. People jumped when she snapped her fingers, ever eager to do her bidding.

Well, most people. Present company excluded. The Toscano empire—and all the money, prestige and privilege associated with it—was certainly impressive and even a bit overwhelming. But it had never intimidated Nick. When he'd joined Frank Toscano's staff ten years ago as a bodyguard for Molina, he'd whistled under his breath at the extravagant mansion she'd grown up in, then put it out of his mind. He'd never let the family's wealth and power affect him. He'd had a job to do—a very serious one at that. Protect the heiress at all costs.

He had that same job now.

Since Frank had phoned him two days ago, Nick had been following Molina all over Manhattan. At night, he'd taken up residence at The Plaza in the suite next door to her. Not an easy arrangement by any stretch of the imagination. On more than one occasion, Nick had to stop himself from tapping on her door and slipping inside, like he'd sometimes done years ago, when they'd finally given in to their passion and engaged in a sexually gratifying, albeit emotionally deficient, affair.

He hadn't seen her in five years, since he'd left the Toscanos behind to pursue a gig with the Secret Service. Being in such close proximity to the beautiful heiress for the past couple of nights brought back all of the memories of the good old days. Well, they hadn't all been good. Most of his days with Molina had been volatile, sometimes downright explosive.

But the nights... Just thinking about the fiery nights he'd shared with the erotically tantalizing woman was enough to make him hard. No matter how frustrating and irritating she could be in the light of day, Molina was the most sexually arousing woman he'd ever known. Exciting, intriguing, and totally uninhibited. What the woman could do to his body with just a sultry look was shameful. What she'd done to him in private—on many heated occasions—was nothing short of sinful.

And five years without her was enough to drive him mad with want. So much so, he'd had to employ his iron will to stay on the other side of the hotel room door, keeping his presence unknown while he sat in the dark, replaying in his mind some of the steamier evenings he'd shared with her. Even now, he had to shift to a more comfortable position in his chair as his desire for her intensified.

He had promised Frank he wouldn't make contact with Molina until she was ready to leave New York and return to Santa Barbara. His task had been to shadow her, keep an eye out for anything suspicious, and ensure her safety at all times. For the past two days, Nick had faded into the background and kept his distance from her. It had been pure torture.

Now, Nick stood as Molina headed to the tall double doors at the entrance of the hotel. As she exited the elegant building, those who remained in the lobby of The Plaza continued to bask in the alluring scent she left behind. It was that arousing.

"Your car, Miss Toscano." Nick heard the valet comment in a polite tone. He crested the steps of the grand hotel as the valet escorted Molina to the sleek, black limousine that would take her to the airport.

She looked anxious to leave the crisp chill of New York. Her cousin's funeral service had been impeccably orchestrated, thanks to Molina's efficient organizational skills, and now she was heading west to a much warmer climate.

Molina had donned a lightweight, flowing overcoat in a soft shade of winter white to ward off the chill. The coat hung open, revealing the smart business suit she wore beneath it, also in the same winter white color that complemented her golden skin.

A gold-and-diamond necklace and matching dangling earrings—created specially for her by Harry Winston, Nick recalled—and a gold Cartier watch accented the ensemble. Her long, light brown hair was pulled back in a sleek ponytail, and her beautiful peridot-colored eyes were concealed behind designer sunglasses.

She looked stunning, as always, he thought as she climbed gracefully into the car and slid across the smooth leather seat. She crossed her long legs, closed her eyes and inhaled deeply.

"Damn chilly out, isn't it?"

The deep voice, which suddenly filled her well-appointed car, did not startle Molina; rather, it sent a spark of excitement straight to the heart of her. She'd suspected she would see Nick Moretti this week at Anthony's funeral. And even though she hadn't caught the slightest glimpse of Nick over the past two days, she had sensed his presence, felt his eyes on her. She hadn't questioned why he'd remained in the shadows rather than make the rounds with her family. Nick was just that way.

Admittedly, she'd been relieved to have some time to prepare herself for this moment. After five years, she'd had no idea how she would respond to Nick's sudden reappearance in her life. She had some thoughts of how she'd *like* the reunion to go—some very wicked, pleasurable thoughts, as a matter of fact. But Molina knew persuading Nick to engage in casual sex was as likely to happen as world peace. Nick took nothing lightly—not his job and certainly not sex with her.

His feelings for her ran deep. The problem with Nick was he always wanted more from her than she was capable of giving.

Too bad, she thought on a wistful sigh. The one place she and Nick were simpatico was in the bedroom. It was unfortunate they'd had trouble playing nice outside of it.

She removed her sunglasses as her eyes swept over him, finding the view to be nothing short of breathtaking. She crooked an eyebrow at him. "You're looking well."

Nick slid into the car and settled into the seat opposite her. "And you look positively ravishing." His gaze was bold and daring.

Nick Moretti didn't beat around the bush, and he didn't bother hiding his appreciation of her assets. Molina had always considered that an admirable quality. She liked to know where she stood with a man. With *this* man, in particular.

Though Nick was too damn stubborn and unyielding for her taste, she could certainly appreciate what he had to offer. Intelligent, savvy and devastatingly handsome, Nick was the ultimate catch. They would have been perfect together, Molina thought, if only he'd let her have her way when she'd wanted it.

Spoiled. That's what he'd called her on more occasions than she could recall. It had been the bane of their relationship, though only one of the many obstacles they'd been unable to overcome.

As thoughts of their tumultuous past tripped through her mind, the valet closed the door and the car pulled away from the curb. This perplexed Molina. She gave Nick a curious look. "Mind telling me what you're doing?"

"Need a ride," he said in an easy tone.

She laughed softly. How presumptuous of him to just climb inside her car without an invitation. "The audacity you possess, Nick. It's mind-boggling, really."

"I didn't think you'd mind." His slow, sexy grin was meant to distract her, quell any suspicions she might have over his unexpected appearance in her car.

He continued to look at ease, as though sharing a limo to the airport was an ordinary, every day occurrence for them. It wasn't. In fact, there was nothing remotely ordinary about his presence in her life, nor had there ever been.

Nick wasn't just hitching a ride. She knew him well enough to know when he was up to something, to recognize he had an ulterior motive.

Perhaps he simply wanted to pass along his condolences in private. She considered the possibility. But her gut instincts, which always served her well, told her there was more to his visit than sympathy over the loss of her cousin.

She eyed him with great suspicion. "What do you want, Nick?"

His deep blue eyes glowed in a seductive way, making her insides flutter all too easily.

"A drink with an old friend." He reached into the silver-plated ice bucket that sat on the side bar and retrieved a bottle of '97 DVX sparkling wine. He held it up for her inspection. "It's not Dom, but it is one of your favorites, as I recall."

"How very clever of you to have stocked the bar." Yes, he was definitely up to something. Perhaps the sparkle in his sapphire eyes was an indication he'd changed his position on casual sex.

One could only hope.

A smile tugged at the corners of her mouth. Molina reveled in the tantalizing sensations sweeping over her at the mere thought of sex with Nick. She found herself mesmerized by the sight of his strong hands as they worked the cork on the champagne bottle until it popped, echoing loudly in the spacious car. She knew what those hands felt like on her body, the erotic sensations they were capable of evoking, the pleasure they were capable of giving.

Nick poured two glasses, passed one to her. "*Salute,* baby."

"Not your most eloquent *brindisi,*" she said of his toast. But she was amused, nonetheless. She sipped deeply, savoring the crisp taste of the sparkling wine.

Nick stretched his long legs out in front of him, making himself comfortable. "It was a nice funeral service."

"Yes," she agreed. "Robert Carmelitano did a wonderful job directing the funeral." *As usual.* The Carmelitanos had been burying Vientis since the turn of the century. There had been many deaths.

All tragic. All suspicious.

"I'm sorry about Anthony. He was a great man."

Molina drew in a full breath. She'd done all the crying she would do over the loss of her cousin. It was too painful to dwell on the senselessness of it. "Yes, he was. He devoted much of his time to the Catholic churches in New York."

"Not many people like that today," Nick commented.

"No. And now there's one less."

They rode in silence, sipping their wine. It occurred to Molina that if this was all Nick was going to say on the untimely demise of Anthony Vienti, V, he could have done it before they'd left the hotel. There was more on his mind, though it was clear he wasn't quite ready to reveal his hand to her.

She studied him over the rim of her glass. Though he vexed her more often than not, he was still the most fascinating man she'd ever known. He was strong and virile, with a commanding presence and a body that warranted the sigh of longing suddenly bubbling up inside her. Taller than most of the men she knew, Nick towered over her even though she neared six feet when wearing her tallest heels. She adored that about him. Tall men just seemed more powerful in her mind.

Yes, Nick Moretti was definitely a man worthy of her most erotic fantasies. And this particular evening, he looked hotter than ever. Dressed in black-as-night jeans, a crisp white dress shirt and a sleek, black leather coat, he looked mysterious and edgy. Downright sinful, in fact. His thick dark brown hair dusted the collar of his coat, adding to his devilishly handsome looks. He needed a trim, but was probably too busy saving damsels in distress to spend twenty minutes in a barber's chair.

Nick was one hell of a bodyguard—she'd had enough of them in her lifetime to provide a solid basis for comparison. She knew she'd been lucky to have Nick by her side for so long, watching over her, protecting her.

The thought gave her pause, and she set her glass aside. He was back in her life because of Anthony's accident. She knew it. And in that instant, a startling, bone-chilling realization occurred to her.

"I'm in danger. Aren't I, Nick?"

Chapter Two

Nick never lied to her. Nor did he gloss over ugly truths. She'd always appreciated his straightforwardness, even when it was something she wasn't particularly fond of hearing. She expected nothing less now, and was pleased he didn't take the high road.

"You may be, sweetheart."

She settled more deeply into the leather seat. "Okay," she said before pulling in a deep, steadying breath. "Tell me."

Nick appeared uncomfortable, rather uncharacteristic of him. He rubbed his hands together and gave her a compelling look.

"Your father hired me back into service. Following Anthony's death he's… worried."

Molina's stomach plummeted. She knew exactly what troubled her father. *The Vienti Curse.*

Some in her family believed a curse had been cast upon the bloodline at the turn of the twentieth century. The dozen Vienti victims—including Molina's cousin, Anthony—had shared two important commonalities, making the curse theory a viable possibility. Each Vienti had died from a fatal accident, each one in their third decade.

Molina's amiable mood instantly vanished. Anger coursed through her, hot and bright. She'd known Nick would show up in New York because of that damned curse. But in her heart, she had wished for something different. She'd wanted him to be here to offer support, not professional bodyguard services.

But Nick was all business.

"You can get out of my car now."

Nick let out a low laugh, filling the small space with his rich, sensual tones. He spared a glance out the window. "Car's moving, Molina. In case you hadn't noticed."

"So?" Her eyes met his dark blue ones and held. Something sparked between them, a certain awareness. The feeling rushed through her for a moment before she managed, miraculously, to rise above it.

She reached for the phone. "Stop the car, Carlos," she demanded into the receiver. The driver did as she instructed, pulling off the busy freeway in a jerky move.

"There's only one explanation I want to hear for why you're in my car."

Nick cocked a dark eyebrow at her. His tone was suggestive. "Trust me, sweetheart. I would love to say I'm here because I missed that gorgeous body of yours. But that's not the reason for my visit."

Irritated, she narrowed her eyes at him. "Fine. Get out."

"Not until you hear what I have to say."

"Okay." She reached for the handle and gave the door a hard shove. "I'll get out."

"Molina—"

She ignored his protest. She slipped out of the car and walked away, trekking along the shoulder of the treacherously busy freeway. Her long coat was caught by the wind and lifted behind her, fluttering noisily. She paid it no notice.

Nick was capable of working a little magic to coax her back into the car. She'd fight him, though, because she wasn't ready to deal with the harsh reality he seemed intent on handing her. The last thing Molina wanted to think about right now was the Vienti Curse.

She heard his boots on the asphalt as he stalked down the shoulder of the road behind her. He reached out for her. His touch was firm on her arm as he turned her, but his tone was gentle. "Let's not make a scene on a busy New York freeway."

"Maybe I feel like making a scene," she snapped. She stomped her heel on the pavement, swore in Italian then in English. "I know why you're here, damn it."

He nodded, eternally forthright. "So let's talk about it."

"I don't want to talk about it," she glowered. "So just… go away." She tried to work her arm free, but he had a firm grip on her.

"I'm not going anywhere, baby. Deal with it."

"Damn you!" she yelled angrily. "You are so arrogant. Don't you see? It doesn't matter how good a bodyguard you are, you can't stop accidents from happening. And if you try to protect me, you may end up dead yourself."

"I'm not going to let that happen to either of us."

She struggled against his iron grasp. The wind picked up and her hair whipped around her. "I turn thirty next week. If the curse holds true, I'm as good as dead."

Nick growled irritably, "You will be if you keep pulling stupid stunts like this."

"Let me go!"

"Not until you hear what I have to say." He jerked her forward, hauling her up against the hard wall of his chest. He glared down at her. "I don't believe in curses, but that doesn't mean there isn't some sort of force working against your family. I'm going to find out what it is and put a stop to it."

A violent shiver chased through her, and it wasn't from the cold evening air that crept inside her coat. The intensity reflected in his dark eyes and the mere thought of her doomed fate rattled her to the core.

"You can't protect me from a century-old curse."

"Damn it," he said angrily. "Would you stop saying that?" And, presumably to shut her up, he bent his head and crushed his mouth to hers.

Molina forgot all about the dreaded curse as soon as his lips touched hers. Nick's kiss wasn't the least bit hesitant or tentative. It was hot and demanding, arousing and seductive... and oh, so delicious.

His mouth remained on hers for only a moment before they both parted their lips. His tongue slid over her bottom lip, tasting her before slipping inside. His arms eased around her waist, and he held her tightly to him as he continued to kiss her hungrily.

Lord, how she'd missed his kisses. Intimate and erotic. They stirred her senses in so many ways. A kiss from Nick could trigger her arousal at the same time it soothed her soul.

She pressed against him, letting all of the old memories come rushing back. Nick turned her on like no other man she'd known.

When he broke the kiss, she was breathless. She stared up at him, saw his feelings for her reflected in his dark eyes. Molina swallowed down a hard lump in her throat. Their passion for each other had not diminished an ounce in the five years they'd been apart.

Maybe Nick wasn't back in her life just because of the curse. Maybe he was here because he still believed they had a future together.

The thought terrified Molina. She didn't believe she had a future to share with him. Yet at the same time, hope entered her heart, swirling around, building slowly.

"Let's get back in the car," he said in a tight voice.

She gave a slight nod, not trusting her voice. He released her and guided her back to the limo with a gentle hand at the small of her back. His touch was familiar and comforting, and it helped to relieve some of the tension—both nervous and sexual—that had her insides coiled so tightly.

She allowed him to help her inside the car. He took her slender hands between his two large ones. He rubbed gently, bringing warmth back to them.

"I'm taking you to your grandmother's. You'll be safe there," he said in a soft tone. All traces of the anger she'd sparked with her protests had vanished, as had her own ill temper.

Rose Marie's estate was nestled in the Santa Barbara hills. The mansion was secluded and quiet. Molina knew Nick felt comfortable there because he could control the environment.

She smiled softly at him. "I know you like a good challenge, Nick. The more intriguing the better, but—"

"Hey," he interjected, "if someone would have told me about this supposed curse a long time ago, things might have turned out a bit differently for us. And for Anthony."

The intense determination in his eyes stole her breath. Her body still hummed and vibrated from the sensations his kiss evoked. For a moment, she wondered how she could have pushed him away all those years ago, when all he'd ever wanted was to be by her side.

But the reality of the situation—and her fear of a doomed fate—had been the catalyst behind their volatile breakup.

He continued. "There has to be some logical explanation to the deaths. I intend to find out what it is."

Hope speared her insides. *Logic* she could deal with.

Still, she'd spent the better part of her life fearing the curse. She didn't latch on easily to the potential of beating it. "Where would you even begin?"

Nick looked taken aback by her question. "You're kidding, right?"

Molina rolled her eyes. "That was a silly question, I'll admit. I suppose your first call will be to Matt."

Nick had a wide array of resources at his disposal—not just through Frank. He'd grown up in D.C., and he came from a long line of FBI agents and private investigators. Nick's older brother, Matt, had been with the FBI for nearly fifteen years, and Molina knew he'd offer all the help he could.

Not to mention, Nick was quite clever and skilled himself.

Molina's pulse quickened. If he intended to engage his brother and his cousins in an investigation, then he believed there was a tangible reason for the deaths.

Tangible meant *conquerable.*

For the first time, Molina began to toy with the possibility of surviving her fate. With Nick's determination and his family's investigative talents, her optimism grew.

She'd lived with this dark cloud looming over her for most of her life, though she'd avoided thinking of the implications. "Out of sight, out of mind" had always been her motto. But deep down, she'd feared what her relatives believed to be an inevitability: she was a woman without a future.

"Well," she said, feeling a bit breathless from the excitement he sparked inside her. "You have my full cooperation. I know you'll do everything in your power to keep me safe."

Nick reached for her and pulled her to him. She snuggled against him because she needed his strength at the moment. She rested her head against his chest, as their fingers twined together in his lap. He smelled of leather, Hugo Boss cologne and glorious male heat. An arousing combination.

Impulsively, she slipped a hand around his neck and pulled his head down. His lips skimmed over hers. He knew exactly how she liked to be kissed. He caught her bottom lip between his teeth and nipped lightly, exciting her. His tongue slid into her open mouth and smoothed over hers. He pushed deeper, tangling, twisting, suckling. She kept pace with him, matching his erotic dance with steps of her own.

It was a long, deep, warm kiss that aroused her with the sheer intimacy of it, sending the most intense sensations to the core of her. When it ended, she sighed against his neck as her heart thumped in her chest.

"Maybe we ought to keep the kissing to a minimum," Nick said on a ragged breath.

"Too distracting?"

"By far."

Molina had missed his amazing body and the spark of passion he evoked inside her. His kisses alone brought her back to life. "I have faith you're capable of vanquishing a demon while still finding time for extra-curricular activities. Besides," she said as she nuzzled his neck and inhaled his masculine scent. "If I'm going to be stuck with you 24/7 until you solve this mystery, I ought to get some pleasure out of it."

Maybe he thought they should keep the kissing to a minimum, but she didn't. In fact, she wanted much more than just his arousing kisses…

She trailed a finger down his skin to the opening of his shirt. How she loved his chest. It was well-defined, with rock hard pectoral muscles. His bronze skin was covered with the finest, softest dusting of dark brown hair. Her fingers toyed with the next button on his shirt. She lifted her eyes to his handsome face as she slipped the small disk through its opening.

"Think of it this way," she continued in a sexy voice. "The closer you are to me, the safer I'll be. Feel free to visit my room and rumple the sheets whenever the mood strikes. You have my permission to guard my body *any-time*—day or night."

"Way to rationalize, baby," he grinned at her. "But, no."

Her lips curled upward. "Now, Nick," she said as she slid her fingers inside his shirt and stroked his hot flesh. "You know the more you resist, the more *I* persist…" To prove her point, she bent her head to him and lightly brushed her lips over his neck. "Mm," she sighed. "You smell heavenly."

Nick groaned, low and deep. "I'm all for some pleasure, too, baby. But we need to focus on business first."

Molina concealed a sly grin. *Foolish man.* He ought to know better than to dangle a carrot in front of her and think she wouldn't reach for it. When it came to Nick Moretti, Molina found it impossible to resist her sexual impulses. She wanted to touch him, and be touched by him.

Her fingers worked the remainder of the buttons on his shirt. She tugged at the hem at the front, freeing the material from the waist of his jeans.

"This is hardly the place to start something, baby," he said in a low tone.

It was dark outside; the limo was dimly lit inside. The partition glass separated them from the driver. Seemed like a perfect place to her.

Despite his semi-protest, his dark blue eyes glowed seductively. It was all the invitation she needed. She pushed gently at his shirt, clearing the material from his chest. He eased out of it, along with his leather jacket. Her fingernails grazed his nipples, drawing them tight, and he shifted in the seat next to her, as though he was suddenly very uncomfortable.

Molina smiled. "Pants getting a little snug?"

Nick pulled the holder from her ponytail. His fingers tangled in her long hair. "You know how to make me hard in an instant, sweetheart."

Her hand left his chest and smoothed over the hard ridges of his abdomen. Her fingers skimmed over the narrow patch of hair leading farther south. She eased her hand lower still, over the erection that strained against the fly of his pants.

Nick's fingers tightened around the strands of hair he held in his hand and he jerked slightly beneath her touch. His head fell back against the seat and he let out a low groan.

Molina smiled wantonly as her hand moved over the full, hard length of him.

"Molina," he whispered hoarsely. His hand closed over hers to still it. "Don't."

She leaned into him, pressing her body to his. Her lips brushed the warm skin on his neck. She traced the tip of her tongue around the outer shell of his ear, then playfully nipped at the lobe. "I've had the most erotic fantasies about us," she whispered. "Do you ever fantasize about me, Nick?"

His jaw clenched then loosened. "All the damn time, baby." He turned his head to gaze at her; the heat in his eyes emphasized his words. By the strained look on his handsome face, he was employing every ounce of willpower he possessed to keep from ravaging her.

Molina hoped to break his restraint. She *wanted* to be ravaged. The mere thought made her ache for him deep inside.

His erection continued to pulse beneath her hand. "Nick..." She said his name on a suggestive sigh.

"This is not a good idea, Molina."

But they both knew they'd left good sense back on the highway with that first kiss. She knew she'd have to deal with the ramifications of her actions later. Nick wasn't a one-night stand man; he'd expect more from her than instant sexual gratification.

She'd deal with the messy emotional stuff later, though. Right now, all she could think about was getting him worked up enough to make him forget about his views on causal sex.

"I think it's a wonderful idea," she said on a soft, seductive note. "I've missed you terribly."

Nick stared down at her. "I've missed you, too, baby."

Molina's stomach fluttered. She eased her hand out of his death grip and reached for the gold fastening on her suit jacket. She slid the zipper oh-so-slowly down its track. The sound echoed erotically in the car. She shimmied out of her overcoat and suit jacket, tossing them to the far corner of the car. She wore a lacy white camisole underneath her suit jacket. Her plump breasts rose above the cups, creating cleavage she knew Nick would appreciate.

"Let me tell you about one of my fantasies." She pressed her breasts against him as she whispered. "It involves you giving me a very thorough, full body massage."

Nick's thumb skimmed across her jaw line, his fingers caressing the side of her neck. He drew her close and dipped his head to hers. His kiss was demanding, and it conveyed a hint of warning. Things were about to get out of control.

When his lips left hers, they grazed her temple. "Take your skirt off, baby," he whispered on a sharp breath.

She did as he asked, and tossed the garment in the corner of the seat where the clothes were beginning to pile high. Nick's gaze turned smoldering and hot as he eyed her lacy thong panties and the garters holding her thigh-high stockings in place. She knew he was a sucker for sexy lingerie, which was why she'd become such a fan of it years ago.

He pulled her against him. With a wicked smile on her lips, Molina straddled him. She splayed her hand over the rigid muscles of his stomach, which flinched involuntarily under her hot, greedy touch. He growled deep in his throat and shifted his body beneath her.

She eased forward, her arms twisting around his neck, her breasts pressing to his chest. She rocked gently against his erection, and his grip on her hips tightened. His hot mouth grazed her throat as she whispered in his ear.

"Candles are flickering all around us, and I'm lying naked on a huge bed, covered in red satin sheets. You rub warm oil over every inch of my body—my arms, my breasts, my belly, my legs. Until my skin is slick and glowing. I writhe and moan under your touch, growing restless and hot and in desperate, desperate need of you."

Nick grew impatient beneath her. His hands roamed her body, up her back, then down over her hips to her bare bottom. He cupped the rounded cheeks and gave a gentle squeeze.

"What do I do to you, baby?" he asked in a tight voice. "In your fantasy?"

"What you always do to me, Nick. Your hands caress my skin, your tongue teases all of my sensitive spots. You make me so hot, stroking my breasts and my clit that I beg you to make me come."

Nick growled. He lifted his hands to her shoulders and his fingers twisted in the straps of her camisole. "You usually beg me in Italian," he said. "Drives me absolutely wild."

He eased the straps of her camisole downward. Without the support of the thin material, the unstructured cups collapsed under the weight of her breasts, completely exposing her to Nick. Desire flashed in his deep blue eyes. He bent his head to her and his tongue glided over a nipple, causing it to pebble tightly.

Molina's breath caught. Everything inside her seized up for the briefest of moments, and then slowly, almost painfully, a fiery sensation began to flow through her. How could she have forgotten how she responded to his touch?

Nick gave her no time to recover from her initial reaction to him, nor did he give her a moment's reprieve to assimilate his touch. His hands cupped her breasts and kneaded them gently. His tongue flicked the other nipple and it puckered to an almost painful point. He drew it into his mouth and sucked, hard.

Molina gasped as the erotic pleasure pricked her deep inside. Her fingers gripped his steel biceps, her nails pressing into his flesh. She looked down at him as he laved and sucked her taut peaks, giving equal attention to each one. She fought for a full breath.

She released his arms and wove her fingers through his thick, lush hair. She pressed his head to her and arched into him, urging him to continue, urging him to drive her mad with desire the way only he knew how. Her long hair cascaded down her back, the silky strands teasing her skin the way his mouth teased her nipples as his tongue and teeth and lips toyed with her ultra-sensitive flesh.

One hand left her breast and eased up the outer side of her thigh. He touched the exposed skin above the lacy top of her stocking, and expertly unfastened the garter with a quick flick. His fingers grazed the damp crotch of her panties.

She started beneath his touch, responding as though a flame had been held against her skin. Nick groaned loudly at her reaction to him.

His mouth relinquished her nipple, and his teeth nipped at the flesh on her neck.

"Touch me, Nick. Put your fingers inside me," she said into his dark hair.

He cupped her mound and pressed his fingertips into her swollen flesh. The thin, drenched wisp of lace covering her there provided little barrier to the heat he emitted. Molina felt her insides coil into a tight fist.

"Baby," he whispered against her throat, "you're so wet for me."

She was also breathless. Her insides hummed and pulsed. She felt hot and restless, just like she did every time she fantasized about this magnificent man.

"Nick," she urged, desperately needing him to touch her. "*Please.*"

"As I recall, you like to be on top. Don't you, sweetheart?"

She moaned. "You know exactly how I like it, no matter what the position. Take me anyway you want me."

He growled, low and primal. He kissed her again. His lips and tongue tangled with hers. He deepened their kiss as his fingers finally pushed aside the material between her legs and brushed over the wet, slightly plumped up flesh.

She broke the kiss and gasped. Sharp stabs of desire pierced her deep inside. Her hard nipples grazed his skin as she fought for a full, steady breath, tightening them further as they brushed against the silky hair on his chest.

Nick stroked her slick folds, making her pant in his ear. She rose up a bit off his lap, giving him better access to her most intimate area. He found that precious nub and rubbed it slowly, skillfully, intensifying the throbbing deep inside her. Her breath quickened. She closed her eyes as he continued to stroke her. Her lips parted slightly as a sigh of lust and longing passed through them.

Then his fingers slid inside her and she cried out, her body responding fervently to the sudden, sweet intrusion. Her nipples were still tightly puckered and begged for attention. Nick's mouth latched onto one as his fingers pumped in and out of her in quick, determined strokes.

The pressure inside her mounted to an unbearable degree as he took her to the brink. But she wanted more than this. She wanted all of him.

"Don't you want to be inside me, Nick?" she asked on a labored breath.

"You know I do, baby."

She reached for his hand. He withdrew his fingers and Molina quickly unfastened the small silver belt buckle at his waist. She unzipped his jeans and slid the denim below his hips. The tip of his hard cock strained above the waistband of his sexy black briefs. Molina's fingers skimmed over the smooth skin, and he bucked beneath her touch. She pushed the briefs down as her hand wrapped around his shaft. Nick's hands gripped her upper arms, as though he needed something steady to stabilize him.

She eased her body over the head of his cock and rubbed it against her wet flesh. Nick groaned. He closed his eyes and rested his head against the seat again. His chest rose and fell sharply with his quick breath. She drove him wild as she used his cock to stroke her hot, sensitive flesh.

Molina slowly drew him into her body, an inch at a time. Nick's hands cupped her breasts and his thumbs teased her nipples. She took him in farther, then eased back toward the smooth, throbbing tip, drawing him out of her. She repeated this action, over and over, until he was writhing restlessly beneath her. His grip on her breasts tightened, heightening her arousal.

Knowing she had such power over him, knowing she could make him so hot and hard, spurred her desire. Finally, she drew him completely inside her and rocked against him. When she knew they were both close, she increased the tempo, riding him hard and fast. His hands grabbed at her hips, and he pressed her down onto him as he arched and thrust himself deeper and deeper inside her.

"I'm going to come, baby," he said on harsh breath.

"Yes, Nick. *Now.*"

She rubbed her tight nipples against his chest. His hands slid to her bottom and he cupped her cheeks. He pushed himself into her and she felt his body shake and convulse from his powerful orgasm.

Moments later, a shattering climax rocked her body and she cried out. She squeezed her inner muscles tightly around him, wanting desperately to prolong the sensations rioting inside her for as long as possible.

She was breathless, a bit dizzy, even. Her heart thundered in her chest and she felt mini-aftershocks rack her insides as her muscles continued to contract around him. He wrapped his arms around her and held her close.

It seemed to take an absurdly long time for her breathing to resume to normal. She climbed off of Nick and slumped against the seat. He reached for a stack of napkins from the bar. He leaned toward her, used a napkin to absorb some of the moisture that had trickled down her inner thigh. He kissed her knee, grinned lazily at her.

Nick cleaned himself up and they dressed in silence. He raked a hand through his disheveled hair.

"Guess we've officially kissed and made up," he said.

Her stomach fluttered. "I'd say so. And let me just add, the real thing is always so much better than the fantasy."

Nick shook his head and let out a low laugh. "You are too much, baby." He glanced out the window. "Looks like we have good timing." They'd arrived at the airport.

"We're flying commercial?" she inquired, still a bit breathless.

"I sent your private plane back to California. I like the idea of commercial better. Bit safer right now." He flashed her a sexy grin. "Don't worry, baby. I booked us first class."

Chapter Three

Molina woke to the sun streaming through the partially open drapes. Golden rays flitted halfway across the enormous room, just reaching the bed she slept in.

Partially clothed, she tossed the eggplant-colored velvet duvet off of her and sat up. Sleepily, she thought about the evening before. She'd been so emotionally drained from the week-long funeral preparations and service, and physically spent from her interlude with Nick in the limo, that she'd slept on the plane and again fell asleep during the ride to Rose Marie's. Nick had carried her upstairs and put her to bed. She'd roused long enough to ask him to join her.

"I'm taking the suite next door," he'd told her. "Close enough to keep my eyes on you."

"But not your hands," she'd said with a sigh of disappointment.

Nick had kissed her on the tip of her nose. "I can't afford to be distracted by you, Molina."

He'd left her room after that, and as she'd drifted off to sleep, she'd realized he'd let her off the emotional hook. For now.

Molina climbed out of the bed and padded across the floor to the bathroom. Nick's iron will had kept him from crawling into bed with her last night. She shouldn't feel so annoyed he'd found the strength to resist her.

But she was annoyed.

She let out a low sigh as she undressed. The hot shower helped to ease some of her tension, but her skin was still sensitive. Thinking of Nick's caresses made her tingle all over. He could tell her he didn't want any distractions while he was working, but it wasn't going to stop her from *being* a distraction.

Her mood instantly brightened. With a wicked grin on her lips, she went to her walk-in closet and selected a sexy turquoise-colored top with thin spaghetti straps and enough boning in it to plump her breasts up over the low dip of the neckline. The perfect top to make Nick drool.

She paired it with black dress pants, pumps and her usual gold jewelry. She noticed her hands trembled slightly when she applied her makeup. The mere thought of Nick sent a shiver of exhilaration up her spine. He made her feel alive and full of hope. She knew he would move heaven and earth to change her fate.

She pulled her long hair into its customary sleek ponytail, then left her room. She traveled the long hallway to the second floor mezzanine, which was an open area above the foyer. She caught a glimpse of Nick ascending the long, sweeping staircase and she waited for him to reach the top.

His eyes swept over her, lingering on the endowments she'd purposely put on display. She could see the heat seep into him as his dark eyes glowed.

Oh, yes. Let the drooling commence.

"Sleep well?" he asked in a strained voice, his gaze still glued to her chest.

Her nipples tightened behind the material from his look alone. She flashed him a flirtatious grin. "My batteries have been sufficiently recharged." She lifted an eyebrow suggestively.

Nick grinned at her, but didn't take the bait.

Dressed head-to-toe in black, he looked mysterious and sexy. His jaw was set in a stubborn line. His broad shoulders were squared and he had a peculiar tunnel-vision look about him. Very intense. Very focused. Nick was all business this morning.

Well, that just won't do, she thought.

"I have the schematics for the alarm system and the blueprints of the house," he said. "I'm going to be working all day on evaluating the current system and determining what improvements need to be made."

"Meaning don't distract you?"

Nick nodded. "I just need to make sure the updates are made. This is the safest place for you to be right now. It needs to remain that way."

She closed the gap between them with two small steps. She lifted a hand to his chest, trailed her fingers over his hard muscles. "You're here. I'd say that makes it the safest place on the planet for me." She stared up at him, a sexy smile on her lips.

Nick's hand closed around hers. He didn't even crack a smile. The serious look on his handsome face didn't waver. "I'm not taking any chances, Molina."

Not sweetheart or baby, she thought. *Molina.* He was being way too intense for her taste, trying to establish boundaries she didn't want established. He was telling her playtime was over. He had serious work to do.

She didn't discount that work by any stretch of the imagination. The mere thought of being able to live her life without the dread she'd become accustomed to feeling was enough to get her on board with his work-related efforts.

What she couldn't understand, however, was why he had to be so grim about it. She was safe here. Nothing sinister would happen to her within these walls. So he hardly needed to pull the all-work-and-no-play act.

Well, she'd simply have to put a kink in his plans, she decided. She didn't intend to waste the time they had together. The opportunity to seduce Nick was just too delicious to pass up.

Yesterday was just the beginning of greater things to come. They'd barely scratched the surface of their desire for each other. Even now, Molina could feel his hands on her body, stroking her, inciting all those wonderful sensations deep inside her. How could they ignore the passion they'd always shared? As far as she was concerned, they couldn't resume a bodyguard-client relationship. She knew, however, she'd have to finesse Nick a bit to get him to loosen up.

"Nick," she said on a seductive note. "You know if you tell me not to distract you, that's exactly what I'll do." She leaned closer to him and the tops of her breasts brushed against his bare skin, just under the hem of the short sleeve of his shirt.

For a moment, he only stared at her. His eyes cast low, they landed on the very assets she'd intended to make good use of for her seduction. His jaw worked rigorously as he mulled over whatever thoughts were tripping through his mind.

Hopefully very naughty, erotic thoughts...

Molina lifted her chin and her lips grazed his cheek. His skin was smooth and warm.

"I know you want me," she whispered. She kissed the corner of his mouth. "I'm all yours." She pressed her breasts against his arm, to emphasize her point.

Nick groaned deep in his throat.

Molina tried not to gloat over the response she'd so easily elicited. She untangled herself from him. "I have to go see my grandmother now." She turned on her tall heels and strolled off.

She traveled the long hall of the west wing to her grandmother's suite, with a noticeable bounce in her step. She had no doubt she'd left Nick hot and bothered.

The French doors leading to the veranda were wide open. White drapes billowed as a gentle breeze caught and lifted the airy material. The sheer panels floated to the marble floor, falling slowly back into place, only to be lifted again, moments later. The aria wafting through the suite was haunting and moving.

And in the middle of the room, nestled comfortably on a sage-colored velvet settee was Rose Marie D'Angelo Vienti. A vision in white, her silver hair swept back in an elegant French twist, her spring dress made of a flowing gauzy material, she was practically angelic.

Until she opened her mouth to speak.

"Damned stubborn fool you are," she said in a chastising tone. But a flash of mischief in her pale green eyes—eyes identical to Molina's—revealed her adoration for her granddaughter.

"Climbing out of a car while on a busy New York freeway. You practically invited the curse to take you."

Molina let out a soft laugh. She crossed the room, kissed her grandmother on both cheeks before settling next to her. She took the older woman's small hand into hers. A hand that appeared frail from age but which held a shocking amount of strength. "Who told?" But, of course, she already knew the answer.

"I spoke with Nicholas early this morning. He told me Frank discussed the curse with him. He's intent on ensuring the 'accidents' cease."

"If anyone can do it, it's Nick. We should have told him about the curse a long time ago. But Daddy didn't want anyone talking about it. When Mama died, it was just too hard from him to accept she'd been a victim of the curse." She knew how difficult her mother's death had been on her grandmother and her father. Ann Marie had been the light in her father's eyes; it had dimmed significantly with her passing. He'd retreated to his work and distanced himself emotionally from Molina, perhaps because he feared she would someday suffer the same fate.

"It has to end," Rose Marie said in a soft tone. "We've all become accustomed to accepting the tragic loss of our loved ones. It's time we stop thinking of premature deaths as inevitable."

"I agree." Molina gave her grandmother a bright smile. "And I know in my heart Nick will save me from that fate."

"He's determined to do so." Rose Marie studied her for a moment, no doubt homing in on the excitement radiating from her. Rose Marie took Molina's hands in hers. "Darling, you have your whole life ahead of you—Nick will see to that. Your father doesn't place his utmost confidence in everyone, you know. He trusts Nick to ensure you have a future."

"I know."

"So, then. Perhaps you ought to start thinking about that future." Rose Marie gave Molina's hands a gentle squeeze.

Molina felt her insides coil. "Nick is back in my life because Daddy hired him back, Gran. It doesn't mean he intends to stay." But Molina certainly intended to enjoy his company while he was here.

"Perhaps he doesn't intend to stay because you never give him reason to."

Molina rolled her eyes. "I admit I have some emotional… *shortcomings*. It doesn't mean I don't want him around."

"Yes. But, darling, you push him away whenever he gets too close." Molina opened her mouth to protest but Rose Marie silenced her with a pointed look. "Now, I will only tell you this once, my dear, so pay attention. You have a bright future ahead of you, and you would be a damned fool not to include Nick Moretti in that future. I want this house filled with laughter and children. Not loneliness and sorrow. We've had enough of that to last an eternity."

Molina swallowed down the lump that had suddenly formed in her throat. She was the last of the Vienti bloodline. Rose Marie had lost a husband, two children and three grandchildren to the Vienti curse. Each death troubled her all the more. She was strong enough to survive a broken heart, but she was incredibly sad.

The passing of her grandson, Anthony, V, had been particularly difficult because Rose Marie's health did not allow her to travel across the country. She'd missed the funeral, and Molina knew that saddened her all the more.

But in typical Rose Marie fashion, she did not dwell on her heartache. "Now," she said as she gave Molina's hand a gentle pat. "I'm going to send you on your way. I have some calls to make regarding the Foundation's gala."

Molina had founded the Ann Marie Toscano Foundation when she'd turned twenty-one. Raising money for underprivileged children was a pet project of hers, and she planned an annual gala to support the Foundation's fundraising efforts. Molina called on her grandmother each year to use her connections in the community to help bring in donations.

"Well, I'll leave you to your business." Molina brushed her lips over the cool, wrinkled skin on her grandmother's cheek and told her she'd return later so they could enjoy lunch together.

Nick spent the entire day assessing the current alarm system and the upgrades needed to bring it into this century. Rose Marie had occupied the family estate for nearly sixty years. She'd done a fantastic job keeping the place in modern opulence, but she'd neglected the security system.

After his initial sweep of the house, he had three pages of notes and half-dozen phone calls to make. By the time he'd wrapped up this preliminary work, it was dark outside. He'd missed lunch and he'd had to contend with Rose Marie's chef, Isabelle, shooting him scolding looks each time their paths crossed.

But Nick had wanted to get as much accomplished as possible while Molina was with her grandmother. He didn't think clearly when she was close by.

Do you ever fantasize about me?

Her words rattled around in his head as he finished his work. Practically every time he closed his eyes, he saw her face. Hell, yes, he fantasized about her. And only her. But she'd been right in the car. The real thing was infinitely better than the fantasy.

His groin tightened. It hadn't been wise to make love with her in the limo. Instead of taking the edge off, it made him want her all the more.

He wandered into the dining room, hoping to find her there.

Isabelle informed him Molina had had an early dinner with Rose Marie in her suite. Disappointment sat like a rock in his gut. He would have enjoyed dining with the two women.

Hell, who was he kidding? He wanted Molina, plain and simple.

He ate his meal alone, then kissed Isabelle on the cheek because she'd made his favorite, Osso Bucco.

He went in search of Molina and found her in the study, making good use of the oversized mahogany desk that had been her grandfather's, the late Anthony Vienti, III. She glanced up from her laptop and reached for her glass of wine as he walked in. Floor-to-ceiling bookcases lined the walls and a sliding ladder rested in the far corner, waiting for someone to come along and select a book sixteen feet off the ground.

Nick poured himself a glass of port from the bar and sank into a burgundy leather chair.

"Foundation work?"

She nodded. Her smile was warm and inviting. Her peridot eyes twinkled in the soft lighting emitted from the crystal chandelier, which hung directly above the desk. "Annual gala."

He propped his feet on the footstool, sipped his wine. He couldn't help but admire the view before him. Molina was stunning. The color of her top complemented her golden skin, and the way the garment fit her was downright sinful.

Molina engaged all of his senses at once, creating a wicked sensory overload. Everything about her spiked his passion—the sight of her feminine curves; the rich scent of her perfume; the sound of her soft, erotic moans; the feel of her velvety skin; and the taste of her luscious mouth.

But she affected him on more than just a physical level. His heart was definitely involved.

The corners of her mouth lifted as he continued to stare at her.

"Am I distracting you?" she asked in a soft, flirty tone.

Nick felt a familiar longing bubble up inside him. "Yeah, baby. You are."

She needed no more encouragement than that. She stood up and came round the enormous desk. She trailed a hand over his broad shoulder as she leaned over the back of his chair.

Nick suppressed the groan that welled up inside of him from her touch. He wanted her. For longer than he could remember, his thoughts had been consumed by her. Erotic images of them making love would flash through his mind with such vivid clarity he'd feel as though she was right there in the room with him, fanning his desire with her heated looks and sinful touch.

As she did now. Her fingers skimmed the side of his neck, then tangled in his hair.

"You're incredibly tense," she whispered in his ear.

No shit. He was trying to concentrate on his job, when all he really wanted to do was play out some of the fantasies they'd both conjured up over the years.

Question was, could he play with fire and not get burned—again? When it came to Molina, it wasn't just his body that ached for her. His heart and soul longed for her as well.

He knew better than to start something with her; she was incapable of seeing it through on an emotional level. The woman was commitment phobic, had been since the day he'd met her. Molina considered everything in her life to be fleeting. She had every right to feel that way, he supposed. She'd lost so many people she'd loved in her short lifetime.

Nick had not understood her reasons for holding him at arm's length, emotionally, years ago. He understood it now that he knew about the curse.

Her hands slid over his shoulders. She gently massaged the tight muscles. "You need to relax. I have a very good feeling everything is going to work out."

Indeed, he wasn't going to let anything happen to Molina. She could count on living a long life. He would see to it.

She leaned closer to him, her hands sliding down the front of him, igniting a fire inside him. Her long hair fell over the back of the chair, the silky strands teasing his neck. The material of his shirt provided absolutely no barrier against her touch. He could feel her warmth, could feel the strength in her fingers. Molina was graceful and feminine, but she was also tough as nails. All of which were qualities he admired in a woman.

His body quickly became one big livewire, looking for an outlet to release the pent-up energy.

"You're much too used to getting your way, sweetheart."

"And you're much too stubborn."

He grinned. With every soft breath tickling his skin, he came that much more undone.

Molina moved back around to the front of the desk. She propped herself on the edge of it, gave him a sexy look.

Nick knew he was in trouble.

She toyed with the straps of her top for a moment before sliding them down her arms. Nick felt a powerful surge in his groin. He ground his teeth together as he forced himself to remain in his seat and not leap forward and grab her.

The buzzing of his cell phone granted him a reprieve. Nick extracted the phone from the front pocket of his dress pants and glanced at the caller ID. It was his older brother, Matt.

"I have to take this," he told Molina. He flipped the phone open and greeted his brother.

He stood up and turned to go, difficult as it was to leave her. As he crossed the study, an idea popped into his head. He told Matt he'd call him right back and snapped the phone shut.

Nick glanced about the cavernous study and said, "Have you ever gone through all of your grandfather's memorabilia?"

Molina cast a curious look at him. Her lips were glossy and plump. Damn tempting. He fought to remain focused on his current train of thought, rather than her luscious mouth.

"What do you mean?" she asked.

Nick's gaze swept over the voluminous collection of books, papers, scrapbooks and photo albums kept by Anthony Vienti, III.

"I don't know," Nick said as he absently rubbed the back of his neck. His hormones were still raging, and it took a great deal of effort for him to concentrate on anything other than the sexy woman standing before him. "The answer to the dreaded curse has to lie somewhere. Given your grandfather was basically the historian of the family, maybe there's something in these books that might help us."

Molina gasped. "I never even considered that. You could be right. My grandfather kept extensive records and personal effects of the Vientis. More so than anyone else in the family."

Nick spied a Vienti family album on a low shelf. He removed it and placed it on the desk.

Molina stared up at him, a frown on her beautiful face. "Okay, here's the problem. I have no idea what I'm looking for."

"I know." He flipped the book open anyway.

She sounded deflated when she said, "Half this library is filled with books on my family, Nick. It'd take years to go through them all. And according to the unwritten laws of the Vienti curse, I don't have that long."

He shot her a hard look. "Don't say that. If we have to stay here until we solve this mystery, we will. And as long as you're here with me, nothing's going to happen to you."

He saw the tension creep into her delicate features. "I believe you, but..." she shook her head as she let out a sigh.

"What?" Nick inquired, his tone turning soft.

Molina looked agitated and uncomfortable and sullen all at once. She flipped absently through a few pages in the oversized scrapbook spread before her. The parchment paper pages were crisp and they made a distinct "whooshing" sound as she turned them over with a flick of her wrist.

Nick waited for her answer, but it wasn't forthcoming. He leaned over and rested a hand on hers, to still it. Her eyes lifted from the book and met his.

"Say it," he said. Words he'd never heard her utter were on her tongue. He knew it. And maybe if he had faced this demon years ago, things would have turned out differently. Maybe they would have conquered the mystery of the Vienti curse before Anthony lost his life. Before Molina's thirtieth birthday loomed so ominously. Before she'd pushed him away.

She shook her head. "I don't know, I just..." she groaned. She snatched her hand from his and reached for the cover of the leather-bound book. She snapped it close and the sound echoed in the room. "I can't believe we're going to find the answers here."

It wasn't at all what she'd intended to say. He could tell. "It's as good a place as any."

She looked frustrated. She threw her hands up in the air. "This is an impossible mystery to solve. Where on earth would we start?"

"Here," Nick repeated as he pointed to the book on the desk.

She shook her head again. "They're just photos and memoirs, Nick. How am I going to find clues to a century-old mystery in here? I'm not Nancy Drew."

His jaw clenched as he tried to keep his own frustration under control. "We've got to start somewhere, sweetheart. So I suggest you start boning up on the family history."

He turned again to walk away. He punched the speed dial number for his brother.

"It's me," he said in a tight voice. "What have you found?"

"Might want to sit down for this, bro," Matt said. "I have some very disturbing news."

Chapter Four

Molina went back to the desk and opened the old scrapbook. She studied the pages, found herself taking notes. By midnight, she had a notebook full of scribbles that meant nothing to her. She tossed her pen on the desk.

She was looking for the proverbial needle in the haystack. She'd gone through over a dozen books so far and had found nothing out of the ordinary to spark her interest or curiosity. She closed the last one and hefted it off the desk. Her grandfather believed in immortalizing the family history in oversize leather books that weighed a good ten pounds.

She climbed the first three steps of the ladder and reached above her head to replace the book in its designated slot on the bookshelf. She lost her footing, swayed and fell backward, landing solidly on the hardwood floor.

"Ow!" she cried out, as she lay sprawled on her backside. She groaned, then rolled onto her hip. She rubbed her sore cheek. "Christ. Who needs a curse to bump you off when you're this clumsy?" she grumbled as she slowly got to her feet. The book lay open on the floor, and she bent down to retrieve it. Several loose photographs escaped the pages and floated to the floor.

Along with a tarnished brass key.

Molina picked up the antique key and studied it for a moment. She glanced around the library. She didn't see anything small enough to accommodate such a tiny key. The books she'd looked at didn't have locks on them, so she had no idea of the key's purpose.

Yet another mystery to solve.

Molina knelt down and scooped up the photos and arranged them in a neat stack. She carted the old black-and-white pictures, the key and the book to the desk and dropped the items on the mahogany top with a resounding thud. As fascinating as her family was to her, she'd had enough of the Vientis for the evening.

She turned off the lights and left the study.

She crossed the enormous foyer and climbed the curving staircase to the second floor. Her tall heels clicked softly as she walked down the long, wide hallway. Molina entered her suite and went straight to her walk-in closet. She rummaged through the lingerie drawers. Nick was doing a good job standing his ground, but he was no match for a woman hell-bent on seducing him.

She dug around and finally located what she was looking for. Between the clothes she'd brought and the clothes she'd always kept at Rose Marie's, she pulled together a sexy outfit Nick wouldn't be able to resist.

She knocked softly on their adjoining door. Waited patiently. She knocked again, a little harder. And again. Molina frowned. It was possible he was avoiding her. Or asleep.

She shook her head and sighed. No. He was elsewhere; she'd find him.

She left her room and went to the far end of the wing to the entertainment room. A large, flat-screen TV and pool table were situated at the far end while a fully stocked wet bar and several plush sofas and chairs filled the front of the room. Warm lighting and soft music created an inviting atmosphere. Molina found Nick at the bar, sipping a cocktail.

She sidled up next to him. "Crown Royal, straight up," she mused. "You're doing some serious drinking tonight."

She went round the bar and took down the bottle of Chivas. She poured the amber liquid into a crystal glass, then set the bottle aside. She took a sip.

Nick gazed at her over the rim of his glass. "That's some outfit you're wearing."

She winked playfully at him. Black corset, black miniskirt, black stockings, black high heels. Oh, and a black lace g-string with a cute little red butterfly embroidered where all of the strings joined in the back. His iron will didn't stand a chance.

"Shoot some pool?" she asked in an innocent tone. She didn't wait for his answer. She rounded the bar, Chivas in hand, and crossed the room to the far corner.

She chose a stick from one of the two racks mounted on the wall then racked the balls while Nick selected his own pool cue. She executed a forceful break, dropping three stripes. She eyed her options on the table, did some quick mental calculations. Nick had taught her to play years ago. He'd taught her a lot of things, actually. How to drive, how to select produce, how to balance her checkbook. Things normal people did.

Before he'd joined her legion of bodyguards, Molina had been a sheltered heiress, stifled and smothered by the small entourage surrounding her from the moment she left her bedroom in the morning until the time she returned at night. She'd had little freedom and very few friends because it was too difficult to build friendships with bodyguards looming so close.

Threats of being kidnapped and held for ransom were the initial cause for the overprotection. After her mother's fatal accident when Molina was ten, her father had heightened the security around her. It had made for a very lonely existence.

Until Nick came along. He appeared on her nineteenth birthday and didn't leave her side for five years. He'd treated her as a young woman, not an assignment, and had opened up a whole new world to her, teaching her things she'd never before considered. Like how to cook gourmet meals, ride a motorcycle, shoot a .357 magnum, execute self-defense moves, sail a small boat. Nick had encouraged her to be more than just a pretty heiress. And he'd empowered her to take personal responsibility for her safety.

He'd been more than her bodyguard, though. He'd been her friend and closest confidante. Her first lover.

Not just the first. The best.

She lingered over the thought a moment as she lined up her next shot on the pool table. She leaned forward, knowing she was giving Nick an excellent view of the tops of her breasts as they rose above the low, sweeping neckline of her curve-hugging corset. She slowly lifted her gaze to see if he was looking.

When his sapphire eyes caught hers, his look was so hot it nearly seared her. She felt the muscles deep inside her clench and quiver, making her shudder.

She forced her eyes away from his, focused on her shot. Normally, she was a great pool player, but tonight... the wayward cue ball hit a solid—one of his balls—and dropped it into the corner pocket. She swore under her breath.

Nick chuckled. *The cad.* He eased past her, his body gently grazing hers, igniting a slow burn.

"Thanks for the help, sweetheart." He quickly assessed the table, took aim and sank two balls.

She knew she was in trouble.

He glanced over at her before lining up his next shot. "Find anything of interest in those books?"

She drew in a long, shallow breath. His look was a scorcher, all sexual awareness mixed with subtle warning—what was he trying to tell her? Seducing him was dangerous business?

And did he really believe she could carry on a conversation with him looking at her like that?

So far, her research efforts had been a waste of time, but there was still hope she could salvage the evening. If Nick would cooperate with her.

Nick took another shot, sank a ball. He looked at her expectantly. He actually thought they could have a conversation when she was this worked up.

She sighed. Tried to focus. Tried to think of things other than him setting her on the edge of the pool table, pushing her skirt up to her waist and taking her. Hard. The way he sometimes did when they were both so hot and bothered nothing else would satiate them.

Molina pulled up a stool, not just because she sensed Nick would be running the table for a while. Her knees practically knocked together at the thought of sex with Nick. She wasn't so sure she could continue to stand without swaying on her tall heels.

Okay, he'd asked her a question. He wanted to know about the books. She pulled in a breath. Funny how she lost every coherent thought when he was around.

"Well," she began. "Considering I don't know what I'm looking for, I'd say my initial investigation was a complete bust."

Nick eyed her over the end of the cue stick. His expression changed, became more serious. "I don't know what you're looking for, either. But it's been my experience that clues to family murders lie close to home."

Molina nearly fell off her stool. "*Murder!*"

Nick straightened. "Yeah, Molina."

"No, Nick." She shook her head, shocked he would say such a thing. "We're talking about accidents, here. You know, tripping and falling down a flight of stairs, falling over the railing of a houseboat and drowning, crash-landing an airplane. Those were all accidents. As were the others."

Nick rested the butt of his cue stick on the marble floor as he rubbed the back of his neck. For a moment, Molina was sidetracked by him. He was so damn sexy, dressed all in black. And he fit in so well at Rose Marie's.

He belongs here. With me.

The thought jolted her. It was enough to make her want to get back to murder and mayhem.

"I got some news earlier from my brother, Molina," he told her. "He's looking into Anthony's death."

"Another accident."

"I don't think so."

She groaned. "Come on, Nick. I can't subscribe to the murder theory. My cousin was hit by a car while crossing a street in Brooklyn. That," she said with conviction, "was an accident."

Nick shrugged a broad shoulder, looking unconvinced.

Molina slid off her tall stool and crossed to where he stood. "Have you been to Brooklyn, Nick? Even with a crosswalk, the green light and the 'walk' sign in your favor, crossing a street in Brooklyn can be deadly. Pedestrians get run over all the time in Brooklyn. It was an accident."

"And what if it wasn't?" he countered, his dark eyes narrowed. "According to Matt, who's seen the police report and talked to the cops handling the case, your cousin was run down by a car doing at least sixty miles per hour in a thirty-five zone. The driver didn't bother slowing down. There were no skid marks on the street, Molina. He didn't apply the brakes *at all*."

She stared at him, trying to comprehend what he was saying. He was talking about cold-blooded murder. All this time, she'd thought the curse was some sort of pre-determined fate. Not murder. Never before had she considered murder.

Perhaps others had. "Does my father know about this?"

Nick nodded.

Molina turned away to go back to the table and get her drink. She could use a good stiff drink. Nick's warm hand slid down her arm until his fingers twined with hers. He moved behind her, wrapped his and her arm around her waist. He leaned close to her ear. "Baby, I didn't mean to scare you."

"I know," she breathed. She felt unsteady, a bit queasy.

Nick's lips brushed her temple. He tossed his cue stick on the pool table and wrapped his other arm around her. "You're safe. I promise."

She nodded her head. She had to work down a lump of fear and dread before she could speak. "Guess I'm better at ignoring uncomfortable thoughts than we'd imagined. Murder never even occurred to me."

"There aren't any witnesses to Anthony's accident—rather surprising in a busy Brooklyn neighborhood. Not a single lead to go on, either." He spoke in soft, soothing tones, which helped to calm her frayed nerves. "Matt is going to investigate further. He'll come up with some answers. In the meantime, you're safe with me."

Nick's older brother had been with the FBI for fifteen years. A brilliant covert agent, if anyone could figure out what had happened to Anthony, it was Matt.

"Next time you speak with him, tell him how much I appreciate his help."

"He'd do anything to help keep you safe, you know that. He's crazy about you."

She smiled. "Hmm. Runs in the family, does it?"

Nick chuckled. The sound was low and deep, and it seeped inside her, warming her. She let him comfort her for a moment longer, let him chase away the fear that had crept over her. She was safe with Nick.

Before the moment became too emotionally overwhelming for her, though, she turned in his arms, wrapping hers around his waist. "I take it we're done playing pool?" she whispered.

Nick glanced down at her. His eyes lingered on her glossy lips for a moment, then followed the path down her throat to the swell of her breasts above the top of her corset.

His breath caught. The lustful look that flashed in his dark eyes sparked something carnal deep inside her.

"I still have a few shots to make."

She gave him a coy smile before she eased out of his arms and took a few small steps to the pool table. She leaned over the lip of the table and reached for the eight ball. She was stretched across the end of the table, bent over it so her skirt hitched up several inches in the back. She rested her elbows on the red-felt top and palmed the black ball. She eyed the table, looking for an opening. Spotting a clear path, she flicked her wrist and the ball dropped to the table and rolled across the felt to the far corner. It fell into the pocket.

Molina glanced at Nick over her shoulder. "Game over."

He grinned at her. "Oh, yeah?" One large, strong hand skimmed lightly up the center of her back, tracing the satin laces on her corset, which led from her waist to just below her bare shoulder blades. The touch sent a jolting current of electricity up her spine. "So who won?"

She could feel his fingers work through the laces, as if he were contemplating how the complicated fastenings worked—and possibly how to get the top off of her in the most efficient way.

"Let's call it a draw."

Nick gently massaged her bare shoulders, then slid his hands back down her spine. One step forward and he closed the small gap between them. He pressed his erection against her tight ass. Thoughts of taking her right there flitted through his mind, making him tremble with want and need. His hands moved over the intricate laces in the middle of her back, down to her waist, then skimmed over the soft swell of her hips.

"I'm dying to know what you've got on underneath this skirt, sweetheart." He already knew she was wearing thigh-high stockings. The hem of her skirt rose well above their lacy tops.

Her eyes glowed with excitement. "Why don't you take it off and find out?"

Nick was already on it. He worked the button and the zipper, then he eased the material over the gentle slope of her hips and let it drop to the floor.

He sucked in a breath. Desire coursed through him, targeting his hard cock, which strained against the front of his pants. Molina shifted, spreading her legs apart. She arched her back, lifted her bare bottom in the air a bit more. It was a provocative stance, made all the more erotic by the lingerie she wore—the miniscule panties, thigh-high stockings and corset.

The g-string definitely made the outfit. Nick bit back a lustful growl and his need to possess her. Right here, right now. His hand smoothed over the small of her back and dipped into the curve of her waist.

"Way to turn me on in record time," he muttered. "The butterfly's a nice touch."

She grinned at him over her bare shoulder. He leaned forward, capturing her mouth with his. He pressed tightly against her as he kissed her, and he put one hand to the table to support his weight. The other hand searched for a way to get her out of her top. He fumbled with the laces for a moment.

He broke their kiss and demanded in a low growl, "How the hell does this thing work?"

Her eyes glowed seductively. "The laces are just for show. The fastenings are underneath."

Nick folded back the material lining one side of the laces. A long line of hook-and-eye fastenings held the corset together.

Nick shook his head. "Oh, hell no, baby." He had neither the time nor the inclination to work all of those tiny hooks. He grasped the material at the top of the line of fastenings and gave a solid yank. He ripped the material from top to bottom.

Molina gasped as the corset dropped to the table.

"I'll buy you a new one, sweetheart."

"It was specially designed for me in Paris, Mr. Caveman."

Nick grinned. His hands smoothed over her sleek back, then moved round to cup her full breasts. "You didn't really want me to waste time on those damned hooks, did you?"

Her teeth caught her lower lip as his fingers pinched and rolled her hard nipples. She shook her head.

"Good. My patience is thin right now."

He leaned against her, trailed his lips down the long delicate line of her spine. His hands left her breasts and slid around and down to her backside, splaying across her rounded, shapely ass. His thumbs skimmed the cleft between her cheeks. He sank to his knees between her parted legs.

"Remember years ago, when we made love on the terrace outside your room?" he asked. Her buttocks tightened as his warm breath caressed her bare skin. "You were bent over the stone railing, in this exact position."

"In the middle of a thunderstorm," she said on a breathless whisper. "We were drenched. But it felt too good to stop for even a minute to step inside."

"You wore incredibly tall, red patent leather shoes, stockings and a red garter belt that looked like vinyl. You had on a matching bra that just barely covered the undersides of your breasts. The rest of your breasts, including your nipples, were exposed." The memory of her elicited a low groan from him. "I almost came the minute I stepped out on the terrace and saw you."

"You remember what I was wearing?" she asked.

"God, yes. It's impossible to forget your lingerie. And how sexy you look in it."

His lips brushed her smooth, silky skin. His thumbs skimmed lower still and slightly forward, until he grazed the swath of satin covering her.

Molina moaned. Nick felt equally turned on. He wanted to touch her and taste her and fill her. He wanted to make her feel as hot and restless as he did. Wanted to make her feel the kind of raw, exquisitely painful need he felt.

Her body trembled under his touch, and she teetered a bit on her heels. He had a steady grip on her though, holding her in place.

Nick's thumbs slid under the tiny bit of material covering her and stroked her slick flesh. Her breathing grew shallow. He rubbed her clit with his thumb, slowly at first, then with purpose. She was deliciously wet. As he continued to rub the sensitive nub, he slid two fingers inside her.

Molina cried out as the pleasure rocked her body. He felt her quiver inside and contract around him. She came instantly.

"Nick," she whispered on a sharp breath. She stretched her arms out so her upper torso lay flat against the top of the table. "Don't stop."

He didn't intend to. His fingers pumped in and out of her making her body rock slightly, causing her nipples to rub against the red felt. He wondered if the friction aroused her further.

The thought made his groin tighten to an almost painful degree.

"Are you going to do to me what you did that night on the terrace?" she asked in a strained voice.

"Yeah, baby. I am." His fingers pushed deep inside her and she came again, calling out his name on a spiked breath.

Nick's restraint snapped. The need to be buried deep inside her was too great. His legs shook slightly from the intense desire gripping him and his insides were a mess. His need to keep her safe and alive, mixed with his need to possess her had him all twisted around.

At the moment, all he could focus on was the way she whimpered in Italian, telling him exactly what she wanted and how she wanted it. It was when she whispered in Italian that she said the naughtiest, most erotic words. All couched in a sexy dialect that drove him wild.

He withdrew his fingers from her, stripped off his shirt, unfastened the fly of his pants and pushed the material, and his briefs, aside so he could enter her.

One hand hooked around her thigh and he lifted her leg off the ground, granting him greater access to her. He groaned loudly as he sank into her warm depths. His other hand went to her waist to help steady her.

Molina came back up on her elbows for leverage as she pushed back against him. The pace he set was fast and frenzied. He pulled out of her and then thrust back inside. Over and over, he hammered into her, making them both wild with desire.

"Harder, Nick," she moaned. "Harder."

He wasn't sure his heart could take it, but he increased the tempo regardless. If he died making love to her, it wouldn't be such a bad way to go.

Molina panted and writhed and moaned and begged for more. It was all he could do to keep from coming. Then she slid her hand down between her legs, and he felt his control slip. She turned at the waist, just enough so she could look over her shoulder at him. Their eyes connected.

"Come with me," she said in a low, tight voice.

"Tell me when, baby," he all but growled.

"Now. Oh, God. *Now*, Nick."

The sensations gripping his body, shaking him to the core, intensified as she came. Her inner muscles squeezed him like a tight fist. She was so damn wet and hot and slick, he couldn't control his powerful reaction to her. He thrust deep, deep inside her, making her scream his name. His orgasm was strong, prolonged by her contractions. She milked him, drawing out every last bit of pleasure, until his body went limp.

He carefully eased her leg down so both feet were firmly on the ground. She was breathing heavy, as was he, and her eyes were closed as she lay sprawled across the pool table.

Nick's hands circled her small waist. He eased her off the table and they both swayed a bit as they made their way to a plush, oversized chair. He sank into it and pulled her into his lap. She curled up against him.

He could feel her heart pounding against his chest and kissed the top of her head. "Back off on the sexy lingerie for a while, huh, sweetheart? I don't think my heart can take it."

Chapter Five

Nick had security equipment arriving by the vanload several days that week, and he worked with a number of specialists to install the cameras, TV monitors, alarm sensors and computer programs that would help to run the entire system. He gave Molina updates from time to time. He had yet to run a full test of the system, which included his expert team running through a number of scenarios to see how the system would detect and alert anything from potential intruders to full-blown home invasions.

Molina was equally busy. She had event planning to manage for the Foundation's gala, having booked the elegant Bacara Resort and Spa for the event. Her assistant, Danielle, managed the work off-site, but Molina gave the final say on everything.

When she wasn't working on the gala, she was in her grandfather's study, poring over books and photo albums. She'd searched the entire study for an antique lock small enough to fit the key she'd found, to no avail.

The only thing remaining locked in the study was a door to the cabinet at the far end of the room. She eyed it from time to time, but knew the lock was too big for the key. Still, the fact that the bottom right hand door of the massive cabinet was locked gnawed at her. She'd found a key for every other lock in the damned place—her grandfather had kept them all on a brass ring, which she'd located in one of his desk drawers. Why hadn't the tiny key been on the ring with the others?

She had a key with no lock, and a lock with no key.

She sighed in frustration. She tried to concentrate on one of the many journals she'd unearthed, but it didn't hold her attention. Her eyes continued to drift to the cabinet. She felt as though it was taunting her.

She shut the book and pushed back her chair. Grabbing the long, thin nickel-plated letter opener from the edge of the desk, she crossed the room to where the tall cabinet stood. She plopped down on the floor in front of it and contemplated what might be so valuable inside it warranted a lock with no key.

She'd worn jeans, button-down shirts and tennis shoes for the past couple of days as she'd worked in the study. The old volumes were dusty and she was often climbing up and down the tall ladder. She'd learned her lesson about wearing heels when she'd taken a tumble off the ladder, and now favored more casual clothing.

Determined to open the cabinet door and find out what was inside—her grandmother had not been able to shed any light on the mystery when Molina had queried her—she stuck the sharp tip of the letter opener into the lock. She worked it gingerly at first, trying to finesse the lock open. But she had no success. She continued to reposition the tip of the opener, twisting and turning it at different angles, hoping to find just the right spot to unlatch the lock.

Frustration quickly set in. She shifted on the floor, coming up on her knees and tried again. Her curiosity grew with every passing minute, until she was poking and jamming the metal device into the small opening with a great deal of vigor.

"You stupid piece of—"

"Whoa!" She heard the amusement in Nick's voice as he entered the study. "Easy there, sweetheart."

He joined her, crouching next to her. He watched her for a moment as she continued her assault on the lock.

"A good thief you would not make," he said with a chuckle. "Are you trying to open that lock or torture it?"

She cast her annoyance on him. "Initially, I wanted to open it, smart ass. But the idea of torture has become much more appealing."

Nick grinned. "Okay, sassy. Hand over the lethal weapon."

She ground her teeth together, irritated, but did as he'd asked. She was sure he was better skilled at breaking and entering anyway.

Nick shooed her out of the way. He studied the lock for a moment, then carefully inserted the letter opener.

"I've tried every way imaginable. I think the lock must be broken."

"What's in here?"

"I have no idea. And it's driving me stark raving mad." She pushed at the long strands of hair that had escaped her ponytail during her fight with the lock.

"Well," Nick said as he gave a quick flick of his wrist, "we're about to find out." The sound of the lock releasing echoed in the quiet room.

"Finally!" Excitement quickly replaced the annoyance she'd felt. She rubbed her hands together. "Open the door," she urged.

Nick grinned at her. "Patience has never been your strong suit."

"Nick!" She playfully swatted at him. "I'm dying to see what's inside. My grandfather was keeping something under lock-and-no-key. It must be incredibly valuable. Even my grandmother doesn't know what's in here."

Nick wagged his eyebrows at her. "Look at you. You *are* Nancy Drew."

She laughed. Anticipation welled inside her. "Come on, come on. The suspense is killing me."

"Okay, cool your jets." He removed the letter opener from the lock and set it aside. He worked the fragile handle on the door and *voila*, pulled it open.

Excited, Molina peered inside. She blinked. Once, twice.

She sat back, stared at Nick in bewilderment. "It's empty."

Nick looked as stunned as she felt. "After all that, you're telling me this cabinet is empty?"

"Bare as a baby's butt."

Nick laughed, despite his apparent disappointment. "Well, sweetheart, I just don't know what to say to that."

Molina's frustration returned. "This makes no sense at all. Why would my grandfather keep this door locked if there was nothing inside?"

Nick appeared to give this some thought for a moment. Then he asked, "How long has this estate been in the family?"

"My great-great grandfather—the first Anthony Vienti—bought it after he married his wife, Josephine. Josephine's family was in the shipping business; her father was quite the tycoon for his day. Anthony came from money as well. And he had great aspirations of being a doctor. He and Josephine married when they were twenty and moved out west, presumably to put a little distance between themselves and Josephine's overbearing father, who liked to meddle a bit too much in their affairs."

She frowned, leaned toward the cabinet and poked her head inside. *Yep. Completely empty.*

She glanced back at Nick. "Why do you ask?"

Nick ignored her question and posed another one. "Is this study the original one?"

She nodded. "For the most part. That far wall over there burned to the ground in a fire in the '20's, but it was rebuilt. The rest of the mansion has been remodeled or rebuilt over the decades, but not the study. My grandmother sort of ended up with the mansion by default, because no one else wants to live in California. She's not of Vienti blood, but the rest of the family took a monetary settlement for their share and she signed a document saying the estate would always remain in the Vienti family, in some capacity. Which pretty much makes it mine, if I want it."

"Hmm." Nick nodded his head, but she wasn't so sure he'd listened to all of what she'd said. He shifted positions so he could lie on his back and stick his head inside the cabinet. "Maybe your grandfather wasn't the one who lost the key. Maybe your great-great grandfather did."

Molina stared at him a moment. His royal blue shirt pulled tight against the rigid muscles of his abdomen and chest. When he lifted his arms to run his hands along the cabinet's inner walls, his biceps bulged.

For a moment, Molina forgot all about the cabinet and the mismatched locks and keys. Nick wore black jeans paired with his black leather boots. The belt he'd worn the night he'd dropped back into her life circled his tapered waist. Her eyes landed on the small silver buckle and she grinned mischievously. He was so much more interesting than a mysterious cabinet.

She placed a hand on his strong thigh.

"Molina, honey," he said, his voice instantly thick with desire. "I'm trying to work here."

"Am I distracting you?" He didn't need to answer. She saw him grow hard as her hand skimmed over his leg.

"Think I've found something, baby."

"Me, too," she cooed as she eased her hand over the hard length of him.

Nick groaned. "You want what's inside this cabinet, or not?"

"I want what's inside these jeans," she purred.

Nick scooted out of the cabinet and sat up. His gaze was hot, his eyes filled with fire. "Trust me, baby. I want you, too. But I think we ought to take a look at what I found, first."

She struggled to rise above her desire so she could grasp what he was saying. "It's empty, Nick. I saw that for myself."

His grin was cocky. "No, it's not, sweetheart. I suspect this piece was built into the wall back when your great-great grandfather had the house constructed. He had a secret compartment built into the top of this cabinet. I felt the lock when I ran my hands over the wood."

Molina's breath caught. "Is it tiny?" It would certainly be antique…

"Yeah, why?"

Her spirits lifted. "I think I have the key." She fished it out of the front pocket of her jeans and handed it to him. She'd been carrying it around for days, trying it in every lock she came across.

Nick stuck his head back into the cabinet and a moment later, said, "Bingo."

Molina felt her heart slam against her chest as excitement shot through her. "Really? Oh, my God! Open it, Nick!"

He did and extracted a small box, which he handed to her. He sat up and Molina set the old, weathered leather-covered box between them. Nick handed her the key.

"Looks like it'll fit in that lock, too."

"It does," she agreed. Her fingers actually trembled as she took the key from him. Nick's eyes met hers, and she saw he was equally curious and excited to see what was in the box.

Exhilaration zipped through her. She inserted the small key in the fragile lock and gave it a gentle turn. The tarnished brass latch released and flipped open. Molina grinned. Her breathing had quickened, she noticed, in anticipation of what she might find.

She carefully lifted the lid of the box and the small, old hinges creaked softly. Molina peered inside.

"Well?" Nick inquired, equally enthralled.

Molina frowned. She wasn't sure how many times in one day she could be let down, but she was quite certain she'd met her threshold. She glanced over at Nick and said in a deflated tone, "More photographs."

She was about to close the lid when Nick stopped her. "Hold on a second, sweetheart. If your great-great grandfather went to such great lengths to hide or protect these photos, don't you think it's worth taking a peek at them?"

"You ever sit around for days and days and look at your family photo albums, Nick?" she challenged.

He grimaced. "That'd be futile. We all look and act the same. Even the FBI has trouble telling us apart."

"Oh, I have no trouble telling you apart. Your brother and your dozens of cousins may be as clever as you, but they're not nearly as sexy." Her voice dropped to a whisper as she added, "And I doubt they know how to please a woman the way you do."

Nick groaned in defeat. "Come here." He reached for her and dragged her down on top of him as he leaned back against the hardwood floor, the box and its contents completely forgotten.

Chapter Six

Much later that evening, as she passed the study on the way back from visiting Rose Marie, Molina remembered the box of photos she and Nick had recovered earlier in the day. She crossed the tiled patio and entered the study from the tall glass doors lining the back wall of the room. She went to the large built-in cabinet and retrieved the box. As she stood, she heard a loud creak that sounded as though it had come from the rafters. Molina looked up. Hanging above her was the massive gold and crystal chandelier her great great grandmother had bought her husband as a first-year anniversary present.

Nothing seemed wrong. Molina continued on her way. She left the study, but halfway down the hall she dropped the box and let out a startled scream when she heard a loud crash, which echoed through the entire first floor of the west wing.

Rose Marie's house staff came running. Molina raced back to the study, her tall heels clicking on the marble floor. She entered the room from the interior just as Nick entered from the exterior. They stared at each other across the room. Between them lay the shattered remains of the massive nineteenth century Palladian crystal chandelier.

"Oh, my!" Isabelle cried as she entered the room behind Molina and pulled up short. "That could have killed someone!"

That was all it took for Molina to go into emotional overload. She felt the room tilt and then everything went dark.

"Molina!" Nick cried out. His heart jumped into his throat.

He dashed across the room, skirting the debris, and sank to his knees next to Molina. He scooped her up in his arms and carried her out of the room. Simone, the medical attendant on Rose Marie's staff, met him in the hallway. The Jamaican woman followed Nick up the long stairs to Molina's suite.

"She's not hurt," Nick said over his shoulder. "She's just scared."

So was he, truth be told. He'd heard the crash, heard her scream. He'd bolted to the glass doors, but quickly assessed that Molina was not buried beneath the rubble and shards of glass. Then she and Isabelle had walked in and his whole world had been turned upside down again. Watching Molina collapse to the ground, when he was fifty feet away and incapable of catching her, made him feel helpless and insignificant. His job was to be by her side at all times, to catch her when she fell.

He laid her gently on the bed, and her eyes fluttered open. She stared up at him, but he could see she was having trouble focusing. He took her hand in his.

"Close your eyes, baby. Just relax."

He heard Simone bustle about the room. She appeared a moment later with a cool, damp towel and a glass of water. Nick moved out of the way and let Simone administer her brand of first aid, which included a lot of tsking and "there, there; ain't so bad, child."

Molina let her fuss for a few minutes, then pushed Simone's hand away. She hauled herself up so she was propped against the plump pillows on the bed. She eyed Nick, who was pacing restlessly and rubbing the knot at the base of his neck.

"You look like you've seen a ghost." She turned her attention to Simone. "Got anything to help him?"

Simone shook her head. "No, child. Can't cure love."

Nick drew up short. His eyes narrowed on Simone's stiff back, then shifted to Molina. She was smiling at him, her pale eyes dancing mischievously. "Well, now. That's an interesting thing for Simone to say."

Nick growled. "I see you're feeling better."

"If my sharp tongue is any indication?" She smiled a bit brighter, then turned her attention to Simone. "I'm all right, Sim. I just lost my head for a moment."

"For a moment? Child, you been losing your head since the day you met that man." The pretty, mocha-colored woman stood. She turned to Nick. "Keep that cold cloth on her head, give her a little aspirin and make her drink some water or hot tea. Call me if she's dying."

"Gee, thanks for worrying about me, Simone," Molina said with a soft laugh. But Nick knew Simone thought the world of Molina. The attendant was probably just as shaken as the rest of them; she just knew how to hide it better.

Nick sank into the mattress. "Gave me a bit of a scare there, sweetheart."

"Sorry." She snuggled against the pillows. "Nick, I have to tell you something." She glanced past him to the few others who were milling about, keeping an eye on her and waiting to be called upon, should they be needed. Molina's gaze returned to his. "In private."

Nick nodded. He scooted off the bed and approached the house staff. He asked Isabelle to inform Rose Marie of the fallen chandelier and the fact that Molina was safe. Then he asked the rest of the staff to see to the damage in the study.

They all scurried off, happy to do his bidding as if he were the man of the house. The thought struck him as odd. In a way, he was the man of the house, and had been for a very long time. More so than Frank had ever been, considering Frank spent such a brief amount of time here.

Nick circled the room, dimming the lights. He undid a few buttons on his shirt and then made his way back to the king-size bed. He stretched out next to Molina and took her hands in his.

"I should have been by your side," he admitted.

She sighed against his cheek. "You can't always be."

"It's my job. No, it's more than that." He rubbed the backs of her fingers against his cheek, then his lips. "I can't imagine a world without you in it to torture me, sweetheart."

She grinned, which was what he'd hoped for. "You can be very charming when you want to be. Now is not one of those times."

He let out a soft laugh. He arched his arm over her head, which rested on a pillow, and brushed the hair from her face. "Baby, I don't want anything to happen to you," he whispered.

"I know." He watched her work down a hard swallow. "But you can't hold yourself responsible if something does happen to me. That's what I needed to tell you. It's not your fault, Nick."

He felt the emotions well inside him. He would give anything—his wealth, his own life, *anything*—to keep her alive.

"We have to make some serious changes, Molina," he told her.

She shook her head against the pillow. "No. I know what you're thinking. But, Nick, I can't have you so single-minded. I know it's in my best interest to have you focused solely on my safety, but I can't do the all-business-no-play thing. My God, it'd be like my childhood again," she said in a grim tone. "I don't want that. I don't want stoic, grave-faced people surrounding me. I don't want to be flanked by bodyguards and restricted to this house. I love it here, but I can't live the rest of my life trapped here."

He started to protest, say it was better than the alternative, but she stopped him.

"Nick. I believe in my future. You made me believe in it. There's an answer to this mystery, somewhere. And somehow we're going to find it."

Tears filled her eyes. She was trying to be strong, he could tell, trying to be brave. Damn if it didn't make him want to do whatever she asked of him.

"Stay with me," she whispered.

He nodded. "Just try to get rid of me, baby."

Chapter Seven

Nick brought the old box to her while she was in bed. He'd stayed the night with her, holding her, soothing her frayed nerves. When she'd waken from a restless sleep, she'd told him she'd dropped the box in the foyer. He returned with it, and she settled herself comfortably in the plush bedding.

"You're going to love this," he said as he handed the old box to her. "It's not just full of photos."

She eyed him curiously. "What else is in here?"

"Well, stuff spilled out all over the floor when you dropped it. Photos, letters, a small gift box. I stuffed everything back into the box."

"Sounds like this has become a bit of a treasure hunt." She anxiously opened the lid. She set aside the small stack of photos and pulled out the letters buried beneath, along with the gift box Nick had mentioned. She spread everything out on the rich velvet duvet and eyed the items curiously, not knowing where to start.

Nick made a fresh pot of coffee from her mini-bar and poured two mugs. He set them on the nightstand and then eased onto the bed. He'd showered and changed into a pair of jeans and a white button-down shirt. He exuded strength, and Molina felt safe in his presence. More so than she ever had with any other man...or bodyguard.

She reached for the stack of photographs and idly sifted through them. She'd been through dozens and dozens of photos all ready. She shuffled them like playing cards, barely gazing at the black and white faces. She'd gone through seven or eight when realization dawned on her. She slowed the shuffle, went through the stack again. She frowned.

"What is it?" Nick asked.

"I've never seen these photos before." She glanced over at Nick. "I don't know who these people are."

She continued to sift through the photos, but she still didn't recognize anyone except her great-great grandfather. She pulled out a photo and handed it to Nick. "That's the first Anthony Vienti. Immigrated to New York in January of 1902. He was twenty."

"And the woman in the photo with him?" Nick inquired. "Is that Josephine?"

Molina shook her head. "No. I've never seen that woman in any other photo."

"A sister, perhaps?"

"He was an only child."

Nick studied the photo for a moment, then turned it over. He slid the photo out of its cardboard frame and handed it to Molina, backside facing up.

"'Anthony and Patricia, Summer 1902.'" Her frown deepened. "That's odd. Anthony met Josephine in the spring of 1902, and he married her in the fall."

Nick grinned. "Looks like Anthony, Sr. was a bit of a player."

"Nick!" She swatted at him and laughed. "What a terrible thing to say. My family claims he loved Josephine very much."

"Hmm. Well, he might have loved Josephine's *money* very much."

Molina gasped. "You think my great-great grandfather had an affair with Patricia?"

Nick only wagged his eyebrows suggestively.

"Oh, my. A family scandal," she quipped. Then more seriously, she said, "I wonder who this woman is." She studied the photos closely. One was taken outside a brownstone. The name "Moreno" hung above the mail slot in big block letters.

Patricia Moreno. Molina had never heard the name before. She set the photos aside and reached for the stack of letters. She untied the leather binding and opened the first ecru-colored envelope. She scanned the letter, her interest growing with each word she read.

Nick stretched out around her. He lightly rubbed her back while she skimmed through the romantic prose.

"These are love letters," she said. She set aside the one she was reading and reached for an envelope further down the stack. She curled into Nick, rested her head on his shoulder as she read a few letters out loud.

"Well, now. It seems you're right. Anthony, Sr. *was* a bit of a player. According to Patricia's letters to him, they were very much in love," she said.

Nick shook his head and grinned. "The scoundrel."

"I'll say." Molina spied the small gift box. She opened it and found an elegant gold pocket watch.

"Bet there's an inscription on the back."

"I bet it was a gift from Patricia." She turned the timepiece over and read aloud, "'With all my love until the end of time. Patricia. 5-13-03.'"

Molina studied the elegant script for a moment, contemplative. She opened the device and was shocked further. A black and white photo of a baby was glued to the inside of the front cover. The edges of the photo had come up and were frayed and tattered.

Molina handed the watch to Nick for his inspection as she reached once again for the letters she'd read. "These letters began in May of 1902. He married Josephine in September of that year. She gave birth to Anthony Vienti, Jr., almost a year later. That watch was given to Anthony, Sr., in April of 1903."

"With a photo of a child."

"That baby is not Anthony Vienti, Jr."

"So he had an affair with Patricia while courting Josephine. Assuming this unidentified baby was born in April and belongs to Anthony, Sr., Patricia got pregnant in July 1902. Two months before he married Josephine."

Molina nodded. "Which makes that baby the real Anthony Vienti, Jr. But because Anthony married Josephine instead of Patricia, that baby was illegitimate, and had no claim to the Vienti name."

Nick started to say something, but his cell phone rang. He scooted off the bed and retrieved the device from the clip on his belt. He flipped the phone open and answered the call.

Molina continued to read the letters, but her concentration waned. Out of the corner of her eye, she saw Nick begin to pace in agitation. He was talking in a hushed tone and rubbing the back of his neck, the way he always did when he was frustrated. A moment later he reached for a pen on the nightstand and the napkin he'd brought from the mini-bar with the coffee mugs. He scribbled furiously then snapped the phone shut.

Molina climbed off the bed. She approached Nick. "What is it?"

Nick eyed her for a moment. Then said, "You'd better sit down, sweetheart."

"Okay," she said in an uneasy tone.

Nick paced the rug in front of the eggplant-colored sofa and chair set. Finally, he stopped and turned to face Molina. "That was Matt on the phone. He managed to track down a couple of witnesses to your cousin's accident. They admitted to being paid not to come forward with information about the accident."

Molina felt her heart constrict and her hands began to tremble in her lap. Nick continued.

"One eye witness got a partial plate number, the other gave a full description of the SUV that struck Anthony. Matt ran the information and discovered the identity of the SUV's owner."

Nick held the napkin he'd written on in his hand. He dropped it on the coffee table before Molina. She stared down at it and knew the color had just drained from her face.

Anthony Moreno, V.

Nick sank into the sofa next to her, reached for her shaking hands. "My guess is, the century-old Vienti curse is actually a century-old Moreno vendetta."

Molina's entire body began to tremble. No longer was murder an inconceivable theory. If they were right about the pieces to the puzzle, it meant Morenos had been picking off Vientis for nearly a hundred years, starting with Anthony, Sr. He'd died in 1912 when passing under construction scaffolding that collapsed on top of him. A freak accident, the family had always thought.

Tragic, too. It had been Anthony's thirtieth birthday.

"So that baby—the one whose photo is inside my great great grandfather's watch—is probably the first Anthony Moreno. And scorned lover Patricia bumped off the father of her child because he married another woman."

"Or one of her family members did it. Or they hired someone to do it. Matt says the Morenos have ties to organized crime."

She felt stricken, as ill as Nick looked. "Oh, this is just too scary for words," she breathed.

She'd been so relieved when Nick had made her believe there was a tangible source of evil to conquer. She'd never imagined 'tangible' would translate to murder. She got to her feet, began to pace where Nick had previously. "Oh, my God. My family was murdered. My mother..." She stumbled.

Nick shot to his feet, grabbed hold of her to steady her. "Okay, let's sit back down, sweetheart."

"No!" She gripped his forearms. "Nick, they're after me now."

Nick cupped her face in his hands, looked deep into her eyes. "They're not going to get you, sweetheart. Don't you see? We know who murdered your cousin. Matt's involved now, and that means the FBI is involved. They're going to find this guy and end the vendetta."

Molina wasn't entirely convinced. "What about the chandelier? Was it just some random accident?"

Nick gave a noncommittal shrug. "I have someone looking into that, to see if the beams were weakened by age and structural damage over time, like from earthquakes. Or if..."

"They were weakened on purpose?" Her blood ran cold.

"Molina, listen to me. I believe that if—and it's only a small possibility—those beams were weakened intentionally, it was done before we got here, before I installed all of the new security and alarm systems. Regardless, I'm not going to let anything happen to you. You have to believe that."

She did. In her heart, she knew Nick would never let someone get close enough to her to murder her. But, admittedly, her hopes for a future had dimmed significantly over the past couple of hours.

She moved away from Nick. Her father would be arriving later in the day and she needed to pull herself together. Her birthday was tomorrow. She prayed it would be an uneventful one.

❦

Nick spent the early part of the afternoon with the structural engineer he'd hired to assess the beams in the study and determine the cause of the mysterious chandelier crash. He rubbed his jaw as he listened to the guy say yeah, maybe the beams were intentionally weakened, possibly the bolts had been loosened. But he needed to investigate further before he could provide a definite answer.

Nick left him to it. He wandered into the living room and found Molina in there. Her skin tone was normal; her eyes sparkled. She was fine, he realized. Too resilient to be more than momentarily set back by such an ordeal. He liked that about her. Not so strong she didn't need him, but strong enough to bounce back, take stock of the situation and then proceed forward.

He crossed to the wet bar and poured a glass of scotch. He was a bit shaken up by all that had happened in the past twenty-four hours, but he also had great confidence they'd found the source of evil that plagued the Vienti family and were capable of putting a stop to it. He expected to hear from Matt and the NYPD this evening.

He took a sip of his drink, then set it on the granite-topped bar. He crossed to where Molina stood, gazing out the tall glass doors. He placed a hand on her hip and a light kiss on her temple.

"Feeling better?" he asked.

"A little." She turned in his arms. "I don't know how we're going to break the news to my father. He'll be devastated to hear my mother was killed in cold blood."

Nick's jaw clenched. He stared down at her. "He all ready knows. He's been on all of my calls with Matt."

She nodded. "I should have known. My father is never far out of the loop, is he?"

Nick wrapped his arms around her and she melted into him, her body fitting so perfectly against his. His hand moved through her hair and tangled in the soft strands. He kissed the top of her head.

"What about us?" he whispered. "Are we better?"

❧⟨♋⟩❧

Molina sighed against his chest. They were getting along fabulously—better than she'd ever dreamed possible. Perhaps the time apart had strengthened their bond.

She'd known he would eventually probe a bit deeper, force her to confront her feelings for him, which she was willing to do, to an extent. She'd done a bit of soul searching over the past couple of days and had actually begun to consider what it might be like to have a long-term arrangement with Nick.

Admittedly, the thought made her uneasy and restless, but she was working through her emotions and finding it easier as time passed to let her guard down around him. Her commitment phobia had not entirely diminished, even though she innately knew the source of it. She was used to having people come and go and she was used to losing people she cared about. She'd stopped being shocked by their fleeting presence when she was a teenager. The only truly steady presence in her life was her grandmother.

What concerned her most was whether or not Nick's presence was equally fleeting. They were unraveling the mystery surrounding the curse. If she survived her presumed doomed fate, she'd no longer need a bodyguard. What would be Nick's purpose for sticking around? He was much too independent and strong to stay just because he had feelings for her. What reason would he have to stay with her here, at the estate, when he could be back in D.C. with Matt, protecting innocent people?

Anxiety roiled around inside her, and she wiggled out of Nick's arms. "I think I'll go take a hot bath before Daddy arrives."

She turned to leave, but Nick's hand captured hers. He pulled her back to him, wrapped his arms around her. "Not yet, sweetheart. You didn't answer my question."

"Nick, I can't." She gave a gentle shove to emphasize her point and he released her. But the dark look flashing in his eyes told her she'd sparked his anger.

His jaw clenched. "I thought we were doing a good job getting past your intimacy issues."

"I don't have intimacy issues; I have commitment issues. There's a big difference."

He raked a hand through his hair. "Christ, Molina. When are you going to stop running away?"

"I am not running away." Her tone held a slight edge to it.

Nick did not heed that warning. "Every time we get close, every time there's a tender moment between us, you squirm."

Her temper flared. She wanted to tell him she was just this minute contemplating their future together, but thought better of it. "Damn it, Nick. I don't want to argue with you. I just… want to go take a bath."

His eyes grew hard and flat. "Yeah, because it was getting just a bit too uncomfortable for you, wasn't it? Things between us were going just a bit too well."

"Yes, they are going well. And I'm glad."

"So what are you doing?"

She shook her head. She felt the storm roll in, knew there was no way to stop it. This was how it always was between them. Stormy and tumultuous and… doomed. Her heart ached and she felt tears well in her eyes. "I don't want to fight with you," she said again in a small voice.

"Then damn it, stop walking away from me," he growled.

Anger took hold of her. "I am not walking away!" she shouted. "And for the record, I'm not the one who walked away last time." She pointed an accusatory finger at him, jabbed him in the chest. "*You* walked away. *You* packed up your stuff and *you* left."

Tears instantly sprang to her eyes as she thought of the pain she'd felt five years ago when he'd disappeared from her life.

He hadn't even said goodbye.

"As I recall," he said in a terse tone, "*you* fired me."

She threw her hands up in the air. "And that was all it took for you to sever the ties?"

He looked aggravated and confused and furious all at once. "I don't know what the hell you want from me, Molina. I don't know what the hell I'm supposed to do from one minute to the next to keep up with your mood swings."

"This is not a mood swing, damn it." She turned to stalk off, but thought better of it. Her anger had turned into something different. Something darker. She felt emotions well up inside her, and thoughts and feelings she'd suppressed for five years collided inside her and begged to be released.

"I needed you," she told him, the tears spilling from her eyes. Her fists clenched at her sides. "I needed you to keep me grounded, to help me through the hard times. But you couldn't see that. You were so intent on packaging everything up in a neat little bundle, tied with a bow."

The tears were flowing now but she didn't care. Nick, it appeared, was at a loss for words. She continued. "You couldn't deal with the messy stuff. And when it got rough, you just... *left*."

He shook his head, appeared to try to reconcile in his mind what she was saying. It took him a few moments, but he dropped his gaze to hers and said, "I thought that's what you wanted."

"No. It's what you needed. To distance yourself." She pulled in a ragged breath. "I made a lot of mistakes, and I'm sorry I hurt you. But you hurt me, too. You left me... just like everyone else in my life has."

She couldn't stand there a moment longer. The pain was too great and the lost look in his eyes only made it worse. He loved her. She could see it; she could *feel* it. He had loved her all those years ago, and she hadn't known what to do with that love; she wasn't sure what to do with it now. But in her heart, she knew one thing: they should have stayed together. No matter how difficult and emotionally trying the times, they should have stuck it out, worked through the tough times together. That's what couples—people in love—do.

She was as much to blame for the split as he was, she knew that. She was an expert at pushing people away. But she needed him to know he'd made mistakes, too. It was the only way they were ever going to learn from them. And rectify them.

She turned to go, but drew up short when she saw a tall, imposing figure standing in the doorway, a look of disappointment on his handsome face.

"Daddy, you're early," she gasped. She swiped at the tears on her cheeks, pulled in a ragged breath. "This is a surprise."

Frank glanced from her to Nick. "This isn't. Don't you two ever try to get along?" He crossed the room and kissed Molina on the cheek. "Why don't you run upstairs and freshen up, dear. Nick and I have some things to discuss."

He clasped Nick on the shoulder. "Good to see you, son."

"Likewise," Nick said in a tight voice. He shot Molina a look, telling her they weren't through with their discussion.

Chapter Eight

Molina visited her grandmother after dinner and entertained her until bedtime. After leaving Rose Marie's suite she returned to the east wing. Nick was climbing the stairs.

"I'm sure that was an interesting manly chat you had with my father, considering it continued after dinner." She was tired and still a little cranky. She could see Nick was wound pretty tight as well.

He let out a low groan. "Hours and hours of a manly chat. The Spanish Inquisition was a tea party compared to it."

"At least you had some expensive booze to ease the pain. I saw my father brought your favorite scotch."

"It did help," Nick commented as they continued down the corridor together.

"I think we should talk," she said. She had some apologizing to do for her earlier behavior. Hell, she needed to apologize for her behavior five years ago. Maybe that was their problem. They'd kissed, but they certainly hadn't made up.

But Nick didn't look interested in hearing what she had to say.

"I can't take much more conversation this evening. Besides, you'll say something that will piss me off, and we'll just start arguing again."

She frowned at his surly attitude. She had to walk briskly to keep up with his long strides as he stalked down the hallway. "Nick, I know you're angry with me, but—"

"No, sweetheart. I'm not just angry with you. I'm angry with me, too. I let things get out of hand." He raked a hand through his hair. "I'm still letting them get out of hand. Christ." He pulled up short, glared down at her.

His look was so intense, she actually halted, then took a step or two backward. Nick came toward her. The volatile look in his dark eyes made her breath catch. "Nick," she said in a tentative voice.

"Shh. Don't say a word." He reached for her and hauled her up against him. "I barely heard anything your father said to me, though I'm sure his words were all scathing, considering the scene he walked in on. All I could think about was making love to you."

The breath escaped her in a painful rush of air. Desire flashed in his eyes, and when she tried to wiggle her way out of his tight embrace, she felt his steel erection.

Passion flared inside her. The raw intensity exuding from him made her shudder with excitement and trepidation.

"Sorry I distracted you so much," she managed to say.

"You're not done yet, baby." He groaned deep in his throat as he pressed her body even tighter to his. All of his hard angles melded to her soft ones. He bent his head to her and kissed her in the hot, demanding way that made her go weak in the knees.

"Nick," she moaned when he pulled away. Her fingers clutched at the material of his shirt. Fear and exhilaration coursed through her, igniting her insides.

He let out a low growl. "Shut up, Molina. I've had enough conversation for one night."

He scooped her up in his arms and marched down the hallway. He all but kicked in the door to her suite, then dropped her not-so-gently to her feet. He kicked the door shut behind him and pressed Molina up against it, his mouth crushing hers.

Excitement tore through her. Every nerve ending sizzled and a wave of passion swept over her at the touch of his impatient hands, his demanding lips. In turn, she went to work on his clothing, tugging on buttons, pushing material off of him. She had no idea how long it took for them both to be naked, but it seemed entirely too long. He hoisted her up so she was forced to wrap her legs around his waist.

His mouth covered hers, their lips and tongues tangled in an exquisite dance.

"Tell me how much you want me, baby," he demanded in a gruff tone.

"So much," she whispered, breathless. He pushed himself deep inside her, and she gasped from the sudden, sharp, but oh-so-sweet invasion at the heart of her. "Oh, Nick. That feels so good. The way you fill me…"

He pushed deeper, stealing her breath.

"You feel so good, baby. Like heaven."

He used the door as a sturdy brace as he drove himself deeper into her. She cried out as the first wave of pleasure rocked her body. Hard and fast, the sensations gripped her, racked her body with violent tremors.

He wasn't done with her.

Her hands clutched at him, her nails digging into his hard muscles as he hammered into her. She felt so very hot. She burned with her intense need for this man. And even though he was deep inside her, she wanted more.

"Nick, please," she pleaded.

"What, baby? Tell me."

She kissed him, her fingers twining in his thick hair. Nick…"

"Whatever you want, sweetheart," he groaned. His mouth was on her neck, his teeth nipping and grazing her skin, driving her positively wild.

Molina felt like her heart was about to leap from her chest. She was so restless inside, she just couldn't get enough of him.

"Talk to me, baby. Tell me what you need."

She couldn't. She didn't know what she was asking for, what she was seeking.

She was close to coming again but found herself wanting to slow it all down. The reckless intensity she'd first felt when they'd entered her room had subsided, giving way to more tender sensations. She wanted to be underneath him, his body stretched out over hers. She wanted to feel his weight on her, feel his hard muscles pressed against her soft body. She wanted to have access to all of him, from head to toe. Their current position, hot as it was, provided none of what she truly needed.

Before she could even stop herself, words tumbled from her mouth. "Take me to the bed, Nick. Make love to me. Slowly. Like you've always wanted to."

His movements slowed and he pulled away from her slightly to stare down at her. His breathing was labored and his chest rose and fell sharply. He looked at her with a mixture of confusion and pleasure on his face.

She closed her eyes. "Don't overanalyze it. Just do it."

He cupped her cheeks and carried her to the bed with her long legs still wrapped around his waist. Gently, he laid her down. Sprawled across the velvet duvet, her raw need for him began to morph into something more substantial. Something tender and warm and beautiful.

Her hands smoothed over his heavily muscled back and she held him to her, feeling the restlessness abate now that he was lying on top of her, settled between her legs. Nick kissed her deeply, conveying emotions they both felt. His hands caressed her as he moved inside her with full, easy strokes.

Molina wanted the moment to last forever. The exquisite feeling of having Nick inside her and the comfort she derived from the closeness they shared—the sheer intimacy of the moment—touched her heart.

They had been open and honest with each other during their earlier argument, and had finally expressed words and emotions they'd both suppressed for far too long. Nick understood her shortcomings and now knew her deepest fears. They did not drive him away this time. If anything, she thought the connection between them was stronger than ever before.

She sighed contently as Nick pushed them both closer to the edge. She arched her back, pressing her body more firmly against his, wanting to feel his heat and his strength. His mouth left hers and skimmed over her jaw, then up to her ear. He whispered sweet words that made her stomach flutter. She held on to the glorious sensations as long as she could before everything erupted inside her.

But even as her breathing slowed and the quivering inside her ebbed, the deep feelings she had for Nick continued to grow.

"Happy Birthday, baby," Nick whispered in her ear.

Molina smiled. She was curled up against him with his arms wrapped around her. Her head rested on his broad shoulder and his fingers were tangled in her hair. Their legs were entwined. All in all, it was a glorious way to wake up.

As the early morning sun streamed across the room, Molina felt a sense of optimism seep into her veins again. Nick had truly made love to her last night. Twice. Their intense physical need for each other had evolved into something emotional, something beautiful. And even commitment-phobic Molina couldn't deny it.

She smiled, dropped a tender kiss on his chest.

"You're not running off to take a bath," Nick commented in a curious tone.

"No. I like it here, in your arms."

"Hmm. This is something new."

"Don't gloat," she warned. She snuggled close to him, traced a finger over his smooth skin. Her fingernail grazed his nipple and she marveled at the way it pebbled under her touch. His body responded quickly to her, just as her body responded to him. "I'm so sorry about yesterday. About... everything."

He kissed the top of her head. "So am I."

"I don't want to fight anymore. I just want to... I don't know. See what happens." She glanced up at him, saw encouragement in his eyes. "Between us."

"God, you take an incredibly long time to come around."

She laughed softly. "I know. I'm sorry."

He sighed. "We both made mistakes. We need to learn from them. I need to learn to be more patient, less demanding."

"And I need to be more open with my feelings."

Silence enveloped them for a few moments. Then Nick said, "I have a birthday gift for you."

Molina giggled. She felt oddly light-hearted. "Oh, I just bet you do." Her hand skimmed low, over the ripple of muscle at his abdomen, across the soft dusting of hair leading to his hard penis, nestled in a dark patch.

Nick groaned. "I meant a real gift, baby."

"Oh," she teased, "the kind that comes in a gift box?"

"I even had them put a bow on it."

"Figures." She laughed, then added, "I would have settled for this." Her hand still held his hard cock.

His arm tightened around her. "You may have to settle for that. You keep touching me, I'm going to forget all about your present."

She disentangled herself from him and sat up. "No, no. I want the gift."

Nick grinned at her. He tossed the sheet off of him and walked to the door, where his pants lay in a wrinkled heap. Molina admired the view—long, powerful legs, tight ass, a wide, muscular back, which tapered to a nice V at his trim waist. He was tanned and toned and one hell of a male specimen. She loved the body. Loved the man.

Desire prickled in the heart of her. Only this time, she let her admiration and her respect for him mingle with her passion. By the time he returned to the bed, she'd lost interest in her gift. Whatever he had in that tiny baby blue Tiffany's box could not possibly be more precious than the gifts he'd already given her. Love. Life. Hope.

Tears instantly welled in her eyes.

"Oh, shit," Nick said in a soft tone as he climbed back into bed. "Already it's the wrong gift."

She laughed. A tear spilled over the rim of her eye and she swiped at it. "I'm going to love whatever's in that box. I just..." she shook her head. "This is all your fault, so I don't want to hear any grumbling about my overemotional state. You're the one who made me... *feel*." She said it so begrudgingly that he laughed. So did she.

Nick grinned at her. Emotion filled his eyes. But he teased her anyway. "So I guess this would be a bad time to tell you I don't want to see you anymore."

"Oh, no," she shook her head. "You created the monster, you get stuck with it."

Nick leaned toward her, kissed her softly. "Deal."

She took the box from his hand. "This better not be an engagement ring. I can only handle so much in one day."

"Are we in some sort of a twelve-step program for the commitment-phobic?"

She shrugged. "Maybe just a three- or five-stepper. I've made excellent progress recently."

He smoothed a hand over her cheek. "Yeah, I think you have."

She swallowed down the lump of tenderness that formed in her throat. She sniffled. "Okay, I've expended myself emotionally," she quipped. "Let's not overdo it." But she didn't feel the usual urge to push him away or run from her feelings. Rather, she felt inclined to embrace them, accept them. Cherish them, even.

She smiled at him again, then removed the white bow and the baby blue lid from the Tiffany's box. Inside was a black velvet box. She crooked an eyebrow at Nick. "I know you have excellent taste in jewelry. I can hardly wait to see what's inside."

She pulled out the box and opened it. Molina gasped from sheer and genuine delight. Nestled against the black velvet interior was a stunning pendant—a pear-shaped peridot, close to ten carats, Molina suspected, surrounded by sparkling diamonds. The jewels dangled from a platinum chain. Matching dangling earrings completed the ensemble.

"They're magnificent," she said, breathless.

Nick took the box from her and released the necklace from the tiny clamps holding it in place against the velvet. Molina scooped up her hair and let him put it on her. She fingered the enormous peridot and smiled at him. "Is it stunning on me?"

Nick looked mesmerized. "More so than I imagined. That color is perfect against your skin. And it matches your eyes."

"I love it," she said. She threw her arms around him and kissed him. The urge to tell him she loved *him* bubbled up inside her, but she suppressed the words. She planned to save them for tonight. After her birthday dinner. She'd tell him *before* they made love, so he'd know the emotion was real and not just a side effect of great sex.

Nick's warm lips brushed over her throat, sending a rush of excitement coursing through her. Her body responded so naturally, so fervently to his.

He rolled back onto the bed, pulling her on top of him. Greedily, his hands roamed over her body, caressing, stroking, sparking heat at the heart of her. She moved above him, taking him inside her. Their fingers intertwined as they moved together, slowly, sensuously at first. As the momentum built, his hands found their way to her hips and he rocked her gently, increasing the tempo. She marveled at how fully he filled her, how complete she felt with him inside her.

"More, Nick," she pleaded. "I want to feel you deep inside me."

Nick groaned. "Oh, yes, baby."

They came together, Nick surging and pulsing deep inside her.

She loved this man. And she intended to tell him so.

Chapter Nine

Dinner was served on the lawn, under the stars. It was an enormous Italian feast. Tall brass garden torches blazed around the myriad of tables set up to accommodate the food and all of the guests. Molina, her father, Nick, and Rose Marie were accompanied by Rose Marie's staff. Each of them had pitched in to make the evening memorable. The soft glow from the votives on the tables created an intimate atmosphere. Rose Marie had chosen Molina's favorite arias from *La Boheme* and *Madam Butterfly* to fill the night air as they dined.

Molina wore a beautiful black strapless dress for the occasion, which hugged her breasts and small waist. The skirt fell to the floor in a straight line, and a provocative slit ran high up the back. Her long, sleek, light brown hair fell over one shoulder, and she wore the jewelry Nick had given her. Of course she'd dabbed just the tiniest bit of her signature scent on her pulse points.

Bella had been created for her mother at her father's request. He'd hired an Italian chemist to produce the unique fragrance, and gave it to Ann Marie on their wedding day. When her mother died, the precious bottle had passed to Molina. She'd worn no other perfume since her mother's death. There was only one bottle of *Bella* in existence, so Molina cherished it as her mother had.

The evening was warm and intimate, the kind Molina adored the most. She would love to have included her cousin's widow, Josie, and her Aunt Ellen, but they hadn't been up for traveling. Understandably.

Molina was content with the small gathering. Her eyes scanned the area and landed on Nick, who was grazing the long buffet table with Rose Marie. He held a plate for her in one hand while he cupped her elbow with the other. She walked unsteadily, even with a cane and Nick's strong hold on her.

Molina could hear his deep voice drift on the night air, mixed with the poignant aria and Rose Marie's delightful laughs. Nick was amusing her, something he normally did. He cared greatly for Rose Marie—and for Frank. And that meant a lot to Molina. She knew they adored him equally.

"I see you and Nick have reconciled your differences," Frank said as he took a seat next to his daughter.

Molina smiled. "We're trying, Daddy." She reached over and patted his hand. "I know how you feel about Nick. I know you'd like to have him as a son-in-law."

"I would. But what I want doesn't matter. What do you want?"

She shook her head and sighed. "I'm not sure. I never thought about marriage and children. But maybe..." she shrugged noncommittally. "Who knows? We're going to take it slow. See what develops."

Molina didn't mention that, although the mystery of the curse had been uncovered, Anthony Moreno, V, had still not been apprehended. Nor had other loose ends been tied up. For instance, exactly why did the Vientis meet their demise in their third decade? What was the significance there? Molina wanted to know. But she kept her thoughts to herself. Everyone was having a wonderful time, and she didn't want to spoil the evening.

Rose Marie and Nick joined them at the table.

Following dessert, Rose Marie suggested everyone dance. It had been too long since they'd had a party at the estate, she said.

"I have the perfect music," Molina volunteered. "Everyone will enjoy it and it's a bit more conducive to dancing than the arias." Molina excused herself, explaining she only needed to retrieve the CD from her suite.

She hurried, rather excitedly, through the house. The evening was so beautiful, so enjoyable. She wanted everyone to dance and drink and enjoy her birthday party.

As she rushed down the corridor to her suite, she sensed she wasn't alone. Nick had followed her. It was comforting to know he was there, keeping an eye on her. She smiled as she rounded a corner and pushed the door to her room open. Nick wouldn't let any harm come her way. He loved her. She was certain of that. And she looked forward to telling him later tonight that she loved him, too.

As Molina entered her suite, she drew up short. She gasped in surprise as she stared at the tall doors leading to her terrace—they were all wide open. The sheer panels blew inward with the evening breeze. Although it was balmy outside, the inside of her suite was freezing cold, as though the thermostat on the air conditioning unit had been turned up to full blast.

She shivered from the cold as she hoisted her long skirt up and hurried across the room to the doors. She shut all six of them, then turned back. Another gasp, this one loud and full of distress, escaped her lips. There, on the floor next to her dressing table, lay the broken fragments of the *Bella* perfume bottle.

Molina let out a strangled cry of anguish. She rushed forward, dropping to her knees beside the table. She reached for a piece of glass and felt the shard pierce her skin. She winced from the sharp pain that shot through her, but held the remnant nonetheless, clutching it in her hand. The glass bottle had apparently blown off the edge of the vanity and hit the marble floor, shattering into hundreds of tiny pieces. The perfume made a small puddle on the floor.

The only perfume she'd ever worn. The only perfume her mother had ever worn.

Tears stung her eyes. She hadn't left the bottle that close to the edge of the table, had she? She could have sworn she'd left it in the center, in a safe spot. She wouldn't have been so careless with something that meant so much to her.

And the terrace doors... She'd closed them all before she'd left the room. She was certain of that. Nick insisted she keep them locked when she wasn't in the room.

Damn it.

Tears flowed down her cheeks as she stared at the shattered bottle. The only bit of *Bella* she owned, would ever own, because its creator was long deceased.

The perfume had been a constant reminder of her mother. Ann Marie was all around her when she wore that perfume. The mother she'd adored, who'd been taken from her too soon.

With tears streaming down her cheeks and blood oozing out of her tightly clenched fist, she stood. Her body shivered violently from the cold air swirling around her. She eased open her hand, pulled the glass from her skin and tossed it on her dressing table. She wrapped her arms around her and went to the fireplace in the corner. The room was thick now with the scent of *Bella*. Molina fought back sobs of grief. She'd lost the one last connection she'd had to her mother.

Hoping to quickly warm the room, she reached for the switch to the gas fireplace.

"Molina, no!" Nick's deep voice filled the suite. He stood just inside the door, taking in the full scene.

"Nick, it's so cold in here."

"Yeah, obviously for a reason. Don't touch that—"

But she didn't heed his warning. Instead, while he spoke, she flipped the switch.

She let out a blood-curdling scream as a loud explosion ignited in the fireplace, rocked the room and rattled the windowpanes. Flames shot out, tall enough to curl out of the hearth and nip at the marble mantle above it. Stunned and almost scorched by the flames, she stumbled backward, falling against the sofa.

"Molina!" Nick called out as he raced across the suite.

For a moment, Molina was too stunned to move, paralyzed by fear. The flames licked at the mantle and the hearth. The room was aglow from the fire. Nick turned off the gas at its source, then used the fire extinguisher, emptying its contents to ensure the fire was entirely put out.

Molina merely stared at him in shocked disbelief.

"Are you okay?" he asked as he dropped to his knees beside her. Her hand was bloody, as was her arm, from when she'd rubbed it to ward off the chill. He gently helped her to her feet.

"Let's clean you up."

Her father and a few staff members rushed into the suite, obviously having heard Molina's scream and the explosion. The hustle and bustle was efficient and orderly. Frank instructed a few of the men to clean the mess in the room.

Simone shooed Nick away from Molina as she'd done two nights before. She studied Molina's cut, determined it was minor, just messy. She snapped at one of the staff members to bring her antiseptic and a bandage.

Molina wondered if Simone had a remedy to chase away the helpless, terrified look in Nick's eyes.

Questions swirled about, but only Molina had the answers to them and she wasn't speaking at the moment. After several minutes, Rose Marie appeared. In her quiet, authoritative voice, she ordered everyone out of the room except Simone, Frank and Nick.

Nick could feel his blood pressure rise. Something had spooked Molina other than the fire. And what had cut her? He glanced around the room, his eyes landing on the broken bottle on the marble floor.

Christ, he thought. He crossed to the dressing table and knelt to inspect the damage. The bottle was shattered. The perfume was wasted. He looked over at Molina and she closed her eyes, sighed sadly.

It broke his heart. And infuriated him.

Simone's assistant returned and they patched up Molina's hand. Frank helped her sip some brandy, which seemed to help. She explained what had happened. Nick and Frank exchanged looks as she described the scene she'd walked in on and the ensuing events.

They were about to hold a private conference when Isabelle entered the room, her face as pale as Molina's had been just minutes before.

"What is it?" Nick demanded.

"Josie. She's…" Isabelle shook her head, apparently too distressed to say the words. She pulled in a ragged breath. "She's had an accident."

The silence that filled the room was deafening. The words that lingered, unspoken, in the air may as well have been scrawled across the wall in blood. *The Vienti Curse.* Or rather, *the Moreno Vendetta.*

"She's in the hospital," Isabelle added. "Stable condition, but shaken up. Broken leg and wrist."

"What happened?" Rose Marie asked in a surprisingly steady tone.

Isabelle's look faltered. She glanced from Rose Marie to Nick to Molina. But her full gaze landed on Frank. She gulped so hard it echoed in the quiet room. "She fell. Down a flight of stairs."

"Oh, no!" Molina cried. She pushed herself out of the chair and propelled herself into motion.

Nick wanted to stop her, to tell her to sit down and regroup. But Molina was on the move. She rushed across the suite to her closet. She appeared a moment later with her suitcase in tow.

Nick watched, stunned, as she quickly and carelessly threw clothing into the carry-on bag. As if everything she'd experienced in the past half-hour or so had not even happened.

Spoiled Molina would have sat on that sofa, pouting over her loss. But the woman before him had a look of fearless determination in her eyes. Nick's respect for her increased tenfold.

"Daddy," she said in a shaky tone. "I need the plane ready. Nick and I are going to New York. Isabelle, please find out what hospital Josie is in, probably Mount Sinai. Book a suite at The Plaza for us, leave the departure date open-ended. Nick," her eyes connected with his. "Can we get someone to stand guard outside Josie's hospital room?"

His cell phone was already in his hand. He nodded.

Everyone around her suddenly jumped into action. Nick would make more calls on the way to the airport. Rose Marie would call the hospital and check in with Josie's family. Frank would contact the pilots and have the jet ready.

Nick stuffed clothes into his own bag and then hustled downstairs. They made it to the airport in record time.

During the flight to New York, Molina paced the cabin of the jet and sipped at a glass of scotch, as though continually trying to calm her nerves. Nick didn't dare ask her to talk about her feelings now. He sensed she'd come completely unglued, and that wouldn't be good for her at this point.

Thank God Josie wasn't seriously harmed. She was alive.

Molina stopped her pacing. "It couldn't have been Anthony Moreno." Her tone was firm, full of conviction and certainty. "Josie's not of Vienti blood."

She said this as though it were the revelation of the century. And she looked damned relieved. "As coincidental as the accident was, falling down stairs and all, as my mother had, it couldn't possibly be related to the… *murders*. It was just a freak accident."

Nick nodded, but didn't commit to whether he agreed or not about the vendetta playing a part in Josie's accident. As a precaution, he'd had bodyguards stationed outside her hospital room. He'd also sent two of his cousins to look after Molina's Aunt Ellen, and he'd called in a few favors to local FBI agents to investigate and search Rose Marie's estate. The agents would also question the staff and keep an eye on things while Nick was gone to ensure everyone's safety.

He'd phoned Matt on the way to the airport and filled him in on the latest developments. Matt had told him the other family members' deaths were being investigated by the FBI.

"Why don't you sit down, sweetheart?"

"I can't. I need to work this all out in my head. Someone was in my room tonight. They did things meant to terrify me, not kill me. Why?"

Nick ground his teeth together. "I don't know, baby. But we're going to find out."

She stopped pacing, turned to face him. "I'm so glad you were there with me. I should have listened to you and not turned on the fireplace. It didn't oc-cur to me that—"

"Molina," he reached for her good hand and eased her down on the sofa next to him. He pulled her to him. "Shh, baby. Just relax for a little while."

She collapsed against. "I need you," she whispered.

"I'm right here with you. Always."

She snuggled close to him. "This is such a nightmare." She looked up at him. "But I know I'm safe with you."

When they touched down in New York at seven the next morning, a waiting limo rushed them to Mount Sinai. They found Josie's floor and greeted her family in the waiting room.

"Oh, you're such a dear for coming," Josie's mother, Grace, said. She took Molina's hands in hers, noted the bandage.

"It's nothing," Molina quickly said before Grace had the chance to inquire. "How is she?"

"A bit shook up. She's sleeping now." Grace looked worse for the wear. "You didn't have to come all this way. It must've been such a long flight. She's fine, really."

"What happened?" Molina asked.

Grace's eyes clouded. "She was coming down the steps at the movie theatre, and she was tripped."

Relief washed over Molina. "She tripped?"

"No," Grace said in an insistent tone. "*She was tripped*. Someone deliberately tripped her at the top of the stairs."

Molina glanced over at Nick, saw the confusion register in his dark eyes.

Grace continued. "She said she felt the hard sole of a shoe against her shin. There's a small knot and a bruise on her leg to show that's exactly what happened. Her wrist broke her fall, but somehow her leg buckled under her and the bone snapped."

"That sounds bad," Molina gasped.

"She's okay," Grace assured them. "She and the baby are just fine."

Molina's own legs buckled beneath her. Nick leapt forward and caught her before she hit the floor and dragged her to the closest chair.

Grace called out, her voice full of concern.

"She's fine," Nick said quickly. "Just tired from the long flight."

"Oh," Grace gasped. "You shouldn't have come!"

Molina waved a hand in the air in a dismissive manner, unable to speak. She glanced up at Nick, pleaded with him with her eyes.

"We should probably check in with Ellen," Nick commented. "Congratulations, by the way."

Grace looked delighted, despite her obvious fatigue. "It's a boy. She's going to name him Anthony Vienti, VI."

Whatever color was left in Molina's face quickly drained, she knew. She reached for Nick's hand. "I could use some water," she all but croaked.

Nick helped her out of the chair and they skirted down the hallway to a nearby drinking fountain. Molina's Aunt Ellen hurried down the corridor toward them. Nick relayed what they'd learned from Grace in a quick conversation.

"Her unborn child is Vienti blood," Ellen gasped.

"He could carry on the bloodline," Molina said. "I was the last of the Vientis, but now..."

A cold, hard look entered Ellen's eyes. She turned to Nick. "No one will hurt these women or my grandson."

Nick nodded.

Ellen grasped his hand tightly. "Promise me."

Chapter Ten

The limo was waiting for them outside, and Nick helped Molina into the back seat. She was perfectly still and quiet during the short drive to The Plaza. Nick checked them in. Isabelle had booked a suite with two bedrooms. Molina sank into a sofa and tried to collect her thoughts. Things were spiraling out of control. It had been a hellish fourteen or so hours.

Nick settled next to her and clasped her hands in his. It tugged at her heart. She was nothing but trouble for him. She'd cause him nothing but heartache in the end. She supposed she'd always known that. It was the main reason she'd kept things between them on a level she could control. She had let him in, years ago, but not all the way. And she'd pushed him away, purposely, when he'd gotten too close. She didn't want him to end up like all the others who'd loved a Vienti and lost them to a doomed fate. She didn't want him to become the next widower in the family. She'd never wanted that for him.

She knew Josie and her unborn child were in danger; so, too, was she. Nick was in danger as well, if he hung around her for much longer.

She had to sever the ties with him. It was the only way to keep him safe. She'd known that years ago. She'd been a fool to get her hopes up, to believe in a future that could never be.

It broke her heart to push him away, but she knew it was for the best. Sadness welled inside her, nearly choking her. Tears stung her eyes, but she knew what she had to do.

"I know you want to keep me safe," she said. "But I don't believe you can without jeopardizing your own life. Nick, I'm releasing you from your duties."

Nick didn't even bat an eye. "Forget it, baby. I'm not going anywhere. And for the record, the only one who can fire me is the man who hired me. So get used to having me around."

"Nick." Why did he have to make this so difficult? She moved off of the sofa, paced the small area between the coffee table and the fireplace. "I've made up my mind. You can't persuade me otherwise. This has to end between us. I don't want this. I don't want us back together."

He nodded, rubbed the scruff of fresh whiskers that had appeared along his jaw line. "I know what's happening inside that pretty head of yours, baby. You're worried something bad's going to happen to you, to me. But it's not. I told you I won't let it."

"My relatives have been *murdered*, Nick." Saying it out loud made her shake. "And those who loved them have suffered. I saw the look on my father's face at my mother's funeral. It broke my heart. All the pain I felt over losing my mother dulled in comparison to what my father felt. He loved her with all his heart."

"The way I love you," Nick said in a low tone.

Molina pulled in a harsh breath. "Exactly the reason why you have to go. It has to end between us." She swiped impatiently at tears that rolled down her cheeks. "Nick, I don't want you to suffer the same fate as my father. The same fate they've all suffered."

His jaw was set in a hard line, his eyes were fixed on her. "For the last time, Molina. I'm not leaving your side. No matter what."

He pushed himself out of the plump sofa and went to her. He reached for her arms, held her still in front of him while he said, "We'll deal with this vendetta. We'll beat it. And then we'll be together."

"No." She shook her head, wiggled against his tight grip. "It's not going to work. We can't survive this."

"Why not?" he demanded.

She struggled against him, desperate to escape the comfort, the lure of his touch. He let her go and she marched across the room. "Because you're going to get hurt. Physically, emotionally, both. I don't know. All I know is it's just as dangerous to love a Vienti as it is to be one." She opened the door to one of the bedrooms, then located her suitcase and makeup bag. She hefted both up and tossed them recklessly onto the floor in her room.

"Is that a fact?" Nick asked.

"Yes. I'll be dead and you'll be alone."

"I'm not letting anything happen to you," he said stubbornly.

"You have no control over any of this. Whoever is trying to get to me—and to Josie's unborn child—is doing a damn good job."

Nick pushed a hand through his hair. He was getting agitated now. "We know who's behind the murders, Molina."

"But the police can't find him, Nick. And in the meantime, he's tormenting Josie and me. Chances are we're both going to end up dead before the cops catch up with Anthony Moreno." She whirled around, pulled the door to her room closed behind her and locked it.

She fell into her bed and sobbed.

Nick found her at the hospital later that day. She'd left the suite around noon, presumably while he was in the shower because he hadn't heard a thing. He'd been expecting something like that from her, so he'd called one of his cousins in from D.C. to tail her.

Dan had been camped out in the lobby, waiting for Molina to make her escape. He followed her limo to the floral shop where she purchased an impressively large arrangement of flowers. Then she stopped at a bakery, emerged with a box that was tied with ribbon. Dan was on the phone with Nick when she came out.

He reported the stops to Nick, and the purchases made. Nick knew Molina was headed to the hospital, so he jumped in a cab. She beat him there, but he was only five minutes behind her.

Nick caught a glimpse of her speaking with Grace. Then she disappeared inside Josie's room with the flowers. The other two bodyguards Nick had called for assistance loitered about the waiting area, pretending to be visitors so as not to alarm Josie's family. They kept watchful eyes on her door.

Nick waited until Molina emerged from the hospital room. She shook her head and rolled her eyes as she marched past him. Dan was off duty for now, so he disappeared down the hall before Molina could spot him. Nick followed Molina to the elevator.

"Sneaky," he mused as he stepped inside with her.

"I don't have to report my every move to you."

"Actually, you do. That's sort of how this bodyguard gig works."

"I told you, you're not my bodyguard anymore."

"And I told you no one but Frank can fire me."

She sighed, exasperated. She looked worn out, he thought. She obviously hadn't gotten much sleep—probably hadn't gotten any at all.

He certainly hadn't. His ear had practically been pressed to her bedroom door to ensure she was safe. He would've invaded her privacy by picking the lock or getting the bellman to open the door, but he knew she needed space. And he'd given it to her.

"Just do me a favor," he said as he walked beside her through the hospital's reception area. "Let me tag along while you're here in New York. We can renegotiate my duties when we get back to Santa Barbara."

Molina never answered him, so he just continued to follow her.

By early evening, signs of exhaustion darkened Molina's delicate features. Nick suggested she retire to her room. She was obviously fatigued because she didn't utter a word of protest or resistance.

Nick reached for a bottle of scotch just as his cell phone rang. He flipped it open.

"Yeah, it's Nick," he muttered, hearing the tension and weariness in his voice.

"We found him." It was Matt. All traces of fatigue vanished. "Moreno checked into a low-budget motel in Brooklyn. Used a stolen driver's license and credit card. Our boy's not too bright."

"An advantage for us," Nick commented as he began to pace. "What's the plan?"

"Well," Matt said on a soft sigh. "We can question him, see if he's got an alibi for the night of Anthony the fifth's death. If my witnesses agree to a lineup, aren't bumped or paid off, and we actually make it to trial, we can get him for hit and run, maybe manslaughter."

"That hardly involves adequate jail time for what he's done. Once he's back on the streets, he'll continue to hunt Molina and Josie." It was a totally unacceptable answer as far as Nick was concerned.

Matt continued on. "My thoughts exactly. We need to prove premeditated murder."

"I'd happily beat a confession out of him."

"Yeah, that's one way to go," Matt said in a droll tone. "But I was thinking something a little more, oh, I don't know, *legal?*"

"Fine. Wire me. I'll get the bastard to talk." Already a plan was forming in Nick's mind. "You said the Morenos have ties to organized crime. Give me a couple of names."

"Vinny Duran, for one. He's small-time in New York, but a menace to society all the same. Racketeering is standard fare, but he also commands a small army of hit men for Paul Delano—a big fish on the FBI's radar screen. To our knowledge, Duran has never pulled a trigger. He serves as the middle man between Delano and the hired killers."

Nick grinned despite the dire situation. His brother had just handed him the perfect cover. "I can make do with that info."

"I trust your instincts and your techniques. Do you have equipment?"

Nick scoffed. "Think I'm slipping in my old age?"

Matt groaned. "Let's not talk about old age. I'm feeling it these days, bro." He was a quiet a moment, then added, "This is dangerous, Nick. Moreno had help in orchestrating those accidents at Rose Marie's. His contact could very well have told him about you. If Moreno IDs you, he'll shoot first and ask questions later."

"Yeah, I know the risk," Nick said. He entered his room and reached for the small black pouch he'd tucked into his duffle bag before leaving Santa Barbara. It held various micro-size high-tech gadgets he used for surveillance, particularly when he was working Secret Service assignments. He began assembling the device he'd need to record Moreno's confession. As long as he could get his foot in the door—and not get shot—Nick had no doubt he could uncover all of Moreno's dirty little secrets. He just needed ten minutes with the guy...

"Nick," Matt's voice held a hint of concern. "I need you to go by the book on this, pal. We can't risk Moreno walking on a technicality."

Nick grunted. "I promise not to bash his face in. Yet. Does that make you feel better?"

"Marginally."

"I know what I'm doing."

"I know. I also know you've got half a mind to tear the guy's arms out of the sockets for even contemplating hurting Molina. You've got to employ some restraint here. You get in, you get the confession, you get out. Hear me?"

Nick deftly unbuttoned his shirt and juggled the phone as he slipped the material from his shoulders. "Yeah, yeah. Restraint. I can do that."

Matt paused again before saying, "Be careful."

"Always."

Matt provided the name and address of the motel Moreno had checked into. Nick disconnected the call and, minutes later, he was wired and ready to go.

He slipped his gun into the shoulder holster he wore and then pulled on his leather coat. He stepped out of the suite.

Dan stood guard at the door. Nick gave him a casual nod. "Keep an eye on her. She's sleeping now, but you can't trust her to stay put if she gets a wild hair to visit her aunt or Josie. She's a definite flight risk." Nick shook his head and chuckled under his breath. As annoying as Molina's obstinate nature could be, he admired her determination and courage.

"She'll be safe," Dan assured him. "Can't say the same about Moreno, can we?"

Nick's jaw clenched. "No one hurts her and gets away with it."

Using his knuckles, Nick rapped twice on the motel room door. "Open up, Moreno. Duran sent me."

Nick heard the soft click of the lock being disengaged. Moreno pulled the door wide and said, "Inside, man. I think I'm being watched."

Nick gave him a disinterested look. "I doubt it," he said, hoping to build a sense of false security from the onset. Nick stepped into the room, careful to keep his back to the wall as he waited for Moreno to lock up and then cross to the small table in the far corner of the room.

He was a portly man, short and stout, with a couple inches of flab hanging over the waist of his jeans. He wore a plaid shirt and scuffed boots. His thick, dark brown hair was neatly trimmed and combed, but he had a couple of days' worth of stubble on his jaw. Despite the excess weight, Moreno could almost be considered handsome. He had a deep tan as though he spent a good deal of time in the sun. Maybe he was a construction or dock worker.

Moreno pulled out a chair and motioned for Nick to sit. Nick ignored the offering and remained standing just inside the doorway.

"I shouldn't be surprised to see you," Moreno said. "I told Duran the cops were after me."

Nick merely nodded. Moreno had yet to look closely at him in decent light. The drapes were pulled closed and the TV, which Moreno muted with the remote, provided the only source of light. Nick hoped Moreno hadn't been diligent enough in his surveillance efforts to snap a photo of him. If Moreno recognized him as Molina's bodyguard… Game Over. It'd get ugly quick. And the promise Nick had made to Matt not to inflict bodily harm on the bastard would be long forgotten.

Nick felt the tension grip his body at the prospect of Moreno identifying him, but forced himself to appear casual and indifferent. He reminded himself that one of Duran's killers wouldn't care about the circumstances surrounding the job he'd been contracted to carry out. He'd simply want the details of the dirty deed so he could fulfill his obligation.

Moreno plopped into a chair and said, "My landlady said the cops have been sniffing around my apartment, asking questions. They want to know about the hit and run. Damn it," he said angrily. "Duran found two people who admitted to seeing me run over Vienti, and I emptied my bank account paying them off. Duran scared the bejesus out them, too, threatening their lives if they uttered a word. But the Feds must've gotten to them and offered protection. Now I'm hiding out in this pisshole for God knows how long."

Nick spared a quick glance about the place. Paisley drapes. Heavily stained carpet and bedspread. Furniture from the 70s. Dingy walls with cheesy pictures hanging on them. It was the kind of place that rented rooms by the hour, Nick was sure. It made your average Motel 6 look like the Ritz.

"So who are you and why'd Vinny send you?"

Back to business. Nick returned his attention to Moreno. He took a few steps closer to the table, forcing his movements to appear easy, though he was ready to reach for his gun if Moreno suddenly ID'd him. He studied the man's face for a moment, but saw not the slightest hint of recognition in his dark brown eyes. Apparently, Moreno had not been smart enough to find out if Molina had bodyguards. Good.

Nick knew it was best not to give a name or address the reason for his visit—he didn't want anything he said to be misconstrued or considered entrapment. He couldn't risk having a confession dismissed in court because he'd misrepresented himself or botched the process in some way. He opted to keep his words to a minimum, hoping he could prompt Moreno into doing all the talking with his intimidating stare and lack of communication.

It seemed to work, because Moreno didn't press the issue when Nick didn't provide a name. He sat in his chair, looking uncomfortable and sullen, beads of perspiration beginning to pop up on his forehead.

Let him sweat, Nick thought. If he revered Duran and maybe feared hit men, he wouldn't ask questions, just answer them.

To that end, Nick extracted a black and white photo from the inside pocket of his jacket and tossed it carelessly onto the table. "I don't give a damn about your problems with the cops or about the hit and run." He'd admitted to the crime, so Nick didn't see any point in dwelling on it, lest his questioning should draw suspicion. "I want to know about the broad."

Moreno reached for the photo. He studied it for a moment, a look of pure hatred marring his features. "Molina Toscano," he said with obvious loathing. Moreno reached for the cigarette lighter next to the ashtray. He flicked it until a steady flame burned, letting it touch the corner of the photo. Nick watched as Moreno held the blazing photo between his thumb and finger until the last possible moment. Then he dropped it into the ashtray and set the lighter back in its place.

"Bitch," Moreno muttered.

Nick's gut wrenched, but he forced himself to appear unaffected by the other man's hostility. "You've been keeping tabs on her family. What's she to you?"

Much to his surprise, Moreno's palms slammed down on the table, making it shake unsteadily. "She's a fuckin' Vienti! Duran knows I want her dead. Isn't that why you're here?"

Nick shrugged noncommittally.

Moreno continued on. "She deserves to die, just like the rest of them!"

His vehement and heated response told Nick it wouldn't be too difficult to get Moreno to not only confess to Anthony's murder, but to also reveal his plan to kill Molina and Josie—and her baby. Moreno's obvious hatred for the Vientis would be his downfall.

"Goddamn it," Moreno spat. "Look at me! Look at this rat dump I'm gonna be living in until the heat lets up. My family's barely had two dimes to rub together and that bitch," he said as he pointed an accusatory finger at the now smoldering pile of ashes, "has lived the lap of luxury her whole damn life. They all have. Her great-great grandfather was loaded to begin with. Then he went and married a shipping heiress and bam! The guy's got more money than God. But the greedy bastard never did nothin' for no one but himself."

Nick had Moreno right where he wanted him. He just needed to keep the guy talking. "Okay, so, like, I've got no idea what your beef is with her, but obviously you think she owes you."

"It's not just her," Moreno said. Anger created patches of pink on his throat and cheeks. He rubbed his scruffy jaw for a moment, then said, "It's the whole family. Starting with the great-great grandfather. Son-of-a-bitch knocked up my great-great grandmother, Patricia Moreno, then left her with nothin'. No name for the kid, no child support. Meanwhile, he builds some Goddamn mansion in the hills of Santa Barbara and raises his other son like a king. And when Patricia was on her death bed, you know, dying from pneumonia, the bastard didn't even come see her. He was a doctor, for Chrissakes! Didn't try to help her with medicine or money. He just let her die."

Nick could understand the distaste that would leave in one's mouth. But murdering an entire bloodline for revenge? Talk about a grudge. Maybe the senior Anthony Vienti was morally defunct for abandoning her and their child—personally Nick couldn't fathom doing anything of the like—but still... it was the first Anthony Vienti's sin, not that of the entire bloodline.

Of course, the true motivation for revenge probably wasn't the fact that Patricia and her child had been left to fend for themselves. Money had an evil way of influencing people.

"What happened to Patricia's kid?" Nick asked. He hoped his voice didn't betray his eagerness to uncover the whole truth behind the vendetta.

But the dark, menacing look in Moreno's eyes told Nick the man was too shrouded in anger and hatred to catch onto Nick's ploy. Moreno's fists clenched at his sides and his jaw tensed. He shook his head and said, "Whaddya think? He grew up as the neighborhood bastard. Illegitimate and poor. His uncle took care of him for a while. You'd think his father would have come for him, but no. He had to fend for himself, you know? He didn't get a good education and didn't have much of a future to look forward to. So he took up with some local gangsters. Made a little bit of money, then lost it gambling. He was in and out of jail… whatever."

Nick shrugged. "Some life. Are we getting to what this has to do with the chick?" Though Nick wanted the full story, he thought it was more in-character to appear impatient and bored.

Luckily, Moreno wasn't to be rushed. Ignoring Nick's prompting, he said, "When the kid was old enough, the uncle told him about how his old man had turned a cold shoulder on him and his mother. Even when she was dying, he wouldn't help her. And she was young, too. Just turned thirty when she got sick. But Patricia's brother evened the score for her and the kid."

"Yeah? How'd he manage that?"

A wide, nasty grin curled the edges of Moreno's mouth. "How'd you think?" He crossed to the battered dresser and opened a large cooler that sat beside it. He pulled out a can of beer, popped the top and handed it to Nick. "He offed him. And the beauty of it was," he said as he retrieved another can and opened it, "he made it look like a freak accident. The cops never suspected nothin'. He totally got away with it!"

"Smart guy," Nick snickered.

"No shit. You don't mess with Morenos, man. We've got a mean streak, and we don't like people hurting our families."

"So, the great-great grandfather bites it and everybody's happy, vindicated."

"Hell, no," Moreno said before taking a long pull from his beer can. "Cuz now we got nothin'. The kid should have inherited some money, you know? *Something.* Vienti had millions, but didn't leave a penny for the kid!" Moreno threw his head back and drained his beer in several long gulps.

"So my family figures," Moreno continued, "an eye for an eye, right? Give them just what they deserved. From way back when, my family figured the Vientis should suffer the way we have. The kid was the rightful heir to a fortune and a good family name for Chrissakes. He deserved his own vengeance, you know? So he did a little homework and found out the Vientis owned a vacation home in New York. He kept an eye on his half-brother, and when the brother turned thirty, guess what?"

Nick's stomach turned. Moreno was so blinded by family pride and the need to carry on this tradition of slaying Vientis it was sickening. "He 'offed' him?"

"You bet your sweet ass he did. And we've been doing it ever since. One by one until we're down to the last of the worthless lot."

"And she's it?"

Moreno shook his head as he tossed his empty can into the trash and reached for another beer. "I thought so. Turns out the wife of the guy I took out a few weeks ago is pregnant. Duran had her followed for a while after the hit and run, and thought it was kinda curious that she kept going back to the doctor. He did a little snooping around and found out about the baby. So there's two Vientis left to kill."

Nick was this close to wrapping his hands around Moreno's throat. He wanted to choke the life right out of him for even considering harming Josie and her baby. Not to mention the irrational emotions that welled inside him at hearing Moreno confess he planned to kill Molina.

That last thought was what helped him to keep his temper and rage intact. He was getting the confession the FBI needed to nail this son-of-a-bitch.

"All right," Nick said. He took a sip of his beer not because he wanted it, but because his throat was dry and tight with mounting anger. "I see where this is headed. Your family's revenge is to make the Vientis extinct. Clever. But let's get back to the girl. How do you plan to do it?"

Moreno paused, arm in mid-air as he'd prepared for another marathon chug. He lowered the can and eyed Nick. For the first time, Moreno looked skeptical. "What's it to you?"

Nick could have kicked himself. He'd pushed too hard, gotten too eager to wrap this whole damn thing up and be on his way. The sooner he got the tape to Matt, the sooner this asshole would be locked up. For a very, very long time. Nick groaned inwardly at his slip, but recovered quickly. "Why do you think?" he scowled, hoping like hell Moreno would draw the appropriate conclusion: that Nick was here under Duran's orders as a hired killer to help facilitate the murder.

Moreno seemed to consider the possibilities for a moment. Eventually, a slow grin eased over his lips. "We could do it simultaneously, which would really throw the cops off my tail! They couldn't suspect me of killin' Toscano and the widow at the same time if they were in different parts of the city when it happened."

Nick nodded. Then he waited. He all but held his breath as Moreno contemplated this new plan. Finally, Moreno shook his head. "Nah. It'd be too much of a coincidence to have Anthony bite it, and the other two Vientis die at the same time, just weeks later. I'd for sure have the Feds breathing down my neck. I mean, hell, that's why I haven't offed Toscano yet. I went after the pregnant cousin because she was an easier target. I used an insider at the mansion to ruffle Toscano's feathers a bit, yeah. You know, let her know she wasn't safe and that I was coming for her." He actually appeared to puff out his chest a bit. "The whole random accident thing has worked all these years. No one has ever suspected the Morenos. And the Vientis just think it's some sort of evil curse that's bumping them off." He laughed heartily and rubbed his hands together. "I'll finish the job with the widow. I didn't intend to kill her initially. Just thought I'd help her miscarry. But she's tougher than she looks. So, fine. She's next to go. And then Toscano. I'll make her the grand finale."

Nick had to employ every ounce of willpower he possessed to remain in character and not reach for his gun.

"That's the plan," Moreno said. "That's always been the plan, starting with the first Anthony Vienti. I'm the last of the Moreno line, so it's up to me to do in the last two Vientis. Just me. I want it over with. *Finito.* You can tell Duran thanks for the offer but I've got it all under control."

Nick shrugged. "Suit yourself."

"I'm just gonna step in the john for a minute. Sit down and enjoy your beer. I could use some company."

As soon as the door closed, Nick was out of there.

Chapter Eleven

Nick returned to The Plaza an hour later, tired from the tension in his body that wouldn't ease up, yet pumped from the successful confrontation with Moreno. He entered the hotel suite and dropped his coat and cell phone on the coffee table. He'd already apprised Matt of his conversation with Moreno, and then he'd doubled the number of bodyguards outside Josie's hospital room. She was obviously the first target; Nick wouldn't give Moreno a chance to hurt her.

Nick removed the small recording device that had been strapped to his chest and handed it to Dan. "Get this to Matt." The FBI would have Moreno in custody within twenty-four hours, according to Matt.

"On my way." Dan grabbed his coat and headed to the door.

Nick went straight to the bar and poured himself a glass of scotch. He downed it quickly and splashed a bit more into his glass. He was strung pretty tight, and was tempted to slip into Molina's room and rouse her from her nap. Instead, he sank into the plush cushion of the overstuffed sofa. He rested his elbows on his knees and his head hung between his wide shoulders. He was emotionally drained.

He let out a long breath and then took another sip. He needed a hot shower and a good night's sleep, which he felt he could manage, knowing Moreno would get no where near Josie. Nor would he be going after Molina anytime soon.

They stayed in the hotel room the entire day, until Molina thought she'd go crazy from boredom. She needed fresh air, so she coaxed Nick into taking her to dinner. They found a quaint outdoor café in the Village, which delighted Molina.

They ate in silence and sipped wine afterward as they watched people walk by. It was one of Molina's favorite things to do when in New York. People were fascinating. She loved to watch the tourists as they gushed with awe and rushed through the streets, trying to cram in as much of the New York experience as they could in the short period of vacation time they had. Lovers strolled, hand in hand, or sat on park benches, stealing kisses, laughing. It was a warm spring evening in Manhattan. A beautiful night to be outside.

A beautiful night to be alive.

Tears suddenly threatened Molina's eyes. *Damn it.* She really was scared. Unable to push her fears aside, she decided to call it an evening. She finished her wine and stood. She wanted to get in the limo, head back to the hotel. Or preferably, back to Rose Marie's. But neither place was safe, was it?

Nick dropped money on the table as she made her quick departure. She stepped out in the street, stalking across the asphalt to the limo.

Suddenly, she heard the revving of an engine, heard the squeal of tires. For a moment, she was temporarily blinded from the flash of headlights that flickered on. In the next instant, an SUV was bearing down on her before she had the chance to move. She was paralyzed with fear.

She opened her mouth to scream, but no words came out.

"Molina!" Suddenly, she felt Nick's powerful body against hers as he pushed her out of the way with such force they both sailed through the air then hit the ground hard. The impact jarred her and pain lanced through her body as her knees, forearms and left shoulder made contact with the asphalt. The breath escaped her, and she barely had time to pull in another one before Nick was hauling her up and dragging her across the street. He deposited her on the curb.

"You okay?" he asked.

Molina numbly nodded her head. Carlos, the limo driver, appeared at her side and Nick addressed him. "Stay with her."

Before Molina could utter a word of protest, Nick bolted down the street after the SUV. The soft glow of the moon and the streetlamps created a silhouette of the car as it weaved in and out of traffic, its lights off.

"You two are damn lucky to be alive," Carlos said.

"I know." Molina's stomach twisted in tight knots. They were fortunate no oncoming cars had struck them when she and Nick had hit the ground. She was damn lucky Nick was never far from her, that he was always close by to keep her safe.

The harrowing incident made Molina tremble with fear, but what really terrified her was that Nick had gone after the driver of the SUV—he'd gone after Moreno.

Her blood ran cold. If anything happened to him, it would be all her fault. She'd never be able to forgive herself...

"Don't worry about him," Carlos said as he draped his jacket over Molina's shoulders. "Mr. Moretti knows how to take care of himself."

Molina's eyes were locked on Nick as he raced down the sidewalk, hurdling overturned trashcans and dodging pedestrians. He was damn quick, able to almost keep up with Moreno because he was now stuck behind several cars at the light a few blocks down the street.

He reached for the passenger door handle just as Moreno veered sharply to the right. Nick managed to get a foot inside the vehicle and he held on as Moreno hopped the curb and then sped down the sidewalk, sending screaming pedestrians scampering out of his way. He floored it and the vehicle went sailing round the corner and back into the street. Car horns blared in the distance and people yelled obscenities at the reckless driver.

Molina gasped when she lost sight of the vehicle—and Nick. Moments later, sounds of a thunderous crash—metal on mental and shattering glass—filled the night air.

Molina jumped to her feet. She darted across the street and raced down the sidewalk, pushing people out of her way. Her pulse roared in her head, and her heart hammered in her chest. Tears spilled from her eyes at the horrifying thought that Nick had just been killed. Her knees threatened to buckle beneath her, but somehow, she managed to keep running.

She rounded the corner, weaving her way through the throng of people that had gathered. She drew up short, her chest heaving, as she tried to suck in some much-needed oxygen.

Anthony Moreno's vehicle had struck a delivery truck. The front of the SUV was smashed into the side of the truck. Moreno was slumped against the steering wheel, and the horn wailed in a solid, continuous stream. The airbag had not been deployed.

Blood splattered on the windshield and dashboard of the SUV.

Molina's stomach turned. Her hand covered her mouth, as if that would really hold back the bile rising in her throat. Then she realized that Moreno was the only one in the car. She glanced about, frantic and scared, seeing no sign of Nick.

A moment later, she heard the rumble of trashcans, bottles and other objects behind her. She turned at the sound of Nick's deep grumble. He lay sprawled on the sidewalk, lodged between debris and the brick wall of the corner building.

"Nick!" she cried. She pushed her way through the growing number of bystanders and dropped to her knees beside him.

Carlos appeared on the other side of him. The chauffer made excited sounds as he eyed Nick's minor cuts and bruises. "That was one hell of a stunt, Mr. Moretti. You are like James Bond! It's always an adventure when you're in town!"

Nick groaned. "Yeah, great fun. Now get this crap off of me, will you?"

As Carlos helped him escape the broken wooden crates and steel garbage barrels, Molina swiped at the paper and trash that had settled on Nick when he'd jumped from the SUV and taken out everything sitting on the street corner. Tears stung her eyes and dampened her cheeks.

Nick's arm eased around her shoulder as she helped him sit up. He glanced past her to the mangled SUV and its lifeless driver.

His grip tightened around her. "Looks like that's the end of Anthony Moreno."

Chapter Twelve

More importantly, Anthony Moreno's death put an end to the Vienti curse.

After answering questions for the NYPD and the FBI, Molina and Nick returned to Rose Marie's manor. They'd learned that the Moreno family had, in fact, been responsible for the deaths of each Vienti since Anthony, Sr.'s untimely death in 1912. A journal, kept for nearly a century by the Morenos, apparently passed down from son to son, revealed the Morenos had kept very close tabs on the Vientis. A Vienti family tree had been drawn and added to over the decades. The dead Vientis had dark black Xs drawn over their names, with a record of how each had met their sudden demise.

The FBI also found extensive reports kept by the late Anthony Moreno, V, on Rose Marie's staff. He'd singled out Angelo Vallero and had paid him handsomely to carry out the accidents at the estate, in an attempt to distract Nick and Molina while Moreno stalked Josie and her unborn child.

Vallero's wife was dying of cancer and the only way he could afford the treatments was to trade his loyalty to Rose Marie for a pay-off beyond his wildest imagination. In apology to Rose Maria, he willingly ID'd Anthony Moreno, V, as the man who'd hired him.

Molina felt as though a tremendous weight had been lifted from her chest. The vendetta had been broken. She and Josie's baby were safe, so Molina and Nick returned to Santa Barbara.

"I have two gifts for you," Rose Marie said as she joined Molina on the gallery overlooking the grounds. One hand rested on her cane, the other held a white gift bag.

"You already gave me a birthday gift," Molina said. "And might I add a gift certificate to Prada is always greatly appreciated."

"I'm glad you liked the gift, dear. Now take this bag," she said. "Open the gift-wrapped box first."

Molina did as her grandmother asked. Inside, the elegantly wrapped box she found a glass and diamond bottle fashioned in the shape of a butterfly. Molina turned the cap and held the bottle to her nose. She tentatively sniffed the fragrance inside. It was deeply stirring. Soft, tantalizing, arousing. She closed her eyes and inhaled. "It's wonderful."

"Nick had it created for you."

Molina's eyes flew open. "What?"

"Your father found a perfumery in Italy that would work with Nick. He described the exact scent he wanted and *voilà*. A one-of-a-kind scent was created for the woman he loved. Exactly how *Bella* was created for your mother."

Molina was stunned. "I can't believe he went to the trouble…"

"Why not, dear? He loves you. And that's what people who love each other do."

Molina shook her head, tamped down tears that threatened her eyes. "He continually amazes me," she mused.

"Now, for my gift," Rose Marie urged.

Molina put the bottle of *Butterfly* perfume back in its ornate box. She then retrieved a tiny black velvet box from the gift bag. She opened it slowly. Inside was a stunning, princess-cut diamond engagement ring.

"It was your mother's ring," Rose Marie said. Tears pooled in her eyes. "I've had it all this time. I guess I just wanted a constant reminder of her, so I kept something she loved close to me. As you did with the bottle of *Bella*."

"Then you shouldn't give it to me," Molina said. "Keep the ring."

"No," Rose Marie said in a steady voice. She gave Molina a pointed look. "I realized something after the bottle of *Bella* broke. I know how it must have hurt you, to see that shattered bottle on the floor. You carried it with you always. Wore the perfume always. It was one of the things that reminded you the most of your mother. When you wore her perfume, she was with you. And then the bottle was broken and the perfume was gone. But you gave such little thought to it because being by Josie's side was much more important."

Molina began to protest, but Rose Marie held a hand up in the air to stop her. "You grieved over the loss of it—over the loss of that one thing that made you feel as though Ann Marie was close to you at all times. But you realized your mother was in your heart. You didn't need the perfume to think of her, to feel as though she were with you.

"You rushed off to Josie's side without a second thought to what you had just lost. You put it all behind you, concentrated on those who needed you."

Rose Marie smiled warmly, her eyes filled with love and pride. "And I suddenly realized I had been holding onto this ring for the exact same reason. I don't need it anymore," she said. "Ann Marie is in my heart. She will always be here. Always with me."

Molina swiped at the tears in her eyes. "And with me."

"Yes. And I want you to have her ring."

Molina smiled through the tears. "I'll cherish it as she did."

"Good. Now you have an important task to attend to, don't you?"

Molina sniffled. "No rest for the wicked? What exactly ought I be doing?"

"Salvaging the best, and only, romantic relationship you've ever had."

Molina gnawed her lower lip. She had pushed Nick away. Again. She'd barely spoken to him since the fateful night at The Plaza when she'd told him she didn't want them to stay together. His job was done. She was safe. And now he was leaving.

The thought made her feel empty inside.

"I suppose," Molina said as a finger absently trailed over the stone railing, "you're right."

"Damned stubborn, you are," Rose Marie scoffed.

Molina hugged her grandmother. "I do love you, Gran. Even when you're meddling." She pulled away, gave Rose Marie an earnest look. "But tell me this. What reason does Nick have to stay?"

"You, my dear."

She found him on the back patio, sipping iced tea and talking on his cell. When he saw her, he concluded his call and snapped the phone shut. He set it on the table in front of him.

Molina wasn't sure what she was going to say to him; she wasn't sure if there was anything appropriate *to* say. Twice now she'd let him in then pushed him away when he'd gotten too close. It wasn't fair to him. He deserved someone who loved him so much, the thought of spending one moment without him would be devastating.

I love him that much.

Molina had to look away from him for a moment as she fought to keep her composure. She was so used to losing people she loved. It'd been happening to her the whole of her life.

But that was all over now.

She sank into a chair next to Nick's. He was waiting patiently for whatever she had to say.

"I love the perfume. Thank you. It was an incredibly thoughtful gift." She held her wrist out to him. "Do you like it on me?"

He inhaled deeply. Smiled softly. "It's definitely you. Now you truly do have a fragrance that's yours alone."

"I love it, Nick. I can't thank you enough."

"I'm sorry you lost the bottle of *Bella*."

Molina shook her head, let out a slow breath. "I was devastated at first, but... my grandmother is right. My mother's always with me. In my heart."

Nick nodded. "I know it must have been hard growing up without her."

"Yes. But I've had other people around me to fill the void. People who love me." She gave him a pointed look.

Nick merely nodded.

"So, what are your plans?" she asked.

"Job in D.C. if I want it," he said in a tight voice. "A senator is being stalked by some radical animal rights activists. They've already picked off two of his aides."

She nodded in acknowledgement, but didn't like the implication. "Secret Service stuff. Dangerous business."

Nick shrugged noncommittally.

"Don't go." The words tumbled out of her mouth before she even knew what she was saying. But even as her plea lingered in the air between them, she was glad she'd uttered the words.

Nick stood. He raked a hand through his hair. "Tell me why I should stay. You're safe. You don't need a bodyguard anymore."

"I'm not asking you to stay as my bodyguard. I'm asking you to stay as... my lover. My boyfriend. You know, my significant other." She tried all the labels, none of them seemed to fit.

Nick pulled in a breath. He closed his eyes for a brief moment, then gave her a compelling look. "No."

Molina felt her heart break. It was such an overwhelming emotion it brought tears to her eyes. "I love you, Nick," she said earnestly. "Please stay with me."

She stood and closed the space between them. She looked up at him. For the first time, she opened her heart completely to him. "You gave me the best birthday gift ever. You gave me a life. And I want to spend the rest of it with you. Every single day of it."

His dark eyes misted. He cupped her face and his thumb grazed over her glossy lips. "Say it again," he said in a hoarse voice. "Slower this time."

"I love you, Nick."

He shook his head, let out a soft laugh. "Took you long enough to realize it, baby."

She smiled, though the corners of her mouth quivered slightly. "I've always known it. Since my nineteenth birthday. It's just been so hard for me to say it because... I was afraid of loving one more person who would leave my life."

Nick nodded in understanding. "I expect to hear it more frequently than every eleven years, sweetheart."

She smiled more confidently now. "Deal."

He pulled her close to him. "Damn, you smell good." He gave her a long, sweet kiss. "I love you, too, Molina."

He kissed her again. His arms slipped around her in a tight embrace. When he pulled away, they were both breathless. Molina rested her head against his chest. "How do you feel about weddings, Nick?"

"Depends on who's getting married, baby."

"Well," she said in a soft voice. "I have this beautiful engagement ring that belonged to my mother. And June is right around the corner. It's a popular wedding month. I thought we could get married out here on the back lawn."

Nick grinned down at her. "You are too much, sweetheart. But don't you think someone ought to propose, first?"

She nodded. "You're absolutely right." She eased out of his arms and gazed up at him. "Nick Moretti, will you marry me?"

Nick shook his head at her, the soft grin still playing on his lips. "Jeez, baby, I don't know…"

"Nick!" she gasped. She reached out to swat him, but he grabbed her wrist and pulled her back to him.

"Sweetheart," he said as he scooped her up in his arms. "You are fabulously unpredictable."

She wrapped her arms around his neck. "Is that a yes?"

"I'm not going to answer you just yet. You made me wait eleven years. I think I'll let you sweat a little."

She laughed.

He carried her across the lawn, but stopped before they entered the house. "Okay, I give. The answer," he said, "is yes."

About the Author:

Calista Fox owns a small communications and PR firm. She lives in Scottsdale, Arizona with her husband and their two mischievous puppies. She is an avid reader of romance novels and believes every life should be filled with passion. This is her first published story. You can visit her at www.calistafox. com.

If you enjoyed *Secrets Volume 13* but haven't read other volumes, you should see what you're missing!

Secrets Volume 1:

In *A Lady's Quest*, author Bonnie Hamre brings you a London historical where Lady Antonia Blair-Sutworth searches for a lover in a most shocking and pleasing way.

Alice Gaines' *The Spinner's Dream* weaves a seductive fantasy that will leave every woman wishing for her own private love slave, desperate and running for his life.

Ivy Landon takes you for a wild ride. *The Proposal* will taunt you, tease you, even shock you. A contemporary erotica for the adventurous woman's ultimate fantasy.

With *The Gift* by Jeanie LeGendre, you're immersed in the historic tale of exotic seduction and bondage. Read about a concubine's delicious surrender to her Sultan.

Secrets Volume 2:

Surrogate Lover, by Doreen DeSalvo, is a contemporary tale of lust and love in the 90's. A surrogate sex therapist thought he had all the answers until he met Sarah.

Bonnie Hamre's regency tale *Snowbound* delights as the Earl of Howden is teased and tortured by his own desires—finally a woman who equals his overpowering sensuality.

In *Roarke's Prisoner*, by Angela Knight, starship captain Elise remembers the eager animal submission she'd known before at her captor's hands and refuses to be his toy again.

Susan Paul's *Savage Garden* tells the story of Raine's capture by a mysterious revolutionary in Mexico. She quickly finds lush erotic nights in her captor's arms.

Secrets Volume 3:

In Jeanie Cesarini's *The Spy Who Loved Me*, FBI agents Paige Ellison and Christopher Sharp discover excitement and passion in some unusual undercover work.

Warning: This story is only for the most adventurous of readers. Ann Jacobs tells the story of *The Barbarian*. Giles has a sexual arsenal designed to break down proud Lady Brianna's defenses — erotic pleasures learned in a harem.

Wild, sexual hunger is unleashed in this futuristic vampire tale with a twist. In Angela Knight's *Blood and Kisses*, find out just who is seducing whom?

B.J. McCall takes you into the erotic world of strip joints in *Love Undercover*. On assignment, Lt. Amanda Forbes and Det. "Cowboy" Cooper find temptation hard to resist.

Secrets Volume 4:

An Act of Love is Jeanie Cesarini's sequel. Shelby's terrified of sex. Film star Jason Gage must coach her in the ways of love. He wants her to feel true passion in his arms.

The Love Slave, by Emma Holly, is a woman's ultimate fantasy. For one year, Princess Lily will be attended to by three delicious men. She delights in playing with the first two, but it's the reluctant Grae that stirs her desires.

Lady Crystal is in turmoil in *Enslaved*, by Desirée Lindsey. Lord Nicholas' dark passions and irresistible charm have brought her long-hidden desires to the surface.

Betsy Morgan and Susan Paul bring you Kaki York's story in *The Bodyguard*. Watching the wild, erotic romps of her client's sexual conquests on the security cameras is getting to her—and her partner, the ruggedly handsome James Kulick.

Secrets Volume 5:

B.J. McCall is back with *Alias Smith and Jones*. Meredith Collins is stranded overnight at the airport. A handsome stranger named Smith offers her sanctuary for the evening—how can she resist those mesmerizing green-flecked eyes?

Strictly Business, by Shannon Hollis, tells of Elizabeth Forrester's desire to climb the corporate ladder on her merits, not her looks. But the gorgeous Garrett Hill has come along and stirred her wildest fantasies.

Chevon Gael's *Insatiable* is the tale of a man's obsession. After corporate exec Ashlyn Fraser's glamour shot session, photographer Marcus Remington can't get her off his mind. Forget the beautiful models, he must have her —but where did she go?

Sandy Fraser's **Beneath Two Moons** is a futuristic wild ride. Conor is rough and tough like frontiermen of old, and he's on the prowl for a new conquest. Dr. Eva Kelsey got away once before, but this time he'll make sure she begs for more.

Secrets Volume 6:

Sandy Fraser is back with **Flint's Fuse**. Dana Madison's father has her "kidnapped" for her own safety. Flint, the tall, dark and dangerousmercenary, is hired for the job. But just which one is the prisoner—Dana will try *anything* to get away.

In **Love's Prisoner**, by MaryJanice Davidson, Jeannie Lawrence experienced unwilling rapture at Michael Windham's hands. She never expected the devilishly handsome man to show back up in her life—or turn out to be a werewolf!

Alice Gaines' **The Education of Miss Felicity Wells** finds a pupil needing to learn how to satisfy her soon-to-be husband. Dr. Marcus Slade, an experienced lover, agrees to take her on as a student, but can he stop short of taking her completely?

Angela Knight tells about reporter Dana Ivory stumbling onto a secret—a sexy, secret agent who happens to be a vampire.She wants her story but Gabriel Archer believes she's **A Candidate for the Kiss**.

Secrets Volume 7:

In **Amelia's Innocence** by Julia Welles, Amelia didn't know her father bet her in a card game with Captain Quentin Hawke, so honor demands a compromise—three days of erotic foreplay, leaving her virginity and future intact.

Jade Lawless brings **The Woman of His Dreams** to life. Artist Gray Avonaco moved in next door to Joanna Morgan and now is plagued by provocative dreams. Is it unrequited lust or Gray's chance to be with the woman he loves?

Surrender by Kathryn Anne Dubois tells of Lady Johanna. She wants no part of the binding strictures of marriage to the powerful Duke. But she doesn't realize he wants sensual adventure, and sexual satisfaction.

Angela Knight's **Kissing the Hunter** finds Navy Seal Logan McLean hunting the vampires who murdered his wife. Virginia Hart is a sexy vampire searching for her lost soul-mate only to find him in a man determined to kill her.

Secrets Volume 8:

In Jeanie Cesarini's latest tale, we meet Kathryn Roman as she inherits a legal brothel. She refuses to trade her Manhattan high-powered career for a life in the wild west. But the town of Love, Nevada has recruited Trey Holliday, one very dominant cowboy, with *Taming Kate*.

In *Jared's Wolf* by MaryJanice Davidson, Jared Rocke will do anything to avenge his sister's death, but he wasn't expecting to fall for Moira Wolfbauer, the she-wolf sworn to protect her werewolf pack. The two enemies must stop a killer while learning that love defies all boundaries.

My Champion, My Love, by Alice Gaines, tells the tale of Celeste Broder, a woman committed for a sexy appetite that is tolerated in men, but not women. Mayor Robert Albright may be her salvation—*if* she can convince him her freedom will mean a chance to indulge their appetites together.

Liz Maverick takes you to a post-apocalyptic world in *Kiss or Kill*. Camille Kazinsky's military career rides on her decision—whether the robo called Meat should live or die. Meat's future depends on proving he's human enough to live, *man* enough, to make her feel like a woman.

Secrets Volume 9:

Kimberly Dean brings you *Wanted*. FBI Special Agent Jeff Reno wants Danielle Carver. There's her body, brains—and that charge of treason on her head. Dani goes on the run, but the sexy Fed is hot on her trail. What will he do once he catches her? And why is the idea so tempting?

In *Wild for You*. by Kathryn Anne Dubois, college intern Georgie gets lost and captured by a wildman of the Congo. She soon discovers this terrifying specimen of male virility has never seen a woman. The research possibilities are endless! Until he shows her he has research ideas of his own.

Bonnie Hamre is back with *Flights of Fantasy*. Chloe taught others to see the realities of life but she's never shared the intimate world of her sensual yearnings. Given the chance, will she be woman enough to fulfill her most secret erotic fantasy?

In Lisa Marie Rice's story, *Secluded*, Nicholas Lee had to claw his way to the top. His wealth and power come with a price—his enemies will kill anyone he loves. When Isabelle Summerby steals his heart, Nicholas secludes her in his underground palace to live a lifetime of desire in only a few days.

Secrets Volume 10:

In Dominique Sinclair's *Private Eyes*, top private investigator Niccola Black is used to tracking down adulterous spouses, but when a mystery man captures her absolute attention during a stakeout, she discovers her "no seduction" rule is bending under the pressure of the long denied passion.

Bonnie Hamre's *The Ruination of Lady Jane* brings you Lady Jane Ponsonby-Maitland's story. With an upcoming marriage to a man more than twice her age, she disappears. Havyn Attercliffe was sent to retrieve his brother's ward, but when she begs him to ruin her rather than turn her over to her odious fiancé, how can he refuse?

Jeanie Cesarini is back with *Code Name: Kiss*. Agent Lily Justiss would do anything to defend her country against terrorists, including giving her virginity away on an undercover mission as a sex slave. But even as her master takes possession, it's fantasies of her commanding officer, Seth Blackthorn, that fuels her desire.

Kathryn Anne Dubois' *The Sacrifice* tells about Lady Anastasia Bedovier who's about to take her vows as a nun, but decadent, sensual dreams force her to consider that her sacrifice of chastity might mean little until she has experienced the passion she will deny. She goes to Count Maxwell and, in one erotic night, learns the heights of sensual pleasure. Maxwell thought he was immune from love, but the nameless novice that warmed his bed has proved his undoing, and despite his desperate search, he can't reach her.

Secrets Volume 11:

Jennifer Probst brings us *Masquerade*. Hailey Ashton is determined to free herself from her sexual restrictions. Four nights of erotic pleasures without revealing her identity. A chance to explore her secret desires without the fear of unmasking.

Jess Michaels's *Ancient Pleasures* tells of Isabella Winslow who is obsessed with finding out what caused her late husband's death, but trapped in an Egyptian concubine's tomb with a sexy American raider, succumbing to the mummy's sensual curse takes over.

Manhunt by Kimberly Deanis about Michael Tucker. Framed for murder, he takes Taryn Swanson hostage—the one woman who can clear him.

Despite the evidence against him, the attraction between them is strong. Tucker resorts to unconventional, yet effective methods of persuasion to change the sexy ADA's mind.

Angela Knight returns with *Wake Me*. Chloe Hart received a sexy painting of a sleeping knight. Radolf of Varik has been trapped for centuries in the painting. His only hope is to visit the dreams of women and make one of them fall in love with him so she can free him with a kiss.

Secrets Volume 12:

In Dominique Sinclair's *Good Girl Gone Bad*, Reagan's dreams are finally within reach. Setting out to do research for an article, nothing could have prepared her for Luke, or his offer to teach her everything she needs to know about sex. Licentious pleasures, forbidden desires… inspiring the best writing she's ever done.

Aphrodite's Passion, by Jess Michaels, tells the tale of Selena, who flees Victorian London before her evil stepchildren can institutionalize her for hysteria, Gavin is asked to bring her back home. But when he finds her living on the island of Cyprus, his need to have her begins to block out every other impulse.

Leigh Wyndfield brings you *White Heat*, where Raine is hiding in an ice-house in the middle of nowhere from one of the scariest men in the universes. Walker escaped from a burning prison. Imagine their surprise when they find out they have the same man to blame for their miseries. Passion, revenge and love are in their future.

Summer Lightning, by Saskia Walker, is about a scupltress, Sally, who's enjoying an idyllic getaway on a secluded cove when she spots a gorgeous man walking naked on the beach. When Julian finds an attractive woman shacked up in his cove, he has to check her out. But what will he do when he finds she's secretly been using him as a model?

Men you've been dreaming about!

Secrets

Satisfy your desire for more.

*F*eel the wild adventure, fierce passion and the power of love in every **Secrets** Collection story. Red Sage Publishing's romance authors create richly crafted, sexy, sensual, novella-length stories. Each one is just the right length for reading after a long and hectic day.

Each volume in the **Secrets** Collection has four diverse, ultra-sexy, romantic novellas brimming with adventure, passion and love. More adventurous tales for the adventurous reader. The **Secrets** Collection are a glorious mix of romance genre; numerous historical settings, contemporary, paranormal, science fiction and suspense. We are always looking for new adventures.

Reader response to the **Secrets** volumes has been great! Here's just a small sample:

"I loved the variety of settings. Four completely wonderful time periods, give you four completely wonderful reads."

"Each story was a page-turning tale I hated to put down."

*"I love **Secrets**! When is the next volume coming out? This one was Hot! Loved the heroes!"*

Secrets have won raves and awards. We could go on, but why don't you find out for yourself—order your set of **Secrets** today! See the back for details.

Secrets, Volume 1

Listen to what reviewers say:

"These stories take you beyond romance into the realm of erotica. I found *Secrets* absolutely delicious."

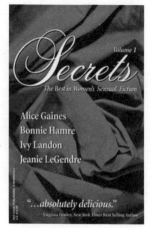

—Virginia Henley,
New York Times Best Selling Author

"*Secrets* is a collection of novellas for the daring, adventurous woman who's not afraid to give her fantasies free reign."

—Kathe Robin, *Romantic Times* Magazine

"...In fact, the men featured in all the stories are terrific, they all want to please and pleasure their women. If you like erotic romance you will love *Secrets*."

—*Romantic Readers* Review

In *Secrets, Volume 1* you'll find:

A Lady's Quest by Bonnie Hamre

Widowed Lady Antonia Blair-Sutworth searches for a lover to save her from the handsome Duke of Sutherland. The "auditions" may be shocking but utterly tantalizing.

The Spinner's Dream by Alice Gaines

A seductive fantasy that leaves every woman wishing for her own private love slave, desperate and running for his life.

The Proposal by Ivy Landon

This tale is a walk on the wild side of love. *The Proposal* will taunt you, tease you, and shock you. A contemporary erotica for the adventurous woman.

The Gift by Jeanie LeGendre

Immerse yourself in this historic tale of exotic seduction, bondage and a concubine's surrender to the Sultan's desire. Can Alessandra live the life and give the gift the Sultan demands of her?

Secrets, Volume 2

Listen to what reviewers say:

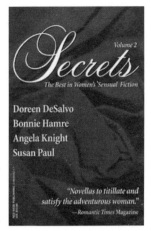

"*Secrets* offers four novellas of sensual delight; each beautifully written with intense feeling and dedication to character development. For those seeking stories with heightened intimacy, look no further."

—Kathee Card, *Romancing the Web*

"Such a welcome diversity in styles and genres. Rich characterization in sensual tales. An exciting read that's sure to titillate the senses."

—Cheryl Ann Porter

"*Secrets 2* left me breathless. Sensual satisfaction guaranteed...times four!"

—Virginia Henley, *New York Times* Best Selling Author

In *Secrets, Volume 2* you'll find:

Surrogate Lover by Doreen DeSalvo

Adrian Ross is a surrogate sex therapist who has all the answers and control. He thought he'd seen and done it all, but he'd never met Sarah.

Snowbound by Bonnie Hamre

A delicious, sensuous regency tale. The marriage-shy Earl of Howden is teased and tortured by his own desires and finds there is a woman who can equal his overpowering sensuality.

Roarke's Prisoner by Angela Knight

Elise, a starship captain, remembers the eager animal submission she'd known before at her captor's hands and refuses to become his toy again. However, she has no idea of the delights he's planned for her this time.

Savage Garden by Susan Paul

Raine's been captured by a mysterious and dangerous revolutionary leader in Mexico. At first her only concern is survival, but she quickly finds lush erotic nights in her captor's arms.

Winner of the Fallot Literary Award for Fiction!

Secrets, Volume 3

Listen to what reviewers say:

"*Secrets, Volume 3*, leaves the reader breathless. A delicious confection of sensuous treats awaits the reader on each turn of the page!"
— Kathee Card, *Romancing the Web*

"From the FBI to Police Dectective to Vampires to a Medieval Warlord home from the Crusade—*Secrets 3* is simply the best!"
— Susan Paul, award winning author

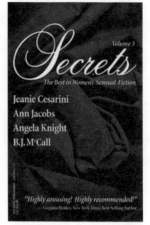

"An unabashed celebration of sex. Highly arousing! Highly recommended!"
— Virginia Henley, *New York Times* Best Selling Author

In *Secrets, Volume 3* you'll find:

The Spy Who Loved Me by Jeanie Cesarini

Undercover FBI agent Paige Ellison's sexual appetites rise to new levels when she works with leading man Christopher Sharp, the cunning agent who uses all his training to capture her body and heart.

The Barbarian by Ann Jacobs

Lady Brianna vows not to surrender to the barbaric Giles, Earl of Harrow. He must use sexual arts learned in the infidels' harem to conquer his bride. A word of caution—this is not for the faint of heart.

Blood and Kisses by Angela Knight

A vampire assassin is after Beryl St. Cloud. Her only hope lies with Decker, another vampire and ex-mercenary. Broke, she offers herself as payment for his services. Will his seductive powers take her very soul?

Love Undercover by B.J. McCall

Amanda Forbes is the bait in a strip joint sting operation. While she performs, fellow detective "Cowboy" Cooper gets to watch. Though he excites her, she must fight the temptation to surrender to the passion.

Winner of the 1997 Under the Covers
Readers Favorite Award

Secrets, Volume 4

Listen to what reviewers say:

"Provocative…seductive…a must read!"

— *Romantic Times* Magazine

"These are the kind of stories that romance readers that 'want a little more' have been looking for all their lives…."

— *Affaire de Coeur* Magazine

"*Secrets, Volume 4*, has something to satisfy every erotic fantasy… simply sexational!"

— Virginia Henley, *New York Times* Best Selling Author

In *Secrets, Volume 4* you'll find:

An Act of Love by Jeanie Cesarini

Shelby Moran's past left her terrified of sex. International film star Jason Gage must gently coach the young starlet in the ways of love. He wants more than an act—he wants Shelby to feel true passion in his arms.

Enslaved by Desirée Lindsey

Lord Nicholas Summer's air of danger, dark passions, and irresistible charm have brought Lady Crystal's long-hidden desires to the surface. Will he be able to give her the one thing she desires before it's too late?

The Bodyguard by Betsy Morgan and Susan Paul

Kaki York is a bodyguard, but watching the wild, erotic romps of her client's sexual conquests on the security cameras is getting to her—and her partner, the ruggedly handsome James Kulick. Can she resist his insistent desire to have her?

The Love Slave by Emma Holly

A woman's ultimate fantasy. For one year, Princess Lily will be attended to by three delicious men of her choice. While she delights in playing with the first two, it's the reluctant Grae, with his powerful chest, black eyes and hair, that stirs her desires.

Secrets, Volume 5

Listen to what reviewers say:

"Hot, hot, hot! Not for the faint-hearted!"

—*Romantic Times* Magazine

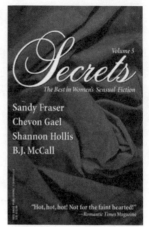

"As you make your way through the stories, you will find yourself becoming hotter and hotter. *Secrets* just keeps getting better and better."

—*Affaire de Coeur* Magazine

"*Secrets 5* is a collage of lucious sensuality. Any woman who reads *Secrets* is in for an awakening!"

—Virginia Henley, *New York Times* Best Selling Author

In *Secrets, Volume 5* you'll find:

Beneath Two Moons by Sandy Fraser

Ready for a very wild romp? Step into the future and find Conor, rough and masculine like frontiermen of old, on the prowl for a new conquest. In his sights, Dr. Eva Kelsey. She got away once before, but this time Conor makes sure she begs for more.

Insatiable by Chevon Gael

Marcus Remington photographs beautiful models for a living, but it's Ashlyn Fraser, a young corporate exec having some glamour shots done, who has stolen his heart. It's up to Marcus to help her discover her inner sexual self.

Strictly Business by Shannon Hollis

Elizabeth Forrester knows it's tough enough for a woman to make it to the top in the corporate world. Garrett Hill, the most beautiful man in Silicon Valley, has to come along to stir up her wildest fantasies. Dare she give in to both their desires?

Alias Smith and Jones by B.J. McCall

Meredith Collins finds herself stranded overnight at the airport. A handsome stranger by the name of Smith offers her sanctuaty for the evening and she finds those mesmerizing, green-flecked eyes hard to resist. Are they to be just two ships passing in the night?

Secrets, Volume 6

Listen to what reviewers say:

"Red Sage was the first and remains the leader of Women's Erotic Romance Fiction Collections!"

—*Romantic Times* Magazine

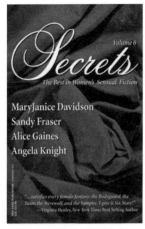

"*Secrets, Volume 6*, is the best of *Secrets* yet. ...four of the most erotic stories in one volume than this reader has yet to see anywhere else. ...These stories are full of erotica at its best and you'll definitely want to keep it handy for lots of re-reading!"

—*Affaire de Coeur* Magazine

"*Secrets 6* satisfies every female fantasy: the Bodyguard, the Tutor, the Werewolf, and the Vampire. I give it Six Stars!"

—Virginia Henley, *New York Times* Best Selling Author

In *Secrets, Volume 6* you'll find:

Flint's Fuse by Sandy Fraser
Dana Madison's father has her "kidnapped" for her own safety. Flint, the tall, dark and dangerous mercenary, is hired for the job. But just which one is the prisoner—Dana will try *anything* to get away.

Love's Prisoner by MaryJanice Davidson
Trapped in an elevator, Jeannie Lawrence experienced unwilling rapture at Michael Windham's hands. She never expected the devilishly handsome man to show back up in her life—or turn out to be a werewolf!

The Education of Miss Felicity Wells by Alice Gaines
Felicity Wells wants to be sure she'll satisfy her soon-to-be husband but she needs a teacher. Dr. Marcus Slade, an experienced lover, agrees to take her on as a student, but can he stop short of taking her completely?

A Candidate for the Kiss by Angela Knight
Working on a story, reporter Dana Ivory stumbles onto a more amazing one—a sexy, secret agent who happens to be a vampire. She wants her story but Gabriel Archer wants more from her than just sex and blood.

Secrets, Volume 7

Listen to what reviewers say:

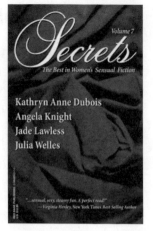

"Get out your asbestos gloves — *Secrets Volume 7* is...extremely hot, true erotic romance...passionate and titillating. There's nothing quite like baring your secrets!"

—*Romantic Times* Magazine

"...sensual, sexy, steamy fun. A perfect read!"

—Virginia Henley,
New York Times Best Selling Author

"Intensely provocative and disarmingly romantic, *Secrets*, *Volume 7*, is a romance reader's paradise that will take you beyond your wildest dreams!"

—Ballston Book House Review

In *Secrets, Volume 7* you'll find:

Amelia's Innocence by Julia Welles

Amelia didn't know her father bet her in a card game with Captain Quentin Hawke, so honor demands a compromise—three days of erotic foreplay, leaving her virginity and future intact.

The Woman of His Dreams by Jade Lawless

From the day artist Gray Avonaco moves in next door, Joanna Morgan is plagued by provocative dreams. But what she believes is unrequited lust, Gray sees as another chance to be with the woman he loves. He must persuade her that even death can't stop true love.

Surrender by Kathryn Anne Dubois

Free-spirited Lady Johanna wants no part of the binding strictures society imposes with her marriage to the powerful Duke. She doesn't know the dark Duke wants sensual adventure, and sexual satisfaction.

Kissing the Hunter by Angela Knight

Navy Seal Logan McLean hunts the vampires who murdered his wife. Virginia Hart is a sexy vampire searching for her lost soul-mate only to find him in a man determined to kill her. She must convince him all vampires aren't created equally.

Winner of the Venus Book Club
Best Book of the Year

Secrets, Volume 8

Listen to what reviewers say:

"*Secrets, Volume 8*, is an amazing compilation of sexy stories covering a wide range of subjects, all designed to titillate the senses. ...you'll find something for everybody in this latest version of *Secrets*."

—*Affaire de Coeur* Magazine

"*Secrets Volume 8*, is simply sensational!"

—Virginia Henley, *New York Times* Best Selling Author

"These delectable stories will have you turning the pages long into the night. Passionate, provocative and perfect for setting the mood...."

—*Escape to Romance* Reviews

In *Secrets, Volume 8* you'll find:

Taming Kate by Jeanie Cesarini

Kathryn Roman inherits a legal brothel. Little does this city girl know the town of Love, Nevada wants her to be their new madam so they've charged Trey Holliday, one very dominant cowboy, with taming her.

Jared's Wolf by MaryJanice Davidson

Jared Rocke will do anything to avenge his sister's death, but ends up attracted to Moira Wolfbauer, the she-wolf sworn to protect her pack. Joining forces to stop a killer, they learn love defies all boundaries.

My Champion, My Lover by Alice Gaines

Celeste Broder is a woman committed for having a sexy appetite. Mayor Robert Albright may be her champion—if she can convince him her freedom will mean a chance to indulge their appetites together.

Kiss or Kill by Liz Maverick

In this post-apocalyptic world, Camille Kazinsky's military career rides on her ability to make a choice—whether the robo called Meat should live or die. Meat's future depends on proving he's human enough to live, man enough...to makes her feel like a woman.

Winner of the Venus Book Club Best Book of the Year

Secrets, Volume 9

Listen to what reviewers say:

"Everyone should expect only the most erotic stories in a *Secrets* book. ...if you like your stories full of hot sexual scenes, then this is for you!"

—Donna Doyle Romance Reviews

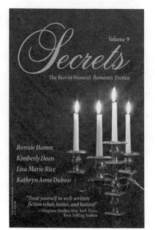

"*SECRETS 9*...is sinfully delicious, highly arousing, and hotter than hot as the pages practically burn up as you turn them."

—Suzanne Coleburn, Reader To Reader Reviews/Belles & Beaux of Romance

"Treat yourself to well-written fictionthat's hot, hotter, and hottest!"

—Virginia Henley, *New York Times* Best Selling Author

In *Secrets, Volume 9* you'll find:

Wild For You by Kathryn Anne Dubois

When college intern, Georgie, gets captured by a Congo wildman, she discovers this specimen of male virility has never seen a woman. The research possibilities are endless!

Wanted by Kimberly Dean

FBI Special Agent Jeff Reno wants Danielle Carver. There's her body, brains—and that charge of treason on her head. Dani goes on the run, but the sexy Fed is hot on her trail.

Secluded by Lisa Marie Rice

Nicholas Lee's wealth and power came with a price—his enemies will kill anyone he loves. When Isabelle steals his heart, Nicholas secludes her in his palace for a lifetime of desire in only a few days.

Flights of Fantasy by Bonnie Hamre

Chloe taught others to see the realities of life but she's never shared the intimate world of her sensual yearnings. Given the chance, will she be woman enough to fulfill her most secret erotic fantasy?

Secrets, Volume 10

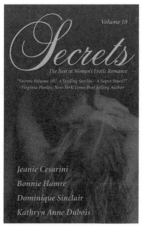

Listen to what reviewers say:

"*Secrets Volume 10*, an erotic dance through medieval castles, sultan's palaces, the English countryside and expensive hotel suites, explodes with passion-filled pages."

—*Romantic Times BOOKclub*

"Having read the previous nine volumes, this one fulfills the expectations of what is expected in a *Secrets* book: romance and eroticism at its best!!"

—*Fallen Angel Reviews*

"All are hot steamy romances so if you enjoy erotica romance, you are sure to enjoy *Secrets, Volume 10*. All this reviewer can say is WOW!!"

—*The Best Reviews*

In *Secrets, Volume 10* you'll find:

Private Eyes by Dominique Sinclair

When a mystery man captivates P.I. Nicolla Black during a stakeout, she discovers her no-seduction rule bending under the pressure of long denied passion. She agrees to the seduction, but he demands her total surrender.

The Ruination of Lady Jane by Bonnie Hamre

To avoid her upcoming marriage, Lady Jane Ponsonby-Maitland flees into the arms of Havyn Attercliffe. She begs him to ruin her rather than turn her over to her odious fiancé.

Code Name: Kiss by Jeanie Cesarini

Agent Lily Justiss is on a mission to defend her country against terrorists that requires giving up her virginity as a sex slave. As her master takes her body, desire for her commanding officer Seth Blackthorn fuels her mind.

The Sacrifice by Kathryn Anne Dubois

Lady Anastasia Bedovier is days from taking her vows as a Nun. Before she denies her sensuality forever, she wants to experience pleasure. Count Maxwell is the perfect man to initiate her into erotic delight.

Secrets, Volume 11

Listen to what reviewers say:

"*Secrets Volume 11* delivers once again with storylines that include erotic masquerades, ancient curses, modern-day betrayal and a prince charming looking for a kiss." **4 Stars**

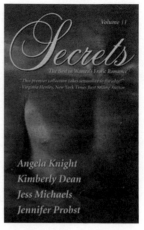

—*Romantic Times BOOKclub*

"Indulge yourself with this erotic treat and join the thousands of readers who just can't get enough. Be forewarned that *Secrets 11* will wet your appetite for more, but will offer you the ultimate in pleasurable erotic literature."

—*Ballston Book House Review*

"*Secrets 11* quite honestly is my favorite anthology from Red Sage so far."

—*The Best Reviews*

In *Secrets, Volume 11* you'll find:

Masquerade by Jennifer Probst

Hailey Ashton is determined to free herself from her sexual restrictions. Four nights of erotic pleasures without revealing her identity. A chance to explore her secret desires without the fear of unmasking.

Ancient Pleasures by Jess Michaels

Isabella Winslow is obsessed with finding out what caused her late husband's death, but trapped in an Egyptian concubine's tomb with a sexy American raider, succumbing to the mummy's sensual curse takes over.

Manhunt by Kimberly Dean

Framed for murder, Michael Tucker takes Taryn Swanson hostage—the one woman who can clear him. Despite the evidence against him, the attraction between them is strong. Tucker resorts to unconventional, yet effective methods of persuasion to change the sexy ADA's mind.

Wake Me by Angela Knight

Chloe Hart received a sexy painting of a sleeping knight. Radolf of Varik has been trapped for centuries in the painting since, cursed by a witch. His only hope is to visit the dreams of women and make one of them fall in love with him so she can free him with a kiss.

Secrets, Volume 12

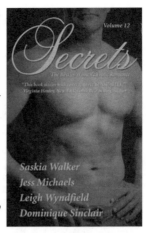

Listen to what reviewers say:

"*Secrets Volume 12*, turns on the heat with a seductive encounter inside a bookstore, a temple of naughty and sensual delight, a galactic inferno that thaws ice, and a lightening storm that lights up the English shoreline. Tales of looking for love in all the right places with a heat rating out the charts." **4½ Stars**

—*Romantic Times BOOKclub*

"I really liked these stories.You want great escapism? Read *Secrets, Volume 12.*"

—*Romance Reviews*

In *Secrets, Volume 12* you'll find:

Good Girl Gone Bad by Dominique Sinclair

Reagan's dreams are finally within reach. Setting out to do research for an article, nothing could have prepared her for Luke, or his offer to teach her everything she needs to know about sex. Licentious pleasures, forbidden desires… inspiring the best writing she's ever done.

Aphrodite's Passion by Jess Michaels

When Selena flees Victorian London before her evil stepchildren can institutionalize her for hysteria, Gavin is asked to bring her back home. But when he finds her living on the island of Cyprus, his need to have her begins to block out every other impulse.

White Heat by Leigh Wyndfield

Raine is hiding in an icehouse in the middle of nowhere from one of the scariest men in the universes. Walker escaped from a burning prison. Imagine their surprise when they find out they have the same man to blame for their miseries. Passion, revenge and love are in their future.

Summer Lightning by Saskia Walker

Sculptress Sally is enjoying an idyllic getaway on a secluded cove when she spots a gorgeous man walking naked on the beach. When Julian finds an attractive woman shacked up in his cove, he has to check her out. But what will he do when he finds she's secretly been using him as a model?

Secrets, Volume 13

Listen to what reviewers say:

"In *Secrets Volume 13*, the temperature gets turned up a few notches with a mistaken personal ad, shape-shifters destined to love, a hot Regency lord and his lady, as well as a bodyguard protecting his woman. Emotions and flames blaze high in Red Sage's latest foray into the sensual and delightful art of love." **4½ Stars**

—*Romantic Times BOOKclub*

"The sex is still so hot the pages nearly ignite! Read *Secrets, Volume 13*!

—*Romance Reviews*

In *Secrets, Volume 13* you'll find:

Out of Control by Rachelle Chase

Astrid's world revolves around her business and she's hoping to pick up wealthy Erik Santos as a client. Only he's hoping to pick up something entirely different. Will she give in to the seductive pull of his proposition?

Hawkmoor by Amber Green

Shape-shifters answer to Darien as he acts in the name of the long-missing Lady Hawkmoor, their hereditary ruler. When she unexpectedly surfaces, Darien must deal with a scrappy individual whose wary eyes hold the other half of his soul, but who has the power to destroy his world.

Lessons in Pleasure by Charlotte Featherstone

A wicked bargain has Lily vowing never to yield to the demands of the rake she once loved and lost. Unfortunately, Damian, the Earl of St. Croix, or Saint as he is infamously known, will not take 'no' for an answer.

In the Heat of the Night by Calista Fox

Haunted by a century-old curse, Molina fears she won't live to see her thirtieth birthday. Nick, her former bodyguard, is hired back into service to protect her from the fatal accidents that plague her family. But *In the Heat of the Night*, will his passion and love for her be enough to convince Molina they have a future together?

The Forever Kiss
by Angela Knight

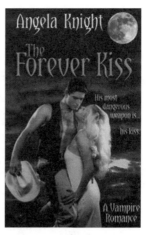

Listen to what reviewers say:

"*The Forever Kiss* flows well with good characters and an interesting plot. … If you enjoy vampires and a lot of hot sex, you are sure to enjoy *The Forever Kiss*."

—*The Best Reviews*

"Battling vampires, a protective ghost and the ever present battle of good and evil keep excellent pace with the erotic delights in Angela Knight's *The Forever Kiss*—a book that absolutely bites with refreshing paranormal humor." **4½ Stars, Top Pick**

—*Romantic Times BOOKclub*

"I found *The Forever Kiss* to be an exceptionally written, refreshing book. … I really enjoyed this book by Angela Knight. … 5 angels!"

—*Fallen Angel Reviews*

"*The Forever Kiss* is the first single title released from Red Sage and if this is any indication of what we can expect, it won't be the last. … The love scenes are hot enough to give a vampire a sunburn and the fight scenes will have you cheering for the good guys."

—*Really Bad Barb Reviews*

In *The Forever Kiss*:

For years, Valerie Chase has been haunted by dreams of a Texas Ranger she knows only as "Cowboy." As a child, he rescued her from the nightmare vampires who murdered her parents. As an adult, she still dreams of him—but now he's her seductive lover in nights of erotic pleasure.

Yet "Cowboy" is more than a dream—he's the real Cade McKinnon—and a vampire! For years, he's protected Valerie from Edward Ridgemont, the sadistic vampire who turned him. Now, Ridgmont wants Valerie for his own and Cade is the only one who can protect her.

When Val finds herself abducted by her handsome dream man, she's appalled to discover he's one of the vampires she fears. Now, caught in a web of fear and passion, she and Cade must learn to trust each other, even as an immortal monster stalks their every move.

Their only hope of survival is…*The Forever Kiss*.

*Angela Knight is the 3ʳᵈ Place winner in Paranormal Romace for **The Forever Kiss***

Finally, the men you've been dreaming about!

Give the Gift of Spicy Romantic Fiction

Don't want to wait? You can place a retail price ($12.99) order for any of the *Secrets* volumes from the following:

① **Waldenbooks and Borders Stores**

② **Amazon.com** or **BarnesandNoble.com**

③ **Book Clearinghouse (800-431-1579)**

④ **Romantic Times Magazine**
Books by Mail (718-237-1097)

⑤ Special order at other bookstores.
Bookstores: Please contact Baker & Taylor Distributors or
Red Sage Publishing for bookstore sales.

Order by title or ISBN #:

Vol. 1: 0-9648942-0-3   **Vol. 8:** 0-9648942-8-9

Vol. 2: 0-9648942-1-1   **Vol. 9:** 0-9648942-9-7

Vol. 3: 0-9648942-2-X   **Vol. 10:** 0-9754516-0-X

Vol. 4: 0-9648942-4-6   **Vol. 11:** 0-9754516-1-8

Vol. 5: 0-9648942-5-4   **Vol. 12:** 0-9754516-2-6

Vol. 6: 0-9648942-6-2   **Vol. 13:** 0-9754516-3-4

Vol. 7: 0-9648942-7-0

The Forever Kiss: 0-9648942-3-8 ($14.00)

Red Sage Publishing Mail Order Form:

(Orders shipped in two to three days of receipt.)

	Quantity	Mail Order Price	Total
Secrets **Volume 1** *(Retail $12.99)*	——————	$ 9.99	——————
Secrets **Volume 2** *(Retail $12.99)*	——————	$ 9.99	——————
Secrets **Volume 3** *(Retail $12.99)*	——————	$ 9.99	——————
Secrets **Volume 4** *(Retail $12.99)*	——————	$ 9.99	——————
Secrets **Volume 5** *(Retail $12.99)*	——————	$ 9.99	——————
Secrets **Volume 6** *(Retail $12.99)*	——————	$ 9.99	——————
Secrets **Volume 7** *(Retail $12.99)*	——————	$ 9.99	——————
Secrets **Volume 8** *(Retail $12.99)*	——————	$ 9.99	——————
Secrets **Volume 9** *(Retail $12.99)*	——————	$ 9.99	——————
Secrets **Volume 10** *(Retail $12.99)*	——————	$ 9.99	——————
Secrets **Volume 11** *(Retail $12.99)*	——————	$ 9.99	——————
Secrets **Volume 12** *(Retail $12.99)*	——————	$ 9.99	——————
Secrets **Volume 13** *(Retail $12.99)*	——————	$ 9.99	——————
The Forever Kiss *(Retail $14.00)*	——————	$11.00	——————

Shipping & handling (in the U.S.)

US Priority Mail:
1–2 books .... $ 5.50
3–5 books $11.50
6–9 books $14.50
10–11 books $19.00

UPS insured:
1–4 books $16.00
5–9 books $25.00
10–11 books $29.00

—————

SUBTOTAL   —————

Florida 6% sales tax (if delivered in FL)   —————

TOTAL AMOUNT ENCLOSED   —————

Your personal information is kept private and not shared with anyone.

Name: (please print) ————————————————————

Address: (no P.O. Boxes) ————————————————————

City/State/Zip: ————————————————————

Phone or email: (only regarding order if necessary) ————————————

Please make check payable to **Red Sage Publishing**. Check must be drawn on a U.S. bank in U.S. dollars. Mail your check and order form to:

Red Sage Publishing, Inc.   Department S13   P.O. Box 4844   Seminole, FL 33775

Or use the order form on our website: www.redsagepub.com

It's not just reviewers raving about *Secrets*. See what readers have to say:

"When are you coming out with a new Volume? I want a new one next month!" via email from a reader.

"I loved the hot, wet sex without vulgar words being used to make it exciting." after *Volume 1*

"I loved the blend of sensuality and sexual intensity—HOT!" after *Volume 2*

"The best thing about *Secrets* is they're hot and brief! The least thing is you do not have enough of them!" after *Volume 3*

"I have been extreamly satisfied with *Secrets*, keep up the good writing." after *Volume 4*

"Stories have plot and characters to support the erotica. They would be good strong stories without the heat." after *Volume 5*

"*Secrets* really knows how to push the envelop better than anyone else." after *Volume 6*

"These are the best sensual stories I have ever read!" after *Volume 7*

"I love, love, love the *Secrets* stories. I now have all of them, please have more books come out each year." after *Volume 8*

"These are the perfect sensual romance stories!" after *Volume 9*

"What I love about *Secrets Volume 10* is how I couldn't put it down!" after *Volume 10*

"All of the *Secrets* volumes are terrific! I have read all of them up to *Secrets Volume 11*. Please keep them coming! I will read every one you make!" after *Volume 11*